This was utter madness, to be allowing a dev... Branford to sti...

He tumbled won... soused himself in the demons of drink, he chased countesses naked through exotic villas. And here she was, allowing his flaming fingers to rove at will over her own exposed flesh. What was she thinking? Only that Lucifer's touch was making her feel sinfully alive.

She knew that an open flame was extremely dangerous, and yet, like a moth mesmerized by a candle, she felt inexorably drawn to the tantalizing heat. It had ignited a conflagration of emotions inside her that she had never experienced before. And while she couldn't begin to explain the urgent need that drew her closer and closer to the source of the fire, there was no way she could pull back now. . . .

THE TIGER'S MISTRESS

First in a sparkling new Regency series from

Andrea DaRif

THE TIGER'S MISTRESS

ANDREA DARIF

POCKET BOOKS
New York   London   Toronto   Sydney   Singapore

This book is a work of fiction. Names, characters, places and incidents are products of the author's imagination or are used fictitiously. Any resemblance to actual events or locales or persons, living or dead, is entirely coincidental.

An *Original* Publication of POCKET BOOKS

POCKET BOOKS, a division of Simon & Schuster, Inc.
1230 Avenue of the Americas, New York, NY 10020

ISBN: 0-7434-6348-X

First Pocket Books printing August 2003

10 9 8 7 6 5 4 3 2 1

POCKET and colophon are registered trademarks of Simon & Schuster, Inc.

Cover illustration by John Ennis

For information regarding special discounts for bulk purchases, please contact Simon & Schuster Special Sales at 1-800-456-6798 or business@simonandschuster.com.

Printed in the U.S.A.

for Barbara Metzger
and Amanda McCabe

Two great writers and
great friends. Thanks for
all your encouragement!

Chapter One

❧❧❧

Snick.

The thin shaft of metal caught on the tumbler but the lock did not open. Shifting slightly, the cloaked figure crouched beside the desk flexed a gloved hand and tried again.

Snick. Snick. Still no luck.

"Oh, bloody hell." The oath was no louder than the faint whisper of the damask draperies framing the open window.

"Well, what did you expect?"

The fingers froze and the figure whipped around, revealing a masked face.

"You are going about it all wrong."

Black silk stretched from the intruder's hood to below the nose, with two holes cut out for the eyes. The pale wash of moonlight did not allow the Earl of Branford to remark on their color—or perhaps, he thought with a wry grimace, the reason had something to do with the fact that he had just polished off his second bottle of brandy in less than an hour. The surfeit of spirits, however, could not drown the sight of the softly curved lips beneath the slash of midnight. No matter how foxed, he was absolutely sure they were not those of an ordinary thief.

"I would suggest you hold the wire between your thumb and your forefinger." He rose from the leather armchair where he had been dozing and moved across the Oriental carpet with surprising quickness. "Like this."

Taking the implement from the young lady's hand, the earl thrust it into the small opening of the drawer and gave a jiggle. "No wonder you're making a hash of it," he muttered after a moment. "A hairpin!" A low snort emphasized his opinion of the implement. "Not only are you harebrained enough to attempt to rob the marquess while he is at home, but you don't even have the sense to bring along the proper tools."

The eyes behind the slitted openings narrowed in indignation. They were green, Branford realized, now that he was much closer. A green the color of molten jade, with sparks of amber shooting up from their depths.

"I don't need some jug-bitten gentleman to tell me that a hairpin is not the ideal choice," she retorted, the sarcasm in her voice every bit as sharp as his had been. "I'll have you know that I started out with a set of excellent picks, only . . . only they somehow slipped from my pocket on the way up."

"I'm sober enough to come up with a better excuse than that." He was also sober enough to note that the heat of her voice was immediately reflected in her cheeks—at least, what little of them was visible below the mask. They turned a deep, glowing pink that put him in mind of the exotic roses that his last mistress used to decorate her boudoir. An apt metaphor, he decided, for, despite being a trifle in his cups, it was clear that the female crouching next to him was a highly unusual specimen of her sex.

Her next words were just as prickly as a *cuisse de nymphe*. "Have *you* ever tried to scale a two-story wall while wearing skirts?"

Branford allowed a devilish grin to spread over his lean features. "I have been accused of a great many ungentlemanly acts in my life, but donning petticoats is not one of them."

The sparks from her gaze would have singed Lucifer. "Well, then, don't smirk. It's deucedly hard with all that fabric getting in the way of your boots, not to speak of snagging on the vines."

"Professionals don't make excuses." His gaze swept from the defiantly tilted chin down to where the bunching of skirts was revealing a nicely turned ankle. "Next time, try wearing breeches. I think you will find the snug fit a welcome change; I know I would."

Her lips parted in outrage.

"But then, I rather doubt you can call yourself a professional at this sort of thing," he went on, his wits still sharp enough to note several telling details. Her speech indicated she was a lady of gentle breeding. As did her cloak and gown. They were of good quality, even though the styles were out of date and the wool slightly frayed around the edges. And a faint tang of lavender, mixed with an undercurrent of verbena, perfumed the lock of hair that had strayed from the confines of her hood—hardly the signature scent of Southwark or Seven Dials. So, that made the question of why she was there an intriguing one.

His musings were cut short as she snatched back the hairpin from his grasp. "I don't intend to call myself anything. I've wasted quite enough time in idle conversation." Her chin came up a fraction higher. "Now kindly take yourself off, sir. You are blocking what little light there is."

Branford leaned back a bit but made no move to rise. "Aren't you worried that I might raise the alarm if I do? After all, I *am* a guest in this house."

"Call the magistrate and be damned," she muttered while renewing her attack on the small brass lock. "It is the Marquess of Dunster who is the real criminal, and I vow I shall prove it, even if I have to swim all the way back to London from a penal colony in the antipodes."

Criminal? The marquess a criminal? If she was looking to arouse his curiosity, she had certainly done it in spades.

Up until the discovery of the masked intruder, the evening had been a crashing bore, like so many others since his return to London. He had agreed to accompany a casual acquaintance to the marquess's private party for no other reason than that the company of strangers seemed preferable to a night alone with his own depressing thoughts. It was, however, a decision he soon regretted. Dunster had struck him as a crude, unsavory character, and the coarse treats being passed around after the port and cigars were not at all to his taste, despite the rumors being bandied about Town.

Oh, some of the whispers were true enough. His skills at coaxing favors from a deck of cards or another gentleman's wife were only slightly exaggerated. And no doubt he did possess a hair-trigger temper and cold-blooded nerve, seeing as two men lay nursing bullet wounds from recent encounters on the dueling field.

But the prospect of writhing about on the carpet in the midst of a debauched orgy held no allure. If a female's thighs were to be wrapped around his hips, he preferred to choose his partner—and achieve his pleasure through seduction rather than brute force. So he had drunk more than was good for him and then wandered upstairs, thinking to pass the time with yet another glass of spirits rather than a hired trollop until the others were all too deep in their cups or otherwise occupied to notice his departure.

Branford certainly had no intention of leaving now. "Try a little more pressure with your index finger," he said. His hand closed over hers and guided it slightly to the left. There was a touch of resistance, then a distinct click. Reaching up, he slid the drawer open. "Voilà."

He smiled, rather expecting some acknowledgment of his expert assistance, but such a notion was rudely shoved aside as the young lady scrabbled to get at it. Without so much as a word of thanks, she reached in and began rummaging through its contents.

"Just what are you after?" inquired the earl, massaging the spot on his ribs where her elbow had caught him a solid blow. "Has Dunster reneged on the promise of a diamond bracelet? Or failed to pay the agreed upon fee?"

A scathing look was the only answer. She then turned her attention back to the sheaf of papers she had snatched up and continued to examine each page.

"Look here," he growled. "Perhaps if you explained—"

A sudden clattering in the hallway interrupted his demand. There was a brief silence, then a trilling squeal, followed by several drunken guffaws. After another moment the steps suddenly turned in their direction.

"Damnation!" The young lady's head jerked up as several elongated shadows fell across the half-open doorway. With the documents still clutched in her hands, she made a quick survey of the room before turning for the voluminous drapes.

"Too late," murmured Branford. It was clear she would never make it to cover in time. Why he should feel any obligation to give further aid to the sharp-tongued chit was as big a mystery as her presence here, but for some odd reason he did.

A spin to his left blocked her path of retreat.

"Out of my—" The rest of her words were swallowed in a squawk of outrage as his lips came down hard upon hers. Ignoring her muffled protests, he twirled her around and lifted her onto the edge of the desk. One hand held her hard against his chest while the other rucked up her skirts high enough so that he could step between her flailing legs. They were quite long and shapely, he couldn't help but note as his fingers grazed the inside of her thigh.

The intimate touch brought an even more furious response. Her mouth parted, trying to manage a louder cry. To cut off any outburst, he deepened the kiss with a thrust of his tongue, filling her with the lingering heat of the brandy.

For an instant she went absolutely still.

Branford took full advantage of the lull. He pressed closer, so that their bodies were locked together, then leaned forward, forcing her head nearly down to the blotter. Tightening his grip around her waist, he then yanked free the knot of his cravat and fell to fondling her breast.

"Well, lookee here. Should ha' known a stallion of Branford's reputation wouldn't take long in mounting one of the fillies."

Out of the corner of his eye, the earl saw the Marquess of Dunster and one of his cronies leaning rather heavily on the half-naked female who stood between them. Both of them looked every inch the proper gentlemen in their tailored evening coats, embroidered waistcoats, and polished Hessians. However, as their breeches were missing, not all of those inches were of the sort that titled lords should be showing in public.

"Seems she's giving you a spirited gallop," said the leering Dunster, for indeed, the young lady had resumed her struggle to break free. "P'rhaps when you're done in the saddle, you'll pass the reins to me."

The other gentleman laughed and added a very lewd comment.

Branford exaggerated the rocking of his hips, using the movement to nudge the desk drawer back into place. Taking care that his back blocked all view of the papers and the masked face, he released her mouth long enough to glance over his shoulder with a wolfish grin. "Find your own rides, gentlemen. I don't plan on finishing with this one anytime soon."

There was a sharp intake of breath from the young lady.

Fearing that an outburst of temper might ruin the whole charade, he gave her a warning shake. "Keep quiet, you little fool," he whispered while appearing to nuzzle at her neck. "Unless you truly wish to be trotted off to Newgate."

Apparently she was not devoid of all sense, for she bit back whatever retort was hovering on her lips.

Raising his voice to a rough growl, the earl turned back to the others, noticing that a third man had approached and was standing in the shadows, half hidden by the marquess's swaying shoulders. "So, gentlemen, if you don't mind closing the door as you leave . . ."

"Like to apply the spurs in private, eh?" Dunster's flushed face took on a petulant pout. "A shame. Would have liked to watch you put her through her paces."

"Aw, come on, milord." The doxy rubbed up against the marquess's arm. After eyeing what showed of the other young lady's willowy form, she gave a slight sniff and a toss of her overly blond curls. "If yer looking for spirit an' stamina, I've a friend downstairs wots got a lot more to offer a fine gentleman than that bag o' bones."

Amid a rumble of laughter and ribald jests, the door slammed shut. Branford slowly relaxed his hold as he heard them stumble off, and started to speak.

The young lady beat him to the punch. "Why, you unprincipled cad!" Yanking one hand free, she wasted no time in landing a hard right to his jaw.

His head snapped back. *Hell's teeth!* he thought

with some amazement. Where had a female learned to hit like that?

"You *might* show a bit of gratitude, you ungrateful chit," he growled, rubbing gingerly at the spot. "I just saved your neck."

"You nearly stole my virtue! And it was *not* my neck you were making sport with, rather . . . several other parts of my anatomy!" Suddenly aware of how much of that anatomy was now in full view, she hastily tugged her skirts back over her knees and slid off the desk.

He gave a throaty chuckle, despite his smarting jaw. "My dear, I am far more skilled at larceny than you are. Had your virtue been the object of my desire, it would now be in my possession."

"Arrogant coxcomb!" She sought to brush off his hand, which still had a grip on her arm. "Damn you, let go of me! I do not wish to suffer any further indignities at the hands of a lecherous rogue."

"Not before you answer a few questions." Drawing his dark brows together, he fixed her with his most intimidating stare. It was a look that had usually reduced the soldiers under his command to quaking in their boots. And as his military experience with Wellington had also involved interrogating a good many traitors and double agents, he imagined he would have a young lady—no matter how defiant—confessing within seconds. "Starting with who the devil are you, and what are you looking for among those papers."

His experience with men of war, however, had not prepared the earl to be on the lookout for a swift kick in the shins.

"Bloody hell!" Caught by surprise, he fell back against the edge of the desk, bruising his hip in the process. The young lady seized the opportunity to twist out of reach and sprint for the window. Off balance, his reflexes still slightly slurred by drink, Branford was a step slow in lunging after her. He grabbed for the collar of her cloak, but his fingers missed by a fraction of an inch. Instead they closed over thin air.

No, not quite thin air, he realized as he felt a slight tug. A thin gold chain had snagged on his hand. It snapped, and the broken links fell to the carpet, along with a ring.

Before he could recover, she jumped onto the sill and, with a theatrical flourish of her cloak, dropped down from sight.

Damn!

In a fit of disgust, Branford kicked at the wainscoting as he watched her disappear into the shadows of the garden below. It was *he* who had made a complete hash of things.

His hand raked through his raven locks. The Black Cat—once Wellington's most trusted intelligence officer—bested by a woman? Good Lord, the thought was more sobering than a Methodist's sermon. If he could be outsmarted, outmaneuvered, and outgunned by a mere female, perhaps it was high time to stop drowning himself in self-pity.

With a last look at the boxwood hedge, he drew the window closed and turned away.

A wink of light suddenly caught his eye.

He had almost forgotten the fallen trinket. Bending down, he retrieved the broken chain, but the ring took a bit of searching to locate. Once he had scooped it up from under the armchair, he carried it over to the desk and lit one of the candles in order to examine it more closely.

It glowed with the soft patina of age. The shape and size indicated it was made for a man, and although the engraving was quite worn, the earl could make out the intricate outlines of a crest.

A husband? A lover?

Whoever he was, his name would be easy enough to trace. And, once armed with that information, he was certain the young lady's identity would not remain a secret for long.

His lips quirked into a grim smile. She may have won the first skirmish, but the battle was far from over.

"Bloody, *bloody* hell."

Miss Portia Hadley could not restrain the unlady-like oath as she threw off her cloak. Dropping the sheaf of papers and crumpled silk mask onto her dressing table, she turned to the unlit hearth of her bedchamber and began pacing. Although it was well past midnight, she was still too furious to feel any inclination for sleep.

Good Lord, the evening had been a complete disaster!

A second look at the stolen documents during the carriage ride home had shown them to be useless—naught but bills from a boot maker and wine merchant on Jermyn Street, mixed in with several highly improper verses. If only she had not lost her set of picklocks, she might have had more time to make a proper search of Dunster's desk.

And if only the information she had overheard at the Framingham supper concert had been more explicit as to what took place at a gentleman's evening at home, she might have avoided a most embarrassing encounter. The next oath was directed at herself. How could she have been so naive! Somehow, the picture in her mind had been of a rather stodgy gathering—a formal supper followed by port and cigars, with nothing more heated than disagreement over politics.

Ha! Heated, indeed! Portia felt her face grow exceeding warm at the mere thought of what she had seen. And felt.

All in all, the evening could not possibly have gone any worse, she fumed. Unless, of course, she had slipped from the vines and broken her neck.

And even that might have been preferable to being mauled by a ruthless rake. Her steps slowed and a shudder of disgust ran down her spine at the recollection of his hands roving upon her person and his mouth plundering hers.

Or was it some other emotion?

The flush of anger suddenly turned a guilty shade of crimson. She could not deny that along with outrage and indignation, she had also experienced a strange frisson of excitement at his touch. It was, she knew, quite wrong—a proper young lady should have swooned from maidenly shock.

But then again, Portia was well aware that she was not a proper lady. And never had been. Given the rather unorthodox nature of her upbringing, she feared her sensibilities were far less refined than they should be, and that her headstrong behavior often caused her to stray far past the boundaries established by Polite Society. Perhaps that was why, unlike most innocent English schoolroom misses, she had allowed herself to be kissed rather thoroughly before.

It had happened several years ago during one of her family's expeditions to Greece. Intellectual curiosity had compelled her to encourage the amorous advances of a native guide on the island of Mykonos. Taking advantage of her father's preoccupation with the ruins of an ancient temple, the young man, aptly named Adonis, had pulled her behind one of the crumbling marble columns and pressed his mouth to hers while sliding a callused palm inside her bodice to fondle her breast. It hadn't lasted all that long, but despite the fact that he had smelled vaguely of donkey and tasted of stale *retsina,* the fleeting intimacy had been undeniably intriguing.

Indeed, she had thought about it often since then. And on more than one occasion had found herself desiring to be kissed again, for surely it could not be *that* wicked to wish for the brushing of a gentleman's lips against hers. . . .

Ha! Such a sentiment caused her mouth to pucker in a wry grimace. *Wicked* did not begin to describe the embrace she had just experienced! It had certainly involved a good deal more contact than a brushing of lips. And the Earl of Branford had certainly been in no hurry!

The Earl of Branford.

Oh, yes, he may not have had a clue as to her identity, but Portia knew who *he* was! How could she not, even though she had only been living in London a short while? Every time the earl entered a ballroom, heads swiveled and the whispers commenced. According to the gossips, he was the Devil Incarnate, guilty of such a multitude of sins that Dante would run out of circles in which to consign him!

The Devil, she repeated, staring at the unlit logs and finding herself slightly surprised they didn't burst into flames. That she could well believe! She had been aware of the heat emanating from those broad shoulders and long limbs as soon as he had crouched down next to her. And then, when his arms had crushed her to his chest, and his hand had raked over the top of her stocking . . . Heaven help her, the sensation had been like a burning match against her bare skin! She was sure the flesh was still singed and smoking where his long, lithe fingers had trailed their fire!

Her own fingers flew to her cheeks, which were now glowing like red-hot coals. They then strayed down to her lips, which were also feeling a bit scorched. "May Lucifer be roasted on his pitchfork," she whispered. She could still taste the sizzle of the earl's mouth, hot with the spice of brandy. He had left her senses reeling, and much as she wished to say she had loathed the sensation, in truth it had made her feel oddly alive.

It was all so devilishly confusing! Was a kiss really supposed to ignite such a . . . conflagration of passions in a proper young lady? She rather thought not.

Still . . .

With an exasperated oath, Portia forced herself to

extinguish such thoughts for the time being. She had much more burning questions to occupy her attention. Such as, how in the name of Hades was she going to prove that the Marquess of Dunster was a liar, a thief, and quite possibly a murderer?

Her lip puckered in concentration as she paced. What if she—

"Portia?" Her door opened a crack, just enough to allow a shadowy figure to slip into her room.

Drat it—yet another male to fend off! This one, however, should not prove nearly as hot to handle.

"Where the devil have you been?"

"You shouldn't swear in the presence of a lady," she replied rather primly. "Nor should you be skulking around in the wee hours of the night."

"Hah—rather the pot calling the kettle black!" Her younger brother flopped down upon her bed. "On both accounts."

She executed another quick turn in order to hide her guilty expression.

"Come on, confess, Portia. Where have you been?"

"Out. Which is where you are going this instant. Back to your own bed, if you don't mind. It's awfully late, and I wish to make use of mine."

His scowl turned every bit as black as hers. "Damnation, don't try to fob me off as if I were a child." He gave a hard look at her black garments and the scuffed toes of her sturdy boots. "And don't try to tell me you were attending the Renfrew ball dressed like that. I may be too young to go about in Society, but I'm not *that* naive."

A flicker of sympathy lit in Portia's eyes. Sixteen

was a deucedly awkward age. With his long, gangly limbs and voice that could range over an octave in one sentence, Henry was not quite a boy, but not quite a man.

"No," she answered softly, but made no effort to elaborate. While she could well understand his frustration, that did not make her any more willing to involve him in the very adult risks she was running.

After another moment of silent confrontation, his gaze shifted away. "You promised you wouldn't do anything rash."

Actually, what she had just done had not been rash, she thought as a grimace tugged at her mouth. It had been insane!

"Did you learn anything about Papa's disappearance?" he continued in a low whisper.

"No."

As she feared, her brother had not failed to notice the papers on the dressing table. "Then what are these—"

"Please, Henry. Don't press me any more tonight. I—I really am exhausted and not feeling up to a detailed explanation."

He must have sensed that the slight tremor in her voice was unfeigned, for he rose without further argument and jammed his hands into the pockets of his dressing gown. "Very well." The growl was obviously meant to sound manly; however, the jut of his lower lip almost caused Portia to smile in spite of herself. He looked more like six than sixteen. "But only for now. I shall expect to hear all about it come morning."

Ha! On no account was she going to tell her

brother *everything* that had transpired in the marquess's study. He would get a highly edited version, and even that, she worried, would be too much. She sighed. As if she didn't have enough to think about, it now appeared she would have to be extremely careful that her brother did not get any wild ideas of his own.

Her weary fingers began to work at the buttons of her bodice. It was bad enough that one member of the Hadley family was flirting with danger and disgrace. But perhaps the morning would bring with it a glimmer of hope, a change of luck.

Ha! And perhaps the Devil would be invited to breakfast with Saint Peter!

Chapter Two

The Devil was not invited to breakfast with Saint Peter. He was invited to breakfast with the Honorable Anthony Harkness Taft.

At the ungodly hour of ten in the morning.

Branford glanced at the clock on the mantel, then rubbed a hand over his stubbled chin. The engagement had slipped his mind until a moment ago, when the note from his friend had come dislodged from the jumble of papers at his elbow. He was tempted to cry off, but there was a veiled urgency to its tone that made him abandon the idea. Tony was not prone to exaggeration, so there must be a good reason for the summons.

Another slight turn of his head brought a momentary flash of his reflection in the mullioned window. *The devil take it!* He supposed he ought to manage a shave and change of linen before presenting himself at his friend's town house. Not that Tony would be overly shocked by his appearance. The two of them had known each other since university days and served as comrades in the Peninsular campaign, so the other man was well aware of the reckless side of the earl's nature. And yet, despite their differences in temperament, the rakish gambler and sober diplomat had become quite close over the years, for they both shared a sardonic sense of humor and a need for intellectual challenge.

However, since his return to England, Branford had seen little of his old friend. It was, he admitted, almost as if he had consciously avoided the sort of social engagements where they might run into each other. Biting back a weary sigh, he ran a hand through his hair. And perhaps with good reason—perhaps he feared seeing a flicker of disappointment in Tony's penetrating gaze.

Well, unfortunately, there was little he could do now about the deep shadows under his eyes or the look of general dissipation that lined his haggard features. Given that it was already past nine, a nap was not an option, and in any case, a short doze would hardly disguise the fact that he had been up all night. But at least he had not spent the entire time drinking or carousing, as had been his wont of late. One of the benefits of his elegant new residence was a well-stocked library, and so he had gone directly home on quitting Dunster's party, retreating to that stately room rather than the boudoir of some high-priced cyprian.

It had not taken overly long to research what he wanted to know. Turning his attention back to one of the books that lay open on his desk, he finished copying the information printed under the detailed engraving, then snapped the pages shut.

Hadley of Waddington. His expression was one of grim satisfaction as he looked over his notes. *Vert, a* _chevron between three stags' heads caboshed. Crest—on a wreath of the colors, a stag trippant proper, gorged with a collar vert. . . ._ He skimmed down a few lines. . . . _issue (3)—Portia Beatrice, Henry Falstaff, Bertram Orlando. . . ._

It appeared the obscure country baron had a fondness for Shakespeare. An interesting coincidence, he noted, seeing that someone close to the family certainly had a flair for theatrics.

Branford folded the sheet of foolscap and tucked it into his pocket alongside the worn signet ring and delicate tangle of gold links. Now that he knew where to start his hunt, he had no doubt that the elusive young lady would soon be run to ground.

With a heavy sigh, Portia forced herself to slip out from beneath the quilt and face the day. It was, she supposed, hardly surprising that the reflection in the small looking glass by the washstand was a rather depressing sight, showing smudges nearly as dark as midnight under her eyes and a grim tautness to the set of her mouth.

Her lids pressed closed as she hurriedly splashed a handful of cold water over her cheeks. It was not the first time she had blinked back the urge to cry over the last several weeks. The news that her father had lost all the family's possessions in a wild night of drinking and deep play had come as a complete shock. Papa foxed? Papa wagering the beloved cottage and his precious books on the turn of a card? _Ha! Not bloody likely!_ She would willingly bet her life on it.

Her father had never imbibed more than an occa-

sional tipple of sherry. And he wouldn't know the King
of Spades from the Prince Regent. Portia's mouth
crooked into a fond smile. The baron was not a worldly
gentleman—not in the usual sense of the word. Oh, he
traveled the globe, but not in search of earthly pleasures.
Eschewing the whirl of the dance floor and the glitter of
the drawing room, he preferred hiking the mountains of
the Andes or trekking the deserts of Palestine in search
of arcane archeological treasures.

Dearest Papa. While most people considered the
baron weirdly eccentric, she thought him a fascinating
father. Brilliant, funny, encouraging, and tolerant—
what more could a child have wished for while growing up?

She patted the towel to her brow. Well, now that
she thought about it, a tad more attention to practical
matters might have come in handy. While her father's
mind had been wandering in centuries past, his attention focused on finishing his *magnum opus* on ancient
civilizations, his present-day finances had slowly
crumbled into ruins. Perhaps if her mother had survived the birth of her youngest brother, things
wouldn't have fallen into such a sad state of affairs. But
she hadn't, and a fourteen-year-old girl, no matter how
sharp-witted, should not have been expected to deal
with bullying tradesmen, senile bankers, and two precocious siblings while her father absented himself for
months and months at a time.

Ah, well, that was all ancient history, she reminded
herself. Unlike her father, she wouldn't allow her
thoughts to dwell on the past. It was the current situation that was cause for real concern.

Her father had gone missing and her little family had been tossed from their rightful home with little more than the clothes on their backs. She sighed. As usual, if there was to be any hope of putting things to right, it was up to her—Practical Portia—to figure out what to do about it.

Opening the small armoire, Portia chose her best dress from among the meager assortment, in hopes that the cheery stripes of cream and azure might help brighten her outlook. However, the sight of the slightly frayed cuffs and discreet bit of mending at the neckline was further reminder of her family's precarious position. She paused, the garment clutched to her chest, and glanced around the bedchamber. It was a cozy little room, with sunlight spilling in through mullioned windows that overlooked a small walled garden. But her eye, well-schooled in noting such nuances, did not fail to observe a number of telling little details—the faded edges of the draperies, the tiny chip on the lip of the washbowl, the darning on the hems of the linens. Her great-aunt, though possessed of an honorable title, had precious little blunt to go along with it. And while the dowager countess had been quick to offer a place of refuge to her destitute young relatives, Portia knew that the addition of three extra people to the tiny household must be putting a strain on the elderly lady's finances.

How long could they continue to impose on Lady Trumbull's generosity? She dared not dwell overly on the future. There were no other relatives to speak of, save for a distant cousin in Yorkshire whose disapproving view of their father's activities was clear in the few missives received over the years. The fellow sounded like a rigid martinet, and Portia rather doubted they would find any welcome there.

With her genteel birth, she might, of course, seek a position as governess or paid companion. But then what of Henry and Bertie? Squire Gillen had subtly hinted that, through an acquaintance at the Admiralty, he might be able to secure a midshipman's commission for both of them. The thought caused her hands to clench into fists. *Over her dead body!* The Royal Navy was a brutal life, dull with routine and the monotony of shipboard life. Her brothers were much too bright to have their talents drowned in cheap grog and petty tyranny. They deserved to attend university. And she would damned well see that they got the chance.

It was, she sighed, yet another pressing reason to concentrate all of her practical abilities on solving the mystery. And quickly.

Her brow furrowed in concentration as she began to dress. The trouble had all started when, out of the blue, the Marquess of Dunster's man of affairs had arrived at their door. Brandishing a gaming vowel supposedly signed by her father, he had announced that the baron had lost Rose Cottage and all of its contents on the turn of a card. The slimy weasel had then gone on to say Portia and her brothers had twenty-four hours to vacate the premises.

She had, of course, refused to believe it, no matter that the man had brought along her father's heirloom ring, claiming the baron had given it over as further proof of the claim. Squire Gillen, the local magistrate and an old friend of the family, had thought it a very peculiar tale too. But without any evidence of fraud or foul play, there was nothing he could do to oppose the marquess's demand.

And that went to the heart of the matter. Her father had simply vanished from the face of the earth, as if Charon had gathered him up and ferried him across the river Styx. The man of affairs had sworn to having seen the baron embark on an East India ship bound for ports unknown, and claimed to have witnesses to corroborate the fact. Portia knew it wasn't true—her father might be a trifle absent-minded, but he would never have gone off on one of his far-flung adventures without telling her. In fact, he had made it quite clear before leaving for London that he only expected to be gone three or four days.

She pulled a face. No matter how many times or how many ways she looked at the facts, she couldn't figure out an explanation for what was going on.

So much for logic and rational thought.

And so she had climbed into the marquess's study, hoping to find some clue to solving the mystery. The gaming debt was a clever forgery, the story of the baron's abrupt departure was a lie. *But why?* A shiver ran through her. It was a chilling question, and caused her hand to steal inside her chemise, feeling for the reassuring warmth of the burnished gold. . . .

The devil take it—the chain was gone!

She had lost Papa's ring!

A sob caught in her throat, but with a hard swallow, Portia forced it away. She would not—could not—afford to dissolve in despair. Tears would serve no purpose, she reminded herself with grim logic. Save to redden her already haggard eyes. Catching a glimpse of her profile in the mirror, she forced her chin up in a martial tilt, then turned and marched for the door.

Whatever battles lay ahead, she would meet them head-on.

"You look like hell." Anthony Taft laid aside his newspaper and began to butter a piece of toast.

Branford regarded his friend with a humorless smile. "As most of Society considers me Lucifer in Hessians, I suppose it is only appropriate."

Taft lifted his brows a fraction, then went on as if he hadn't heard the cynical remark. "I would have thought a man of your exalted talents would be bored to perdition by spending his time in . . . mindless pursuits. At least, that is what it appears you have been doing since your return from the Peninsula."

Branford couldn't keep the edge from his voice as he took a seat at the dining table. "A man of my exalted title is not supposed to use his mind." A warm, syrupy light was pouring into the breakfast room, but rather than brighten his own glum mood, it only exacerbated the feeling that a pitchfork was pounding against the back of his skull. "Except, of course, for really important decisions—like choosing the color of a waistcoat or whether to become foxed on claret or on brandy." With a pained grimace he reached for the coffee that the footman had just poured, hoping the steaming brew might help dull the throb.

"I would guess brandy got the nod last night. Claret

doesn't usually cause such a wicked hangover. Or a snappish mood." His friend indicated the chafing dishes heaped with beefsteak, beacon, and creamed kidneys. "Speaking of snappish, care for a bite?"

The sight of food caused Branford's stomach to give a queasy lurch. "I'm sure you have heard through the grapevine that I only breakfast on small children— that is, when I am not feasting on innocent maidens. So I'll decline the kind offer."

"Good Lord, whatever female you feasted on last night, she certainly left a sour taste in your mouth."

The cup came down on the table with a thump. "If you've invited me here simply to discuss my tastes in wine or women, I'll leave you to your sirloin and shirred eggs. I'm in no bloody mood for it."

Taft cut off a morsel of his kippered herring and chewed thoughtfully before replying. "Hmmm. You *are* in a devil of a mood. In all the years we've known each other, I've never seen you quite so out of sorts."

"I've never been accused of cheating unsuspecting young men out of their inheritances." Branford couldn't keep the bitterness from his voice. "Or of being little more than a . . . murderer."

"In the past, you have never cared a whit about what people said or thought. It's hardly the first time scurrilous rumors have swirled around your name."

The earl turned away from the window, a bleak expression shadowing his face. It was true. At Oxford he had been dubbed "The Black Cat," for his presence at the gaming tables usually cursed the other players to a night of deep losses. It was also true that his uncanny luck was due to applying the same sort of careful calculation and cool nerve that had made him one of Wellington's most reliable intelligence officers, rather than the result of any dark tricks. There were, however, some disgruntled gentlemen whose whispers implied otherwise. Branford had simply shrugged off the mutterings, for innuendoes had seemed a small price to pay for his winnings. The blunt had purchased far more than mere physical comforts. By allowing him to be in control of his own destiny, beholden to no one but himself, it had brought him some measure of freedom from the demons of the past.

His jaw clenched on recalling his youth. Lord, how he had hated those years. His father, a charming but feckless younger son, had somehow managed to kill both himself and his wife in a carriage accident, leaving their only child an impoverished orphan. Branford still remembered with haunting clarity how angry he had felt at being left alone, and then how ashamed he had been at his own feeling of vulnerability and sense of loss. He had been cared for by various relatives, all of them kind and well-meaning. But he had sensed their pity as well as affection, and it had only exacerbated his uncertainty and the rawness of his youthful pride. It was then that he had vowed to stay well clear of emotional attachments.

"It's not what other people are saying that has you wallowing in drink and despair, is it?" pressed his friend after the silence had stretched to some minutes. "It's what you yourself are thinking."

The tightening of Branford's fingers threatened to crack the delicate china. He had remained true to his promise, enjoying the pleasures of the moment and the fleeting company of more than a few females without ever allowing himself to need or care for anything deeper. That is, until his young cousins, the two scampy pups who had followed his footsteps with dogged devotion in their youth, grew old enough to join the army's same regiment.

"Let it go, Alex. There was nothing you could have done about it. My God, over sixty officers and seven hundred soldiers died at Badajoz, along with Ranleigh and Wilford."

"I could have ordered them to the back lines." Well aware that his words were hardly more than a whisper, Branford cleared his throat and tried for a more dispassionate tone. "Or, at the very least, forbidden them to carry the dispatches between cavalry commanders."

"No, in good conscience you could never have done such a thing. You were far too good a soldier to play favorites." Taft had laid aside his silverware and was regarding the earl from over the tips of his steepled hands. "Besides, they would never have forgiven you. And, being as hardheaded as their revered cousin, they never would have obeyed you. They would simply have found another officer to countermand such an order."

There was another lengthy silence before the earl looked up, the shadows turning half his face as dark as a crypt. "Christ Almighty, Tony," he whispered. "They were so young. So full of life and promise."

"And so you mean to ride hell for leather after them into an early grave, just because you feel sorry for yourself?"

Stunned by the accusation, Branford recoiled. "What the devil do you mean, feel—"

"Self-pity exacerbated by sheer boredom. That, I imagine, is the real reason for your self-destructive behavior since you returned to England as the new earl."

"I never wanted the damn title!" Though he realized he was perilously close to shouting, he couldn't contain his outrage.

"I'm well aware of that, Alex," answered his friend softly.

"Nor ever expected to have it. Not with my uncle hale and hearty, and his two sons just entering the prime of their youth." Suddenly feeling very old and very tired, Branford rubbed at his temples and tried to swallow the taste of bile caught in his throat. "Hell's teeth, quite likely it was the shock of their loss that caused Fitzwilliam to fall victim to a sudden stroke."

"Ah. You blame yourself for that too?" Taft paused long enough to pour a fresh cup of tea and add a splash of cream. "So now you think yourself the Almighty as well as the Devil? What hubris, Alex! Though God knows, you try to convince yourself otherwise, it is foolish to imagine that you, and you alone, control the destinies of others."

Branford opened his mouth to protest, but found himself utterly incapable of speech.

"Well, you can't. And no amount of drinking, dueling, deep play, or dallying with other men's wives will change that fact." Taft left off stirring. "There is a certain fate—or call it what you will—that shapes our lives. I would have thought a clever fellow like you could have figured that out by now."

Turning white as the damask tablecloth, he finally managed a response. "Is the lecture over?"

"Not quite. I've yet to take you to task for snubbing my company in favor of carousing with strangers, for ignoring your old comrades, and for refusing Cecilia's entreaties to call on her. You've been a damn shabby friend, Alex. And it is as wounding to me as any bullet or saber."

Branford felt as if he had taken another punch to the jaw, this one even more stinging than the one of the previous night. "Have I been as bad as that?"

"Worse." Taft gave a faint smile. "However, I am about to allow you to make it up to me."

"Oh, bloody hell. No doubt I shall regret it. . . ." The earl shifted in his seat. "But I suppose I might as well listen to what you have in mind for my penance."

"Start talking."

Henry punctuated the demand with a jab of his knife, unmindful of the dab of strawberry jam that fell onto his breeches.

Portia could still hear the faint rustle of papers and pleated silk as their great-aunt made her way down the hallway toward the library. To forestall having to answer, she broke off another bit of toast and popped it into her mouth, taking care to chew very slowly. From beneath her lowered lashes she watched him spear a morsel of ham and winced. Such savage manners might pass unnoticed around a campfire in Crete, but here in London, amid fine china and silver, the lack of polish was glaring.

Good Lord, had she really neglected to school her siblings in proper table etiquette?

The crumbs suddenly tasted dry as sawdust. No,

she assured herself, she had tried to teach them how to behave as gentlemen, along with a good many other things since their mother had passed away. But perhaps now that they were growing older, they needed a firmer hand than that of an elder sister. Even one who had reached the ripe old age of twenty-four.

Her grip tightened on the damask napkin as her gaze moved up from the offending piece of silverware. The sorry state of their wardrobe was even more pronounced in Henry's clothing. As he had shot up several inches over the past few months, a wide expanse of bare wrist now protruded from the worn cuffs of his shirt, and his jacket looked uncomfortably tight across the shoulders. Somehow, she would have to manage the expense of new garments before he was reduced to walking around in his nightshirt.

Unaware of the scrutiny, he stood up and turned to the sideboard for a second helping of eggs. Portia suddenly realized he was almost as tall as she was. And, she noted with a rueful quirk of her lips, unfortunately the resemblance didn't stop there. The stubborn jut of his jaw was suspiciously familiar, as was the arrogant tilt of his rather long nose and the strong-willed glint of his gaze. The frown now furrowing his forehead was softened somewhat by the shock of hair falling in boyish disarray. Several shades darker than her own wheaten tresses, it needed a good trimming, but as she had grown adept at wielding scissors, the expense of a barber could be saved. . . .

"*Well?*" repeated Henry, upon resuming his seat.

The growing impatience of his tone, along with another noisy attack on the jam jar, finally jarred her from her musings. "There is really not much to tell," she murmured. "I paid a visit to the marquess's study. Unfortunately, I did not have a great deal of time to look around." Her fingers turned the remainder of the toast into a pile of crumbs. "You saw all that I managed to turn up. Nothing but bills and bawdy verse."

"Dunster's study?" It took a moment for her brother to digest the import of what she had said. "But how—"

"Never mind."

"But what if he recognized—"

"He didn't."

"But surely he will suspect—"

"He won't."

Thoroughly confused, Henry balled up his napkin and threw it down upon the table. "The devil take it, I don't understand—"

"Good."

"Portia!"

Deciding that it might be better to provide a few more details so that his imagination didn't go off half-cocked, she relented. "Look, Henry, I can assure you that Lord Dunster will assume that one of his, er, guests was looking to steal some bauble or bit of blunt when he discovers the riffled desk drawer."

"I would think you would be one of the first to fall under suspicion," replied her brother.

"Trust me, the marquess has no idea I was among the . . . females present."

"The black clothing—" His eyes narrowed. "Are you telling me you were not invited to the festivities?"

Portia felt a faint tinge of color rise to her cheeks. "Not exactly."

"That was devilishly dangerous of you—"

They both fell silent as the door swung open.

"Ha! I thought so." The eyes beneath the thatch of wheaten hair were perhaps not quite as emerald as those of his older siblings, but held the same hard-edged glitter. "What are the two of you discussing behind my back?"

"Never mind," answered Henry, his curt dismissal an unconscious echo of his sister's earlier rebuff. "Go back to your logarithms."

"Don't play the high and mighty prince with me, Henry Falstaff!" cried the youngest Hadley. "Just because you are four years older doesn't give you the right to order me around." Wiping the smudge of ink from his cheek, he turned an imploring look on his sister. "I'm *not* a child, Portia, to be locked away in the schoolroom when something important is afoot. If you two are conspiring on some plan concerning Papa, I want to be part of it."

Portia gave a silent sigh and found herself eyeing the casement window with longing. In fact, if given the choice at that moment, she might rather face one drunken rogue than two adolescent boys. However, as flight was not an option, she marshaled her wits to deal with the latest dilemma.

"No one would mistake you for a mere child, Bertie," she replied. "And both Henry and I are well aware of how useful your talents can be in a pinch."

In that statement, at least, she did not have to stretch the truth. While she and Henry had inherited their father's gift for languages and history, the youngest Hadley was a mathematical prodigy. As a toddler, his skill at arithmetic was such that the local tradesmen quickly learned not to try adding an extra halfpenny onto their bills. And by the age of ten, his grasp of complex theory had some of the baron's Oxford acquaintances mumbling in awe—or pique—as the lad was wont to solve problems they had been struggling with for months.

"If it would be of help, I could figure out the exact position of the East India merchant ship at this moment." Encouraged by his sister's praise, Bertie's words came out in a rush of enthusiasm. "All I would need is a tide table and some information on the average prevailing winds."

The statement drew a reluctant grin from his older brother. "We know that, Bertie. And if we have to move the pyramids to get at where Papa is being imprisoned, we shall count on you to calculate the weight and mass, and what size lever is needed."

Bertie made a face, not sure whether he was being teased. "Even a five-year-old could figure that out. Now, if we needed to postulate the cubic—"

"I have no doubt you could solve any logistical conundrum that might arise," interrupted Portia, determined not to let the conversation turn into one of the usual arcane family discussions. They could be quite fascinating, but tended to go on for hours if not nipped in the bud. And this morning she had a number of things she wished to get done. "However, the problem is, we have no idea as of yet whether Papa is locked away on ship, hidden under the pyramids, or on his way to the moon! And without any notion of where to start looking, it's deucedly difficult to formulate a plan."

The two boys turned to her and waited expectantly.

"So what do you suggest we do?" Henry finally asked, when it became clear she was not going to continue.

"*We* are not going to do anything," she said firmly. "You know very well that on account of your ages, you cannot move about in Society."

"It's deucedly unfair," grumbled Henry.

A rueful smile tugged at Portia's lips. "I don't like the rules any more than you do, but flaunting them would only do more harm than good right now. We have no idea what—or whom—we are up against, so we have to proceed slowly, and with a great deal of caution and discretion."

Caution and discretion. She was one to talk! If her brothers had any idea of how little of either quality she had exhibited of late . . .

"I suppose that makes some sense," allowed Bertie. "One should always tackle a difficult problem with cool detachment and calm reason."

Despite the gravity of the situation, it was only with great difficulty that she kept from chuckling aloud.

Henry looked none too happy about it, but nodded his agreement. "Very well. For now." His brow then puckered. "Speaking of caution, you aren't planning to go back to Lord Dunster's town house, are you?"

"I'd like to have another look around," she admitted, "but I am not sure when the opportunity will present itself." One thing was sure, she vowed. The next time she would choose a night when she was absolutely certain the marquess was not entertaining at home. "In the meantime there are still several people I have not had a chance to speak to. Sir Reginald Huffington is someone with whom Papa corresponded quite often, so it is possible he may know something that could prove useful. And as luck would have it, I happen to have learned he is attending Lady Fotherington's ball this evening."

"A document has gone missing, and the fate of the nation may depend on its recovery."

"A single document?" Branford rolled his eyes. "Aren't you waxing a bit melodramatic?"

"Hear me out before making a face." Taft set down his cup and tilted back in his chair. "As you know, our government is desperate to coax Russia into another alliance with us, rather than France. However, since Austerlitz and the Treaty of Tilsit back in 1805, Tsar Alexander has proved reluctant to commit himself to either side—"

"Christ, Tony, my brain is not so fuzzed with last night's brandy that I need a blasted history lesson."

"Then you are well aware that for years, Alexander has been warring with the Ottoman Empire and Persia over annexing territory around the Black Sea. Well, at present, unrest in the Caucasus is threatening to erupt into full-scale revolt—something the Tsar must avoid at all costs, seeing as his domestic reforms have already created resentment among his own people. One more crisis might cause the Romanov dynasty to topple from its throne."

"So, what does that have to do with us?" demanded Branford.

"I am getting to that," replied Taft patiently. "The

leaders of a powerful religious sect in Shemakka have issued a challenge of sorts to Russia. If Moscow can decipher the meaning of its most sacred relic, known as the Riddle of Rafistan, they will take it as a sign from God and guarantee peace. So, in turn, Alexander has passed the word on to London—and to Paris. Whoever can give him the answer to the Riddle will gain the Russian bear as an ally. Needless to say, if Bonaparte succeeds, it could spell certain disaster for England. The Little Corsican might very well be able to make good on his threat to hang the Bayeux Tapestry in Westminster Cathedral."

The earl let out a low whistle.

"Aye, it's serious business, Alex. However, our envoy in Moscow somehow convinced the tsar to give us first crack at the Riddle. It was passed in utmost secrecy to a British Navy frigate in Constantinople, which made all haste to Portsmouth. A special courier took charge from there and set off for London. The trouble is, word of it apparently leaked from the inner sanctum of Whitehall. The messenger was ambushed and the document was stolen."

"Bloody hell."

"Aye, bloody hell, indeed, if we cannot retrieve it." Taft tugged at his cuff. "So far, the only clue my men have managed to uncover is a rumor that it is here in London and being offered to Bonaparte for an astronomical sum. If that isn't bad enough, the tsar's envoys are already making inquiries about our progress and Whitehall doesn't dare let it slip that we have lost the damn thing."

"An interesting story." Branford rubbed at his chin.

"Assuming, of course, that your information is correct."

"I'm quite sure it is." Taft's mouth compressed in a tight line as he glanced down at the newspaper's account of the turbulent diplomatic negotiations with the Tsar of Russia. "What I need to discover—and quickly—is who took the damn thing and how to get it back."

"And you think I may be of some help?"

"As I have said, the situation is highly sensitive. My superiors at Whitehall would prefer that it be, er, resolved without any of the interested parties learning that the item has gone missing." His fingers beat an urgent tattoo upon the folded newspaper. "Wellington considered you the best man he ever worked with."

"Much has changed since then." A bitter smile ghosted across the earl's features. "I fear my skills at espionage may have become a bit rusty, Tony."

"Somehow I doubt that, though God knows they have been soaked with enough brandy to corrode the keel of a forty-gun frigate." After a flash of his teeth, Taft's expression once again became serious. "The only thing that has changed since Portugal is that you are bored out of your skull. What you need is a challenge to get your wits back in working order." He paused. "Besides, your reputation and your scandalous behavior of the past six months only serve as an advantage in this case."

Branford felt a spark of the old fire kindling inside him. "Why?"

"We have reason to suspect the person we seek is someone who not only moves in the very highest circles of Society but has contacts among the hardened denizens of the stews," explained his friend. "Someone who may also have access to the inner sanctum of Whitehall."

"You are not without a certain expertise in clandestine activities. Have you no idea who he—or she—may be?"

"*She?*" The legs of Taft's chair came down with a thump. "How the devil did you know that a lady's name is on my list of possible suspects?"

"I didn't." Branford rubbed unconsciously at an old scar on his ribs. "But my wartime experience taught me that women may be even more dangerous than men."

"Hmmm. You have a point." Taft fiddled with the folds of his cravat as a wry note crept into his voice. "After several years of marriage I am ready to concede that the female mind is every bit as capable as that of a male when it comes to Machiavellian subterfuge and scheming."

The thought of emerald eyes and black silk flashed into Branford's mind. "As am I." Although he had sworn never to stir up the coals of his old life, he couldn't help but inch forward in his chair. "I must say, the story is beginning to take on an even more intriguing angle."

"I rather hoped it might." Taft was trying not to look too pleased with himself. "I imagine you now see why, in order to have any prayer of success, an investigation must be handled outside the official channels of the government, and yet by an individual who can move freely among the *ton* without raising the least bit of alarm. That certainly rules out any of our usual agents, or ministers like myself, whose positions are no secret. Our culprit is much too clever to be caught by either."

"But I—"

"But you, on the other hand, are a titled lord. And you have established yourself as a dissolute wastrel, uninterested in aught but reckless pleasures. It is a perfect cover for moving in both the lighter and darker sides of Society."

Branford unconsciously rubbed at his jaw. "What makes you think I might be interested in taking on such an assignment?"

"A number of reasons. One, because you owe me a rather large favor to make up for your neglect. Two, because I see a certain light in your eye that tells me the real Alexander Sheffield is ready to return to life." The grin returned to Taft's face. "And three, because if you don't, I shall lock you in a room with Cecilia for a half an hour and allow her to give full vent to her feelings of neglect." He gave a mock shudder. "Trust me, you would rather the sultan of the Ottomans hung you upside down from the palace gates and let the crows pick at your eyes."

Branford found himself grinning as well. "Enough said. So where in hell do I start looking?"

Chapter Three

❦❦❦

The elderly lady brushed back a silvery wisp of hair from her forehead, which was now furrowed in puzzlement. "How very odd." She removed her spectacles, wiped absently at a few smudges, then set them back on the bridge of her nose. "Well, send him in, Stevens."

A few minutes later the caller was shown into the cozy study.

"I do hope you will forgive the informality of receiving you here, sir, but I am in the middle of translating a particularly thorny passage of Virgil. . . ." She looked up from her manuscript. "I don't suppose you are here to drop off the Latin lexicon that I ordered from Hatchards?"

Branford's mouth twitched in amusement as he inclined a polite bow. "I regret to say I do not have the aforesaid parcel in my possession, Lady Trumbull."

"No, of course an earl would not be acting as a messenger boy," she murmured. Still, a twist of disappointment was evident in her expression. With a sigh she gave one last, longing glance at the half-finished page before turning back to her guest. "Hmmm." Her eyes narrowed into a squint. "Well, then, if you don't mind my asking, why *are* you here? Your grandmother and I were good friends, but Adelaide cocked up her toes several years ago, if I recall correctly. . . ."

He strolled toward the desk and peered down at the tattered volume that was propped open against a marble bust of Aristotle. After a moment of study he reached for her pen. "May I?"

She blinked several times but allowed him to pluck the quill from her fingers without protest.

There was the sound of rapid scribbling upon a scrap of foolscap. "Have you considered this?" he asked, handing over the finished lines.

Lady Trumbull scanned the paper once, then twice, and a smile of delight slowly spread across her face. "My dear man, it appears you are as accurate with your Latin declensions as you are with your pistol! I've been struggling with that dratted sentence for hours!"

Branford gave an inner wince. His behavior must be the talk of the Town if even an elderly dowager was up-to-date on the latest scandal surrounding his name. However, he managed to keep a bland expression on his face. "Sometimes a fresh perspective can make all the difference, Lady Trumbull."

"Indeed. One often fails to see what is right in front of one's nose." She rubbed at her lenses and the smile broadened. "How can I ever thank you?"

"Well, since you asked . . ." He unfolded the sketch he had made earlier that morning and smoothed it out upon her blotter. "You could do me one small favor by looking at this and telling me whether you recognize it."

"Of course I do. It is my nephew's crest."

"Julian Hadley?" he said. "Of Pevensey?"

"Y-yes," she replied, clearly puzzled by his line of questioning.

"And this?" Branford took the ring from his pocket and held it out in his upturned palm.

"Why, that is Julian's as well! But"—Lady Trumbull paused—"how did you come to be in possession of it, sir?"

"It was dropped by a young lady as she took her leave from a certain party yesterday evening, but I was not quite quick enough to catch up with her before she . . . disappeared." His fingers closed over the dull gleam of gold. "As I didn't catch her name, I did a bit of research and came up with the Hadley connection to you, Lady Trumbull. So I thought I would start my inquiries here." He cleared his throat. "I should like to return it to its rightful owner."

"Well, you make an excellent Bow Street runner, Lord Branford, as well as a scholar and . . ." She gave a little cough. "Er, not that I pay attention to what the tabbies are saying. You seem like a perfectly pleasant gentleman to me."

He acknowledged her words with a faint smile.

Lady Trumbull fingered an ink stain on her cuff. "My grandniece will be delighted to find her father's ring is not lost."

"Unlike her parent."

There was a heavy sigh. "So you have heard about that too?"

"As you well know, rumors are hard to avoid in this Town." Seeing the lady's face grow even more clouded, Branford changed the subject. "Perhaps if your niece is in . . ."

"Unfortunately, she is not. But you may, of course, leave it with me."

"I would prefer to hand it over in person, if you don't mind."

"Somehow I doubt it would make much difference if I did," she replied dryly. "However, she has taken her brothers for a tour of the Tower, so they will likely be gone all afternoon."

"No hurry, Lady Trumbull." He slipped the ring back in his pocket. "I'm sure the young lady and I will be meeting again in the near future."

"No doubt, sir." There was a wink of light from off the freshly polished lenses. "Especially if you are planning to attend Lady Fotherington's ball this evening."

The violin twirled on a high note, then capered on to the next measure, leading the couples through the steps of a lively country set. Muted laughter, the clink of crystal, and the whisper of swirling silk added a subtle harmony to the music, as did the buzz of conversation coming from the perimeter of the dance floor.

"This is all the information I've been able to gather on the theft," murmured Taft as he edged deeper into the shadows of the potted palms. While making a show of brushing a large frond from his lapel, he slipped a small packet into the pocket of the earl's black melton evening jacket. "Along with the latest reports from Constantinople, which, as promised, just arrived at Whitehall this afternoon. Even so, it's not much to go on, I'm afraid. You have your work cut out for you."

Branford shrugged and surveyed the crowded ballroom. "The answers in this sort of business rarely appear on a silver platter." He signaled for a passing servant and took a glass of champagne from the ornate tray. "What about the list of possible suspects that you came up on your own?" he asked, once they were alone.

"It's there with the other paper—though, as I warned you before, my guesses are only gropes in the dark."

"Your intuition has always been as sharp as your intellect, so I would be a fool to ignore them." Stepping back, the earl leaned against one of the fluted columns, his own profile becoming no more than a black outline among the jagged leaves. "However, the lists could have waited until the morrow. Is there another reason you asked me to meet you at such a dreadfully dull party?"

"As a matter of fact, I wanted to point out two recent arrivals to Town whom I knew would be here tonight." Taft was watching a heavyset gentleman who was sporting a bottle-green swallowtail coat and thick whiskers spin his partner through a series of intricate figures. "Roxleigh, there, is certainly someone to keep an eye on. He gambles heavily and spends a good deal of blunt on horseflesh, with no discernible source of income to support such extravagant habits. Add to that the fact that his wife's family has ties to America—a younger son in the Carolinas with vast rice plantations and a vested interest in seeing our embargo lifted from European ports."

His gaze shifted toward the far corner of the room, where a small crowd of gentlemen were gathering around a striking raven-haired lady attired in shimmering scarlet. "Then there is the mysterious Mrs. Grenville, recently returned from India. She's said to be fabulously wealthy, and a widow. . . ."

"And, by all appearances, hardly mourning the loss of her dear departed husband," remarked the earl dryly. Even from a distance the clinging lines and low cut of her gown were readily apparent.

"If he ever existed," replied Taft. "For although we can verify that a Grenville and Company, headquartered in Madras, has made a fortune in ginger and cloves, any information concerning Mr. Grenville is proving deucedly hard to uncover."

"Perhaps I shall have better luck in uncovering what, if anything, the lady is hiding." The earl's lips curved into a sardonic smile. "I've always enjoyed spicy fare—the hotter the better."

"Just have a care you don't get burned."

"You think the Black Cat cannot handle a kitten?"

"If this lady is the person we seek, she's more dangerous than a Bengal tiger! As you yourself said, don't underestimate the threat, simply because your opponent may be a female."

"My dear Tony, I fear that marriage has indeed put you under the cat's paw—" Branford stopped abruptly. The dance had come to an end, and as the couples drifted off into the milling crowd he suddenly caught sight of Lady Trumbull. She was seated in a shallow alcove, along with a number of other matrons. However, amid the turbans and ostrich plumes, the earl also spotted a twist of wheat-gold curls that could only belong to a lady of much younger years. "By the way, speaking of recent arrivals to Town, what do you know of a Miss Portia Hadley?"

"Miss Hadley?" His friend frowned as he followed Branford's gaze. "What the devil makes you ask about her?"

"I am merely . . . curious."

"Well, don't be. She is not at all your type." The lines deepened around Taft's mouth. "No matter what sort of rumors are being bandied about, I cannot believe you have developed a taste for seducing green girls. She may be older than most chits fresh out of the schoolroom, but she's still naught but an inexperienced country miss who is much too innocent to understand the rules of Society's games."

Ha! though the earl to himself. For an inexperienced country miss, Miss Hadley seemed quite willing to play with fire.

"Besides," continued Taft in a low growl, "speaking of rumors, although she has only been in Town a short while, the young lady has already earned a reputation for eccentric behavior."

That was putting it rather mildly, thought Branford with an inward grimace.

"In short, she is said to be an odd sort of bluestocking who is unfashionably outspoken and opinionated. It must run in the family, for her father and great-aunt are both noted scholars—and noted quizzes." His friend brushed at another frond. "The truth is, I can't think of a young lady less likely to attract your interest."

The earl drained his glass in one swallow and set it in one of the terra-cotta pots. "You will have to excuse me, but a new set is forming."

"Hell's teeth—"

"Don't worry, Tony. I assure you my interest in Miss Hadley is purely academic."

*   *   *

"I cannot imagine why you have forced me out here on the dance floor, Lord Branford." Portia stiffened her right arm, trying to put as much distance between her and the earl as possible. "Especially as we have no previous acquaintance with each other."

"On the contrary, Miss Hadley, I would say we know each other most . . . intimately."

To her dismay, she felt her cheeks turn hot as Hades. "How *very* ungentlemanly of you to mention the incident. That is, it would be if I had any idea what you are talking about. And—"

He laughed softly and, with an effortless grace, spun her around. "Let's not dance in circles, Miss Hadley. You know very well we have met before."

When she came back in his arms, she brought her foot down rather hard upon his. "Don't waste your breath if you are looking to blackmail me over it, you odious man," she shot back. "If I had any blunt—which I don't—I would rather pay it to the Devil himself than fork over so much as a farthing for your silence."

Portia was gratified to see her retort had finally wiped the smile from the earl's face. His sapphirine eyes darkened to a stormy hue, more slate than luminous blue, and his voice had an ominous rumble, as if it might deepen into thunder at any moment. "Have a care, Miss Hadley. To be called a blackmailer is even worse than to be accused of cheating at cards. If you were a man, I would be forced to call you out for such an insult to my honor."

"And if I were a man, I would probably be idiotic enough to accept. Why, you and your sort are worse than grubby schoolboys, wanting to bang away at each other with pistols over a matter of words." Ignoring the tightening of his hand over her glove, she went on. "And how dare you speak of honor! It is *I* who should be calling *you* out over your crude assault to my person. Or do you simply forget your gentlemanly scruples whenever it is convenient?"

Although his voice remained low and his step lost none of its smooth rhythm, Portia was aware that the earl was now angry. Very angry.

"My hands around your waist were to help you avoid a set of manacles around your wrists, you ungrateful chit." His expression twisted into a sardonic grimace. "Trust me, my actions were prompted not by any attraction to your person but merely by a sense of obligation to help a lady in distress."

"More likely they were prompted by a hogshead of brandy! By the slur of your speech and the reek of your coat, it appeared that you had consumed at least that much, you dissolute wastrel."

His jaw clenched so tightly she could almost hear his teeth crack. Fearing that in her own anger she may have charged in too far, Portia drew in a sharp breath and sought to bring a halt to the hostilities. An explosion in the middle of the ballroom would only blow up any hope she had of making a few discreet inquiries later on.

"Oh, let us stop taking potshots at each other, sir, and get down to the real reason we are here." Her eyes narrowed. "Which is . . . ?"

"I thought you might have a sentimental attachment to a certain trinket that was dropped last night."

"You have my ring!" Portia restrained the urge to

stamp on his foot once again. "Why didn't you say so in the first place? Give it back to me this instant!"

"Why should I? It would, of course, be the gentlemanly thing to do, but you have made it clear that you think me no gentleman."

In spite of her resolve to keep a rein on her temper, she couldn't help but fire back, "Are you telling me you are a thief as well as a drunken lout?"

"Thief!" His lip curled in a mocking sneer. "It was not *I* who was stuffing papers down my bosom—"

The music was by now drawing to an end, and the earl left off speaking in order to concentrate on the last few figures of the dance. He contrived that the last notes left them standing at a spot to one side of the glass doors, where the angle of the open casement afforded a bit of privacy. The brief pause appeared to have given him time to marshal his ire, for when he spoke again, his voice was under rigid control.

"I have known a great many soldiers whose sabers could not match the sharpness of your tongue, Miss Hadley. But have a care how you wield such a weapon." His own movements were so dexterous that Portia was not aware that her hand was in his until she felt the hard contour of the ring through her glove. "One small slip, and you may very well end up doing yourself serious harm."

She stared down at the wink of gold, grimly determined to avoid his glittery gaze. There was, she knew, a prick of truth in his words, but she was certainly not going to admit it. "If I do, it is certainly none of your concern." Her hand closed tightly. "Seeing as we have taken care of business, sir, I trust we will not have reason to meet again any time soon."

"I devoutly hope not."

Branford polished off another glass of champagne, hoping to douse his still smoldering temper. How dare the outspoken country chit accuse him of outrageous behavior! Rather the pot calling the kettle black, he thought, recalling his first glimpse of her face, half shrouded in midnight silk. The memory caused his frown to deepen. She had been right in accusing him of being deep in his cups the night of their first encounter. And perhaps his handling of the situation had gone a trifle beyond the bounds of propriety. However there had been good reason for his actions.

What the devil was her excuse?

Rather unwillingly, he let his gaze drift to where she sat, the angle of her chin and rigid set of her shoulders indicating that she was still seething from their encounter. Indeed, he wondered, what possible reason could a young lady have for seeking to burglarize a gentleman's town house? She had let fall a vague accusation, but it still made little sense, even now that he was sober.

Branford raised the glass to his lips and took a hurried swallow, determined to wash the sour taste of the young lady from his mind. Miss Hadley and her fanciful claim were not his problem, he chided himself with some heat. He had returned her ring, and that was the end of any obligation. Why, with any luck, he would never see the outspoken chit again.

A whirl of red caught his eye, reminding him that

his thoughts should be focused on an exotic widow rather than an irritating bluestocking. The sultry Mrs. Grenville was dancing with a tall gentleman whose glossy hair was artfully arranged in the latest style. The exaggerated nip of his coat and snug pantaloons were further evidence of his pretensions to dandyism. Branford didn't recognize him until the steps of the dance brought him into the ring of light cast by one of the crystal chandeliers.

Hawkins. The earl thought for a moment. The baron's wits were dull as dishwater, and his manners lacked any sort of polish, though he fancied himself a great favorite with the ladies. It was highly doubtful he could be the mastermind Whitehall sought—not unless his acting skills rivaled those of Edmund Kean. Still, Branford edged closer to the dance floor in order to overhear what they were saying.

". . . a magnificent bloom, my dear Mrs. Grenville. I vow, you put all of our English roses to blush."

Branford winced inwardly. The baron's compliments were nearly as oily as the Macassar dressing on his cropped curls.

The widow's response was a throaty laugh. "Surely not, sir, for it appears to me that there is a great deal of beauty among your homegrown blooms."

"They all pale in comparison to you."

She seemed to be tiring of such florid sentiments, for she merely inclined her head a touch. Her eyes, however, remained riveted on a spot somewhere over the gentleman's left shoulder.

Branford turned slightly to see if he could make out what had caught her attention. There was a stirring in the shadows, and a brief flash of white that might have been the wave of a handkerchief. Then, just as quickly, it was gone. The earl craned his neck, searching the recessed alcoves to either side of the hallway, but could not make out any further sign of movement.

He might have dismissed it as a mere quirk of the light had not Mrs. Grenville paused in mid-step and pressed a gloved hand to her brow. "La, I fear I am still unused to the rigors of the social whirl here in London," she murmured. "I—I feel a trifle faint. Would you mind escorting me to a less crowded spot, sir?" With a flutter of her lashes, she leaned in heavily against her partner and indicated the alcove on the right. "Then I'm sure I would feel much revived if you were to fetch me a glass of ratafia punch."

Hawkins patted her arm and nearly tripped over his own feet in his haste to lead her away—though to the earl's cynical eye, it was debatable as to who was leading whom. A rather affecting performance, he decided. It would be interesting to see how quickly the lady recovered once her escort had hared off for the requested refreshment.

Moving with an air of deceptive nonchalance, Branford began to make his way to the opposite side of the ballroom.

Sapphire blue. Portia somehow managed to repress a shudder as she stared at the stripes of Sir Reginald Huffington's waistcoat. She had devoutly hoped she would not be seeing that exact shade anytime soon, but Sir Reginald was a very large man, and an arrangement of tulips and chrysanthemums to her rear prevented any turning of her head.

"No, your father said nothing to indicate any upcoming journey. Quite the opposite, in fact." The pursing of the baronet's mouth was followed by a slight shake of his head. "Deuced odd, if you don't mind my saying, Miss Hadley."

"I don't mind at all. It struck me quite the same way." Portia gave a forced smile. "You wouldn't by any chance happen to remember exactly what he said in his last letter?"

Sir Reginald stroked his chin. "Hmmm."

There was a lengthy pause, during which she kept her hands clasped together, so that she might feel the touch of her father's ring and the broken chain. For safekeeping, she had slipped them inside her kid glove, and the familiar warmth against her skin was rather comforting.

Insufferable man! Not Sir Reginald, of course—the Earl of Branford. At least he had had the decency to return her property. Portia's fingers tightened. Though clearly, very little else about him was decent. Her breath seemed to catch in her throat as she recalled the husky murmur of his voice and the glittering intensity of his gaze.

Her own gaze suddenly shifted to follow his progress toward the far end of the room. Even at a distance, the earl radiated an aura of raw masculinity. There was something in his movements that gave hint of the powerful beast lurking beneath the finely tailored evening clothes. All too aware of the coiled strength of his limbs, Portia felt a certain prickling heat spread over her as she watched the subtle rippling of muscle stretch the fabric of his coat.

She blinked, and yet found herself still staring at his face. It was a devilishly handsome one, she had to admit, the chiseled leanness softened by a tumble of gleaming black hair that curled around his ears and collar. The texture looked to be as smoothly sensuous as the finest silk, and for a moment she couldn't help wanting to thread her fingers through it, then let them trail across the high-cut cheekbones and down to the firm lips that looked ready to whisper all manner of intimate . . .

With an inward oath, Portia wrenched her eyes away, determined to stop thinking of the earl and the highly improper thoughts he stirred within her. *Intimate, indeed!* How dare the dratted man have referred to that embarrassing interlude as if it had been anything other than . . . repulsive.

He would not make that mistake again, she thought, her chin unconsciously rising just a fraction. She knew that her cutting words had wounded his vanity, for on top of being arrogant, odious, and ill-mannered, the earl apparently had a hellish temper. Nearly as fiery as her own, judging from the flaming scowl and the heated retorts he had hurled back at her.

A faint tinge of color suffused her cheeks. In all fairness, she had to admit that her accusations had been designed to ignite his anger, so it was not to be wondered at that he had been goaded into such rudeness. Still, to imply that *she* was the one who ought to curb her tongue. . . !

Hmmph! The earl should learn to control his own heated tongue—along with his roving hands . . .

"—a package, I believe."

Hell's bells! How could she have allowed her thought to stray so far from the matter at hand! "Er, what was that?" she stammered.

"A package," repeated Sir Reginald. "At least, I believe that was what your father was referring to in the letter. His references were a bit harder to follow than usual. Come to think of it, he was making even less sense when he stopped by my rooms to drop off a book. Seemed rather more preoccupied than usual. And a good deal more agitated than I had ever seen him. Couldn't make hide nor hair out of what he was mumbling about." He shook his head. "Odd, I say. Deucedly odd."

"What was odd?" pressed Portia.

"Both his mumblings and the fact that he insisted I keep a little volume of Persian miniatures, despite the fact that my specialty is medieval French poetry. Wouldn't take no for an answer."

Portia felt a strange prickling at the back of her neck. "Where is the book now, Sir Reginald?"

"Why, er . . ." He had to think for a moment. "Still on my desk somewhere, I imagine. To be honest, I didn't give it much thought."

"Then, you wouldn't mind if I had a look at it?"

"It's all yours, Miss Hadley."

Vaguely aware that the musicians were striking up a lively country tune, Portia felt as if her thoughts were swirling as rapidly as the notes of the violins. "And what of his mumblings?"

He scratched at his ear. "Dam—er, deucedly peculiar, I tell you. Sounded as if he were speaking some unfamiliar language. Couldn't catch above half what he was talking about."

That was not much of a help, thought Portia. "Could you please be a bit more specific?"

"Well, er, along with a number of phrases that were totally foreign to me, he kept muttering something about a 'Jade Tiger' and the 'Lotus of the Orient.' " Sir Reginald appeared perplexed. "Didn't know your father had an interest in the East."

"My father's interests ranged in a good many directions," she sighed. Unfortunately, his person seemed to have followed along in their footsteps to some unknown point of the compass, she added to herself.

"Well, if I understood him correctly, those were the phrases he kept repeating."

"Jade Tiger? Lotus of the Orient?" Portia frowned. "Have you any idea what they might mean?"

He lifted his shoulders. "None whatsoever."

"Was there nothing else he said that may give some hint as to what he was talking about?"

A baleful look came over Sir Reginald's face. "I'm sorry, Miss Hadley. I wish I had more to offer, but . . ." His expression suddenly lightened. "Wait! Now that you ask, he did mention a name several times. Grenville. It leaps to mind because . . . I have, er, heard it mentioned more than a few times this evening."

Portia imagined there wasn't a male in the room who hadn't been talking about the lady in red.

"A Mrs. Grenville, newly arrived from India, is present. No doubt it is merely coincidence, but perhaps you might wish to ask her if she knows anything concerning your father."

"Thank you, Sir Reginald. You have been an enormous help." Already her eyes were scanning the crowd. It shouldn't be difficult to locate the lady in question, even if the telltale blaze of scarlet was hidden from view. She had only to look for wherever the gentlemen were clustered like flies around a piece of ripe fruit.

"Let me know if there is anything else I might do. I'm quite fond of old Julian, even if his chronology of the Punic Wars is all wrong." He tugged at the corner of his waistcoat, causing a ripple of sapphire and cream across his broad belly. "Er, do be careful how you go on, Miss Hadley. Something deucedly odd is afoot, and I would hate to see a nice young lady like you caught between its paws."

Her mouth thinned to a grim line. "Don't worry about me, sir. Any predator seeking to toy with me will soon discover I am no country mouse."

The satin slippers made hardly a sound upon the polished parquet. Branford moved stealthily as well, and was just able to catch a flounce of red ruffle before the figure disappeared around the corner of the darkened hallway. As he reached the turn, a faint tapping seemed to indicate that the lady was descending a set of stairs.

He paused.

There was the soft click of a door opening, then shutting. The earl waited another moment before following.

The curved staircase wound down to an arched entryway that opened onto the walled gardens at the rear of the town house. The lamps to either side of the mullioned door were not lit, but enough moonlight was filtering in that Branford could make out the pale twist of a graveled path leading through a boxwood hedge.

His fingers found the door handle and he slipped noiselessly outside.

A balcony at the rear of the ballroom overlooked the dark expanse of plantings. The torches set along the stone balusters flickered in the breeze, and the sound of several voices drifted down from among the tall urns of ivy. Other than that, the gardens appeared deserted.

Branford moved across the grass, avoiding the crunch of stones that might alert anyone to his approach. The path skirted a large marble fountain, whose cavorting dolphins and cherubs were bathed in a light splashing of water. From there it wound deeper into the tall holly hedges, and the twists and turns became nearly as convoluted as a maze.

Pausing to survey his position, the earl could make out a high brick wall directly ahead. He listened for footsteps, but the only sounds were the chirping of an occasional cricket and the distant bass of the violoncello.

Where the devil was *she?* he wondered. And what was the wealthy widow up to that required such secrecy? A simple assignation? Or something more sinister?

The snap of a twig brought him instantly on guard. It was followed by the catch of cloth against the foliage and then, from close by, a low whisper. He inched forward, straining to pick up any hint of speech.

". . . another delay."

"Why?" The other voice, though scarcely audible, betrayed a nervous agitation.

"The negotiations are taking longer than— Shhh! Did you hear a noise?"

The earl held his breath as the two conspirators fell silent.

"No," came the terse reply. "It was naught but the wind."

"Listen, it's too risky to meet like this. We cannot be seen together—" Again there was an abrupt hesitation.

The earl was almost certain that one of them was a female, but to be sure, he decided to chance another step closer to the twined benches. If he could just manage to catch a peek of red . . .

At that instant, something smashed down hard upon his head, and suddenly all he saw was black.

A kidskin glove gave a tentative shake to the limp arm.

"Sir! Sir! Can you hear me?"

"Would that I couldn't." Branford groaned and slowly sat up, blood dripping down his nose from the gash in his scalp. "You! I might have guessed that when trouble leaps out of the bushes, you would not be far behind!"

"And I might have guessed that the first words out of your mouth would be yet another rude comment." Portia set her hands on her hips. "It wasn't *I* who coshed you over the head—though it's a tempting thought."

"Who did, then?" He managed to fish out his handkerchief and apply it to the rising lump.

"I'm not really sure. I heard a noise and called out. It was well for you that I did, because as I rounded the hedge, it looked like your assailant meant to finish off the job. I caught just the shadow of someone dropping the weapon, and what looked to be a flash of yellow, followed by the sound of footsteps running off." She pointed to the wall. "A gate slammed, so I assume there is a way out of the garden through there."

"Hmmph." His wits were still working a bit slowly, but her explanation only served to raise more questions than it answered. "And what, may I ask, were you doing out here in the first place, Miss Hadley?"

The note of military authority in his voice seemed to startle her into making a quick response. "I saw Mrs. Grenville come out to get a breath of fresh air, and as I wished to have a word with her in private, I—" Her eyes suddenly narrowed. "Now wait just a moment, sir—I might ask the same of you."

Ignoring her query, Branford fixed her with a sharp look. "Why would you want a private word with Mrs. Grenville?" he demanded.

"I don't have to answer any of your questions," snapped Portia. A contemptuous curl came to her lips. "Speaking of Mrs. Grenville, I suppose I don't really have to inquire why *you* were out here. Tell me, was it the lady herself who took exception to your advances, or did some rival seek to beat you to the punch?"

His head jerked up. "Are you saying you saw another gentleman out here? Someone you recognized?"

"I saw no one prowling the bushes but you, sir," she replied. Bending down, she fingered the brick. "Hmmm. Perhaps I should consider carrying one of these in my reticule. It appears to be an effective weapon in warding off rogues."

Branford swore under his breath and began to rise. However, as he was still a trifle woozy, he sat back down abruptly.

Portia peered at the wadded cloth, which was slowly turning a mottled crimson. "That appears to be a rather nasty cut. Here, I better have a look." Brushing aside his fingers, she made a quick inspection of the gash, then reached into her reticule for a fresh handkerchief. "Messy, but not overly serious. Head wounds tend to bleed quite a bit." Folding the soft linen into a neat pad, she pressed it up against his brow. "The trick is to apply pressure. That usually works to stanch the flow—"

"Damn!"

"Good Lord, stop squirming. You are worse than a twelve-year-old. Do you also scream bloody murder when you skin your knee?"

A twelve-year-old? His teeth clenched. "Miss Hadley, I'll have you know that I've suffered my share of wounds on the battlefield without blinking an eye," he muttered. "As for screams, most normal females would be shrieking for their vinaigrette at the sight of so much blood."

She grinned. "I have raised two younger brothers, sir. Blood, mud, broken bones, frogs, snakes—there is precious little that can throw me into a fit of vapors."

"So I have noticed." He also noticed that her touch was quite light, and that with a bit of gentle massaging she had eased the worst of the throbbing.

Her smile promptly disappeared.

It was, he thought hazily, a rather nice one, especially considering its source.

"Can you stand up now?" she asked, giving a none-too-gentle tug at his sleeve. "Let me help you up to the house, and then I shall ask Lord Fotherington to summon a physician. That wound should be properly cleaned and stitched."

Branford shook off her hand. "No!" He got to his feet. "I'll leave the same way my assailant did. If at all possible, I would prefer to keep word of this little accident from getting out."

She didn't fail to catch his meaning. "Don't worry, sir. I have no more interest than you do in making mention of it."

He watched as she nudged the brick into the bushes with her toe, then turned back to face him. As the moon moved in and out of the scudding clouds, he thought he detected a glint of humor in her jade-green eyes.

"Afraid it might ruin your reputation?" she asked softly. "I mean, the fact that a lady could resist your charms . . ."

Was the impudent chit actually laughing at him?

"Perhaps you would have better luck if your manners were to improve," she continued.

"I doubt it, Miss Hadley," growled the gentleman known to his close friends as the Black Cat. "I am beginning to think it is *you* who are the omen of bad luck."

Chapter Four

❧❀❧

Twitching a ruffling of dust from her hem, Portia ventured a tentative step into the room. "Mr. Dearborne?"

"In here, Miss Hadley. Behind the statue of Septimius Severus."

It took a moment for her eyes to adjust to the dim light. "Thank you for agreeing to see me on such notice."

"Not at all, my dear. I apologize for the untidiness of the office, but judging by the urgency of your note, I assumed you would wish to meet right away." Making a bit of space on the crowded blotter of his desk, the gentleman set aside the book he had been perusing. "Even if the Caesarian Society's housekeeping does tend to be a trifle lax."

"Oh, please don't give it a thought." She edged sideways past a crate filled with pottery fragments. "As you know, I am quite used to the conditions of scholarly research."

"Yes, yes, of course." He rose hastily and removed a pile of manuscripts from one of the side chairs. "Do have a seat. I am only too happy to provide whatever assistance I can in this puzzling affair."

Portia took a moment to settle her reticule on her

lap. Mr. Dearborne was not nearly as intimate a friend of her father as Mr. Huffington. In truth, the two of them were rivals of a sort, and their exchanges had, on occasion, led to some rather heated disagreements within the pages of the *Historical Journal*. However, she was determined not to overlook any possible source of information. "That is very kind of you," she replied. "Then, I trust you will not mind if I dispense with the usual pleasantries and get right to the point of my visit." Opening a small notebook, she turned to a fresh page. "Might I begin with a few questions?"

"By all means." Dearborne leaned back in his leather chair. "Fire away."

"Do you perchance recall my father speaking of any new acquaintances in Town?"

"No, I can't say that he did, Miss Hadley."

Portia stifled a sigh of disappointment. "I don't suppose he mentioned any upcoming sea voyage, either, did he?"

The gentleman's hazel eyes flickered with concern as he fingered his chin. "No, I am afraid not. Your father did seem rather, er, edgy at the Terra Incognita Society meeting shortly before his disappearance, but gave no indication as to why. I assumed he was preoccupied with some new theory or the prospect of an unusual discovery—you know how strangely we scholars can behave about such things, especially with each other."

"Yes." Her hand tightened around her pencil. Unfortunately, she knew all too well the darker side of brilliance.

Throat tightening, Portia let her gaze steal to the

overstuffed bookshelves and crowded cabinets. It all looked achingly familiar—her father's cluttered study at Rose Cottage looked much the same, and she felt a sharp, almost physical stab of pain in her chest from the sense of loss. Lord, how she missed the cozy chaos of his study, and the sight of his lean, ascetic face lighting up with a crooked smile on making some new discovery among his ancient manuscripts. Ever since she could remember, she had thought of that room as a magical place, one that transformed her father into a magical man. Like a modern-day Merlin, he mesmerized her and her brothers with what seemed like a never-ending stream of fascinating stories and arcane facts that made the world appear a sphere of limitless wonder.

Despite their modest circumstances, the gifts he gave them were priceless—he taught them the value of imagination, curiosity, persistence, and passion, as well as to believe in one's self, no matter what people whispered.

And yet, brutal honesty compelled her to admit that genius was not without its own sort of shadows. The baron had also used his room as a retreat from reality, and his travels as an escape from the dullness of everyday existence. There were times when Portia wondered whether he truly realized what weighty burdens he had shifted to her shoulders—the constant anxiety over finances, the pressing worries over household and the overwhelming responsibility of raising her younger siblings. Just as there were times when she had felt a tiny twinge of resentment at having no choice but to become Practical Portia.

But for all his very human faults, she understood his obsessions and forgave him his foibles. All that really mattered now was the fact that she loved him very, very dearly. The thought of life without him only made her more determined to put her practical skills to bear on restoring him and her family to their rightful home. . . .

"Miss Hadley?"

She blinked. "Sorry. I was just—I was just thinking on how well I understand what you mean."

"Of course you do. Especially as you are an expert in your own right on Etruscan art." His head gave a bob of acknowledgment. "Let me add that your last paper interpreting the vase paintings was quite impressive."

Given the fact that she had once written a rather sharp challenge to his findings on the same subject, it was a handsome compliment. So, despite the distracted state of her thoughts, she forced a wan smile. "Thank you, sir. How kind of you to say so, especially given the fact that we have not always seen eye to eye on the subject."

"Pfffff. That little disagreement is long forgotten." He then paused, and a shuffle of papers was followed by a nervous cough. "Getting back to your father, I certainly understand your reluctance to accept his rather, er, precipitous departure. But much as it pains me to say it, there is the possibility that, er, the rumors are true. After all, we scholars may engage in a bit of friendly bickering between each other, but we hardly stir up the sort of passions that result in foul play."

Portia acknowledged the truth of the last observation with a pinched grimace.

Dearborne cleared his throat. "And though perhaps I should not speak of such things before an innocent young lady, a gentleman sometimes does not tell his family everything. There are things he might wish to keep hidden from those closest to him, like a penchant for gambling. And if he had, in a moment of madness, wagered his home and possessions on the turn of a card, he might very well have made a hasty departure out of . . . embarrassment."

"I appreciate your plain speaking, sir, but despite Father's many eccentricities, somehow I simply cannot accept that he would be involved in anything like that." Her mouth pursed as she paused in thought. "There is just one last question I would like to ask. Did he mention anything to you about a 'Jade Tiger' or 'Lotus of the Orient'?"

Dearborne looked bewildered. "No, I cannot say that he did." His lips crooked in a self-deprecating smile. "But my specialty, as you know, is art and mythology, so I imagine he would not have thought to share any Eastern discovery with me. Is it, er, important?"

"I wish I knew," she replied, unable to keep the frustration from her voice. "Mr. Huffington said he kept mumbling something about a Jade Tiger and the Lotus of the Orient, but I haven't a clue as to what it means."

"How very, very odd." The gentleman lifted his shoulders. "I wish I could help, Miss Hadley, but it sounds equally baffling to me." After a slight pause he added, "The only thing I can think of to mention about our last meeting is that your father did appear quite anxious over the imminent arrival of a package."

Another mention of a package. What mysterious delivery had her father been expecting? And why on earth had he made no mention of it to her?

"I told him that he was welcome to have it delivered here to my rooms if he were expecting to be out of town, but he refused the suggestion." Once again Dearborne's mouth gave a tiny twitch upward. "I assumed it was out of professional jealousy. We all guard our little secrets very carefully, don't we?"

Portia forced an answering smile. "Well, as many of you toil for years at your research, it is not to be wondered at."

"Again, I am sorry I cannot shed much light on the matter, Miss Hadley. However, if I can be of any further assistance, please do not hesitate to call on me again. Julian and I have had our little disagreements over the years, but I respect him immensely and would be delighted to be of any service to his family."

"Thank you, Mr. Dearborne. It is a generous offer. I only wish that I may soon uncover a clue that would allow me to take you up on it."

Still wondering where to look next, Portia let her gaze wander over the crowded ballroom, but the winking jewels and smiling faces did not appear to offer much encouragement.

Hell's bells, she thought as she stared back down at her lap. It was high time to start making some real progress in her investigation. For the past few days she felt as though she had been shuffling in circles. . . .

"Ahem." Her great-aunt's elbow punctuated the discreet cough. "Mr. Kettle is asking if you are free for the next set, my dear."

Lost in thought despite the gentle nudge, Portia looked up with a vague frown.

The gentleman standing before her chair bore an unfortunate resemblance to his name. Short, stout, and well-rounded in the middle, he also had a gap between his front teeth that cause a slight whistling sound as he spoke. "M-mayhap Miss Hadley finds the idea of dancing too frivolous a notion." His feet shuffled, as if he were standing on a red-hot hob. "I would, of course, understand. . . ."

Her expression quickly softened to a sympathetic smile. She had become acquainted with the gentleman over the last few meetings of the Society for Arcane Antiquities, and she knew that beneath the unprepossessing appearance and nervous habits lay a very sharp mind.

"Why, Mr. Kettle, I would be happy to stand up with you."

"Y-you would?"

"Yes. We did not have a chance to finish discussing Mr. Pottinger's lecture on the Temple of Dendur the other evening, so I am looking forward to hearing your views on the funerary objects recovered from the antechamber." Portia rose and placed her hand upon his arm. She knew all too well what it was to feel awkward and unsure, yet it was not mere pity that prompted her quick acceptance. A spin around the dance floor would also allow her to making a closer scrutiny of the other guests.

The look of delight that spread across Kettle's face caused only a momentary twinge of guilt. She *did* wish to hear his opinions. However, there was no harm in using her eyes as well as her ears. As an unmarried young lady, she was quite constrained in her freedom to wander about the room alone, so she must make use of every opportunity she had to observe who mingled with whom. . . .

". . . would not have expected a statue of Amon-Re, Lord of the Silent, to be present."

"Uh, no?"

"The workmanship of the gold and lapis looked to have more in common with Twentieth Dynasty—" He gave a slight hop as Portia, her mind wandering, trod upon his toes for the second time. "Miss Hadley, I fear I am boring you with such tedious details of ancient tombs." A rueful twitch of his lips accompanied his words. "I imagine most young ladies would rather hear talk of dashing military heroes or the latest fashions than long-dead pharaohs. Unfortunately those are subjects on which I have precious little expertise."

Portia sought to keep her cheeks from coloring as she caught sight of Branford's profile among the crowd.

"You are ever so much more interesting to talk to than most people I have met in London," she assured him, quickly looking away from the arched entryway. "And I much prefer intelligent conversation to idle gossip." Distracted by a movement near the card room, she paused for a fraction, her eyes following a tall figure who at first glance appeared quite handsome. His thick, reddish locks were swept back from a high forehead, accentuating well-defined cheekbones and a patrician nose. However, a moment of further scrutiny revealed a certain furtiveness to his gaze and a petulant pout upon a rather weak mouth. Clearing her throat, Portia added, "Though, having never experienced a Season in Town, I do admit to a bit of curiosity about Polite Society. For instance, do you know that gentleman in the claret coat who is approaching Lord Dunster?"

Kettle glanced to his left. "Hmmm. I believe that is Lord Roxleigh. Definitely not the sort you would be likely to encounter at one of our meetings, for he spends his time with the betting books rather than any scholarly tomes. Indeed, word has it he will wager on anything." The crinkling of his rather large nose summed up his opinion of such mindless pursuits. "Why, just last week he is said to have bet a thousand pounds on whether a certain fly would land in the soup tureen at Whites."

"What was the outcome?" asked Portia, though in truth she was more interested in observing the surrounding faces than hearing of the viscount's wins and losses.

"On that occasion he came out on top. However, he is not always so lucky." A mournful sigh added a bass note to the faint whistling. "A month ago he lost a collection of Shakespeare first folios on the single roll of the dice."

Rare books? That brought her attention back to the ginger-haired lord.

"It is said his profligate habits should have exhausted the family coffers several times over, though in truth he always appears able to make good on his vowels, no matter how high the stakes. Perhaps his wife's family bails him out of any trouble—I hear her younger brother has married into a highly profitable shipping business based in the Carolinas."

Merchant ships? Portia's gaze remained glued on Roxleigh as her partner maneuvered her through a series of turns.

"Lord Dunster is another inveterate gamester."

Portia's mouth tightened as she shifted her attention to the marquess. Several inches shorter than his companion, Dunster's once trim middle was now running to corpulence. His face, too, betrayed the signs of overindulgence, with its features slightly blurred and a florid flush to his skin.

After a short, wheezy pause to catch his breath, Kettle continued. "Rumor has it that he, too, always seems to come up with the blunt to honor his vowels, though his losses seem to far outweigh the income of his estates." For someone who claimed to have little knowledge of privileged peers, Portia found that he was proving surprisingly well informed. "Rumor also has it that gambling is not his worst vice. If you don't mind me saying so, the two of them are not all the sort of gentlemen a nice young lady like you should seek acquaintance with. Now, take a fellow like Lord Bethel. He is not wont to squander his blunt. . . ."

He began an entertaining commentary on an elderly baron standing near the punch bowls, but Portia was listening with only half an ear. Her eyes were still on Roxleigh and Dunster, who had slowly edged away from the other gentlemen lingering by the doorway. As she watched with increasing interest, they began a hurried exchange of whispers. After several moments the conversation looked to be getting more heated. Indeed, both gentlemen appeared to be scowling, and the marquess had gone so far as to jab a finger at the other man's chest.

If only she could move a bit closer . . .

Gritting her teeth, she turned against the flow of the other couples, all but dragging her startled partner with her. "So sorry," she murmured, once they had squeezed through to the perimeter of the dance floor. "I—I fear that I have two left feet when it comes to dancing."

"Not at all, Miss Hadley," replied Kettle with a show of gallantry. "Actually, you, er, move with great . . . agility."

A final trilling note of the violins signaled the end to the set. After stumbling to a halt, he took a moment to dab a handkerchief to his brow. "I hadn't realized the waltz required, er, quite so much effort. May I fetch you a glass of ratafia punch after I have escorted you back to Lady Trumbull?"

"Oh, as to escorting me back to Aunt Octavia, it looks as if that won't be necessary, sir." Ducking her head, Portia made a show of examining her skirts. "I seem to have suffered a slight tear to the hem of my gown. No doubt it would be best if I withdraw for a moment and see if it can be mended."

"Why, er, of course." Clearly flustered by mention of female necessities, he took a step backward. "It's been a—a pleasure, Miss Hadley. I look forward to our next meeting."

Just as long as it wasn't on the dance floor, thought Portia, feeling a bit ashamed of herself for the blatant lie. However, she quickly squashed such feelings with the sharp reminder that she couldn't afford too many scruples these days, not if she wished to solve the mystery of her father's disappearance.

A quick glance showed that Roxleigh and Dunster were still together in the small alcove near the card room. Taking a deep breath, she turned and slipped between the potted palms.

Ignoring the affronted stare of Lady Trowbridge, his nominal hostess, Branford handed his overcoat to one of the liveried servants and crossed the polished parquet of the soaring entrance hall. He had not received an invitation to the elegant soiree, but Tony had sent around a note informing him that both Roxleigh and Mrs. Grenville were sure to be present.

Manners be damned, he growled to himself, finding his steps slowed by the crush of guests slowly making their way up the curved marble staircase. He turned his head to avoid being blinded by the Duchess of Hampshire's diamonds, only to find his gaze blocked by the scarlet regimentals of several high-ranking cavalry officers in deep conversation with a minister from the Admiralty.

The earl muttered another oath under his breath. The crowd looked to include the very highest sticklers of the *ton,* so he could only pray that Tony's information was accurate. Time was of the essence in finding the stolen document, and still he had not managed to strike up an acquaintance with either of the two suspects, no matter that he had put in an appearance at a number of deucedly boring entertainments over the last few days.

With a scuff of impatience, Branford squeezed by Lord Heywood, who was growing nearly as fat as the

Prince Regent. As he passed, Lady Heywood, resplendent in a gown of apricot watered silk threaded with gold, gave a disapproving sniff, her nose rising in unconscious imitation of the ornately framed formal portraits gracing the walls. Several of the other ladies close by favored him with considerably warmer looks, but their fluttering lashes and brilliant smiles were unnoticed.

Branches of lilac and hydrangea spilled out from two enormous urns flanking the head of the stairs. The earl ducked around the pale purple blooms, and finally gained entrance to the festivities, where the orchestra was just striking up a waltz. Pausing to down a glass of the watery punch, he made a quick survey of the dance floor and the surrounding crowd. Of yet, there was no telltale flash of red, but he was almost certain he spotted the viscount at the far end of the room, in deep discussion with another gentleman whose face was hidden by the ornamental shrubbery.

Branford watched for a moment longer, wondering what subject was bringing such a pinched expression to Roxleigh's face. Whatever it was, it looked to be a good deal more serious than a casual comment on the weather. His interest piqued, he set down his glass and started off.

Set between the hallway leading off to the with-drawing rooms and the entrance to the card room was a towering arrangement of palm and orange trees. The hidden nooks and leafy shadows looked to provide the perfect cover for approaching the gentlemen unno-ticed. He would, however, have to hurry if he hoped to manage any meaningful eavesdropping. Maintaining an air of nonchalant ennui, he moved through the throng with deceptive quickness, though for a short stretch of time, his path forced him to lose sight of his quarry.

Quick, but not quick enough, he realized.

Alert to any sudden movement, the earl stepped back and leaned up against one of the fluted columns, just in time to avoid a head-on collision with the viscount as he stormed by. While pretending a keen interest in the pretty blond heiress dancing nearby, Branford kept a close eye on the other man's countenance before it disappeared in the crowd. It did not require an expert in covert surveillance to discern that Lord Roxleigh was in a state of great agitation. Jaw quivering, the fair skin of his cheeks mottling to a bruised purple, he looked to be seething with anger. But it was not mere rage that gave his eyes such a hunted expression.

The earl had more than enough battlefield experience to recognize fear when he saw it.

Hell and damnation. Adding another, more blasphemous oath under his breath, Branford turned back to the doorway, but Dunster was nowhere to be seen. So who the devil had caused Roxleigh to . .

The slight movement came from among the jagged fronds. A pert nose, a twist of unruly curls—the earl gritted his teeth as the profile emerging out of the darkness became all too recognizable. The young lady paused, shooting a quick look right and left before edging out from behind one of the tall terra-cotta planters. It wasn't until she turned in the direction of where her great-aunt was sitting that she realized she was being observed.

Their eyes met, and Branford couldn't help but note that her face turned nearly as scarlet as the gowns favored by Mrs. Grenville. A gloved hand flew to her cheek, then, with a gulp of air, she hurried off without a backward glance.

The earl's mouth thinned to a grim line.

For an innocent young lady, Miss Portia Hadley was certainly developing a knack for turning up in the most compromising situations.

Grateful for the cover of darkness, Portia stole down the deserted hallway, seeking a brief respite from the glare of the candles and the press of the crowd. A quick turn led her into a side wing of the stately mansion, where the lilt of the violins and trill of laughter faded to a welcome silence. Slowing her steps, she noticed the small conservatory to her left and, after hesitating for just a moment, eased open the heavy leaded glass doors and stepped inside.

The cool air, redolent with the scent of damp earth and lush blooms, felt soothing against her burning cheeks. *Drat the man!* Why was it that he, of all gentlemen, seemed to catch her in the most awkward of situations? Portia frowned as she moved between two rows of flowering lemon trees. It was not as if she should care a whit what the dissolute Earl of Branford thought of her. After all, he had already made his loathing abundantly clear. And the feeling, of course, was mutual. However, for some strange reason, she did not like the idea of him thinking her a hopeless hoyden.

The ghosting of moonlight through the glass ceiling cast a pattern of light and dark across her path, causing her to halt for a moment. As the circumstances of her father's disappearance were still shrouded in mystery, she had no illusions that the slightest misstep in trying to track down the truth could end in disaster. So, she scolded herself, she could not afford to be distracted by a devilish rake, no matter that he possessed a pair of sinfully seductive eyes. Not when her family's future depended on her success.

Be practical! added the same voice of reason. Only a nitwit would think that a handsome blade about Town might ever see anything of interest in a plain country spinster. And only a nitwit would wish him to.

That settled, Portia directed her gaze out to the flickering torches of the ballroom balcony and forced her mind to begin reviewing the information she had coaxed from Mr. Kettle. Were any of the random bits useful? The mention of—

The rattle of the brass latch caught her completely off guard. Biting back a cry of dismay, she slipped deeper into the foliage as a lush laugh followed the soft creak of the hinges.

"La, I believe you are right—we shan't be disturbed in here." The lady's voice sounded a trifle slurred. "No doubt you have a great deal of experience in choosing just the right spot for . . . intimate conversation, Lord Branford."

"I have a great deal of experience in a number of things, Lady Roxleigh."

Roxleigh. Portia felt her jaw go very rigid.

"Mmmm. So I have heard."

"Tell me . . ." Taking the lady's hand, the earl drew her away from the door.

Portia held her breath as they moved closer to where she was hidden, praying that the shifting shadows and the cover of the trees would keep her presence from being noticed.

With a bit of adroit maneuvering, Branford spun his companion around so that her back was pressed up against one of the fluted iron columns. "You do not worry about us being interrupted by your husband?"

Lady Roxleigh's lips pursed. "Harold doesn't give a fig what I do. He is only interested in carousing with his cronies."

"He must be a fool, and blind in the bargain," murmured Branford, which earned him a brilliant smile. "I take it Dunster numbers among his friends?"

"The two of them are thick as thieves," she replied with a pout.

The earl gave a casual laugh and leaned in closer, teasing his thumb along the curve of her bare collarbone. "Surely you do not think them up to no good?" he said lightly, his voice dropping to hardly more than a whisper.

Portia could not make out the answer. Gritting her teeth, she strained to catch what else was being said, but their voices had dropped too low to be overheard. *Hell's bells!* she swore to herself. Just when the conversation appeared to be getting interesting. However, it quickly became apparent that an intimate exchange of words was not the only thing the two of them had in mind.

A surreptitious peek showed that Branford's fingers were now hooked inside the cleavage of the lady's gown, but rather than protest such intimate liberties with her person, she laughed and gave a slinky wiggle that caused the silk to slip down off her breasts. Portia bit back a gasp as the earl, smiling wolfishly, yanked the gown down to Lady Roxleigh's waist and began to fondle the mounds of bare flesh.

A breathy giggle from the lady was cut off as his mouth seized hers. The kisses took on a hard hungriness, moans intertwined with eager lips and probing tongues. Portia was close enough to hear the ragged breathing and frenzied rumpling of fabric against flesh. A prickle of consciousness tingled across her own skin, almost as palpable as the earl's roving touch. Acutely aware of his overpowering masculinity, she could not help recalling the searing taste of his brandied mouth and the faint stubbling of his jaw rasping against her cheek.

For an instant she blinked, then, as her gaze refocused, the earl suddenly lifted his head and, baring his teeth, ducked down to suck in the nub of the lady's left nipple.

"Oh, God, yes!" Arching into his embrace, Lady Roxleigh raked her hands through his hair, jeweled rings winking wildly in the faint light as she twisted the raven locks around her fingers. "Yes!"

Branford appeared to need no urging. His knee was already wedged between her legs, causing her skirts to hike up above her stockinged calves. Moaning softly, the lady lifted them higher and guided the earl's hand into the frothing of delicate lace. Her own touch had now shifted to the front of his pantaloons, and was fumbling with the fastenings of the flap.

Portia felt her throat go very dry, and yet was aware of a strange, licking heat centered between her thighs.

She knew it was sinfully wrong to be watching the wanton encounter, but she could not seem to tear her eyes away from the sight of such naked and unrestrained desire.

They suddenly grew wider as buttons popped loose and the earl's shaft sprang free, a dark silhouette jutting out from the tangle of his white linen shirt.

None of the books she had read—not even the one written in Italian, which contained a good many pictures and detailed captions—had quite prepared her for the rampant reality of his arousal.

"Ohhh," crooned Lady Roxleigh, the pink tip of her tongue protruding from her smile. "I see the rumors are not exaggerated—you may no longer be wearing scarlet regimentals, but you possess a magnificent sword."

Indeed, as Portia stared at Branford's unsheathed manhood, it looked to her as rigid as tempered steel, bringing to mind a cavalry saber ready to plunge into the heat of battle.

"I assure you, sweeting, I may have sold out of the army, but I have not lost any expertise in wielding a blade."

"So I have heard." Circling his girth with her thumb and forefinger, Lady Roxleigh stroked up and down its length. "Am I in danger of being pricked, sir?"

His answer was a rough laugh. Sliding his hands beneath her buttocks, the earl lifted her off her feet and thrust himself forward.

Portia bit down hard on her lip to keep from making a sound.

It was Lady Roxleigh who cried out. However, the sultry echo was not one of pain, but of pure pleasure. Indeed, she seemed to be enjoying it. Immensely, judging by the eagerness with which she had wrapped her legs around Branford's middle, and the lushness of her moans at each surge of his hips. The tempo grew more frenzied, and in the tilt of the scudding shadows their movements became a bit blurred.

The crescendo came quickly. With one last shuddering cry, the lady stiffened, then went very limp in the earl's arms. He, too, appeared suddenly spent, his broad shoulders slumping forward so that he was leaning heavily against the fluted column. There was a brief silence, save for the panting of breath, then the lady slid her feet to the ground and began to rearrange her clothing. She gave a coquettish flourish of her white lace undergarment before smoothing down her skirts. "Anytime you wish a conquest, my lord, you may count on a full and unconditional surrender from me."

"What generous terms, my dear. Be assured I look forward to another heated engagement." Branford tucked in his shirt and restored his cravat to some semblance of order. "However, for the present, let us not give the tabbies any ammunition for gossip. I suggest you return to the ballroom alone. I shall follow along shortly."

Lady Roxleigh paused just long enough to press a last, lingering kiss on his lips, then hurried out the door.

Turning, so that his face was completely in shadow, the earl stood rigid and unmoving for several minutes before spinning abruptly on his heel and taking his leave.

So *that* was what it was like to be ravished by a ruthless rake, thought Portia, her grip on the branch of the lemon tree tightening to steady her knees. The air, redolent with the scent of spicy perfume and an earthier muskiness she could not quite identify, filled her lungs as she finally dared draw in a deep breath. To her dismay, the thud of her heart was as loud as gunfire in her ears, punctuating the still-vivid image of the earl's sinuous hips rocking in and out. It took her a few more gulps and gasps to regain her equilibrium and still the racing of her pulse.

Satan be sizzled! The man was a randy alleycat, and from what she had just witnessed, she should consider herself fortunate indeed to have escaped from their first encounter relatively unscratched. And yet . . .

It was odd. As the earl had passed through a flicker of moonlight, a stark profile against the dappled leaves, she could have sworn she spied a rather bleak expression lingering on his features. No doubt it was merely an illusion, but at that instant the look had resembled something akin to regret.

Don't be daft, she scoffed. He was worse than an alleycat—he was a dangerous predator, all lithe muscle and raw power beneath the tailored ennui.

Dangerous, indeed!

There might be a great many unanswered questions swirling around in her head, but of one thing she was certain—any further contact with the Earl of Branford would be asking for trouble.

Chapter Five

❧❀❧

"I don't know why Hermione kicked up such a dust over the earl making an appearance at her soiree. After all, the presence of a rogue or two always adds a bit of spice to an affair." Lady Trumbull added more sugar to her cup and stirred. "Actually, I found him to be quite charming."

Portia refused to meet her aunt's gaze. That she had failed to overhear even a word of the conversation between Roxleigh and Dunster the previous evening was made even more galling by the fact that *he* had caught her skulking in the greenery. For nearly a week now, he had somehow contrived to turn up at every party she and her aunt had attended. And while he had made no attempt to speak to her, she had been acutely aware of his eyes following her every move. Especially last night. The sensation had been extremely . . . uncomfortable, which was no doubt exactly what he intended.

Not to speak of what she had witnessed when his gaze had been glued on another female.

To her consternation, she felt her skin take on a tingling flush. "*Charming* is not precisely the adjective I would use for Lord Branford."

"Well, you must admit, it was quite thoughtful of him to go to all that trouble to learn your identity in order to return your ring. Extremely clever of him too," murmured the elderly lady, paying no heed to her niece's acid comment. She sipped at her tea, then her lips quirked up at the corners. "No wonder he shot Grantley. The man is an insufferable bore, as well as a pompous ass."

"Bam!" Bertram fired a pellet of bread at his older brother. "The earl is said to be the deadliest shot in Town—nailed him right between the eyes!"

The wad glanced off Henry's cheek, drawing an exasperated snort. "Don't be a gudgeon, Bertie. He merely winged Lord Grantley. If he had killed him, he would have been forced to flee the country."

"Must have been aiming at an arm, then, for word has it that he never misses a wafer at Manton's." Bertie's spoon hung in midair over his bowl of porridge and his voice took on a note of awe. "Dab hand with a sword and his fives as well. Why, Lord Branford is probably the most dangerous blade in London."

"Especially if one is a female," muttered Portia to herself. In a louder voice she added, "Good Lord, Bertie, I should hope you have better sense than to admire a man who does naught but engage in fighting, gambling, drinking, and . . . other such debauched activities. I assure you, the earl is an ill-mannered wastrel. And an unprincipled cad."

A rare silence fell over the breakfast table. Her aunt's brows rose a fraction, Bertie's face scrunched in question, while Henry's mouth compressed in an ominous frown. "What do you mean?" he inquired softly.

Oh, dear. Portia took a bite of toast, wishing she could swallow her last words. "Nuffing," she mumbled with her mouth full. "Except that he is hardly a pattern card for a proper gentleman."

Henry looked as if to speak again, but a rustling of papers and thump of china cut him off. "Time to attack Virgil—however, I mean to use a pen, not a pistol." Lady Trumbull added one last flutter of notes to her stack. "Portia, would you kindly help me carry all this to my study. I would like your opinion on several swatches of fabric, for I fear if I don't soon replace the draperies by my desk, they will disintegrate around my ears."

"Yes, of course." Moving with great alacrity, Portia gathered up an armful of books.

The choice of colors and stripes was quickly decided upon, and Lady Trumbull tucked the damask samples back into her desk. But rather than turn to her manuscripts, she remained with her eyes fixed on her niece.

Portia shifted uncomfortably. Pretending not to notice the scrutiny, she picked up her reticule from one of the side chairs and started to sort through the contents.

"My dear, I cannot help but notice that you are looking terribly fatigued of late."

"I—I suppose I am not used to the late hours and whirl of activities here in Town."

The elderly lady's mouth gave a tiny twitch. "Especially the ones where an unescorted young lady might run into a certain rakish rogue?" Her expression then took on a much more sober mien. "I shall not ask the details, but—"

"It was the result of a minor indiscretion," said Portia quickly, hoping to squash any further discussion on the subject. "I will be more careful in the future."

Her great-aunt was not put off so easily. After taking a moment to arrange her pens in a careful row, she cleared her throat and continued. "I know you are dreadfully concerned about Julian. Lord knows, so am I. However, the risks involved in searching for answers all by yourself are terrible. Surely we must trust the authorities to—"

"To do nothing!" Portia was unable to refrain from interrupting again. "You cannot deny that they have dismissed his disappearance as just another example of Papa's eccentricity." Her voice took on a brittle edge. "What is to become of us if I can't discover what has happened to him? What sort of future awaits if we cannot regain our home and our income, however modest?"

"You and the boys will always have a home here, Portia," replied Lady Trumbull quietly. "I should hope you would know that."

"I do, Aunt Octavia. It is beyond generous, for I am well aware of the burden it places on your finances." She drew in a ragged breath. "Please do not think me ungrateful, but I don't wish to be dependent on you. Or anyone. So I simply cannot let it go."

Lady Trumbull gave a rueful smile. "You have the same sort of dogged determination as your father, though it comes out in a different way."

"What you mean to say is *stubborn*." Her jaw tightened. "I have had to be stubborn."

"I am well aware of that, my dear. Just as I am

aware of the courage and compassion that you have shown in accepting the responsibilities thrust upon you at such an early age. But you have also learned to be practical, so I count on your good sense to weigh the consequences of your actions." Lady Trumbull adjusted the set of her spectacles. "I am not as blind as you young people may think. Over the years I have noticed that a number of your admirable qualities—your fearlessness, your curiosity—have also combined to create a reckless side to your nature, my dear."

Portia kept her eyes averted. Her great-aunt's insight was apparently not limited to discerning the nuances of ancient poetry.

"I don't mean to lecture, but I should be terribly remiss in my responsibilities if I did not remind you that a young lady must exercise caution. For example, have you considered the risk to your reputation?"

"As I am already considered a rather odd, eccentric bluestocking, my reputation is probably no worse off than it was," muttered Portia, "even if the earl is ungentlemanly enough to mention the details of our encounter to one of his dissolute friends."

Lady Trumbull's brow furrowed. "Are you saying his lordship made improper advances?"

She sought to allay the elderly lady's concern with a touch of humor. "You needn't worry, Aunt Octavia. Henry's lessons in the art of boxing came in very handy. Once I hit the cad with a right cross—a very credible one, I might add—he backed off."

"Hmmm. Despite his reputation, I would not have imagined . . ." Her great-aunt rubbed absently at her spectacles. "Did he actually . . . lay a hand on you?"

She forced a smile. "The, er, incident was a trifling one. Laughable, really."

Lady Trumbull was not laughing. "My dear, you must guard your own future, as well as that of your brothers. A young lady jeopardizes her chances of marriage by—"

"I have no desire to be married!" exclaimed Portia. "Ever!"

Her great-aunt's lined countenance turned even more clouded.

"Besides, I doubt there exists a gentleman who would choose to be leg-shackled to an outspoken, opinionated ape leader."

"Portia . . ."

"Please! Let us drop the matter. I understand your concern, but there is really no need to worry about me. I am just as anxious as you are to avoid further trouble." Portia surreptitiously checked her pocket for the slip of paper on which she had jotted a certain address, then finished packing up her reticule. "Trust me— from now on, I have every intention of watching my step very carefully."

Before Lady Trumbull could reply, she rose quickly and shook out her skirts. "Speaking of which, I have a number of errands I wish to run this morning, so I will let you get back to Virgil." Seeing that her great-aunt was still regarding her with a scrunched expression, she tried to lighten the mood. "I assure you that while Lord Branford has been somewhat of a nuisance lately, he won't be seeking another intimate interlude with me anytime soon."

"That's for bloody sure," muttered Henry under his

breath as he removed his ear from the keyhole and crept away from the study door.

"Ah, there it is." The frail gentleman shuffled to the far end of the bookcases and plucked down one of the printed journals from the top shelf. After blowing a bit of dust from its cover, he handed it to Branford with an apologetic smile. "At my age, it sometimes takes me a trifle longer to recall just where everything is located."

"Your memory still seems sharp as a razor, Mr. Yount." The earl thumbed open the pages. "The information you have shared with me has been very helpful."

"Happy to be of service, my lord." He brushed at the sparse strands of silvery hair still clinging to his pate. "I consider Miss Hadley to be one of the leading lights of our Art and Antiquities Society. She possesses quite an agile intellect for one of such tender years."

Her intellect was not all that was agile about the young lady. Branford's lips gave a wry quirk as he recalled a willowy form slipping over a window ledge. "Indeed? Then, no doubt I shall find her essay illuminating." He turned for the long reading table set before the bow front window.

After a slight hesitation, Yount followed him, tugging nervously at his frayed cuffs. "She isn't in any trouble, is she? Naturally I have heard a swirl of rumors concerning Julian and his rather abrupt departure from Town. I should hate to think that such a remarkable young lady is being forced to deal with any unpleasant consequences." He gave a sigh. "She has certainly had more than her share of responsibilities to shoulder over the years, what with running a household and raising two brothers."

Branford paused in his perusal of the pages. In light of recent events he had decided it might be prudent to do a little more research on Miss Hadley. He had already learned a few things—her age, her parentage, and the fact that she possessed the tongue of a shrew and the temperament of a hellion. But a few discreet questions around Town had led him to Mr. Yount, and over the last half hour, the elderly expert on ancient art had sketched out quite a different portrait of the young lady.

"I trust Miss Hadley has no real cause for concern," he answered. Then, in spite of his own rather harsh opinion of her, he found himself curious. "You speak as if you are fond of the young lady."

Yount's lined face brightened. "Oh, I am, sir. Immensely. Not only do I admire her intellect and inquisitiveness, but she is patient with our dottier members, is tolerant of other points of view, and has a delightful sense of humor. Which," he added with a rueful grin, "comes in quite handy at a number of our meetings."

Patient? Tolerant? Humorous? The earl's brow creased. Those were hardly the adjectives that came to mind when he thought of her.

"But enough of my prattling." The other man rubbed his gnarled hands together. "I shall leave you to your reading, my lord. If you have any further questions, you may find me in the back room with my painted vases."

A short while later, as he snapped the journal shut, Branford had to acknowledge that Yount's praises were not without merit. Miss Hadley's writing revealed a lively intelligence, thoughtful reasoning, and surprising insight, not to speak of a sly wit. Rather intrigued, he realized that she had taken on a unique individuality, though when he tried to picture her face, he could recall only a vague impression of features. Indeed, he found himself wondering what it might be like to discuss ideas on art with such a knowledgeable young lady. Unbeknownst to even his closest friends, games of chance were not the only subjects that he had mastered at Oxford. Italian art and literature had been secret passions, ones the coolly calculating Black Cat did not care to reveal, lest it hint at some soft spot beneath the claws and cunning.

The notion of an intellectual exchange with a female brought a sardonic curl to his lips. No doubt it would be a novel experience, for the idea of engaging in a lively discussion had never been foremost in his thoughts when in the company of the opposite sex. A lady's mind was not usually the portion of her anatomy that attracted his attention. However, Miss Hadley was a most unusual female, he admitted. He might not like her, but he could not help admitting to a certain grudging respect.

And a compelling curiosity. For while some light had been shed upon the subject, there was still a great deal about Miss Hadley that remained in the dark.

Portia looked up at the knocker and blinked. It was, after all, hardly the sort of thing one expected to see in the heart of fashionable Mayfair. The polished brass was carved in the shape of a massive elephant's head, the truck curled in a fanciful loop that was designed to strike down upon a tiny monkey. After a moment of hesitation, she took hold of the appendage and gave a firm rap.

The door opened to reveal a servant whose appearance was no less exotic. A white turban sat upon his head, its thick wrappings coming down to touch the tops of his shaggy brows. His eyes were the color of coffee and the nose thin, with a pronounced hook at the tip. Beyond that, it was impossible for her to make out any other features, as a heavy black beard obscured the rest of his face.

Like his turban, the servant's flowing shirt and pants were white, but any lack of color was more than made up for by the sleeveless tunic he wore over them. Dyed a brilliant saffron, the silk garment came down past his knees and was decorated with an intricate pattern of jungle beasts and birds, all embroidered in vivid jewel tones. The effect was rather mesmerizing.

With a strange growl, the man gestured for her to enter.

"Ahhh." Portia finally managed to clear her throat. "Is Mrs. Grenville at home?"

He simply stared.

Determined not to be deterred so easily, she asked the same question, this time using the smattering of Hindi she had learned from Henry.

Her effort was rewarded by a slight stirring in the liquid brown of his eyes. From the folds of his tunic appeared a small silver tray.

"Card."

At least, that is what she thought he said. She quickly handed one over, adding an additional request to the engraved name. "Please tell her it is a matter of pressing urgency. As well as one that calls for . . . discretion." She had no idea whether the message would be passed on to the lady in question, but it was worth a try.

He gave a slight wave of his bejeweled hand, indicating that she should wait in a small parlor set off to the right of the entrance foyer.

The slap of his sandals echoed off the marble floor as he padded down the hallway, leaving Portia alone at the doorway. She entered the room and once again found herself gaping.

It appeared that the wealthy widow was inordinately fond of reds, no matter what the shade. The draperies were a luscious damask stripe of pomegranate and cream, while the sofa and matching settee were upholstered in a deep burgundy velvet, accented by occasional pillows of shell pink. A Persian carpet picked up the berry tones, along with a muted swirling of off white. The overall effect should have been garish, but somehow it was not. There was a certain mysterious allure to the combinations—slightly raffish yet boldly refined.

Rather like the lady herself.

On closer inspection, the appointments were just as interesting as the choice of furnishings. Gracing an elegant Hepplewhite side table were two Greek busts from Hellenic times—Minerva and Athena, if she was not mistaken. Sublime in their simplicity, they were superb examples of the period. No less striking was the ornate Louis XIV ormolu clock that sat between them. The filigree goldwork and delicate enameling couldn't have been more different than the stylized sculpture, yet the juxtaposition was extremely pleasing.

Portia chewed thoughtfully at her lower lip. Clearly Mrs. Grenville was a most unusual lady, one who had an unorthodox imagination and the self-assurance to display it. Not to speak of the money to afford such freedom. There was no mistaking the quality of the widow's choices, thought Portia. Each of them was worth a bloody fortune.

Her gaze then turned to the large painting over the marble fireplace. It was a work from India depicting a bizarre and rather fascinating composition of figures intertwining—

"The three main gods of the Hindu religion," came a soft voice from behind her. "Brahma has the power to create, Vishnu has the power to preserve life, and Shiva . . ."

She spun around.

". . . Shiva is the great destroyer," continued Mrs. Grenville. "Having spent a number of years in India, I feel a certain affinity for their outlook on life." The widow inclined her head a fraction, allowing an enigmatic smile to flit across her lips. "Forgive me if I startled you. Vavek said you wished to see me on a matter of great urgency. Miss—" She glanced down at the card—"Hadley?"

Portia managed a nod. "Yes."

"Indeed?" The announcement elicited a look of cool appraisal from the widow. "Have we met?"

The idea of calling on Mrs. Grenville had seemed quite logical when she had come up with it at home. Yet now, on finding herself face-to-face with the lady in red, Portia was suddenly aware that the dratted Earl of Branford might have been right when he warned her about the dangers of charging headlong into the fray.

It was not always wise to seek a direct confrontation, especially when the opponent's strengths and weaknesses were unknown. *Was Mrs. Grenville a friend or a foe?* It took no more than a quick look at the well chosen possessions and well guarded features to discern that the wealthy widow was a sharp and sophisticated woman of the world. One who would be a formidable foe to cross swords with.

It was, of course, too late to turn back, but Portia quickly marshaled her thoughts, determined to proceed while guarding her misgivings.

"No." She took care not to flinch under the other lady's gaze. "But your name has been mentioned in a matter of great importance to me and my family. One that, for a number of reasons, I wish to discuss in private."

Heaving a sigh, the widow took a seat on the sofa and motioned for her visitor to do the same. Portia couldn't help but notice how she assumed a position of calculated nonchalance, her rose-colored gown falling in perfect folds around her leg. And, like the Greek statues, her face remained an inscrutable mask, lovely to look at but revealing no hint of emotion.

Brahma. Vishnu. Shiva.

For which of the three did the Lady in Red have the greatest affinity?

"My dear Miss Hadley, if you are about to accuse me of seducing your husband, or any other male relation, let me forestall the rantings and the tears." Mrs. Grenville's mouth curled up at the corners, though there was little real humor in her expression. "Despite what the gossips might wish to believe, I've no interest in inviting every male of the *ton* to share my bed."

"I've no intention of wasting either your time or mine by falling into a fit of vapors," replied Portia, matching the other lady's measured tone. "I've come merely to ask a few simple questions, if I may."

The smile became a bit more real. "In my experience, questions on personal matters are rarely simple."

Portia acknowledged the statement with a smile of her own. "Perhaps not. Does that make you unwilling to hear them?" she asked, deliberately letting a note of challenge slip into her voice.

The widow reached for a small lacquered box on the occasional table by her side. Flipping open the lid, she withdrew a thin cheroot, then offered the rest of its contents to her guest. "Do you smoke, Miss Hadley?"

She shook her head.

"No? You might wish to try it sometime. New experiences are always . . . interesting, and you strike me as a more adventurous young lady than most." Mrs. Grenville lit the tobacco and exhaled a plume of fragrant smoke. "So, what is it you wish to ask?"

Portia decided there was no harm in trying a straightforward approach. After all, her mere presence there had already made a certain subtlety impossible.

"Are you acquainted with anyone by the name of Hadley, Mrs. Grenville?"

A perfect smoke ring floated out from the cherry red lips. "Besides you?"

"I was thinking of one gentleman in particular— my father, Julian Hadley."

There was not the slightest change in the widow's expression as she shifted against one of the plump pillows. "Why do you ask?"

"Because he has gone missing." Portia was gazing at the painting of the three deities, but out of the corner of her eye she watched to see if the statement provoked any sort of reaction from the other lady.

The first flicker of emotion appeared in Mrs. Grenville's eyes as she turned to tap a bit of ash into the small brass bowl on the table. "What—"

She was interrupted by the tinkling of a bell, followed by the reappearance of the turbaned servant bearing a copper tray laden with the normal accoutrements for tea. However, the aroma wafting up from the silver pot was unlike any that Portia had encountered before.

"It is *chai*," explained Mrs. Grenville as she motioned for the man to pour. "An Indian mixture of tea, milk and spices that I find so much more interesting than the ordinary beverage you proper English gentry favor. Will you try it?"

"I should be delighted." Portia accepted a cup from the servant. "Like you, Mrs. Grenville, my father is a great believer in trying new things."

"Ah, back to your father. Tell me, what makes you think *I* know anything about his disappearance?"

Deciding two could play at countering question with question, she took a sip of the *chai,* then set it aside. "Do you?"

Mrs. Grenville took up a small silver grinder and added a dash of fresh nutmeg to her drink.

Repressing the urge to dump the steaming brew into the other lady's lap, Portia gave up on that line of inquiry and tried a different tack. "How about the name Roxleigh? Is it any more familiar to you than Hadley? Or perhaps the words 'Jade Tiger' ring a bell?"

For the first time in their meeting, the widow betrayed an unrehearsed emotion. Her face turned a shade paler and the cup came down upon the saucer with a slight rattle. However, instead of answering, she shot a glance at the French clock. "Miss Hadley, I trust you do not think me rude, but I am expecting . . . another guest."

"On the contrary, it was I who was presumptuous in dropping in on a perfect stranger." Portia gathered up her reticule and rose. Whether it had been worth the effort was difficult to say. She felt she had learned rather more about the widow than she had expected, and rather less about the mystery concerning her father than she had hoped.

"I am sorry that I was not able to be of more help to you." A last puff of smoke obscured Mrs. Grenville's expression before she stubbed out the cheroot. "Did you enjoy the *chai?*"

"It's hard to say—a drink of that complexity should be sampled several times before an opinion is formed."

"I imagine it is . . . an acquired taste."

"That can be said for a good many things in life." The door to the parlor suddenly swung open, seemingly of its own accord. Catching a glimpse of saffron hovering behind the paneled oak, Portia took the hint and moved toward the foyer. "Thank you for your kind hospitality, Mrs. Grenville," she added politely. "It has been most fascinating to meet you."

"The feeling is mutual, Miss Hadley. Perhaps we will have a chance to further the acquaintance. But in the meantime, I wish you . . . good luck in your search."

Good luck? thought Portia dourly. The front door fell closed behind her and she started walking for home. Of late, there seemed to be precious little of *that* commodity to go around.

As if to drive home the notion, a fancy curricle came tooling around the corner, its brightly painted wheels cutting close to the curb and sending a splatter of mud over the hem of her best gown. Muttering several unladylike words, she shook out her skirts, then whipped around to glare at the young buck who was handling the ribbons in such a reckless manner. The daggered look was pointless, for the driver was already careening through the turn into Half Moon Street.

She did, however, catch sight of a nondescript hackney drawing to a halt by the widow's town house. A man emerged, a shapeless hat drawn low over his brow, the collar of his unfashionable coat turned up to hide his features. He hurried up the marble steps and darted through the narrow opening that appeared to greet him.

Sun glinted off the brass elephant as the door fell shut with a thud.

"You mean to do *what?*" Bertie blinked in disbelief. "Are you mad? Have you any idea what the force of a bullet, traveling at that velocity over that distance, does to bone and flesh?"

"Stubble the physics lesson, Bertie." Henry scowled and kicked at the fringe of the carpet. "You don't have to come along if you don't want to. I could ask, er, Joshua, I suppose."

"You can't ask the boot boy to serve as your second! Has to be another gentleman—at least, I think it does. Aren't those the rules?"

Henry lifted his shoulders. "How the hell should I know?"

"Well, it doesn't matter," replied his younger brother, "because of course I'm coming with you." His chin rose. "Even if it means that my skull is going to explode in a million and forty-seven pieces and my brains get spattered in a sixty-four-degree arc—"

"He is not going to shoot *you*," snapped Henry. "Besides, I—I am tolerably good with a pistol myself."

"That's right," agreed Bertie, though his voice had a rather hollow ring to it. "The scarecrow in Squire Gillen's field has died a thousand deaths."

"That's right," echoed Henry. "Anyway, we can't just allow the earl to insult Portia and get away with it."

There was a sharp gasp. "He insulted Portia? Why the devil didn't you say so? Where do we find the miserable cur?"

"As to that, I think I have a good idea. . . ."

Head bent, her thoughts engaged in puzzling over the widow's enigmatic words as she cut through Green Park, Portia was unaware of company until a gloved hand reached out and touched her elbow.

"Are you in training for the Newmarket races, Miss Hadley?" The earl fell in step beside her. "Or would you mind moderating your stride to a more ladylike gait?"

She noted that his long legs appeared to have no trouble keeping pace with hers. Nonetheless, she slowed to a more measured pace. "As you have discovered, sir, I very rarely behave like a proper lady."

There was a momentary glint in his eye that might have been sparked by amusement. But as the sun was shining square in his face, she decided it must have been a mere reflection, for the Earl of Branford did not strike her as a gentleman who possessed much of a sense of humor.

He most certainly did not possess any notion of proper courtesy, for his reply was exceedingly rude. "It appears there is at least one thing we agree on."

"Hmmph! It is not as if *you* behave like a proper gentleman." Turning sharply, she took one of the more secluded paths, hoping he would take the hint that his company was unwelcome.

No such luck. The earl remained stuck to her side like a cocklebur.

Inwardly seething, Portia marched on in silence for another few moments before stomping to a halt. "Is there some reason you are following me?" she demanded.

He brushed a speck of mud from his buckskin breeches. "Actually, there is."

She couldn't help but notice that the breeches were skintight, showing every contour of his muscled thighs. As well as slightly higher. Furious at herself for allowing her eyes to linger there, even for an instant, she wrenched them upward, feigning a studied interest in the simple gold buttons of his waistcoat. "What is it, then?"

"I thought we might try to have a friendly chat. Seeing as we got off on the wrong foot the other night, so to speak."

The unexpected answer startled her into meeting his eyes. Her breath caught in her throat as she realized how easily one might drown in the glittering depths of their sapphirine blue. Dangerous. Like the currents of Heraklion, where an unseen undertow could sweep even the strongest swimmer out to sea.

And yet, for an instant, she felt the oddest urge to let herself fall overboard. Which only exacerbated the strange mixture of spark and fire that was starting to tingle through her limbs. Fascination mingled with fury as she noticed the sensuous spread of his smile. *Hell's bells!* No wonder virtue swooned in surrender at the sight of those chiseled lips. Full, yet firmly masculine, they mouthed the promise of unspoken pleasure. . . .

Suddenly aware that her own lips had parted in unconscious anticipation, she formed them into a fierce scowl. "You must be cupshot or crazy to think we might ever be friends, Lord Branford."

His mouth thinned to a tight line. "Why?"

"Because we have absolutely nothing in common. Just what would you suggest we talk about?"

"We might begin with art," he replied quietly.

"Art!" she scoffed. "Pray, what does a gentleman such as yourself consider art, sir? The sort of lewd pennyprints one can buy in an alley, depicting a naked man with his member jutting out from his hairy thighs? Or a woman's legs wrapped around his waist? No doubt such scenes would prove quite familiar, judging by your actions last—" Too late, she realized she had let anger run away with her tongue. Indeed, she was painfully aware of having made a complete hash of the whole encounter. But she was not about to back down and admit it.

"You seem to have a penchant for prowling in the places where you ought not be, Miss Hadley. I wonder why that is?"

"And you, sir, have a penchant for pawing and snabbering over anyone who wears a skirt." Portia's voice grew more sneering. "I have no need to wonder why— the reason was quite . . . straightforward. So to speak." With that parting shot, she turned and stalked off.

This time, the earl did not follow.

Chapter Six

The black stallion tossed his head and gave a snort.

"I, too, would prefer a rousing gallop, but at this hour we must confine ourselves to a sedate canter," murmured Branford. However he loosened the reins just a touch, allowing the spirited animal to pick up his pace.

The thud of hooves quickened upon the bridle path. The far corner of the park was enough removed from the fashionable haunts of the *ton* that there was little chance of encountering some other rider, and so the earl leaned forward in the saddle, hoping that physical exertion and the slap of wind on his cheeks might help relieve some of his anger and mounting frustration. So far, his efforts in the investigation had resulted in naught but trips and stumbles.

Damnation! His skills must have grown dull with disuse—just like an old saber stuck away in an attic to gather cobwebs, he thought rather sourly. And as for the confounding country chit, his brain must have become permanently clouded with claret to think that he might have an intelligent conversation with a lady—

The stallion suddenly shied, nearly throwing him from his seat.

"What the devil!" With expert hands Branford quickly regained control of his mount, then looked down at the cause of the trouble. "Hell's teeth, watch where you are going, lad! Have you no more sense than a flea? You could have done yourself serious injury." He calmed the still skittish animal with a reassuring pat. "Not to speak of the damage you might have done to Hades." It was clear from his tone which of the two possibilities was of greater concern. "Now, if you don't mind, kindly step aside."

The young man standing square in the middle of the path did not budge.

Branford's brows drew together in a menacing frown. His temper, already dangerously frayed about the edges, was in danger of snapping altogether. "Is your hearing as bad as your judgment?" he demanded, in a tone that would have set a regiment of seasoned soldiers to flight.

Rather than send the lad scurrying for cover, the earl's sharp words had the opposite effect. He stared in some surprise as another young man—this one a mere child—joined the first one in blocking his path.

"Y-you are Lord Branford," began the elder of the two, trying manfully to imitate the earl's scowl.

"I damn well know who I am," he answered. "Who the devil are you?"

"Sir, be advised that—"

A sudden tug on his sleeve interrupted his speech. His companion then stood on tiptoes and whispered in his ear.

"I don't *have* a cursed glove, Bertie," came the harried response.

"But that's how it's done! Dash it all, Henry, haven't you read *The Stranger from Castile?*" The smaller lad began a hurried search of his pockets and finally fished out a ball of crumpled kidskin. "Here, I brought one along, just in case you forgot."

Henry blinked in horror. "B-but it's pink!"

"Well, I was in somewhat of a hurry," answered his companion, his voice taking on a somewhat defensive tone. "I had to borrow one belonging to Aunt Octavia."

"I can't slap Lord Branford with a pink glove!"

In spite of his foul mood, the earl found it impossible to contain his curiosity. "And just why, may I ask, do you wish to slap me with a glove of any color?"

"Why, to challenge you to a—*mmmph!*"

"Put a cork in it, Bertie. I'll handle it from here." Henry removed his hand from his brother's mouth and straightened his collar. "Lord Branford, I wish to call you out on a matter . . . of family honor."

"Family honor," repeated Branford slowly. After a closer look at the two upturned faces revealed an all-too-familiar glint of green, he rubbed at the bit of sticking plaster still affixed to his recent wound and added a silent oath.

Somehow it was not difficult to guess just which family they were referring to. Henry Falstaff. Bertram Orlando. Unless his wits had been permanently addled by the recent blow from the brick, it would appear that Lady Portia Hadley's Shakespearean siblings had taken center stage.

"Yes, family honor. You may think that our sister is fair game, just because our father has gone missing. But I will have you know—"

"*We,*" corrected Bertie, his elbow digging into his brother's ribs.

"—*we* will have you know that she is not without protectors," continued Henry. "Ones who will not stand by and allow her reputation to be shredded by a contemptible cad." Jaw clenched, the young man threw back his shoulders and crossed his arms—a rather Byronic pose that was immediately imitated by his younger companion. "So, sir, name your second, and I will have the, er, gentleman acting in my behalf meet with him and arrange the details."

"Let me get this straight," drawled Branford. "*You* are challenging *me* to a duel?"

"That's right, sir." Bertie took aim at the earl's forehead with a stubby finger and squeezed off an imaginary shot. "Pistols at dawn."

"Good Lord, stop acting like a child, Bertie," muttered Henry.

High drama or farce? Branford was not sure whether to be outraged or amused at the scene being played out before him. "Are you aware of what happened to the last two gentlemen who paced off against me?" he inquired softly.

"Y-yes, sir." The young man's chin tilted to an even more acute angle. "Your prowess with a pistol is the talk of the Town. But whether you have sent two or two hundred men to meet their Maker, I should be a craven c-coward were I to let f-fear override p-principle."

"Henry is very good with firearms as well," piped his younger brother with some loyalty. "I have seen him knock an apple from a tree at a distance of thirty paces."

"An apple is not aiming a bullet at your heart, lad."

The Hadleys exchanged rather queasy looks. Henry in particular turned a bit green around the gills. However, he quickly recovered, and waved his hand in an even more melodramatic gesture than before. "Perhaps not, but I am willing to lay down my life for my sister's honor."

"Aye. Me too," chimed the younger lad.

The sight of the jutting young jaws, gothic posturing, and pink glove was suddenly too much for the earl. He began to laugh.

It was now embarrassment rather than apprehension that colored the young man's face. "Honor is no laughing matter, sir," he said in a voice made tight by injured pride.

Branford was not so far into his dotage that he didn't remember the awkwardness of adolescence. "Indeed, it is not," he replied, taking care to smooth all trace of amusement from his expression.

He was now faced with an awkward problem—how was he to extricate himself from the ridiculous challenge without doing any injury to the lad's self-respect? He could, of course, simply ignore it and spur his stallion past them. But for some odd reason he found himself loath to trample on such youthful spirit. However comical their attempts at playing the knight in shining armor, the two Hadleys were displaying more raw courage and steadfast loyalty than many grown men would have done. And that was nothing to laugh at.

A slight constriction squeezed at his chest as he recalled two other boyish faces, alight with an eager idealism undimmed by loss and disillusionment. *Bloody hell*. This was no time for maudlin memories, he swore at himself. A seasoned officer should be able to devise a strategy to outmaneuver—

A loud whisper interrupted the earl's thoughts. "You still haven't slapped him across the cheek, Henry. I have read all about these affairs of honor. They must be conducted by the book."

"Actually you may dispense with the glove," said the earl, seeing his opening and quickly pouncing on the initiative. "It's an optional part of the process."

Henry looked a bit relieved.

"Therefore, without further ado, I acknowledge that a challenge has been issued," continued Branford. "And I will be happy to name my second. That is, as soon as you inform me of the exact offense of which I am guilty."

There was dead silence. After a moment Bertie looked up expectantly at his brother, but was met by a blank stare.

"Er, couldn't we simply say that you have offended my sister?" asked Henry.

The earl gave a solemn shake of his head. "I'm afraid not. The rules are quite strict on this point."

"But you must have done *something* to provoke her," insisted the elder Hadley. "Portia doesn't hit someone without good reason."

An intimate fondling and a forced kiss were reasonably provoking, allowed Branford, but he wasn't about to voice such sentiments aloud. "Be that as it may, you will have to ask her exactly what the incident was." Despite her penchant for headstrong action, the earl trusted that Miss Hadley had enough sense to remain silent on exactly what had occurred between them.

"She won't tell us," sighed Bertie. "You see, she feels she has to look out for us. Especially now, since that slimy slug Lord Dunster stole our home and kidnapped our father."

The earl's brow furrowed. The lad's announcement certainly added a new wrinkle to the scheme of things.

"Put a cork in it, Bertie," growled his brother. "His lordship isn't concerned with our family troubles."

That was quite right, Branford assured himself. He had a much bigger problem to deal with. Still, he couldn't help but seek to probe a bit deeper. After all, Miss Hadley's behavior of late had aroused justifiable suspicions, so it would be well to establish her true motives. On top of that, his investigation would run a good deal smoother if he could arrange it so that he wasn't tripping over the young lady at every turn.

"Tell me, what reason has your sister to suspect that Lord Dunster has anything to do with your father's disappearance?"

The two lads quickly outlined the gist of the story.

"It's deucedly difficult for us," finished Henry, unable to repress a fierce scowl. "I mean, Portia is as smart as most men—"

"Smarter," amended Bertie.

Henry didn't argue. "Very well—smarter. But a female shouldn't have to shoulder all the responsibilities. Not now, when we are old enough to take over."

"Right. It should be us, and not her, who goes sneaking off in the dead of night," added Bertie. "Whatever she is up to, it must be dangerous."

"Amen to that," muttered the earl under his breath. It might be an underhanded tactic to squeeze information out of children, but given the gravity of the situation, he brushed aside any momentary scruples. "Have you any idea what she is looking for during these, er, nocturnal sojourns of hers?"

"Proof of Dunster's perfidy," answered Bertie.

"As well as any clue as to where Father is being held captive," said Henry.

Branford thought for a moment. Was it possible that Miss Hadley's outrageous claim had any truth to it? It was clear that the two lads believed every word of what they had said. But then again, it was highly unlikely that their sister would reveal the real reason for her actions if she was involved in some nefarious plot.

"Hmmm," he murmured aloud, as he mulled over what he had just heard. It took an impatient whinny from his mount to remind him of how long they had been halted in the middle of the bridle path. With a low oath, the earl reached for his pocketwatch. "The devil take it, I'm going to be late for an important appointment." He snapped the gold case shut. "I'm afraid I must be on my way. . . ."

"B-but Lord Branford! Er, about the duel . . ."

"Ah, yes, the duel." Good Lord, he had nearly forgotten about that small detail. "Why don't you make a few inquiries of your sister while I consider the nature of your accusations a bit more carefully. Then let us meet back here tomorrow at the same time and we will discuss the matter further."

"Very well, sir." With a rather endearing show of

dignity, Henry made a formal bow and stepped out of the stallion's way. The grand gesture was somewhat marred by the fact that he had to reach out and yank his younger brother from the path.

As he spurred his mount to a canter, Branford caught a whisper of Bertie's parting words.

"Lord Branford seems a rather decent villain—mayhap he will only cripple you for life instead of spattering bits of your brain from Houndslow Heath to Kew Gardens."

Muttering several unladylike words, Portia threw down her pen and stared at her notes in disgust. No matter how she arranged the sheets of paper, they still did not form a clear picture.

And it certainly didn't help matters any that her brain was having trouble staying focused on the scrawls of black ink, straying instead to the recollection of a raven-haired rake. *Damn the man!* she swore to herself, trying hard not to dwell on certain graphic details. How dare he suggest they might have anything in common! They didn't, save the misfortune of having bumped up against each other in the dead of the night. She took pleasure in intellectual activities, while he—well, it was quite clear how he pursued pleasure.

She meant to see that their paths didn't cross again.

Just as she meant to shake all thoughts of sapphire eyes from her head and concentrate on the matter at hand. With a toss of her curls, Portia propped her chin in her palm and forced her attention back to the items on her desk.

Nothing! She had learned absolutely nothing that might further her quest, despite all the risks she had taken. The papers stolen from Dunster's desk had been naught but useless scraps of paper. And, despite a minute examination, the book she had collected from Mr. Harrington appeared no more than a handsome little volume of miniature paintings, with no subtle messages or clues hidden within the detailed brushstrokes.

Jade Tiger. Lotus of the Orient. What was the meaning of such odd names? A wealthy widow. A malevolent marquess. A wagering wastrel. Which one—if any of them—was the real villain?

A sigh stole forth. She had collected nothing but a handful of seeming random pieces to a puzzle. And she had no idea of how they fit together.

Or *if* they fit together.

Think! Though Portia felt her shoulders sag a bit under the weight of her own expectations, she chided herself to concentrate. There must be a way to go about finding some tangible clue, some hard evidence, as to why her father had been abducted, if only she used logic and reason . . .

Her fingers suddenly paused in their shuffling of the papers. *Hell's bells!* Why hadn't she seen it before? The answer was staring her right in the face! She arranged the notes in a neat row across her desk, then took up her pen and a fresh sheet of paper. The first thing she wrote was a short list of people—Julian Hadley, Lord Dunster, Mrs. Grenville, and the gentleman she had observed in conversation with the marquess, Lord Roxleigh. Next to each name she penned in the one thing they all had in common:

Merchant ships.

Her father had last been seen on the London docks, and the others were in one way or another connected to the shipping trade. What a nitwit she had been! Of course the Isle of Dogs was the logical spot to explore, rather than the town houses of the *ton!* The only question was where to begin. . . .

Portia took her time sorting through the alternatives, determined this time not to make a foolish mistake. No matter how she considered it, Mrs. Grenville's name had to be placed at the top of the list. Grenville and Company no doubt had an office among the many warehouses. Late at night, when the area was sure to be deserted, it should not be so difficult to avoid the few watchmen and gain entrance through a back door. She had, after all, been practicing her skills with a new set of picklocks.

In and out.

This time around, she would not make a hash of the job.

"Still nothing?"

"Nothing. Not even an intimate interlude with Roxleigh's wife yielded much—"

Taft's lip curled slightly.

"—in the way of information. And trust me, it was duty that compelled me to action. The experience was not as pleasurable as your smirk seems to imply." Branford made a face. "I asked as many questions as I could, but aside from learning the names of his closest cronies and the fact that she suspects him of devious behavior, I came away with the impression that she truly doesn't know any specifics about his activities." Branford stared into his brandy. "Damnation, Tony. You needn't rub in the fact that I am making little progress."

"I'm not," assured his friend. "I know full well what a difficult task I have set before you."

"Perhaps I'm simply losing my touch," muttered the earl as he fingered the remnant of sticking plaster on his brow. "I have naught to show for my troubles so far but a cracked skull."

"Still no idea who might have coshed you? That is, other than the Lady in Red?" Taft's mouth twitched. "Though in truth I find it hard to imagine there is a female in existence capable of bringing the Black Cat to his knees."

Branford gave an inward wince as the jibe struck home. He had not mentioned Miss Hadley in his earlier report to Taft for two reasons. First of all, because it seemed unlikely that her presence had anything to do with the crisis at Whitehall. And secondly, because, if truth be told, his pride as well as his skull had suffered a hard knock. He had not wanted to admit to a fellow soldier that a female may indeed have gotten the drop on him.

However, the stakes were much too high for pride to take precedence over prudence. After spotting her in close proximity to Roxleigh, he could no longer deny that the coincidences were becoming too frequent to ignore, despite the explanations offered by her brothers. She might very well be as innocent as they claimed, but until he knew that for a certainty, he had no choice but to inform Taft of his suspicions.

"You yourself warned me not to underestimate the wiles of a woman," he reminded his friend. "Well, it seems the lump on my head may have been dealt by that confounded country chit rather than the Wanton Widow."

"Who?"

"The bluestocking—Miss Hadley. Apparently she, too, wished to ask a few questions of Mrs. Grenville. At least, that was her excuse for being out in the garden when I came to and found her crouched beside me."

Taft's expression sobered considerably as he sipped at his sherry. "Why?"

"She claimed it had to do with her father's recent disappearance." Branford took a swallow of spirits. "You may have heard mention of it circulating around the clubs."

"A word here and there, but the baron is well known for wandering the globe in pursuit of his arcane studies. No doubt the rumors of anything havey-cavey having occurred are simply the result of the young lady's flighty imagination. I expect it will turn out to be just another one of his bizarre journeys."

Whatever her other faults, Branford did not think Miss Hadley flighty or prone to hysteria. "His family seems convinced otherwise." After toying with the fob on his watch chain he asked abruptly, "What do you know of Lord Dunster?"

"Dunster?" His friend shrugged. "Drinks and gambles to excess, like a goodly number of other gentlemen. And while he and his cronies are said to engage in a number of debaucheries at their private parties, they are welcome by all but the highest sticklers of the *ton*. Why?"

"It is just a hunch, but I should like for you to dig a bit deeper and see what you can turn up on him and his activities."

Taft pulled a face. "Have you considered that there is a more nefarious explanation for the young lady's activities?" He shuffled at the papers on his desk, his frown deepening. "Think on it, Alex—an ancient document containing a priceless secret goes missing, and now a noted scholar, however eccentric, has disappeared as well. Perhaps it is she and her family who are involved in something shady."

"I have not overlooked that possibility," admitted Branford. "However, you have not seen or heard the young lady in action. Unless she is a consummate actress, Miss Hadley appears utterly incapable of subtlety. Or subterfuge."

Taft's hands went very still, and when he spoke, it was very softly. "I trust you have not forgotten Lillian de Montfort. She, too, seemed the very soul of innocence, yet it took a goodly number of stitches to keep your liver from dangling down around your knees."

The earl drained his glass in a single gulp. "No, I have not forgotten." Ever the diplomat, Tony had been too tactful to add mention of the others. Two Portuguese agents had been fished out of the river Tagus with their hands and tongues cut off, due to the lady's betrayal. But Branford needed little jostling of his memory to recall yet another set of youthful faces, their features running red with blood. "I am well aware of how skilled a female may be in hiding her true nature." His mouth compressed. "Still, I cannot shake a deucedly odd feeling about the marquess. . . . Look, it isn't as if your men are turning up anything of use, anyway. Humor me on this."

"I have learned over the years not to argue with your instincts, Cat," replied his friend. "I will have someone get on it, even though I think you are clawing up the wrong tree."

"Perhaps." The earl couldn't help thinking that, of late, his instincts seemed to have been as bad as his luck. "In any case, you may be sure I am also keeping a close watch on Miss Hadley."

"Well, it doesn't appear as if you have eyes in the back of your head," quipped Taft. On noting the darkening of the earl's features, he gave a small smile. "Now, don't go falling into a black study, Alex. What I meant was, you seem to have your hands full with pursuing the elusive Mrs. Grenville." There was a slight pause as he searched through a pile of papers and extracted a folded note. "Any luck yet in arranging an introduction to the lady?"

"Contrary to your information, she did not put in an appearance at the Trowbridge ball," replied the earl. "However, Fieldston has assured me she will be present at the Harrington soiree tomorrow evening, and has promised to make sure that we meet. In the meantime I have a few ideas on how to learn a bit more about our mysterious widow." The earl rose and started for the door. "Keep me informed if you hear anything that may be of use. I have no qualms in admitting that I can use all the help I can get."

"Then perhaps you would be interested to know that Cricket is in Town."

Branford stopped in his tracks. "Max? Here? Why, last I heard, he was running the entire intelligence network in southern Portugal." His brow puckered. "Since when has he taken his leave from Wellington's staff?"

"Since a French saber nearly cut out his left eye." Taft's sigh held an edge. "I only learned of it yesterday, and not from him but a visiting attaché from headquarters in Lisbon. Apparently, Max spent some time recuperating at his family's estate in Yorkshire and then, just a fortnight ago, took up residence in Davies Street." Another sigh followed. "Though why he chose such an out-of-the-way location over his former rooms is beyond me."

"Why the devil hasn't he sent word to either of us?" growled the earl.

His friend fixed him with a probing stare. "As to that, Alex, you may have a better idea than I on why an old comrade would choose to avoid his closest friends." He held out the scrap of paper he had pulled out from his notes. "Here is his direction in case you are interested. I stopped by yesterday but was told he was out."

Branford tucked it into his waistcoat pocket, taking care to avoid meeting the other man's eyes.

Taft's words were still echoing in his head as he swung into the saddle. Much as he wished to deny it, his friend's keen observation had cut uncomfortably close to home. Oh, yes, he understood all too well how the blackness of despair could be blinding. So much so that any ray of light—the glimmer of laughter, warmth, and camaraderie—hurt enough that one had to turn away.

But then, mused the earl, he had always had a darker side, one given over to black moods and brooding introspection. Tony, on the other hand, had always been steadiest of the three of them, and the most even-tempered. The consummate diplomat, even as a student, he had on many an occasion talked their way out of deep trouble.

And Max? Branford sighed. There was no better companion to have when facing the horrors and hardship of military life. Cool under fire, loyal to a fault, his only shortcoming might be that his shyness sometimes overshadowed his dry wit and sharp sense of humor. Analytical by nature, Viscount Davenport was more comfortable sifting through a stack of reports than facing a roomful of strangers. He tended to appear stiff and aloof, especially around females.

The earl's mouth quirked at the irony of it. With his tall, muscular form, tawny locks, and chiseled features, Max had a legion of ladies ready to swoon at his feet. But, with self-effacing modesty, he seemed unaware of his effect on the opposite sex. There was a deeper reason, of course. The very soul of honor, Max had been deeply hurt and humiliated by the young lady he had fallen in love with. She had jilted him for a loftier title and richer purse, and he had yet to recover his self-confidence on that particular field of battle.

However, to those few who knew him well, the viscount revealed a very different side of his character.

When his guard was down, he could be wickedly funny and quick to laugh. Lord, there were many dismal nights in Spain when Max had kept their spirits buoyed with perceptive observations on the absurdities of life.

Branford tightened his grip on the reins. Friends, foes, females. He had an unsettling feeling that nothing about this particular assignment was going to prove easy to handle.

"I ain't sure this is a very good idea, Miss P.," grumbled her faithful retainer as he scrambled down from his perch. The door of the carriage opened a crack, revealing a gap-toothed grimace that might have spooked the Devil himself. "I got a bad feeling right now in the marrow of me old bones."

"You say that every time it is about to rain, Owen." Ignoring the prophesy of doom, Portia pulled up the hood of her cloak. "There's no reason to be nervous. I'll be quick about it."

"Oh, aye, I've heard *that* before." His eyes rolled heavenward. "Ye best move yer gams—them clouds is getting thicker by the minute. And this time around, try not to lose them pokers. Hairpins might ha' worked in a pinch on a measly desk lock, but they ain't gonna be worth spit in opening one of these doors."

"I shall keep a firm grip on the picks," she assured him. Just as she would the pistol she had tucked away in the other pocket. In light of her first foray into criminal activities, she had decided it was wise to be prepared for the worst.

Though how much worse it could get after The Incident in Lord Dunster's town house was not something she wished to contemplate.

Her boots kicked up a swirl of vapor as they slipped down to the rough cobblestones. A heavy fog had floated up from the river, making it difficult to make out anything more than the blurred edges of the buildings ahead of her. Though she was grateful for the cover it provided, Portia couldn't help but feel a chill shiver course through her at the prospect of having to brave the ominous gloom.

"Ye want fer me to come with ye?" asked Owen, on noting her hesitation. "I'm still pretty handy wid me fives—though one o' them's only a four."

"That won't be necessary," she replied, with a good deal more bravado than she was feeling. However, to forestall any further remonstrances from her companion, she flashed a quick smile and forced her feet forward. The grizzled ex-pugilist had provided stalwart support in any number of dicey situations over the years, but she refused to involve him in this.

As her shoulder pressed up against the side of the first warehouse, Portia let out a small sigh of relief. Perhaps this wasn't going to be so difficult after all, she told herself. There was no sign of life as she peered into the alleyway, save for the faint scratching of claws in a nearby pile of rubbish. Owen had described the exact location of the door she sought, but in the ghostly darkness it was impossible to make out a single landmark. She bit at her lip, surprised at how dry her throat had become despite the mizzled dampness of the thickening mists. The choices were rather simple—admit defeat and retreat, or push forward, relying on touch rather than sight to find the right spot.

Sucking in a deep breath, she disappeared into the narrow gap between the two buildings.

Thirty-six, thirty-seven, thirty-eight . . . Portia paused in the counting of her steps to feel at the wall. *Thank heavens*—the turn was just where her coachman had said it would be. Stepping around the corner, she kept her fingers on the grimy brick, letting them brush along the pitted surface until they passed over the first doorway, then the second. . . .

At the third door she stopped. The fog was thick enough to cut with a knife, yet she couldn't help but cast a furtive glance in both directions before removing the sturdiest of her picks from its case and setting to work.

Much to her surprise, the door eased open at the first jiggle.

Perhaps luck was on her side tonight, for it appeared that a careless clerk had neglected to check all the locks before closing up. Offering up a silent prayer of thanks for her good fortune, she slipped inside, taking care to draw the iron-banded oak door shut behind her.

Her words ended in a muttered curse as her knee knocked into a stack of crates. It was dark as a crypt in the cramped space, and she realized she hadn't thought to bring along a candle or flint. *So much for luck,* she fumed, fumbling to find a way into the main part of the office. But no doubt there would be some sort of light on one of the desks.

After one or two more stumbles and bumps, Portia finally located the other door. Two small windows on the opposite wall allowed a pale wash of light to seep in from outside. It was just enough to prevent her from tripping over yet another item of merchandise— this one looked to be a rolled carpet that had somehow fallen to block the narrow aisle between the copy desks.

She stepped over it and reached for one of the oil lamps. If *she* were the owner of Grenville and Company, she would certainly not tolerate such sloppiness from her employees, thought Portia. Removing the globe, she turned up the wick. Not only were valuable goods being left in disarray, but a sticky substance was puddled on the floor by her boots. *Spilled Madeira?* Perhaps a scrivener was tippling. . . .

Flint struck steel and a flame sparked up.

She would have let out a small scream at the sight of the wine-dark blood if a hand had not clamped tightly over her mouth.

"Be still!" came a rasping growl close to her ear.

Too shocked to twitch a muscle, Portia did exactly as her captor ordered.

The hand slowly slipped away and the man who had come up behind her knelt down beside the bloody corpse. Removing his glove, he lay a finger against the ashen cheek. "He's not been dead for very long." He looked up and made a swift survey of the place. The sight of the riffled drawers and strewn papers drew a string of invectives from his hidden lips. "The murderer may still be lurking close by," he added as he scrambled to his feet. "So you had best come with me, whoever you are, if you do not wish to have your own throat sliced from ear to ear."

"I—I prefer to make my own way out," she said, trying manfully to imitate his own gruff growl.

"Not a good idea, when—" He stopped abruptly, then whipped around and yanked back the hood of her cloak. "Bloody hell! I might have guessed it would be you."

"There is no call for sarcasm, Lord Branford. I assure you, I am no more happy than you are at yet another tête-à-tête."

"Then, what the devil—"

The whine of a bullet cut off the question. Grabbing at Portia's arm, the earl dove for the cover of a desk, pulling her along with him. His reaction came just in the nick of time, for the next shot shattered the lamp that had been standing only inches from her heart.

"First bricks and now bullets. What will it be next, Miss Hadley—an eruption of Mount Vesuvius?"

Portia finally managed to recover her breath—no easy feat as the earl was sprawled on top of her. "Why is it you always blame *me* for these attacks on your person?"

"Because you always seem to be perilously close to me when they occur, that's why!" He rolled to one side and felt around in his pocket. "Damnation, my pistol! It must have slipped out when—"

"I thought professionals didn't make excuses," she whispered. "Here—would you care to use mine?"

He stared at the old-fashioned weapon she thrust in his hand. "Who gave this to you—Oliver Cromwell?"

"At least I came prepared, which is more than I can say for you. Speaking of which, why *are* you here?" She winced as yet another shot exploded close by. "And why is someone shooting at you?"

"What makes you think our unknown assailant is aiming at *me?*"

Portia swallowed hard. "You mean—"

A loud crash sounded from the storage room. She tried to lift her head and see what was going on, but the earl jerked her back down. Turning to face him, she saw he was hurriedly checking the priming of the old pistol and testing the tension of the tarnished trigger.

"Stay down," he ordered.

"What—"

"And for God's sake, stay quiet." Without further ado, he slithered off into the darkness.

Portia wrapped her cloak a bit tighter around her shoulders and hunched up against the side of the desk. Now that the initial shock was wearing off, she found her hands shaking so badly that she could scarcely keep a grip on the napped wool. Indeed, her nerves were so frayed that the faint scrape of a boot against wood nearly tore a scream from her throat. *Had the earl fallen victim to their unseen attacker?* Despite her dislike of the man, she did not wish for him to end up like . . . the other body.

She pressed her eyes closed, hoping to blot out the hideous image of the gentleman's face. The sightless eyes had been open wide in surprise, the lips drawn back in a cruel parody of a smile. And the throat . . . She choked back a retch. Instead of a neatly knotted cravat, there had been only a wide slash of crimson.

The Lady in Red. A shudder passed through her as she recalled the painting of Shiva, whose arms spun around in a blur of sharpened knives. The widow had not admitted an acquaintance with Lord Roxleigh, but the viscount was certainly aware of sultry Mrs. Grenville.

Why else would he be lying dead on the floor of her place of business?

Portia had little time to ponder the question, for in the next instant there came a thunderous explosion, followed by a piercing scream.

Chapter Seven

❧❦❧

"Hurry!"

Branford tossed away the smoking pistol and vaulted over the back counter. "There are at least four of them, all armed to the teeth. I locked the door from this side, but I doubt that will hold them for long."

The sound of splintering wood served to punctuate the surmise.

To his relief, the young lady didn't waste what little time they had in arguing. She shot to her feet, grasped his outstretched hand, and followed along toward the front entrance without so much as a stumble. No sign of tears or hysterics, either, he noted with grudging approval as he worked the bolts free and kicked the door open.

It wasn't until their boots hit the cobblestones that she hesitated a fraction.

"Now what?"

Footsteps were already echoing from off to one side of the building. The earl didn't answer but hustled her across the narrow loading area and crouched down in the lee of a large barrow, praying that the fog would serve to hide what the rough wood did not.

The man rushing in from the rear of the Grenville

and Company office was met by another who had come around by way of the neighboring warehouse.

"Any sign of 'em headed back for the main road?"

"Naw, but Weber is waiting to cut off any retreat in that direction. They won't slip past his blade. Wot about you—you didn't see nuffing?"

"They must ha' slipped through the fog into them alleyways." There was a shuffling of feet. "Bloody hell, 'tis thick as a French whore's perfume out here. An' soon likely t' be wetter than a mermaid's tit. Gonna be a devil of a time t' flush 'em out."

"Aye, but there will be th' devil t' pay if we don't." The words were followed by a lengthy curse. "Take Grimmell an' work yer way down from over there. Me an' Allbeck will start from here. We'll meet up at th' docks."

"Son of a poxy slut, we was supposed t' be watching fer jes' th' gentry cove hisself," grumbled the other man. "The boss didn't say nuffing about there bein' more than one throat t' slit."

"Stop jawing an' get moving, afore it's yer own windpipe that's whistling in th' wind."

Branford waited several minutes, until he was sure the men had moved into the warren of alleyways. "This way," he whispered, taking Portia's hand and signaling for her to stay low. Hugging close to the shadows, he led them straight for the water's edge.

The docks were a tangle of old rigging, sails, and spars. As one of their assailants had predicted, a steady mizzle began to fall, making the briny planking underfoot even more slippery than usual. However, the chill drops were accompanied by a thickening of the swirling mists, something the earl was counting on to make his plan work. Picking his way past the coils of rope and bundles of netting, he suddenly turned and crept out along one of the loading wharves that jutted into the rippling current.

"W-won't we be t-trapped out here," began Portia, her teeth starting to chatter from the chill night air.

"Sssshhh."

Tied to one of the barnacled pilings was a small sailing dinghy. He lifted a corner of the tarpaulin hung over its boom and peered into the shallow well. There was not much room, but after surveying the items stowed inside, he decided it would do the trick. "In here."

"I don't think—"

He cut off the protest by lifting her none too gently over the gunwales and thrusting her down onto the floorboards. "You're right," he muttered. "If you would take a moment to exercise a modicum of rational thought, you would not be engaging in such harebrained stunts at every turn."

"I—ummphh!"

For the second time that night, Portia was rendered speechless by the earl's full weight landing on top of her.

The low whoosh of air caused a grim smile to flit over his features. *Served the audacious chit right,* he told himself.

"Your conduct is outrageous, sir. I'll not be manhandled yet again—"

"Stop squirming. I need to get my arm free."

His hand started working its way up the length of her thigh, and despite the urgency of the situation,

Branford suddenly found himself distracted by the contours of her body. He had forgotten how long and shapely her legs were, and how the softly rounded curves of her slim hips fit snugly up against his. Shifting slightly, his face grazed her hair and he was conscious of the faint perfume of verbena sweetening the musty odor of damp canvas. The same movement rolled his chest across the swell of her breasts. They were firm yet yielding, and he imagined that they would fit perfectly in the cup of his palm. . . .

"Why?"

His fingers jerked free. "*Must* you ask so many infernal questions?" he demanded as he reached out from under the canvas and groped for the bowline. It took a bit of awkward maneuvering to undo the rope from the rusting cleat, but once it slipped free, he gave a hard shove to the edge of the jetty and sent the little craft drifting out to catch the tide.

Portia wrinkled her nose. The bilge water reeked of dead crabs, and the air trapped under the tarp was heavy with the odor of seagull droppings. She tried to draw in a deep breath, only to find herself enveloped in a distinctly different scent. Leather, musky with undertones of sandalwood and bay rum, cut through the acrid scent of burnt gunpowder and the briny pungency of the surrounding waters. It was not at all unpleasant, simply a bit overpowering. But as her nose was squashed hard up against the earl's shoulder, it was no surprise that she was having difficulty in getting her lungs to work properly. . . .

"If you would try not to keep your spine as stiff as

the planking, you might find a more comfortable position."

"Ha! Not with an overbearing oaf lying on top of me. A large and heavy oaf, I might add." She tried to move her shoulders, but between the narrowness of the boat's hull and the bulk of the earl, she had precious little room to maneuver. "Can't we at least turn back a corner of the canvas to allow for a breath of fresh air?"

Branford caught her hand. "Not quite yet, Miss Hadley. I am counting on the fog to hide our movement, but if anyone spots us, it is best that the boat appear unoccupied. That way it will look as if it were only some carelessness with the mooring lines that caused it to go adrift."

"M-movement?" she repeated. She hadn't realized that the lapping of the waves against the planking meant they were now drifting along in brackish water. "How is it that we are no longer tied up to the dock?"

"I undid the rope and pushed us off," he explained. "The current will do the rest. While our adversaries are combing the alleyways, the incoming tide is carrying us slowly but surely out of their reach. We will soon be far enough downstream to row to shore without being observed—I did take care to check that a pair of oars were stowed under the combing, in case that was your next question."

It was, but she wasn't about to admit it.

"I assume you have a coach waiting somewhere not far off," he continued with an irritating smugness that set her teeth on edge. "So we should be able to return to Town with no further trouble."

Very clever, allowed Portia, but only to herself. Lord

Branford might be arrogant and obnoxious, but it also appeared he was not quite as dull-witted as she had first supposed. The plan had shown a sharp bit of ingenuity on his part, especially under the circumstances. "When it's not pickled in brandy, your brain seems able to function half decently."

He gave a throaty chuckle. "I assure you, Miss Hadley, all of my body parts are in perfect working order."

Odious man! Did he think of nothing but wanton pleasure? She shifted abruptly, causing his hand to knock up against an iron stanchion.

He muttered a curse. "All save for my scorched fingers. By the way, what the devil was loaded in that weapon of yours? The explosion nearly blew me clear to Bombay."

"Naught but shot and . . . a bit of black powder."

"How much black powder?"

"Er, rather a lot, I suppose," she answered a bit defensively. "I couldn't quite remember the exact proportions." In spite of her dislike for the earl, she could not forget how he taken the rusty old pistol without hesitation and rushed to confront their attackers. "I—I am sorry if you were hurt."

"Hmmph. It's only a scratch. . . ."

A sudden gust of wind rattled through the rigging, tipping the boat to one side and throwing Branford hard up against the gunwales. This time his injured hand grazed her cheek as he grabbed for one of the cleats to steady himself.

Portia gave a slight gasp at the touch of tattered leather. "Why, your glove has been torn to shreds! And your hand"—she reached up to feel his fingers—"your hand is bleeding. And chilled to the bone."

"I assure you, I have suffered far worse cold during the siege of—" His words turned into a grunt of surprise as she tugged his arm down and tucked the singed knuckles inside her cloak. "What do you think you are doing?"

"Making sure you do not contract a bout of pneumonia," she replied evenly as she stripped off the remains of the glove. "In my experience, males are uncommonly silly about taking proper care of themselves."

"It's not necessary to make a fuss over a scrape, Miss Hadley," he said gruffly. "Contrary to your low opinion of me, I am not some grubby schoolboy in need of a nursemaid."

As if she needed to be reminded of that!

In truth, Portia was all too aware that the earl bore not the slightest resemblance to a child. He had shifted back into place, and though his elbows supported some of his weight, there was a raw, undeniably masculine physicality about him that was impossible to ignore. The broad planes of his chest were taut as whipcord where they pressed against her, and the hardened muscles of his thighs felt as unyielding as tempered steel. Not to speak of his bare fingers, long and lithe, spreading a flush of heat at the base of her throat.

She felt her pulse begin to quicken beneath their calloused tips. A few moments ago she had been shivering from the damp cold seeping up through the floorboards. Yet now, for some unaccountable reason, it seemed uncomfortably warm within the cramped space. Indeed, she could feel a strange heat stealing through her, and was grateful that the darkness covered the telltale burn of red that she knew must be coloring her face.

Portia swallowed hard. The boat may have come back to an even keel, she thought, but her own reactions seemed to have lost their equilibrium. Surely her reaction was not due to any sort of attraction to a lecherous libertine. Feeling slightly dazed, she once again tried to catch her breath.

The earl was certainly doing nothing to help matters. The dratted man seemed infuriatingly relaxed and gave a languid stretch, rather like a large cat settling itself for a nap. If anything, his lanky form pressed a bit closer.

"How much longer do we have to stay squeezed in here?" Her voice had a rather singed crackle to it.

"You might try thinking of something . . . pleasant to take your mind off the present circumstances."

"Impossible," she muttered.

"Is it?" His breath was a warm zephyr on her cheek.

"S-stop that."

He didn't. If anything, the sensation became more physical, as if something warm and pliant were trailing along the line of her jaw. Her insides gave a lurch that had nothing to do with the gentle rocking of the boat. She began to demand again that he cease whatever it was he was doing, but much to her befuddlement the only sound to come out was a soft sigh.

It was quickly silenced as his lips came down teasingly upon hers. Unlike the night in Dunster's study, they were not slurred with a surfeit of brandy but bore a tantalizing trace of sea salt and an earthy spice she could not define. Intrigued in spite of herself, Portia ran the tip of her tongue along their length, seeking a fuller taste.

Suddenly, as if she had struck a flint to steel, her mouth was filled with a searing heat, the hard thrusting of the earl's tongue matched by the steeling shaft of his manhood beginning to press against her thigh. Portia knew she should protest. And fiercely. A proper young lady was expected to fight tooth and nail for her virtue. Yet, at the moment the battle she was waging was not with Branford but her own flaring desires.

This was utter madness! she railed at herself, trying to ignore the surge of warm pleasure shivering through her. She quite disliked the dratted man, so why was his rampant maleness and roving touch sparking anything but anger and revulsion? It was, however, not outrage that was igniting the strange tingle in her limbs. Try as she might to muster a righteous fury, she found herself thinking of the frenzied coupling she had witnessed in the conservatory and wondering what it would be like to be aroused to a burning passion. . . .

The earl's embrace had slowed to a more deliberate pace. His tongue now slid with rhythmic ease over her lower lip, entwining with hers in a sensuous curl that sent a liquid heat spiraling down between her legs. At the same time he had left off his feathery caresses to the shell of her ear to work his bare hand beneath the folds of her cloak. Taking the nub of her breast between his thumb and forefinger, he began a circular teasing through the thin layers of her dress and chemise. The pinch of his touch and the friction of the light lawn cotton soon had the sensitive flesh feeling like a point of fire.

Portia gave a muffled moan. The practical portion of her brain was screaming that it was beyond folly to allow his plundering of her person to go on a moment longer. And yet, in the back of her head a defiant little voice would not be silenced. When, it asked, would she ever have another chance to experience the sizzling kisses of an experienced libertine? Or feel so gloriously, wickedly alive in every fiber of her being.

The earl's knee was now wedged between her legs, urging them apart.

The whisper grew louder, insisting that she didn't have to like the devilish rogue to be fascinated by what his touch was doing to her body.

Hell's bells! Consigning caution—and the last shreds of common sense—to the wind, she arched up against his thigh and let her hand steal inside his shirt, marveling at the unfamiliar contours of his broad chest and the rough silkiness of the curling hair.

Why the devil was he kissing the feisty Miss Hadley again?

This time around, realized Branford, an excess of brandy was not to blame for his addled wits. Nonetheless, he felt an odd intoxication as his lips came down upon hers. He had begun nuzzling at her throat merely to annoy her. Still smarting from her rejection of his intellectual overtures, he had, in a surge of ungentlemanly spite, intended to see if he might tease her body into admitting a physical attraction to him. But, much to his amazement, he suddenly found himself awash in a strange rush of heat.

Even more baffling than his own response was the young lady's reaction. He had expected an indignant squawk of protest. Or perhaps even another punch—though under the circumstances she would find it a bit difficult to swing a fist with any effectiveness. However, she made no move to protest. Quite the opposite, in fact. To his utter surprise, her lips softened under his, then parted slightly, the whispered breath of air sounding a primal invitation to deepen the embrace.

Her heated response, innocent yet eager, sent a jolt of unexpected arousal through him. Abandoning any attempt to make rational sense of it all, the earl slipped his tongue inside her mouth, aware of a subtle sweetness as she opened herself fully to his advance. He took his time in savoring the heady taste, probing her depths, sucking at her unresisting lips, filling her with wave after wave of lush, intimate kisses.

"S-sir!" Portia finally broke away long enough to manage a coherent sound.

Aware that her hands were fluttering against his shoulders, he raised his head slightly and steeled himself for a full scale verbal assault. After all, he had already experienced how sharply honed Miss Hadley's words could be when she was provoked.

But once again her reaction was not at all what he had anticipated.

"T-there is no audience now, Lord Branford," she stammered. "So there is no need to pretend an attraction to my person." The canvas covering had been blown askew by the gust of wind, allowing a winking of light to spill in from above. It was barely more than a glimmer, but bright enough so that the earl did not miss the spasm of vulnerability that flitted across her features. She tried to look away, but his fingers stilled her chin.

"You think I am pretending?" He regarded her face with a searching frown. "Why?"

"Because my limbs are too gangly, my mouth too wide, my cheekbones too angular, and my eyes . . ." She bit at her lip. "I am well aware that my eyes betray a lack of the proper sort of docility expected in a lady."

He couldn't suppress a chuckle. "Docility? You have all the docility of a tiger, as I can well attest, having felt the sharpness of your claws." She tried to look away but he kept his palm against her chin. "It's true that your eyes always seem to spark with fire. But trust me, Miss Hadley, there are many men who would find them infinitely more intriguing than those of a biddable young lady. To begin with, they are an interesting shade of green. Rather like the color of smoky emeralds." He paused, his face mere inches from hers. "No, that is not quite right," he amended. "They are more opaque than emeralds. More like . . . molten jade."

His words seemed to stir a glittering intensity within their depths. Blind to all reason, the earl lowered his mouth and kissed her again. He could feel her pulse quicken, and as his tongue licked from the jut of her lip to the hollow of her throat, her flesh took on a throbbing heat. She gave a small shiver at the intimate touch, but instead of pulling away, she pressed up into his embrace. His fingers had splayed to cup her breast, and through the thin fabric he could feel the nipple hard and erect against his palm. With a low growl he thrust his knee between her thighs and reached down to pull the bunched tangle of damp wool and crumpled muslin up over her hips. . . .

How far into uncharted waters they might have strayed, he wasn't sure, but the boat suddenly bumped up hard against some obstacle in the water, jarring them apart.

Rocked to his sensed, Branford sat upright. "I had best go see where we are," he said gruffly.

What the devil had got into him? he wondered as he hoisted himself out onto the narrow transom and took hold of the tiller. Since when had a simple kiss left him feeling so deucedly . . . odd? The answer was never, he admitted with a pinched grimace. It was usually the other way around, with his amorous advances leaving the lady in a dazed swoon.

His intentions had been no different with Miss Hadley. So why did he feel as if the ancient pistol had not been the only thing to send a shower of sparks burning through his flesh? It made no bloody sense at all. But then again, there was nothing remotely sensible about the maddening Miss Hadley. Or his own unaccountable actions.

Damnation! He didn't need to recall Tony's warning to know he had no business kissing her. Disgusted with himself, he vowed to make sure it didn't happen again.

With a harried sigh he forced his attention back to more practical concerns. The bow of the boat had become snagged against a large buoy marking the middle of the channel. He reached inside the combing for the oars, and began to maneuver the small craft out of danger. Another quick glance around showed that the warehouses and loading jetties were now far behind them.

Dipping the blades into the eddying crosscurrents, he rowed for shore.

"Are you awake?" The question had been asked in a low whisper, but as Bertie's toe had stubbed up against a chair, knocking a number of books to the floor, the attempt at circumspection went all for naught.

"I am now." Henry yawned and ran a hand through his mop of curls. "What's wrong? Having another bad dream, Bertie?" The initial sarcasm softened to a show of concern. "If you like, you can stay here with me until you are sure it's passed."

"It's not that. It's . . . Portia. She's gone."

The news caused his brother to sit up straight. "B-but I heard her tell Aunt Octavia that she had a headache and was going to retire early."

"The scullery maid says females have used that excuse since the time of Adam." He made a face. "Whatever *that's* supposed to mean."

"What it means is, she has given us the slip. Again." The expression he added under his breath made Bertie blink.

"I don't think you are supposed to say that out loud."

"Of course I'm not." Henry's bare feet slapped down upon the carpet and he reached for his dressing gown.

"What are you doing?"

"I am getting dressed, that's what!"

"Right, but . . ." Bertie shuffled his feet. "The thing is, if you mean for us to go after her, where do we start looking?"

"Ahh . . ." Henry's arm hung suspended in his sleeve. "Damnation." He uttered another oath as he sat back down on the bed. "I haven't the foggiest notion. Why, she could be anywhere!"

"Actually, if she went on foot, based on an average pace of eight minutes and forty one seconds per mile, she would be within a radius of—"

"Oh, stop that, else you'll give *me* a headache," ordered Henry, though not unkindly. "I was not meaning to be literal, only to suggest—"

"That we haven't a chance in hell of figuring out where she has gone," finished Bertie glumly. "Which means we're stuck here, helpless as children."

Henry punched at his pillow, then leaned back and tucked it behind his head. "It looks that way for now. But mark my words, Portia is going to have yet another question to answer come daylight." His mouth scrunched in a determined frown. "Headache or not."

"Miss P.! By the horns o' Satan, I was beginnin' t' get a bit worried about ye!"

"Can't imagine why," quipped Branford.

Portia shot him a scathing look. The strange truce that had come over them while out on the water had seemed to dissolve the moment they set foot back on dry land. Indeed, the earl had been muttering a number of sarcastic comments under his breath as they had picked their way back through the mud and detritus of the riverbank to where her carriage was waiting.

As if the situation were all her fault!

Good Lord, it was no wonder she felt a twinge of pain in the back of her head as she turned to her coachman. Seeing that Owen's mouth had fallen agape at the sight of her disheveled clothing and bedraggled hair, she essayed a nonchalant shrug. "Sorry for the delay," she murmured as a piece of seaweed fell from the folds of her cloak. "I ran into a spot of trouble."

"I can see that for meself." His gaze traveled from the tips of the earl's muddy boots to the damp tangle of raven locks hanging over his forehead. "Who the devil is that?"

"Oh, er, Lord Branford was kind enough to provide an escort past a group of several unsavory individuals. In return, I have offered him a ride back to Town."

Owen scratched at his grizzled chin. "I ain't sure it's quite proper for ye t' be alone with a gentleman in a closed coach, Miss P."

The earl twitched his shoulders in impatience, sending a shower of icy drops over the slick cobblestones. "Do you mind if we dispense with formalities for a bit longer?" he growled through clenched teeth. "After what the young lady and I have been through this evening, another brief interlude in my company can hardly do her any further damage."

Ha! thought Portia, although her coachman, on mulling over the statement for a moment, seemed to agree with Branford.

"I suppose yer right, milord. Climb on in, both of ye, and let us be off afore any more trouble sneaks out o' the fog."

Once inside the cab, Portia readied herself for another round of hostilities. She certainly had ample reason to launch an attack! The earl had deliberately set out to embarrass her—no doubt in retaliation for piquing his male pride during their first few skir-mishes. How else to explain his whispered teasing and seductive assault on her person? Even now, her face was growing flushed as red-hot embers at the recollec-tion of his intimate caresses.

Yes, *assault* was the only way to describe how his skilled lips had sought a complete surrender of all her senses. Including any semblance of rational thought. And he had won with ridiculous ease, she admitted, though a part of her was not sorry.

Portia found herself biting back a confused sigh. She knew she should be furious, but with whom? If blame was to be placed anywhere, it should lay squarely on her shoulders. She *could* have hit him. She *should* have hit him. She *would* have hit him. If only she hadn't been so dratted distracted.

Well, she wouldn't have to worry about it happen-ing again. She was practical enough to have no illu-sions about a handsome rake feeling the least bit of real attraction for her. For him it was only a casual game, like tumbling dice or scattering skittles.

Perhaps he was already enjoying a moment of laughter at how quickly she had fallen. . . .

From under her lashes, she ventured a glance at his shadowed features but caught no sign of smirking tri-umph, only an expression that seemed nearly as pen-sive as her own. It was strange but he, too, appeared in rather a subdued mood. Was the earl actually going to behave like a proper gentleman for once and refrain from making any mention of this latest Incident?

He turned his gaze from the curtained window. "Miss Hadley, I think we had better have a little chat."

Ha! And pigs might fly.

"I'm in no mood for conversation, if you don't mind."

"But I *do* mind," he replied pleasantly. "I fear the matter cannot be put off until later."

"If you mean to bring up The Incident, don't. I see no reason why it can't be forgotten. Just like the first one."

Branford blinked, then a small smile of comprehension spread across his features. "Ah, the Incident. Are you, perchance, referring to my kissing you?"

"You see," she muttered, "it had already slipped your mind."

"Indeed it had not." He cocked his head. "Was it really so forgettable?"

She averted her gaze. "Quite."

His smile broadened for a moment, then disappeared. "We shall return to that topic at some other time. But what I wish to discuss now is exactly what you were doing in the offices of Grenville and Company this evening."

"Actually, I asked you first, if you will recall." Refusing to be intimidated by his steely countenance, she brought her chin up a notch. "Were you hoping to find the lovely widow alone with her ledgers?"

His fist smacked into his palm. "Hell and damnation—enough of these foolish games, Miss Hadley! Have you not yet realized that you are playing with fire?"

His voice reverberated through the carriage like a saber clashing against steel. She sat back, surprised. For the first time in their acquaintance, she caught a glimpse of why a good many gentlemen quaked in their boots at the mention of the earl's name.

"Yes, you should look shocked," he went on roughly. "In case it escaped your notice, that was a very dead Lord Roxleigh splayed out on the floor, and very real bullets seeking to lay you down beside him." The earl edged forward on the seat. "Had you arranged to meet him there?"

"N-no!"

"I hope for your sake that is true." Appearing somewhat mollified, the earl lowered his roar, though his tone still held a note of authority. "You still haven't explained your presence."

Portia hesitated. Under normal circumstance she would have responded to such typically male bullying tactics with a mulish silence. However, there was something about the underlying urgency of his demand that prompted her to tell him the truth. "I—I wondered whether Mrs. Grenville might know something about my father's disappearance."

"Why?"

"Well, she was rather evasive when I questioned her the other day—"

"You questioned her?" he interrupted. "How the devil did you arrange that?"

"There is no great mystery to it, Lord Branford." She allowed a faint quirk of her lips. "I walked up to the front door of her town house and knocked."

"Hmmph." He made a wry face. "Go on."

Slowly recovering a bit of her usual bravado, Portia proceeded to explain her reasoning. "My father was last seen around these docks, supposedly boarding a ship for some faraway port. As Mrs. Grenville is involved in the shipping trade, with a business that deals in exotic goods, it seemed logical to inquire if she knew anything about his disappearance."

"What did she tell you?"

"Precious little." Her face screwed into a rueful grimace. "I would have had better luck trying to squeeze a straight answer out of the oracle at Delphi. So I decided to have a look around her offices."

"Hmmm." he rubbed at his chin. "I suppose you might actually be telling the truth."

"*Might* be! W-why in heaven's name would I be lying?" she sputtered in indignation.

"I don't know. *Is* there a reason?"

Portia folded her arms across her chest and scowled. "I do not appreciate being interrogated as if I am a . . . a criminal."

"Breaking and entering is a crime," he replied dryly, "and I have caught you at it twice."

She found herself shifting uncomfortably under his gaze. "I have explained that there is a logical explanation for my actions," she muttered. Deciding that she, too, was owed a few explanations, she added an inquiry of her own. "Why are you asking me these questions?"

"That is none of your business, Miss Hadley," he said with a cool dismissal that immediately made her regret her earlier acquiescence.

"Oh? And yet, I am to tolerate your poking your nose into my affairs without complaint? And answer every impertinent question you wish to ask?" she retorted. It gave her grim satisfaction to see that her words caused a momentary crack in his stony expression. Seeing that she had him on the defensive, she pressed her advantage. "Give me one good reason why."

"There *is* a good reason." His mouth thinned with an irritation that seemed to match her own. "However, I am not at liberty to divulge it."

"Ha! Next you will be adding that it is for my own good that I be kept in ignorance." She gave a low snort. "Men certainly find *that* platitude extremely useful. If I had a penny for every time I have heard it from some overweening idiot, I would be rich as Croesus."

Her caustic reply seemed to stop the earl in his tracks. But only for a moment. Like a seasoned soldier, he quickly regrouped and attacked from a different flank. "What about Roxleigh? You claim you had no meeting arranged with him at the Grenville offices, and yet, you were seen emerging the other evening from what looked to be a private conversation with the gentleman."

It appeared that in addition to his other faults, the odious man had been spying on her! Her jaw clenched in outrage. "I think I have answered quite enough of your questions, sir."

With a deliberate flounce of her wet skirts, she turned to stare out the window. For a lengthy stretch of time, the only sound inside the cab was the creaking of the carriage wheels and the muffled thud of hooves. However the mention of the murdered gentleman suddenly sparked another question of her own. One that caused the tiny hairs on the nape of her neck to stand on end. How could she have forgotten that the earl was acquainted—intimately acquainted—with Roxleigh's wife. Was she sitting next to a murderer as well as a lecher?

Without pausing to consider that if such were the case, perhaps it was not wise to confront him over it, she snapped out a challenge. "Speaking of Roxleigh, sir, it has just occurred to me that perhaps it is you who have reason to wish the man dead." With an exaggerated sneer, she added, "A crime of passion, perhaps?"

He fixed her with a hooded stare, then flicked a speck of mud from his sleeve. "If it were, you are not very bright to bring it up, are you?"

She swallowed hard.

"However," he went on, "I assure you that it was not I who put a period to the gentleman's existence. As you witnessed, there was no need to do away with the lady's husband in order to enjoy her favors."

Portia felt her face flooding with color at the memory of the torrid scene, but managed to keep a cool voice. "Perhaps you wished to marry the lady."

"And perhaps you have been reading too many horrid novels, Miss Hadley. That would, of course, account for your penchant for the melodramatic." The earl's equally cool answer was tinged with a touch of sardonic amusement. "And speaking of your lurid imagination, it that what sparks your desire to spy on sexual encounters?"

"S-spying!" To her dismay, she felt her cheeks shade from a vivid scarlet to a guilty crimson. "I-I was not spying! It was *you* who forced such a show of depravity upon *me*."

"Did I? It seems to me you could have spoken up or, at the very least, closed your eyes. But it appears you felt compelled to watch. Perchance you found it . . . stimulating."

"I found it disgusting," she muttered, though a flutter of conscience took most of the air out of her denial. It was a lie and she knew it—she had found the experience fascinating. But on no account did she wish for him to know how close to the truth his guess had come.

"You did not seem disgusted earlier," he said softly, "when I was kissing you."

He had moved a bit closer, and it took all her considerable willpower not to stare at his lips and recall the sweet thrill of their touch. "Let us forget about the mistakes of the evening and concentrate on the important issues at hand," she replied, her tone a bit more shrill than she had intended. "Like your interest in Lady Roxleigh."

Branford looked about to argue the point, then crossed his legs and leaned back. "I assure you, my interest in Lady Roxleigh is casual at best. I have no intention of finding myself caught in the parson's mousetrap. Why should I, when I may enjoy all the benefits of matrimony without all the tedium?"

No doubt he was telling the truth, allowed Portia. At least about that. And yet, though he might not be a cutthroat criminal, there was still another unpleasant matter to consider. "What will happen when the authorities find Lord Roxleigh's body?" she asked after a moment. "Do you think they will find any clue that may set them to looking for . . . the two of us?"

His eyes narrowed. "Don't worry. The authorities will have no reason to seek you out for this particular crime."

"You seem very sure of that."

"I am."

His words were somewhat reassuring, and yet they also carried an ominous undertone. How could the earl be so sure? she wondered.

Unless . . .

Unless the Earl of Branford knew a good deal more than she did about what had just occurred. He claimed to have good reason for his presence, but for all his glib words he had not been forthcoming with any real explanation. If only she could think of a reason for such reticence. One that did not bode of no good.

Unconsciously, her hands tightened into fists. Aggravating though the dratted man was, she found it difficult to think of him as . . . evil. But was she as wrong about that as she had been about so many other things of late?

Suddenly too tired to wrestle with any more questions, she shifted uneasily against the squabs and sighed. "We are drawing near to Mayfair, sir. I think it best if you get out here and find a hackney to take you the rest of the way to your door."

The earl slid across the soft leather seat. But before cracking open the door, he laid a hand on the young lady's knee. "Be assured, you haven't heard the last of my questions on this, Miss Hadley." Ignoring the sparks of anger shooting out from her gaze, he leaned in a bit closer. "However, there is one last matter between us that can't be put off. One of a . . . personal nature." He paused, realizing the subject was a rather awkward one to broach. "I would like for you to give me—"

"Don't you think you have gotten quite enough

from me for one night, sir?" she muttered under her breath.

Despite his exasperation with the young lady's stubbornness, he gave a soft chuckle. "It is naught but a promise that I ask for."

Her eyes narrowed. "A promise of what?"

"That you will, on no account, make any mention of the Incidents—as you so quaintly refer to them—to your brothers."

"Tell my brothers! Are you stark, raving mad?" Portia fixed him with a look of horror. "Good Lord, what makes you think I would ever do such a cork-brained thing as that?"

"Well . . ." He cleared his throat. "They might ask."

"Lord Branford, for all their precocious talents, they are only children. They haven't a clue as to the rather complex nature of . . . relationships that can arise in the . . . adult world."

The earl listened to her halting words with an inward smile. He couldn't help but sympathize with her predicament. He had, after all, had experience with two headstrong nephews. "Perhaps you underestimate the comprehension of, er, children. A pair of boys in particular."

"Don't be ridiculous." She gave a brittle laugh. "Why, you sound almost concerned. What's the matter—afraid they might challenge you to a duel?" The very notion of such a thing caused her laughter to grow louder. However, it died away quickly as she noted his expression. "Oh, no. Lord Branford, you don't really mean . . ."

"I believe 'pistols at dawn' was how Bertram phrased it."

"They wouldn't . . . they couldn't . . . they didn't . . ."

"As I said before, perhaps you have underestimated your younger brothers."

"I have never before underestimated their ability for getting into mischief," she said through gritted teeth. "But this"—with a harried sigh, she buried her head in her hands—"this is truly outside of enough."

"You might wish to curtail young Bertram's reading of Mrs. Radcliffe's novels. He seems to have developed some rather melodramatic ideas concerning honor between gentlemen." His slight cough was suspiciously close to a chuckle. "Though, I must say, the pink glove was a stylish touch. I shall have to keep it in mind for future reference."

She looked up. "Really, sir, this is no laughing matter."

He stilled his twitching lips. "No, indeed."

"Oh, dear," she mumbled after a moment, and her brow furrowed in consternation. "I will, er, have to figure out a way to handle the situation without causing any wounds. To my brothers, that is. Boys of that age can be devilishly sensitive to any cut to their pride."

"You don't say?"

"Yes. You see, they are wont to believe—" She stopped and blinked. "Oh, you are teasing me."

"Just a little," he admitted. In truth, he was impressed by her insight. And her sensitivity to the fragile feelings of her siblings. "Actually, why don't you let me handle things. It is, after all, a concern between gentlemen."

Portia looked at him as if he had suddenly sprouted two heads, green scales, and a pair of horns.

"Though you may find it hard to believe, Miss Hadley, I was once their age. You may trust me to deal with the matter without leaving any scars."

Branford readied himself for a sarcastic retort, but instead the young lady stared at him rather thoughtfully. "I may?" she asked after a lengthy pause.

He nodded.

The warring of emotions was plain on her face. It might have been comical had not he understood the crux of her dilemma. "I know you have no high opinion of me, but despite all you have heard bandied about in the drawing rooms, I assure you that I have never deliberately injured an innocent person—female or male."

She thought for a moment longer, then drew in a deep breath. "Very well, sir. I—I accept your offer of help, even though you have a reputation for being a very dangerous man." Her mouth pursed. "I am counting on you to handle Henry and Bertie with kid gloves."

"Their color will be York tan rather than rose pink." He cracked a fleeting grin as he opened the door and stepped down to the pavement. "However, I promise you that their touch will be light as a feather."

"Lord Branford . . ."

He looked back over his shoulder.

"T—thank you. For that, and for your earlier . . . assistance."

The earl inclined a slight nod, then motioned for the driver to move on. Feeling oddly restless, he decided to walk the short distance to his town house. It wasn't until he traversed several streets that he realized he was whistling, in spite of his singed fingers, water-logged boots, and sodden coat.

Not only that, but the recollection of the two earnest lads—chins thrust out in precise imitation of their sister—and their pink glove suddenly caused a bark of laughter to escape from his lips

Laughter? The squish of sodden leather stilled upon the wet cobblestones. He could not remember the last time he had been moved to real laugher. Or, for that matter, the last time he had felt any emotion, save for a brooding remorse that no amount of brandy could ever fully submerge.

His mouth pursed once again as he resumed walking. Miss Hadley and her siblings had certainly managed to provoke a whole gamut of emotions from him during the last twenty-four hours, from humor to exasperation to anger to some strange stirring he could not quite put a name on.

Shoving his hands in his pockets, Branford lowered his head to the spatter of raindrops and quickened his pace. It was just as well that the reaction remained nameless, he told himself. For despite the young lady's inexplicable allure, he had no intention of finding himself in such close proximity with her again. To do so would only be asking for trouble.

And yet, as he turned the corner his breath came out in another soft tune. A rather more jolly one than the circumstances seemed to warrant.

Chapter Eight

"Where is she?"

Lady Trumbull brushed a crumb from her manuscript and looked up. "Still in bed, I imagine. She sent down word that she was feeling a bit under the weather."

Henry muttered a word that earned him a look of reproach from his great-aunt. "Henry Falstaff, that is no way for a gentleman to speak." She paused and then winked at Bertie. "At least, not in front of women and children."

The elder Hadley struggled to hide a grin. "Yes, ma'am. I apologize."

"Apology accepted." Lady Trumbull reached for the gooseberry jam. "Tell me, is there a particular reason you are so anxious to see Portia?"

The brothers exchanged uneasy glances.

"Er, no reason," replied Henry after clearing a crumb of toast from his throat.

"No reason," echoed Bertie through a mouthful of porridge.

Their great-aunt arched a silvered brow but turned another page of her latest Latin translation without further comment.

Breakfast proceeded in silence, save for the clatter of

cutlery. Indeed, the sound of the forks attacking plates filled with shirred eggs grew so loud and so hurried that it took on the staccato rhythm of musket fire. Spoon in hand, Lady Trumbull shot her nephews yet another quizzical look as she stirred at her tea.

"MayIbeexcused?" asked Henry, bringing his napkin across his mouth in one hurried swipe.

"Of course."

Bertie scrambled to his feet as well, his elbow nearly knocking over a pitcher of cream in the process.

"And yes, you may be excused, too, Bertie," added Lady Trumbull, seeing that the youngest Hadley was going to have great difficulty in voicing his request. "That is, just as soon as you have swallowed that enormous bite of scone and strawberry jam." Her smile grew more pronounced on seeing the lad struggle to down the mouthful without falling into a fit of coughing. "What have the two of you planned for today?"

Henry's hand was already on the door handle. "Oh, not much. I, er, thought I might take Bertie for a walk in the park later on. Perhaps point out some of the interesting sights in Town. It would be . . . educational."

"Educational," agreed Bertie. "One must not forget, exercise is considered a very important part of a gentleman's routine. *Mens sana in corpore sano.* The ancient Greeks——" A quelling look from his older brother cut short what was promising to be a long-winded explanation.

"I am familiar with how the ancient Greeks viewed knowledge and sport," she said dryly. "A commendable philosophy to be sure. I trust you will enjoy a pleasant stroll outdoors."

Once outside the breakfast room, Henry sprinted for the stairs. Taking them two at a time, he reached the top of the landing just in time to intercept the maid carrying a tray of breakfast toward Portia's bedchamber.

"I will take that in to my sister, Mary," he said rather breathlessly. "I was just going to inquire as to how she was feeling."

"Yes, we are very concerned about her," piped up Bertie, nearly tripping on the top riser in his haste to catch up.

Mary gave a bob of the lacy cap as she handed it over with an approving smile. "What thoughtful brothers ye are," she murmured. "Miss Hadley must consider herself a fortunate young lady."

What bloody bad luck! Portia sneezed just as the door flew open. Not only was her head feeling as if it were stuffed full of wool, but now it appeared she would have to face off against not one but two agitated males, and without so much as a sip of the strong Jamaican coffee she had requested from the kitchen! *She might as well have ordered up a pot of hemlock,* she thought with a harried sigh. If looks could kill, *she* would be dead within a few moments anyway. . . .

"Where were you last night?" The tray came down upon the side table with a decided thump.

She winced, wishing her siblings might be a tad less theatrical in their emotions. "Actually, it is none of your business."

"The devil take it, Portia, you are—" Henry was interrupted by another loud sneeze. Looking a bit taken aback, he fished in his pocket for a handkerchief and offered it up. "You *are* feeling poorly."

"There was a good deal of rain and with the wind blowing in from . . ." Deciding it might not be wise to go any further, she stopped to blow her nose.

"From where?" demanded Henry.

Portia reached for the pot of coffee.

"With whom?" pressed her brother. "You didn't have another run-in with Lord Branford, did you?"

A rich aroma floated up from the steaming brew as it splashed into her cup.

"Did you?" Henry was now perilously close to shouting.

Seeing that she would have to say something before things really came to a boil, she set her coffee aside. "Do gentlemen discuss with their friends the particulars of a private encounter with a lady?"

He looked appalled at the very notion. "Of course not! It would be considered a gross breach of honor."

"Well, ladies have a code of honor too. And honor demands that I not divulge anything of a, er, private nature, that may have occurred between myself and a gentleman."

The revelation was greeted by a stunned silence.

After much shuffling of feet and a hurried exchange of whispers, it was Bertie who finally ventured to speak. "Y-you are sure of this?"

"Oh, yes, quite sure," answered Portia firmly. "The rules are very explicit on such things."

His mouth scrunched in dismay. "Polite Society certainly has a hell of a lot of rules."

"Including one which absolutely prohibits an eleven-year-old from swearing," she pointed out.

Bertie colored. "Sorry."

"But that means . . ." began Henry.

Picking up her cup of coffee, she eyed him innocently from over the delicate rim. "Means what?"

Eyes widening in alarm, Bertie made a frantic gesture for his brother to keep quiet.

His efforts drew a glare from Henry. "Stop hopping around like a cat on a griddle," he whispered out of the corner of his mouth. "Of course I wasn't going to tell her."

She couldn't resist the temptation to give her brothers a taste of their own medicine. "Tell me what?"

Henry did his best to dodge the question. "Have you any plans for the afternoon?" he inquired quickly. "If you like, Bertie and I could escort you to Hatchards later—"

"Thank you, but I mean to attend the meeting of The Geographical Exploration Society. I have been sadly remiss in keeping up with my own scholarly studies since we arrived in Town." She had been far too busy with more active pursuits, she thought with a wry sigh. "Ah, you still have not answered me, Henry," she added, seeing the two of them about to slink off. "Tell me what?"

"Well, since you insist," he mumbled. "I have to admit that Bertie also used a bad word in front of Aunt Octavia." Ignoring his brother's squeak of protest, he rushed on. "But don't worry, I shall see that he's made to do some disagreeable task for his penance." His hand took hold of Bertie's collar and aimed him toward the door. "Like figuring out the latitude and longitude of every bloody island in the Dutch East Indies."

*   *   *

Branford was no longer whistling as he surveyed the facade of the modest lodging house tucked away at the far end of Davies Street. The brick was grimy, the paint was peeling from the trim, and the marble steps were dull and discolored from years of neglect. His boots scuffed through dried mud as he climbed to the landing and rapped on the door. It took a repeated pounding before a middle-aged woman, her garb as unkempt as the surrounding, finally shuffled up and threw back the bolt.

"Hold yer water," she muttered, motioning with a jerk of her head for the earl to enter. "I ain't Princess Charlotte, wid a passel o' servants at me beck an' call."

"I am looking for Lord Davenport," said Branford, schooling his features to hide a grimace of disgust. The Princess was known for her slovenly habits, but nothing could match the general level of filth that now assaulted his eye.

"Third floor."

"Is he at home?" he asked, wondering how anyone would choose to spend a moment more than necessary amid such squalor.

The woman spat on the carpet, narrowly missing his foot. "Whether he is or not, yer wasting yer time, not t' speak o' risking yer neck. He don't see nobody." She added a harsh cackle. "Not wid that peeper, he don't."

The earl kicked aside a broken chair and moved toward the stairs. "Nonetheless, he will see me."

With a careless shrug she picked up a bucket filled with filthy water and laughed again. "Suit yerself. But don't say I didn't warn ye."

Regardless of the warning, Branford was not quite prepared for the greeting he received. At first there was no answer to his knocking, but as he kept up the racket, a slurred voice called out from within.

"Go to th' devil, else I'll send you to see him m'self!"

The earl set his jaw and tested the door. It was not locked, so he nudged it open with his shoulder. "Ma—" he began, only to have his words interrupted by a loud explosion. Nearly blinded by the flash of light that flared from out of the gloom, he instinctively ducked and threw himself to one side. The bullet, however, was aimed nowhere near him. It lodged with a dull thud in the ceiling molding, adding yet another splintered hole to the section above the door.

"Son of a Spanish she-wolf, Max! I haven't spent all those bloody years on the Peninsula dodging French bullets only to have *you* send me to my Maker." As his eyes adjusted to the shadows, Branford thought he detected a spasm of movement from the far end of the sitting room.

"You were in no real danger," replied the shadowed figure who lay sprawled in a worn armchair. Dropping the spent pistol, he reached for the glass by his elbow. It was only after he swallowed what remained of the drink that his visitor's voice seemed to register. "A-Alex?" he croaked.

The earl moved to the narrow window and pushed back the curtain.

Maxwell Wescott Bingham, Viscount Davenport and heir to the Saybrook earldom, squinted as a shaft of light cut across his unshaven features. With a muttered oath he ran a hand through the tangle of tawny locks and covered his brow, but it hid only a part of the jagged slash that puckered his sunken cheek.

Struggling to keep the shock from showing on his face, Branford bent down to retrieve the discarded weapon. After a casual inspection of its markings, he laid it down on the side table. "You certainly offer a warm welcome to an old friend," he remarked, striving to keep his voice light.

"Didn't invite you to come," came the sullen reply.

"No, you didn't—and I am wondering why not. I've heard you have been in Town for over a fortnight, and yet, you sent not a word to me or to Tony."

As he waited for an answer he took another quick look around the room. The rug was unswept, a collection of dirty dishes was stacked on the sideboard, and a number of wrinkled garments lay strewn over an old settee. More disturbing was the sight of several bottles of brandy on the table by Davenport's side, along with a large glass vial that looked by its color to contain a potent tincture of laudanum.

Letting his gaze move back to his friend's face, the earl once again had to bite back a sharp intake of breath. *The devil take it.* Max looked like a nightmare sprung up from the very depths of hell. The raw scar, still an angry red, sliced from Davenport's temple to the hollow of his cheek. The puckering of the skin had pulled his left eye into a slight slant, which gave his appearance a malevolent twist. The dilated pupils and dull stare did nothing to soften the impression, nor did the snarling twist of his mouth.

Aware of Branford's scrutiny, the viscount gave a

mirthless laugh, which trailed off into a hostile growl. "What the devil do you want?"

"To say I'm damn glad to see you, Max."

"You wish to welcome me back from the grave?" The viscount's tone grew more sardonic. "Don't bother. I wish the poxy Frog officer's saber had cut several inches deeper."

"Ah, so you intend to finish the job for him?" Branford nudged at one of the empty bottles on the floor with his toe. "That pistol of yours would be quicker. And, all things considered, less messy." His gaze strayed to the vial of laudanum. "Never thought you, of all people, to turn craven coward, Max."

That brought his friend's head up with a jerk. "Go to hell."

"I imagine that is eventually where I am headed. But it looks like you will be there to greet me." Flicking a mote of dust from his sleeve, he shrugged. "A pity. I thought you might be interested in helping me with a particularly thorny conundrum. One that concerns a grave danger to our eastern alliances."

"I'm not in a condition to help anyone," muttered Davenport.

"Not at the moment," agreed the earl. "But perhaps you would be if you ventured to pull your boots on and step back into the land of the living."

"Not interested in living," came the sullen reply. "Not interested in helping a damn soul, either."

Branford let his gaze make another sweep of the cramped quarters, taking in the dusty floor, the dirty dishes, the disheveled clothing draped over the furniture. "No, I can see you are not." He took one of the crested calling cards from his pocket and dropped it atop the crumpled linen on the settee. "However, I am leaving my direction in case you have any need to reach me." After a last look at his friend's haggard profile, he turned for the door.

"A-Alex."

The earl paused, and looked back over his shoulder.

"I—I was sorry to hear about Ranleigh and Wilford. Even sorrier I was not there to lend you some support." A bleak expression clouded his friend's face. "The past . . ." His words were momentarily choked off in a convulsive swallow. "Hell's teeth, memories are sharper than any French saber." With shaking fingers he picked up one of the brandy bottles and took a long gulp.

Memories all too fresh in his own mind, Branford could think of nothing to say that might dull his friend's pain. Leaving him to the temporary oblivion of the brandy and opium, the earl quitted the room. However, as he picked his way down the darkened stairs, he promised himself the retreat would be only a temporary tactic. Along with devising a strategy to win his own wars, he would somehow have to come up with a way to help Davenport fight the powerful forces of cynicism and despair.

They were, after all, enemies with which he was all too familiar.

"How fascinating." Portia placed the brightly colored sketches back in the portfolio and passed them on. "The jungles of Jaipur appear to be filled with all manner of wondrous flora and fauna," she sighed as the artist began to explain some of the details of his work to the other members who had gathered for a closer look.

"Monkeys, cobras, parrots, and tigers are indeed an exotic lot."

Looking up, she found that Mr. Dearborne had edged up beside her. "Speaking of tigers, Miss Hadley," he added in a low voice, "have you discovered anything more about your father? Or the meaning of his odd words?"

"No." She felt her lips quiver and tried to force them upward. "Indeed, I feel rather at wit's end. If only I had some clue as to where to look next."

He patted her arm. "Do not feel too discouraged. You possess a sharper mind than most. And, with all due modesty, perhaps I can be of some help. You see, I have been giving the matter some thought. . . ." Drawing her aside, he pulled out a sheet of paper from his pocket and then a pair of spectacles. "Call it vanity," he murmured as he perched them upon his long nose, "but I prefer not to wear these dratted things unless absolutely necessary."

Portia's tentative smile turned genuine. "They make you look very . . . regal."

His eyes widened in mock horror. "Good heavens, let us hope I am nowhere near as delusional as our dear king." After another tweak to the gold-rimmed frames, he cleared his throat. "All joking aside, Miss Hadley, I could not help mulling over your conundrum, and I came up with a few ideas." The paper crackled. "As I thought it safe to assume your father was not referring to a real beast, I began wondering what the Jade Tiger could be. Naturally the first thing that came to mind was an animal carved out of the stone. So I did a bit of research into the ancient cultures of the countries where tigers exist, to see if I could come up with any reference to a legendary relic with that name."

"How very rational, sir. And very clever." Portia gave herself a mental kick for not having tackled the problem from such a practical perspective.

His eyes raised for a moment from his notes. "Oh, well, not really. Knowing Julian's penchant for the arcane, I just tried to figure out what he would be interested in. Unfortunately, I had no luck. No mention of any sort of jade statue of note."

"Perhaps it is not meant literally," she replied thoughtfully. "It could be something else—a book, a document, a painting . . ."

"Precisely." Dearborne nodded in approval. "That is just what I was going to suggest. It's a rather large subject to research, but I mean to poke around a bit and see what I can discover. Iverton has an extensive collection on Eastern lore, so I thought I would start there."

"I am immensely grateful, sir."

He looked a trifle embarrassed. "Well, I have not really done anything as of yet. But perhaps we will be lucky and learn what it is your father was referring to—"

"And whether it has anything to do with his disappearance," she finished. Again, she wondered why she had not given more thought before to what the strange phrase could mean. She sighed. *Yet another thing to try to puzzle out.* But at least in this she appeared to have an ally.

"Yes." Dearborne shuffled his feet. "Though I caution you once more that your father may, er, have departed for reasons that have naught to do with the Jade Tiger, Miss Hadley."

"I realize that, but I am determined not to leave one stone—gem or not—unturned in trying to determine that."

"Then I shall get to work immediately, and let you know the moment anything turns up." He removed his spectacles and tucked them away. "I take it the package Julian was expecting has not yet arrived?"

Portia shook her head.

"Well, if it does, do let me know. I should be happy to help you inspect it to see if it offers any clues."

"I will indeed." The crowd was breaking up and making for the doors. She was just about to turn and join them when a slight hesitation caused her step to still. "One last thing, sir. . . ."

His head cocked in expectation.

"I think it would be best if you don't mention this to anyone." Seeing the perplexed expression that came to his face, she was forced to add, "You may think *me* a bit delusional, but I have reason to think someone may be shadowing me and my family. So let us be safe rather than sorry."

"Have you any idea who?"

"No," she lied. She certainly was not going to mention the earl's name. Or any of her own exploits that had brought her in contact with him. "I may very well be wrong. But I would rather err on being safe than sorry."

Dearborne thought for a moment. "Lord St. Vincent's secretary is a fellow member of the Numismatic Society. If I were to speak to him, perhaps he might be able to use his influence to begin an official investigation. . . ."

Portia sucked in her breath. That was the last thing she wanted right now. It would be she who would be hauled off to Newgate, not Dunster or Branford. "No, no, that is really not necessary."

Although his brow furrowed in dismay, he made no further argument. "As you wish. But do have a care yourself, my dear. London, for all its veneer of civility, can be as dangerous as any exotic jungle."

"What are we going to tell Lord Branford?"

Henry shoved his hands in his pockets and kicked at another pebble. "Dunno." It ricocheted off a nearby bench, drawing a reproving glance from the governess seated at its other end. "Probably the truth," he added after several more strides, "though it's deucedly galling to have to admit that two able-bodied males can't force a simple answer out of their sister."

Bertie took several moments to mull over his brother's words. "But Portia isn't an ordinary sister," he pointed out. "I wager that not even the Iron Duke could make her do something she didn't want to do."

"Isn't that the truth!" muttered Henry. "But the earl doesn't know that, so we are still going to look like bloody idiots having to withdraw our challenge." A cloud of dust swirled around his boots as he picked up his pace. "My first duel, and I about to make a royal mess of it!"

Bertie trotted along in his brother's wake. "He must have an inkling that Portia isn't quite like other females—after all, she said she hit him. How many ordinary young ladies would do that?"

"Not many, I suppose," admitted the older Hadley, but his expression remained glum.

Branford was waiting for them when they reached the appointed spot. He had already dismounted to loop the reins of his big stallion over the branch of an oak, and as the lads approached he made a show of consulting his pocket watch. "Another one of the rules of Polite Society is that a gentleman never keeps his opponent cooling his heels."

Henry's face, already a dull red, turned positively crimson. "M-my apologies, sir," he said stiffly.

"I had to finish my morning lessons before I was permitted to leave the schoolroom," piped up Bertie, seeking to ease his brother's embarrassment with a detailed explanation. "And Henry had to mend Aunt Octavia's pens for her. She doesn't see too well these days, but if he does the job, she doesn't have to admit—"

"For God's sake, Bertie, put a cork in it!" Henry's elbow nearly knocked his younger brother onto the seat of his breeches. "His lordship doesn't want to hear any childish excuses."

His brother shot him a wounded look as he rubbed at his shoulder. "I was just trying to help."

The earl found himself repressing a grin. He knew he should be aggravated at having to deal with yet another distraction to his investigation, but the guileless charm of the two lads was like a breath of fresh air after his last encounter.

"Actually, the needs of a lady always take precedence, so on this occasion you are forgiven." Seeing the tension ebb from the youthful faces moved him to make a further effort to put them at ease. Turning to the younger Hadley, he essayed a bit of banter. "So, Master Bertram, what sort of onerous lesson were you forced to do battle with today?"

"A mathematical equation, sir."

"Ah." The earl gave a nod of sympathy. In what was meant to be a joking quip, he added, "They can be devilishly tricky. I hope it was not anything as difficult as having to figure out the height of a window based on two other measurements."

"No, sir."

Of course not, thought the earl with an inward laugh. After all, how many eleven-year-olds were conversant with the principles of trigonometry? "What was it, then?" he asked, expecting a basic example of long division.

"I was figuring out the exact size of the hole that your bullet would put in Henry's skull."

"Bullet hole?" Surely he had not heard the lad correctly.

"Yes, sir," replied Bertie smartly, the enthusiasm unmistakable in his voice. "And since you are said to be the best shot in Town, I based my calculation on your drilling him right between the eyes."

Branford felt his jaw go rather slack. "Impossible—"

"Oh, not at all. It is actually quite easy, once the variables are factored in. You see, you take the distance, mass, velocity, diameter of the projectile—"

"*Bertie!*"

The younger Hadley blinked. "But Lord Branford asked me a simple question."

"Simple?" drawled the earl, his initial shock giving way to wry bemusement. "Are you telling me you actually figured out the answer?"

Without a fraction of hesitation the lad rattled off a number. "Twenty-one-point-zero-three-four-three-seven-five millimeters. That's rounded off, of course." He turned to his brother. "I had a feeling I had made a silly mistake yesterday, and sure enough, when I recalculated the equation, I was off by point zero-zero-five millimeters."

"The scamp is making this up." Brows winging up in a skeptical arch, Branford looked to the older Hadley for confirmation.

"I'm afraid not, sir. Bertie is rather gifted when it comes to mathematics."

"That is a bloody understatement," said the earl under his breath. "Assuming that he is correct."

"He usually is." Irritation with his younger sibling had given way to a touch of fraternal pride. "Even Professor Tillinghast has been known to seek out Bertie's opinion on certain of his postulations."

Good Lord! The eccentric Hadleys were certainly proving to be a source of constant amazement, thought the earl. Though he was not overly familiar with the abstract world of theorems and equations, he recognized the name of one of the leading mathematical minds in England. His gaze shifted from the diminutive prodigy to the older lad. "Are you a wizard with numbers as well?"

Henry shook his head. "My specialty is languages."

Branford was almost afraid to ask, but curiosity got the better of him. "How many do you speak?"

"Twenty-two."

"Twenty-one and a half," corrected Bertie. "You only know a smattering of the Szechwan dialect."

"Wrong. Over the last two days I have mastered the grammar of . . ."

Fascinating as the discussion was becoming, Branford realized he would have to move things along if he was not going to be late for a rendezvous with one of Tony's messengers. "Whatever the precise number, it is impressive," he interrupted. "It would indeed be a pity to let such a prodigious amount of knowledge spill out of a twenty-one-point-zero-three-four-three-seven-five-millimeter hole."

As he expected, the statement caused both Hadleys to fall deathly silent.

"However, there is no getting around it, if we are to meet over pistols at dawn." Unable to resist a bit of mild teasing, the earl rubbed at his chin. "Though perhaps if we were to make it twenty-five paces instead of the usual twenty, the hole would be a tad smaller."

The boys took it like men. Henry betrayed no outward sign of emotion, save for a slight whitening of his lips, while Bertie's wince lasted only a moment before he, too, stiffened his spine.

"You *did* find out from your sister what offense I am guilty of?" he went on.

"N-not exactly," answered Henry.

"No?" Branford looked at Bertie. "Well, that certainly throws off the equation, doesn't it." When neither lad answered, he exaggerated a grimace. "Hmmm. Let me think on this. . . ."

Perhaps it was an underhanded trick, he thought with a small twinge of guilt, but he decided he could not pass up the opportunity to pump the lads for any further information they might have about their sister's recent activities. "You've told me the reason why your sister ventures out alone, at certain hours of the evening, where a . . . misunderstanding with a gentleman might arise, but you have not said whether she had discovered any proof as of yet. Has she?"

Henry looked down at his boots and kicked at the dust. "I'm not sure I should be discussing intimate family problems with a stranger, sir."

The younger Hadley, however, did not seem to subscribe to the same set of scruples. Ignoring a hissed warning from his brother, he blurted out an answer. "She says no, but she was out again last night—"

"Blister it, Bertie!" A hand clapped over the lad's mouth, strangling any further explanation. Muttering a more fiery oath, Henry yanked him back several steps and began to whisper in his ear.

The earl rubbed at his chin as he watched the heated exchange taking place between the two lads. There was certainly no question as to their sincerity regarding the facts of their father's disappearance and the reasons for their sister's nocturnal forays. And for all her suspect behavior, Miss Hadley struck him as a most unlikely candidate for a villain. However, Tony's warning could not be dismissed out of hand. *A family left destitute and alone.* A young lady—especially one who was intelligent, clever and resourceful—might be driven to undertake desperate measures to save them all from ruin.

Until he was absolutely sure she was innocent, he would have to keep an eye on her. Not, to be sure, for any other reason than—

A consensus of opinion appeared to have been reached between the two lads, for Henry straightened and cleared his throat. "Family honor dictates that we refrain from further discussion of personal matters. I think we had better return to the matter of the insult to my sister, sir, and how we are going to resolve it."

"Family pride is always a devilishly ticklish matter." There was a long pause and then the earl smiled. "However, in regard to your sister, I believe I have come up with a solution that may satisfy honor on both sides while avoiding any bloodshed." Seeing that he had their full attention, he went on, "But all parties would have to agree to the compromise. Would you care to hear what I have in mind?"

"Yes!" chimed the Hadleys in unison.

"Very well, here is my proposal. As an apology of sorts for any offense I may have given to your sister, I will undertake to look into your father's disappearance. In return, you will withdraw your challenge."

Henry tried to mask his enthusiasm by clearing his throat. "That sounds, er, quite acceptable, sir."

Bertie was a trifle less guarded with his feelings. "Don't be a gudgeon, Henry! It's more than acceptable." He looked up at Branford with a look of undisguised awe. "Only an idiot would turn down an offer of help from such a top-of-the-trees Corinthian! Why, there is no other gentleman in all of London who can culp thirty wafers in a row at Manton's, or race his stallion—"

The earl gestured for silence, causing the younger Hadley's mouth to snap shut in mid-sentence. "I'm not quite finished," he added a bit gruffly, though in truth the lad's obvious admiration caused a slight catch in his voice. "There is just one last detail— you must also convince your sister to stop poking around in places where she is likely to run into trouble."

"We will?" Henry's newfound optimism quickly turned to consternation. "Bloody hell."

"Trust me, we have tried, sir. And she won't listen," added Bertie. "She thinks she has to be braver than Boadicea in looking out for us."

"Why don't I have a chat with her? With your permission, and following all the rules of propriety, of course." Branford's lips gave a wry twitch. "I imagine I have a bit more experience in dealing with ladies than you do." Though perhaps not with a Warrior Queen, he added to himself, with a slight rub of his singed fingers. However, it seemed unlikely that Miss Hadley would be able to cause further injury to his person within the confines of a drawing room.

A new wave of hope brightened their faces. "You are welcome to try, sir," answered Henry for the both of them.

"Good. I shall pay a visit on the morrow at four o'clock, as that is deemed a respectable hour to call on a lady." Untying the reins, Branford led his stallion back to the bridle path and thrust his boot into the stirrup. "Try to make sure that your sister will be at home."

"Oh, she will be at home," muttered Henry. "Even if it means nailing her skirts to the floor."

As the earl spurred Hades to a brisk canter, he wasn't sure whether to pat himself on the back or kick himself in the arse. It had been either extremely clever to offer his help. Or extremely foolish. Probably the latter, he thought with a self-mocking screw of his lips. He had warned Tony that his once finely honed skills had been sadly dulled by drinking, gambling, and wenching. Now such an assertion was proving too damnably true. *Melancholy Max. A fiery female.* How was he to begin helping them solve their dilemmas? He was having a difficult enough time trying to fight off the urge to abandon the impossible task his friend had set for him and sink back into his own solitary despair.

Hell's teeth! Branford's jaw clenched so tightly that his molars were in danger of cracking. And as if that were not enough, the two lads were a haunting reminder of his nephews—and his own past inadequacies. In youth, one had such fierce loyalty, deadly earnestness, and reckless courage, he mused. *And wrenching vulnerability.* It had been *he* who was supposed to possess wisdom and experience, yet he had failed miserably in keeping Ranleigh and Wilford from harm. What made him think that he could be of any help to anyone anymore?

The glint of admiration he had seen in the eyes of the two Hadleys caused a stab of pain somewhere deep in his chest. The Black Cat suddenly felt very ancient, very toothless, and very scared.

However, the soldier in him wasn't quite ready to admit defeat. There were still a few maneuvers he meant to try. And, oddly enough, although the Hadleys—each and every one of the eccentric clan— had certainly added an unexpected twist to an already knotty investigation, he found himself rather looking forward to the next encounter.

One thing was for damned sure—it was not likely to be dull.

Chapter Nine

❧

A muffled sneeze accompanied the turning of the page. *Damn that man!* Although she had thought herself fully recovered from her excursion of the previous evening, Portia realized she must still be feeling a few lingering effects from the exposure to the natural elements. How else to explain the slight flush stinging her cheeks and the odd fogginess clouding her brain?

Her chin rose. Well, she wasn't about to let a little thing like physical frailty to deter her from the work at hand. And she certainly wasn't going to allow any weakness of flesh distract her concentration! Her fingers shuffled the papers into several neat piles, but as she stared morosely at the lot of them, she couldn't help but find her thoughts straying from business to . . . pleasure.

How was it that a kiss from a devilish rogue could ignite such a fiery response deep in her core? She had only meant to taste a bit of pleasure, not allow herself to be swept off her feet by the sheer animal magnetism of the earl.

Ha! Her face screwed into a mocking twist. Swept off her feet? She had been pinned flat on her back on the two occasions that the earl had kissed her. The first time should have been warning enough of the danger in playing with fire, but like a moth drawn to a flame, she had flown willingly back toward the flash and spark. And found the second time around had been an even more searing experience. Like before, his mouth had been hard and hungry, his fingers lithe and nimble, his body hot and demanding. Yet, there had also been a strange sort of awareness to his touch, as if pure animal lust were not the only reason for his torrid embraces.

Don't be a ninny! she chastised herself. The Earl of Branford did not feel a whit of tender sentiment for her. And the feeling was, of course, mutual.

And yet, at the recollection of those wanton embraces, heat flared in her face and spiraled down her spine, igniting a glow at the very center of her being. She knew a proper young lady should be feeling nothing but guilt and shame at having allowed a notorious rake to take such liberties with her person. However, if truth be told, she had found the experiences incredibly pleasurable. But more than that, they had stirred sparks within that went far beyond pleasure. What they were, she couldn't begin to describe, much less understand, yet she found herself passionately longing to experience them again.

The trouble was, that would mean another encounter with the dratted Earl of Branford.

With a defiant tilt of her chin, Portia slapped down a fresh sheet of foolscap and took up her pen. Such odd yearnings were simply the result of . . . intellectual curiosity, and nothing more. It was not as if something important were missing from her life, aside from her father. She was happy with her life—her responsibilities, her scholarly interests, her independence. There was certainly no room in it for a large, arrogant gentleman, no matter that his shoulders had a solid, reassuring strength to them.

What was wrong with her? She didn't need a shoulder to lean on. She could take care of herself and those she loved. However, the chilling recollection of the latest brush with danger caused her grip to tighten on her pen. Didn't she have enough problems to solve at the moment without trying to make sense of an unaccountable attraction to a roguish earl?

Still, she couldn't help but sigh. As an admitted bluestocking, she was conversant enough with the principles of chemistry to know that the combination of two active ingredients in a confined space could sometimes result in unexpected fireworks, especially if a flame was lit under the mix. Well, she was already putting herself into enough danger these days without flirting with the prospect of a full-blown explosion. The most practical course of action, as any sensible spinster knew, was to stay far back on the shelf, away from any spark or catalyst.

No matter how tempting it was to embrace the source of the heat.

Enough of the earl! Pulling her dressing gown sash a bit tighter, as if the action might help rein in such wayward thoughts, she bent over her scrawled notes and, with a determined scowl, fell back to studying each entry. There *had* to be a discernible pattern to the seemingly random events, if only she would pull her head down from the clouds and look at them from the right angle.

The tip of her pen tapped against her chin.

An absentminded genius and a cottage full of arcane books—why would anyone go to such great lengths to steal them away? It was not as if they possessed any real intrinsic value. And what of the mysterious Jade Tiger? If Dearborne's assumptions were right, it, too, might only be a bit of paper or . . .

Tap-tap.

The sound was growing more insistent. Realizing that it was coming from across the room, Portia grimaced and took her head in her hands. Men! Of late, all the ones in her life were proving to be nothing but a deuced nuisance.

"I don't suppose it would do any good to tell you to go away," she called. "So you might as well come in."

After a quick glance at the locked window and her slippered feet, Bertie's face relaxed considerably. "I—I saw a light from under the door, so I thought I would stop by to say good night."

Standing in his floppy nightgown, tousled curls framing his slender face, her youngest brother looked achingly small and vulnerable. Portia felt her throat constrict at the sight. It was sometimes hard to remember he was a rather undersized eleven-year-old when listening to him explain a mathematical theorem or rattle off the answer to a complex equation. But, for all his intelligence, he was only a child, and one who was depending on her to keep them together.

"We said good night several hours ago, if you recall. You should be fast asleep by now, not wandering the hallways in your bare feet." She indicated her as yet untouched bed. "But since you are up, get your toes beneath the eiderdown before you catch a chill."

He climbed up and pulled the coverlet over his knees. "I'm not sleepy."

"Have the dreams come back?" she asked gently.

Ever since early childhood, Bertie had been plagued by nightmares. She feared it may have stemmed from the time her father had been excavating an ancient barrow in the Scottish Highlands. So engrossed was he in piecing together the delicate fragments of a gold chain that it wasn't until they had all sat down for supper that anyone noticed he had left the young toddler in one of the tunnels, along with the shovels, buckets, and chisels.

Dear Papa. His brilliance as a scholar was sometimes eclipsed by the fact that he was forever forgetting the small details of everyday life.

They had, of course, turned the occurrence into a family joke of sorts, with Bertie grinning as widely as the rest when it was referred to. And yet, Portia could not shake the suspicion that the abandonment, however temporary—coupled with their father's long absences and the unorthodox household arrangements—had left the youngest Hadley feeling a bit uncertain about his place in the world. Indeed, the dreams might vary, but they always involved being left behind in a dark, confining space, never quite able to climb to the top of the wall or turn the knob of the door. Though Bertie tried manfully to hide it, there were many a night he woke sobbing at the thought of finding himself utterly alone, utterly abandoned.

Her jaw set—it was yet another reason to locate the baron.

"They haven't been so bad," answered Bertie. "I have only had one or two since we left Rose Cottage," he answered.

She knew he was lying but overlooked the transgression. "Then why aren't you in your own bed instead of mine?" she inquired a bit absently, her attention already turning back to her notes. Drawing the candle a bit closer to her elbow, she began rereading the first few pages.

"I thought I had better check that you were here where you should be, and not out gallivanting about Town." He crossed his arms and tried to imitate the menacing curl of his older brother's lip. "I don't like it that you venture out alone at night. Neither does Henry."

"Mmm." Listening with only half an ear, she dipped her pen in the inkwell and started to draw up a fresh list of questions to consider.

"And neither does Lord Branford."

With an audible snap, the nib split in two. "How the devil do you know Lord Branford's sentiments on my nocturnal activities?"

Bertie gave an owlish blink. "Ladies aren't supposed to swear, either. The rules are very explicit on that point."

"I damn well know the rules!" exploded Portia. "What I don't understand is what my brothers were doing talking about *me* and *my* activities with the infamous Earl of Branford." She was already beginning to question her judgment in giving the dratted man carte blanche to deal with the lads. What was he up to? He was supposed to have been discussing their behavior, not hers!

"Blister it, Bertie!" Still struggling to tug his dressing gown on over his nightshirt, Henry shouldered in through the door, then kicked it shut behind him. "You ought to have waited for me before—"

"Before what—telling me of your clandestine conversations with Lord Branford?" The scarlet hue suffusing Portia's face was now due to anger. Unable to sit still any longer, she rose and set her hands on her hips. "This is outside of enough. The two of you have been sneaking around behind my back!" she accused.

"No more than you have done to us," countered Henry with an infuriating logic that only fanned the flames of her rising temper.

"How dare you consort with . . . the enemy! And against your own sister!"

"The enemy?" Bertie looked crestfallen. "Lord Branford seemed rather a great gun to me—especially when he suggested an alternative to blowing a twenty-one-point-zero-three-four-three-seven-five millimeter hole through Henry's skull."

"Stop saying that—he might have missed, you know," replied his brother, though a moment later he, too, had the grace to appear embarrassed. "We were not exactly consorting. . . ."

"Not at all," assured Bertie.

"Merely discussing a matter of honor between, er, gentlemen," finished Henry. "And I must say, his lordship came up with an excellent plan."

Her eyes narrowed. Somehow she had a feeling that she was not going to agree with her brother's choice of adjectives. "What plan?"

"Er, well, as to that, he would rather explain it to you himself."

"Forget it." With a flounce of her dressing gown, she sat back down and began to cut down another quill. It was a good thing the earl was not present, she thought with some heat. Otherwise it might have been his tongue rather than a goose feather that was being trimmed by her knife.

"But, Portia, he will be calling here on the morrow so that the two of you may have a private chat!" exclaimed Bertie.

"He may wait in the drawing room from then until doomsday, for all I care," she ground out between gritted teeth. "I have no intention of spending any more time with the dratted man than I already have."

Henry's face fell. "You must hear him out! It is a matter of . . . family honor."

"A pox on men and their childish pride." She immediately regretted her acid retort on seeing his cheeks flush and his lower lip come perilously close to quivering. Her fingers drummed a harried tattoo upon the desktop. "Oh, very well," she relented after a moment or two. "I suppose it will do no harm to listen. But I warn you right now, that is all I intend to do."

Branford set aside his pen. It was a last-minute change in strategy, but his military experience had taught him that it was often useful to keep an opponent off balance with an unexpected move.

Not that he had any further reason to think of Miss Hadley as the enemy. The earl steepled his fingers and stared down at the small stack of periodicals on his desk. After reading a selection of her essays, and interviewing several more members of the Art and Antiquities Society, it was hard to believe the young lady capable of deception or betrayal. It was true that her logic, cleverness, and imagination were qualities that would come in handy for villainous purposes. Yet, as each bit of new information helped paint a clearer picture of her character, what he saw was a young lady who appeared . . . innocently intriguing.

Branford found his lips turning up in an involuntary quirk. There was no denying that she was smart, bold, and inquisitive. In short, a highly unconventional lady. And while he hadn't much experience in assessing the intellectual attributes of the opposite sex, he thought wryly, he had handled enough females to know Miss Hadley also had a well-endowed body to go along with a well-endowed mind. With a slight shake of his head, he found himself puzzling over why that was proving such a potent attraction.

A hot temper and fiery tongue were precisely the sort of things a gentleman took pains to avoid in a woman. But on recalling the passionate response to his touch, he felt his flesh take on a slow, burning tingle. His eyes closed, and he felt an unwilling rush of desire. *Damn the chit!* How the devil had she gotten under his skin? And why did it rub him so raw that she thought him naught but a dissolute wastrel, interested in naught but debauched pleasures?

His fingers drummed upon the leather blotter.

Perhaps it was because he could no longer view her as just an outspoken bluestocking. She had taken on a unique aura of individuality, and for the first time he could recall, Branford found himself captivated by the prospect of a female who would not be boring out of bed. Why, he almost pictured the two of them sitting comfortably before the fire, discussing the nuances of Botticelli's symbolism or Da Vinci's brushwork. And strangely enough, that was nearly as alluring as the image of her naked, with her wheaten tresses fanned out in glorious disarray upon his sheets.

Bloody hell! Had he become such a toothless old tabbie that he was growing disgustingly sentimental in his dotage? Surely he wasn't giving any mind to settling down, perhaps even setting up his nursery? He gave a scoffing growl, yet found it difficult to banish thoughts of Miss Hadley at the breakfast table each morning, impish laughter echoing through the now empty hallways of the town house, children hurtling down the polished banisters . . .

Ignoring the tiny lurch deep inside his chest, Branford quickly folded the note he had written and quitted the room. It was an absurd notion. Marriage to Miss Hadley would definitely not be one of convenience. She would be a constant challenge—a provocative, alluring, compelling presence in his life, demanding the sort of intense emotional commitment that he had no intention of embracing.

No, if he ever contemplated taking a wife and having a family, it would be out of duty, not need, he assured himself. After all, experience had taught him that the best way for the Black Cat to survive was to remain a solitary beast.

Tea?

Portia squinted at the crested stationery, wondering whether her eyes were playing tricks on her. But no, the three letters were clearly written, as was the hour—a time considered quite acceptable for paying a call. And as her brothers were included in the invitation, she could hardly cry off on the grounds of propriety. Tucking the paper away, she began to pace before the hearth. The sudden change in plans couldn't help but provoke a certain suspicion. And a certain curiosity. She wasn't quite sure what the earl was up to, but the prospect of stepping inside the lair of a notorious rake was too intriguing to pass up.

A short while later she found herself almost disappointed as she stared up at an imposing limestone facade. The town house looked quite respectable, as did the elderly butler who had answered Henry's eager knock.

"Good afternoon, Miss Hadley." Stepping aside with a measured bow, the retainer indicated a formal sitting room to his left. "If you and the young gentlemen would care to wait in here," he intoned, "I shall inform his lordship of your arrival."

Portia made to follow with the same show of decorum, then discovered her brothers had already rushed for the far wall of the entrance hall, which was bristling with an impressive display of vintage firearms.

"Oh, look, a rare double-barreled dueling weapon

from the time of King Charles," said Henry in a reverential tone.

"And the one to the left of it looks to be a ceremonial pistol of an officer of the King's German Legion," breathed Bertie.

Mortified, she turned to chide them for forgetting their manners, only to find herself rendered momentarily speechless by the sight of the large painting hung over a gilded pinewood console table. All thought of proper etiquette went out the window as she moved closer and leaned up against the piece of furniture, intent on a more careful study.

"Do you like it, Miss Hadley?"

She started, unaware of the earl's approach until his shoulder was nearly touching hers. "It's absolutely marvelous." Without thinking, she blurted out a detailed cataloguing of its technical merits. Then, embarrassed at her show of girlish enthusiasm, she straightened and ended abruptly with a show of sarcasm. "It dates from the Italian Renaissance and is quite valuable, in case you did not know it. Though it would be a pity for posterity were you to sell it to fund your gaming habits." Her eyes shifted back to the canvas. "The artist was a student of a famous artist by the name of Michelangelo. Who, for your information, also hammered a bit of stone and painted a few church frescos."

"Buonarroti was a bit of a poet as well." Branford smiled faintly. " 'Love, your beauty is not a mortal thing. There is no face among us that can equal the image of the heart, which you kindle and sustain with another fire and with other wings.' " He, too, turned his gaze on the lush color and masterful renderings of the human form. "A passionate fellow, eh? Whether expressing himself in marble, pigment, or the written word."

Portia blinked, sure that her reddening cheeks gave more than vivid expression to her own conflicting emotions.

"Though there is a slight question as to whether his feelings—or that of his student—were inspired by the appropriate gender." The earl appeared not to notice her confusion as he continued on with a lucid critique of the painting's allegorical meaning.

Much to her amazement she regained enough of her composure to be drawn into a lively discussion on Quattrocento art. It must have gone on for some time, for there finally sounded a slight but unmistakable cough from Henry.

"I say, sir, is that weapon at the far left really one of the new dueling pieces made by Hevey and Sons? The new design of the hammer looks deucedly strange. How does it work?"

Branford began to explain the details of the new mechanism, but he had managed no more than a few words before Bertie interrupted him.

"Have you any idea what measure of powder is needed to achieve the proper velocity? And why—"

"Put a cork in it," ordered Henry with a jab of his elbow. But then he, too, let fly with another flurry of technical queries.

The earl chuckled and held up his hands in mock surrender. "Hold your fire, lads. I shall endeavor to answer all your questions, but let me face them one at a time."

As he turned his attention to her brothers Portia

sought to catch her breath and regain a measure of equilibrium. The dratted man had once again succeeded in knocking her completely off balance. She certainly hadn't expected a ruthless rake to possess such an erudite knowledge of art and poetry.

Or, for that matter, such a good-humored tolerance of two unruly boys.

And yet, she couldn't help but overhear how patiently he was dealing with the barrage of their youthful exuberance. Did the Earl of Branford possess a more complex character than she had given him credit for? Was it possible that beneath the obvious attributes—the handsome face, broad shoulders, and ramrod manhood—was a man of real substance? She had already glimpsed a hint of his courage and coolness under fire. And now, on observing him with her brothers, she found herself forced to acknowledge that he was also . . . rather nice.

She turned abruptly, glancing back at the painting to hide her dismay. The last thing on earth she wished to discover was that she was beginning to like him.

His next words proved even more unsettling.

"Perhaps if I were to show you the finer points of a pistol's working in action, it would all make a bit more sense." The earl gave a casual shrug. "You are welcome to come along on my next visit to Manton's."

Her eyes widened in surprise. It was, she knew, a truly magnanimous offer. There was probably not another gentleman on earth who would dare to pass through the portals of London's most exclusive shooting club with two boys in tow, and Portia watched as both of her brothers were rendered momentarily mute.

"Y-you mean it, sir?" stammered Henry, on recovering his voice. "I—I am invited to accompany you to Manton's?"

"And me as well?" added Bertie in a awed whisper.

He nodded. "That is, if your sister has no objection." He slanted an amused look her way. "A gentleman should have some practical experience with firearms, don't you agree, Miss Hadley? After all, one never knows when the occasion may arise where the knowledge will prove useful."

Practical.

Portia gave herself a mental kick as she answered the pleading looks from her brothers with a curt nod of assent. She repeated the word several times as Branford led the way into the drawing room, reminding herself to take it to heart. She could not afford to let passion—over art or anything else—override pragmatism. To do so might be more dangerous than any explosion of gunpowder and bullets.

The earl smothered a smile behind his teacup. The real reason for the change in venue of their meeting had been for her to see him in a different light—an educated aristocrat surrounded by his tasteful furnishings and stunning collection of art rather than a drunken lout groping at anything that moved in the dark. And so, he had taken a measure of satisfaction in seeing a flicker of admiration stir in her eyes as they had discussed Italian art. It had been fleeting, yet Miss Hadley had been forced to acknowledge he was capable of grasping ideas as well as a handful of feminine flesh.

Leaning back in his chair, he regarded the mulish

scowl now darkening her downturned features. The two lads had quickly quitted the room when he suggested they might care to have another look at the arsenal in the entrance hall. However, it was clear their sister was not as enthusiastic as they were over the prospect of a private chat with him.

"What's all this about a plan?" she demanded without preamble. "When I gave you leave to speak with my brothers, I did not mean you should fob them off with some fanciful farrididdle—"

"I meant what I told them, Miss Hadley."

"What is it you are proposing?"

"To help you."

Her eyes narrowed to sharp slivers of jade. "Why?"

"To begin with, I am tired of tripping over you at every turn."

Muttering an unladylike expression, she reached for her reticule. "I can see it is pointless to prolong this conversation."

His earlier regard for her character quickly evaporated as he thumped down his cup in exasperation. *Damnation!* he had nearly forgotten that for all her intelligence, Miss Hadley had a remarkably stubborn streak that was irritating in the extreme. "Wait! For once will you listen to reason, rather than charge off in a temper?"

She hesitated.

Seeing that he had at least slowed her down a step, the earl continued on. "If bricks and bullets were not enough, hasn't a slashed throat convinced you of the grave perils in pursuing your current course of action?"

"I am not a bloody idiot, Lord Branford. Of course I realize the danger of what I am doing. But the alternative is not much better." Her fingers tightened. "You do not lie awake at night worrying over how many farthings are left in your purse, or whether tomorrow night you will have a roof over your head. No, you are free to indulge in your fancies, as you have no one depending on you to—" She broke off with a sharp tug to her shawl. "Not, of course, that it is any of your concern."

The earl's lips compressed. She was right—he was unencumbered by emotional attachments. And damn glad of it. His offer of help was pragmatic rather than personal. It was only for Tony's sake that he had gotten involved with such a maddening minx.

"I am offering to make it my concern." He recrossed his legs. "Why not at least listen to what I proposed to your brothers? You can always tell me to go to the devil after I have finished."

One of the logs snapped, sending up a shower of sparks. Portia started, then stared at the glowing coals as though she feared she was about to get burned. "I suppose I had better hear you out, if only to tell Henry and Bertie that I did as they asked."

Branford could not help but note the wariness in her eyes. She could hardly be blamed for not quite trusting him, he admitted. As he had discovered during the carriage ride, she was much too intelligent not to have formed questions of her own regarding his role in their recent nocturnal adventure. He would have to handle the young lady very carefully so as not to arouse further . . . suspicions. Forcing his gaze away from her face—and his mind from tantalizing memory of how perfectly her curves had fit up against his form—the earl cleared his throat and began to speak.

"It's really quite straightforward, Miss Hadley. What I suggested was a plan that would help us avoid getting entangled with each other in the future. Not to speak of saving me the aggravation of having to constantly dodge a duel with a minor."

"What, exactly, do you have in mind?"

"For you to stop poking about in places where you are likely to stir up a hornet's nest of trouble."

Her lips pursed as if she had been stung. "And?"

"In return, I shall undertake to solve the mystery of your father's disappearance." He gave a slight cough. "I believe I am better equipped to make certain inquiries than you are." Seeing the indecision warring on her face, he seized the advantage and pressed on. "You speak of responsibilities—what of Henry and Bertie if something were to happen to you?"

Portia turned deathly pale.

"Why don't you at least think on it a bit before rejecting the idea out of hand?"

"I—"

"Are you attending the Harrington soiree?"

She shook her head. "I have no plans for this evening."

"I am glad to hear it," he quipped. Rising swiftly to forestall any retort, Branford offered his arm and escorted her back into the entrance hall. "Then I shall come around to your great-aunt's on the morrow for your answer. Shall we say at four?"

He took her silence as an affirmative. As the young lady stalked off, he allowed a faint smile. It appeared that with the right tactics, the impetuous Miss Hadley could be made to see reason.

"Y-you promise you aren't planning any nocturnal sojourns?"

Looking up from her desk, Portia shifted the newspaper, hoping that Henry had not caught a good look at what lay beneath it. "The only journey I plan on making tonight is the one from my chair to the bedstead."

His expression brightened. "I told Lord Branford not to worry, that you would be sensible about this."

"If I were *sensible . . .*" Portia left the sentence unfinished.

"What's that you are reading?" Bertie, his older brother's outgrown nightshirt bunching up around his ankles, had climbed up to the head of her bed.

"A highly diverting tidbit concerning the Duchess of Devonshire." It was not exactly a lie, she told herself, glancing down at the gossip column that was prominently positioned on the newspaper's front page. She had skimmed over the article several hours earlier. "Would you care to hear the latest *on dits* from Lady Jersey's *musicale?*"

Both of her siblings made faces.

"I didn't think so." She folded the newspaper in half. "Now that you two have finished checking up on me, would you mind retiring to your own rooms? I would like a bit of peace and quiet in which to peruse the *Historical Journal* before I put out the light."

"Well, then, er, good night."

Bertie looked loath to relinquish his comfortable position among the soft pillows and down quilt, but at a warning look from his brother he slid his bare toes down to the floor.

As the door finally fell shut, she reached toward the inkwell. It was then that her gaze fell on the fine print of the newspaper's back page. Her eyes went from the folded page to her notes and back again.

As the words sank in, a frisson of excitement coursed down her spine.

At last! After all her stumbling around in the dark, she had finally come upon a sign that she was on the right track.

Chapter Ten

❦

"Ah, so the Black Cat finally crosses my path. Should I be worried?" Mrs. Grenville's tone conveyed a teasing coyness, but her gray eyes had the look of polished steel as they swept over the earl in an undisguised appraisal. "After all, I have heard a great deal regarding you and your activities, sir, and it seems that those who challenge you have a habit of ending up . . . unlucky." She proceeded to mention not only the recent duel but several of his gambling wins that were not common knowledge.

"You are remarkably well informed about London Society," replied Branford, making it just as obvious that his eyes were studying her person.

So, he imagined with a flicker of sardonic observation, were the eyes of most every other gentleman in the room, for the widow was once again dressed in an exotic shade of scarlet, the hue made even more vivid by the unusual design of her gown. Baring one shoulder, it clung tightly to the curves of her breasts, then fell in lush folds from the hip—a bold and imaginative interpretation of an Indian sari, he realized. The lady's nerve was apparently as steely as her gaze. She was certainly not afraid of standing out in a crowd.

He would do well to remember that.

Ignoring the affronted stare of the gentleman penciled in next on her dance card, he kept her fingers in his and led her out onto the dance floor.

"I have found that in business it pays to be well informed," she murmured, making no protest over the change in partners.

As the waltz began, Branford was aware that the two of them were actually engaged in a far more subtle dance. "And what business is that, madam?"

The lady appeared to be as cool under fire as any seasoned soldier. "Why, somehow I assumed you knew—the sale of precious commodities."

Knocked a bit off stride by the directness of her answer, the earl's foot grazed her slipper.

"Do you, perchance, know someone who might be interested in my wares, Lord Branford?" she continued softly. "I have found that the best deals are usually made through . . . word of mouth."

Recovering quickly, he vowed to keep pace with her next move. "That depends on what you are offering. And, of course, the price."

She matched his faint smile. "If you would care to send someone around to my offices, I could provide you with a full list."

He spun her in a series of slow twirls before answering. "You are an unusual lady, to have taken on the challenge of running your late husband's company. From what I have heard, foreign trading is a highly competitive business. Indeed, one might even consider it rather . . . cutthroat." His eyes remained locked on her angled profile, watching for any reaction, however small, to his carefully chosen words.

The combination did not throw her off balance. "It appears that you, too, are remarkably well informed as to what goes on in Town. I had thought the authorities wished to keep the incident hushed up for a while longer."

"Like any good merchant, I have my reliable sources, Mrs. Grenville." Branford quickened the pace while at the same time moving forward with his questions. "Rather a peculiar place for a gentleman to meet his Maker, wouldn't you agree?"

"Bow Street has spent a good part of the day questioning me as to Lord Roxleigh's unfortunate demise." She appeared to be watching the movements of the couples nearby. "As I am sure your sources have told you, I am at a loss as to how to account for his presence in my company's office."

"I have a feeling you are rarely at a loss over anything," he murmured close to her ear. Wondering whether he sensed a slight tensing of her spine, he pressed on. "You have no idea why he would be there in the dead of night?"

She shrugged. "I would imagine he was searching for something other than a jar of curry powder."

"Nonetheless, he found things a bit too hot for his taste."

A soft laugh stole forth. Like the lady herself, it was a touch exotic, reminding Branford of the rustle of leaves in a tropic rain. His hand shifted slightly on her back, the glove sliding smoothly over the lush silk of her gown. *Seductive.* He would have to be on guard not to let the wily widow lead him astray from his primary objective.

"If not a particularly tasty blend of curry," he continued, after the sound of her amusement had died away, "what would tempt a gentleman such as Roxleigh to break into your place of business?"

"As the viscount was a complete stranger to me, I cannot speculate as to his . . . desires. But every merchant possesses a wealth of information that would be valuable to the competition."

"You think him involved with someone who wishes to steal your business?"

She lowered her lashes. "I imagine you, as a titled gentleman of the *ton,* would be a good deal more familiar with Lord Roxleigh and his activities than I, sir."

Good Lord, he felt as though he was doing naught but spinning in circles.

With an adroit turn and nimble moves, he guided them toward the far edge of the dance floor, where the doors to the gardens were open to admit the evening breeze. "Not really. In truth, I am far more interested in becoming familiar with you. Perhaps you would care to take a walk in the gardens—I have observed that you seem to have a fondness for seeking the night air."

For the first time that evening the widow betrayed a flicker of emotion. Her face paled and her eyes suddenly lost their steely cast. The earl had seen far too much of war not to recognize the look. It was not precisely fear but a wary apprehension.

Yet, in an instant she had marshaled her composure and reassumed her self-assured smile. "I am afraid I am engaged for the next set." Her own steps stopped along with the music. "You dance extremely well, sir. But then, I would expect a cat to be quick on his feet."

Quick, but not nearly quick enough, he thought. Despite their minutes together he had learned nothing, save that the lady was a more agile opponent than many of the men he had come up against in the course of his wartime activities. He would have to move very carefully if he hoped to maneuver her into revealing any secrets.

For there was no question that she was hiding something.

However, on seeing that Mrs. Grenville's next partner was already seeking her out, the earl decided to relinquish her hand without further probing. Then abruptly, in a sudden shift in strategy that he had not really planned, he slipped in one last question: "You say Lord Roxleigh was a perfect stranger. But what of Baron Julian Hadley? Is he someone with whom you are acquainted?"

"Hadley? Why would I, of all people, have reason to know an eccentric country scholar who appears to have gone missing?" Without waiting for a reply, she glided off on the arm of an admirer, leaving the earl standing alone in the shadows.

A good question, Mrs. Grenville, he mused. And one he meant to get more than a glib answer to, no matter how skillful she was at evasion.

Portia gave the last of the plump pillows an extra thump as she stuffed it beneath the coverlet. She still couldn't believe she had to resort to such a schoolboy trick, but her brothers had left her precious little choice. Time was of the essence. It was imperative that she act tonight if she were to have any hope for her plan's success, and another glance at the clock on her mantel warned her that she could not afford to dawdle a moment longer.

As for Lord Branford's plan . . . she had only given her word to *think* about his offer. Which she would do. In the morning. After all, it wasn't as if she needed his help, especially now that she had a vital clue to pursue. Even if she ran into a spot of trouble along the way, she had plenty of experience in handling it on her own.

Flexing her knees, she marveled yet again at how liberating the feel of breeches was. She must remember to thank the earl for his suggestion—though she highly doubted he had meant to be helpful. Still, he had reminded her of how useful such a garment could be. In the country, she had on occasion worn a pair of Henry's castoffs for riding, but until Branford's acid comment it had not occurred to her to make use of them here in Town.

A good thing it had, she thought, eyeing the window. Just as it was a good thing that her destination was within walking distance. Owen was proving almost as intractable as her brothers over her investigations. On arriving back in the mews after the trip to the docks, the little Scotsman had sworn on the bones of Saint Andrew that he would not be wheedled, cajoled, or manipulated into doing something as corkbrained as allowing a lone female to venture into the stews of London again.

As if she ever wheedled, cajoled, or manipulated!

At least, not unless it was absolutely necessary, she sniffed, trying to hold back a sneeze. However, for the time being, it would probably be wise not to press the matter with her long-suffering retainer.

Ah-choooo! She rubbed at her nose with the back of her sleeve. *Hell's bells!* Hadn't she enough problems without having to cope with a bout of sniffles? It was all the fault of the dratted earl and those damp floorboards. . . .

No, she was not going to start thinking of *that*. Nothing—not the odd thoughts in the back of her mind, the echo of the earl's disquieting warning or the irritating tickle in the back of her throat—was going to keep her from pursuing a vital clue.

After tucking her father's ring beneath her shirt and giving a final hitch to her breeches, Portia climbed out onto the window ledge and swung into the branches of the gnarled elm. Years of keeping pace with two brothers had made her agile as a boy in scrambling down through the branches. Dropping noiselessly to the soft earth of the flower beds, she threaded her way through the ornamental yews and rhododendrons to the back of the walled garden. The heavy hinges of the gate made nary a squeak, thanks to the liberal dabs of grease she had applied while out for a breath of fresh air that afternoon. She needed only a small opening to slip into the alleyway.

Then, just as silently, the stout oak fell back in place.

She had counted on the fact that no one would take any note of a rather shabby young man making his way through the side streets of Mayfair to his place of lodging. Sure enough, by keeping to the shadows she drew only the attention of an overfed pug, but its yapping growl was quickly cut short by a tug of a leash. Murmuring an apology, the tired maid hauled her charge back toward the marble steps of the town house while Portia, hand over her face to muffle a sneeze, hurried by.

There had been no chance for a proper reconnoiter, but she prayed the residence would be similar to that of her great-aunt's. A quick survey of the back wall seemed to confirm her hopes. Gaining entry to the garden should be a snap. The chisel she had brought along looked to be strong enough to pry off the hasp of the gate without much of a problem. Or, if she chose to employ the other method of entry she had come equipped for, the length of rope would loop over the iron rail set atop the brick with plenty to spare.

Portia debated the alternatives for a moment. There was a chance, however slight, that some vigilant Charley would walk through the alley and notice the broken latch. After eyeing the height and the numerous footholds afforded by the crumbling mortar, she made up her mind.

Breeches were indeed a godsend, she thought, straddling the wall in between the spaced spokes and flipping the thick hemp line over to the other side. The rear of the house showed no sign of life, save for the faint glimmer of a candle through the draperies of a top-floor window. No doubt it was just a servant making ready to retire. Swallowing a sniffle, she assured herself that if she was quiet, her presence should not raise any alarm.

Using the knots she had added for handholds, she quickly lowered herself to the ground and moved in a low crouch to the shelter of the bushes. A few moments later she was under one of the large diamond-paned windows that flanked the arched doorway, her gloved hands stealing up to the sill. To her relief the heavy casing was already slightly ajar. No need for the chisel or the thin blade of the knife tucked in her boot—she had only to wedge her fingers in between . . .

She froze as a wraithlike swirl of smoke curled out from the narrow opening. Despite her stuffy senses, the strange sweetness was nearly overpowering, and it was all she could do to keep from falling into a fit of coughing. *Good Lord,* she thought, venturing a tentative sniff after the cloud had dissolved into mere wisps of haze. Her father had brought back all manner of pungent tobaccos from his travels, but none quite as cloying or . . . odd as this particular scent.

Raising her eyes just to the level of the casing, she risked a peek into the darkened study. At first she saw nothing, but suddenly a red-hot coal flared up out of nowhere, glowering back at her like some malevolent Cyclops. Its resemblance to some living entity was reinforced by a deep sucking sound and the gurgle of water. Biting back a startled cry, she was about to make a hasty retreat when she noticed that the fiery glow had grown just bright enough to shed some illumination on the bizarre scene. By squinting, she was able to make out the outline of an ornate brass jug, perhaps three feet in height, and two figures seated cross-legged on the floor before it.

Despite the danger of being spotted, Portia found she could not tear her gaze away from the extraordinary sight. The jug was actually a pipe of some sort, she realized. The coal was sitting in a shallow bowl atop a curved spout, and one of the figures—a gentleman, by the look of his elegant evening clothes—had a snaking length of hollow tubing wrapped around his forearm like a serpent, the carved amber end of which was clamped firmly between his teeth.

"Excellent stuff." He took another long pull at the mouthpiece, his languid features taking on the blissful expression of a kitten that had just fallen into a pitcher of cream. "I trust the rest of the shipment is of the same high quality," he grunted through a whooshing exhale of the smoke.

Portia now recognized the other figure as the turbaned servant who had greeted her on her first visit to the town house. On this occasion, however, his English was as crisp as the swat of a cricket bat. "Unlike many Englishmen, *memsahib* is not a cheat or a liar."

The gentleman's senses were not so befuddled as to miss the note of contempt in the Indian's voice. "Why you bloody savage! I should cut out your heathenish tongue for daring to slur a proper gentleman—" The rest of the harangue was lost in the shuffle of hurried steps coming down the hallway.

Springing to his feet, the servant pressed his palms together and bowed low to the ground.

"Good evening, Vavek." Mrs. Grenville had not bothered to remove her cloak. Indeed, the hood was still turned up over her raven curls, the folds of dark wool obscuring all but the tip of her nose. Portia, however, would have recognized the sultry voice anywhere. "Ah, I see our honored guest has already had a chance to sample the merchandise," she remarked, placing the single taper she carried upon the side table. "Good.

Then, I assume we need not waste time with any of the usual tedious preliminaries."

The widow turned to her servant and held out her hand. Wordlessly he withdrew a small velvet pouch from the pocket of his tunic and placed it in her palm. "You appear well satisfied that all is in order, Lord Mirkham," she continued. "So, why don't we conclude our dealings without any further delay."

Mirkham lounged back against the leather hassock, clearly in no hurry to be going anywhere. "Still all business, my dear Olivia? A pity, for while you evidently have developed a mind for commerce since you were a girl, you also have developed a body for sin." Smirking at his own wit, he inhaled deeply. "Is it, perchance, for sale, like the rest of your goods?"

Ignoring the lewd suggestiveness of his comment, Mrs. Grenville tipped the contents of the bag into her hand. "Sapphires, rubies, emeralds—all of them the size and clarity that you requested." She nodded at the bit of ash still remaining in the pipe. "A bale of the other commodity will be delivered wherever you wish. Now, kindly hand over the promised papers."

"You can hardly expect me to give them over before I have actually received the goods in hand."

She dumped the jewels back into the pouch and tossed it onto his lap.

With a casual flick of his finger, he nudged it into his waistcoat pocket. His hand then stole inside his jacket, but when it emerged a moment later there was a small pistol wrapped in its grip, rather than the requested sheets of vellum. "These may serve as, say, an advance payment, but I'm afraid the actual price has gone up considerably since we last spoke. As a merchant, you understand the laws of supply and demand."

His bushy beard quivering with rage, the servant started forward, but the widow stopped him with a curt command in his own language. Her own visage remained impassive. "How much are we talking about? Another sackful of gems? Another chest filled with Bengali hashish?"

He shook his head, a slow smile parting his moist lips.

"What, then?"

"*The Lotus of the Orient,*" he whispered. "My sources tell me she was due to arrive today, and I want what she brought."

The Lotus of the Orient! Portia somehow managed to repress a gasp, though her knuckles went white from the force of gripping the edge of the sill. If only she hadn't given over her only firearm to the earl, she would be in a perfect position to take control of the situation. Cursing the missed opportunity, she leaned in a bit closer to the paned glass, straining to overhear the next words. As she did, the butt of the chisel pressed up against her thigh.

Did she dare attempt such a bold ruse? Her hand slipped down to her pocket. In the darkness, the shaft would no doubt resemble the barrel of a gun. Holding her breath, she edged one step to her right, hoping to get a better angle. . . .

Thumph!

If the angle of her chin hadn't been buried in the folds of Melton wool, she might have let out a yelp. As it was, she quickly recovered her equilibrium and didn't need the Earl of Branford's hard squeeze on her shoulders to tell her any movement or noise might betray their presence.

"Shhhh," he added as a precaution, his whisper softer than the zephyr stirring the leaves.

She gave a twitch of assent and he relaxed his hold just enough to allow them both to turn back to what was happening inside the study.

On receiving no response from Mrs. Grenville, Mirkham let the pipe's mouthpiece slip from his hand and levered to his knees, all the while keeping a surprisingly steady aim on the widow's heart. "I want it, and I want it now," he snarled, the treacly tone of his voice hardening to a brittle edge. "You don't really think that at this stage of the game I will allow you to cross me up and sell it to anyone else."

The hood slipped from Mrs. Grenville's head, revealing a profile as white as Carrara marble and just as emotionless. "Or else I, too, will end up with my throat slit?"

His face tightened, and a sheen of sweat broke out upon his forehead. "He forced our hand! Don't you!" His tongue flicked over his lower lip. "Come now, it is not so very much to ask for, considering what you get in return."

"Given what happened to Lord Roxleigh, you don't imagine that I would be imprudent enough to keep such a valuable commodity here," she replied.

His brow furrowed. Clearly that particular thought had not occurred to him. "W-where is it?" he demanded.

Portia suddenly felt a sneeze coming on. Biting her lip, she buried her nose in the earl's coat and managed to muffle any sound.

"Ill from your last foray?" breathed Branford in her ear. "A young lady with any normal sensibilities would be home in bed."

"I can't afford to have any normal sensibilities," she whispered back, "seeing as I no longer have a home or a bed of my own." With one last sniff she lifted her head. "What *is* that peculiar odor?" She inhaled deeply. "I don't recognize the tobacco—"

"I wouldn't do that if I were you," he muttered. At her quizzical glance he merely shook his head. "Never mind." Seeing the widow turn, he pressed a finger to her lips. "Now hush, so we don't miss what's going on."

Mrs. Grenville was taking her time in answering. She picked at the hem of her glove, glanced at a tall case clock, then finally gave a small lift of her shoulders. "Very well, I'll tell you. It's in my warehouse."

"We checked!" Mirkham rose rather unsteadily to his feet. "Every bloody inch of the place."

The widow allowed the briefest flicker of amusement to pass over her lips. "Really, Mirkham, do you take me for a fool? Only a bloody fool would use such an obvious spot as the main office. Naturally, I have another, more private place of business in Town."

Eyes narrowing in suspicion, he sucked at his lower lip. "Ain't a nitwit. You'll see." After a moment of hesitation he thumbed back the hammer of his weapon. "Take me there. But not with him." With a jerk of the gun he indicated the glowering servant. "The organ-grinder's monkey stays here."

"As you wish." She was able to add a few quick words to the Indian before Mirkham cut her off with a stamp of his foot.

"None of that gibberish!" he ordered.

"I was just making sure Vavek understood my orders. His English sometimes leaves something to be desired." She took up the taper, holding it in such a way that the servant all but disappeared in the shadows.

Mirkham blinked in consternation but waved her on. "You first. And no tricks, or my pistol will add another shade of deathly scarlet to your gown."

She shrugged and stepped into the hallway. He was just about to follow when a series of slashing blows exploded like lightening from out of the blackness.

The whirling blur of arms reminded Portia of the strange Indian deity depicted in the painting above the widow's mantel. *The Destroyer God*. Did Mrs. Grenville simply mow down anyone who stood in her path? Portia went numb at the chilling thought. If so, her father . . .

A shiver must have caused her to sway slightly, for Branford's arm clamped more tightly around her waist.

The widow moved nearly as quickly as her servant. She spun around and was down on her knees in a flash, her hands hurriedly searching through the unconscious Mirkham's clothing. "Damn," she muttered. "It appears the bastard isn't quite as stupid as I had hoped—they are not on his person." Dusting off her gloves, she sighed and got to her feet.

The servant reached down and dug into Mirkham's waistcoat. "There are ways of extracting information, *memsahib*." The servant cracked his bejeweled knuckles, then tucked the velvet pouch back into the pocket of his tunic. "Especially from such a crawling dung beetle as his lordship. I could then squash the filthy bug and dispose of the carcass in the stews of St. Giles."

It seemed to Portia that the servant had an extremely good command of the English language. *Too good.* She gave a convulsive swallow, drawing another warning nudge from the earl.

Mrs. Grenville appeared tempted by the suggestion. However, after a brief consideration, she shook her head. "It would no doubt be a wasted effort. I am beginning to suspect that he is not the brains behind all this—it's clear he has none. Nor the nerve to commit murder." The toe of her slipper nudged at the slack jaw. "Just dump him, liver and lungs intact, in St. James's Street, along with all the other jug-bitten gentlemen who will be littering the gutters."

A ripple of emotion stirred in the Indian's coffee-colored eyes, but he offered no reply, save for a slight bow.

The widow, however, paused in stepping back from the body. "Damn," she repeated, one finger coming to rest upon the tip of her chin. "I wonder . . . how in the name of Kali did he know the *Lotus of the Orient* was due to arrive in London?"

There was a winking of light as the servant's fingers stroked through his oiled beard. "I take it *memsahib* has not yet read the morning newspaper?"

This time, the expletives that came from Mrs. Grenville's lips would have put a pirate to blush. Tacking on several words in Hindi, she bent down and retrieved the pistol from beneath one of the gilded side chairs. "Bloody hell, it is *I* who have naught but smoke for brains. I should have remembered that such things are published every day." She pulled her hood back up over her hair. "I had better go check that Sanjay is not in need of reinforcements while you dispose of Lord Mirkham."

"Perhaps you should wait until I return—"

"No, no!" She gave a wave of the weapon. "We must move quickly, Vavek. Speed is more important than brawn. I kept the carriage waiting in the side alley, just in case there were any complications. Anschul will have me there and back again before anyone is the wiser."

With a deft twist the servant lifted the beefy body as if it weighed no more than a flea and slung it over his shoulder. "As you wish, *memsahib*."

Darkness once again filled the room as the two of them disappeared into the hallway.

Branford glanced around the garden, his gaze coming to rest on the back gate. "For once your penchant for picking locks may serve a useful purpose."

"Actually, I came over the wall this time, not through it."

"Bloody hell."

"Stop saying that. Using the rope takes only a few moments longer than—" Portia was left talking to thin air, as the earl took off at a dead sprint.

Grabbing hold of the knotted line, he scaled the wall with a catlike agility, and although the iron rail made maneuvering a bit awkward, he managed to lean far enough out over the ledge to look toward the street. Sure enough, at the far end of the alleyway the dark silhouette of a coach loomed out of the mist.

The reconnaissance had taken barely more than the blink of an eye, but when he reached back to yank up the rope, it held firm.

Branford felt sorely tempted to repeat the oath for the third time in as many minutes. Any attempt to halt her ascent would most likely alert the widow's coachman to their presence, so in lieu of ringing a peal over her head, he had to content himself with squashing her flat on her stomach as soon as she wriggled up over the lip of the ledge.

Her chin hit the limestone with a dull thump.

"Bastard," she whispered a moment later as she had lifted her head enough to catch sight of the Indian servant ghosting toward Green Park, the comatose Lord Mirkham slung over his shoulder.

The earl's lips twitched, although he wasn't sure to whom she was referring. Then his amusement disappeared as quickly as the flutter of silk. "Try to keep quiet," he warned. "It's a bloody miracle they haven't spotted us yet, for you made more racket than a regiment of raw recruits scrabbling up here."

"Bastard."

This time he had no doubt for whom the slur was meant. "My manners may be suspect, but my antecedents are not, Miss Hadley," he snapped. However the retort may not have reached her ears, for he had already unlooped the rope and started to crawl in the direction of the waiting equipage.

The scrape of leather on the rough stone told Branford she was hot on his heels.

On reaching the end of the widow's property, he looked to both sides, then suddenly let the rope fall back into the garden and made a grab for the over-hanging branch of a pear tree.

Ha! That should shake her loose from his tail, he thought, working his way hand over hand until he was hanging out over the footpath between the two walled gardens. The drop was a good twelve feet down to the ground, but he had noticed there was a large pile of grass cuttings waiting to be hauled away, which should serve nicely to muffle the sound of his fall. And, as luck would have it, the jog in the neighboring brickwork would hide any flurry of movement.

Smiling grimly, Branford let go of the branch.

The impact drove his knees to his chest, but with a smooth roll sideways he quickly recovered his footing and in several strides had positioned himself at the corner of the wall. It appeared that his timing was impeccable, for just as he pressed up against the mossy brick, there came the sound of Mrs. Grenville's front door falling closed.

The earl listened intently to the widow's hurried footsteps echoing over the cobblestones. He heard the creaking of the seat as the coachman shifted his whip, the snorting of the horses as they blew small puffs of vapor in the chill night air, the jingling of the harness as the coach inched forward. . . .

And scrabbling of boots in the dry cuttings as Portia picked herself up off her rump.

"I don't suppose you have a carriage waiting nearby?" she demanded, a wheezy snuffle making her words a bit difficult to make out.

"No." He knew he should leave it at that, but for some reason he didn't wish for her to think it due to bumbling incompetence. "It would be foolish to give chase in another vehicle. Not only would it scare her away from her real destination, but it would alert her to the fact that someone other than Mirkham was privy to what took place in the study."

"That makes some sense. In that case . . ." She appeared to be thinking.

Out of the corner of his eye, he saw that Mrs. Grenville was coming around the corner. He would have to move fast if—

". . . the best plan would be for us to stow away in the boot of the carriage, but we had better hurry!"

That Portia's suggestion was exactly the strategy he had in mind added an extra burr to his growl. "*We* are not going anywhere. Not together, that is." He found himself wishing he hadn't tossed away the rope, for it would have proved handy in tying her to the nearest immovable object, so that he might conduct his surveillance with a modicum of professionalism. "*I* am getting in the boot, while *you* are going back to your great-aunt's."

"You a-arrogant jackass. I am b-b-bloody well not—" The sneeze she had been battling finally won out. With a sudden spasm her head dipped down and her shoulders jerked forward.

"Quiet!" he hissed.

It took a fraction of a second to realize that the whoosh of air that had just ruffled his hair was not due to her worsening megrim but rather to the velocity of a whizzing bullet.

As it thumped into something solid, all hell broke loose. One of the horses reared in its traces, the coachman screamed a curse, and the widow managed to yank open the door of the carriage and scramble inside. Another bang echoed off the bricks as the wheels skidded over the pavement and the vehicle shot out into the street.

While watching the commotion, the earl was vaguely aware that the young lady had slumped against his coat. "Come, Miss Hadley. Don't choose this moment to start behaving like a normal young miss. We haven't time for a maidenly faint."

For once, his sarcasm failed to draw a retort from her.

"Miss Hadley!" he repeated, giving a none-too-gentle shake to her shoulder. He opened his mouth to chide her again, but the words caught in his throat at the sight of his glove.

It had come away covered with blood.

He looked right and left. Lights were already beginning to bob in the windows of the neighboring town houses, and from several streets over came the faint cry of the watch.

Damnation!

Sweeping her up into his arms, Branford spun around with his burden and loped back down the alleyway.

Chapter Eleven

❧❧❧

Portia felt as if she were trapped in one of Bertie's worst nightmares. The darkness, seemingly blacker than Hades, was threatening to suffocate her within its enveloping shroud. Blindly, she clawed against its hold, heedless of the pain shooting through her arm. . . .

"You must try to be still, Miss Hadley. Thrashing about like that, you only risk doing further injury to yourself." The earl shifted her weight in his arms, hugging her tighter to his chest. His pace, however, did not slow. "I dare not stop to examine the wound, not until we are safely off the streets and hidden away from prying eyes. Can you hold out a bit longer?"

"Y-yes."

"Good girl."

She closed her eyes and let her cheek fall back against the crook of his neck. The collar of his coat had come slightly askew, and despite her wooziness she was acutely aware of the scent emanating from the thick wool. Brandy, smoke, a tang of citrus and sandalwood. And an earthy undertone she had come to recognize as distinctly his own. Breathing deeply, she nestled a bit closer.

"It's not so bad," she murmured. "No worse than when Henry accidentally knocked a bolt off one of the spring-loaded gates Squire Gretham employed to keep out trespassers."

"What happened on that occasion?"

"The latch exploded, sending a four-inch nail into my thigh. But he managed to pull it out without too much difficulty—that is, once he had finished casting up his accounts." She gave a soft laugh at the memory. "Good Lord, I was madder than a wet hen. It ruined my only decent riding outfit, but we did steal away with a sackful of apples." Her voice faded into a rather dreamy murmur. "Mmmm. As I recall, they were delicious."

He laughed as well. "Hellion."

"I suppose I was." She gave a small sniff. "Not that I have turned into a paragon of propriety. No wonder you think me a beastly nuisance."

"A very brave beast," he replied, his breath tickling her ear. "You have the courage of a lion, Miss Hadley. And the heart of a tiger."

Her insides gave an odd little lurch that had nothing to do with the earl's hurried steps over the uneven stones. It must be that her head cold was taking a turn for the worse, she reasoned, because all of sudden her cheeks had a warmth to them that could only have been brought on by fever. So it was understandable that her arms should wind around the earl's neck in order to steady her spinning senses. After a moment she felt recovered enough to make a reply. "I would have expected you to compare me to a mule, seeing as you have accused me on more than one occasion of being awfully stubborn."

He laughed again, and it struck her what a pleasant sound it was—low and melodious, like cool river water rippling over granite. "You are, but with your green eyes and sinuous grace, it would be a rather inelegant metaphor. I prefer to think of you as a tiger."

Her arms tightened, seeking to fight off yet another strange yawing, and much to her surprise, Branford seemed to cradled her even more closely.

The earl was actually being uncommonly decent about the whole thing, she decided as she listened to the muted thud of his steps. Having to skulk through the byways of Mayfair with a helpless female in his arms was not only a taxing feat of strength, given the fact that she was the size of a small ox, but one that would require a great deal of explaining if he was caught in the act. Portia grimaced. If only she were more like the fashionable young ladies of the *ton,* petite as a china doll and weighing no more than a feather.

Ha! If she had anything in common with those demure young ladies, she would not be fleeing through a shadowy side street in the arms of a notorious rake. Nor would she be spoiling his expensive overcoat with blood from a bullet wound. A small groan slipped from beneath her gritted teeth. It was no use, she thought, burying her nose a bit deeper in the earl's coat. She would never get the hang of being a proper female.

"Try to bear it just a bit longer, Miss Hadley." Portia was startled at the gentleness of Branford's voice. Even more surprising was the fact that he didn't appear to be breathing hard. "We have not much farther to go."

Usually the one who had to consider all the practical ramifications of a plan, Portia suddenly realized she had not given a thought to their present predicament. "W-where *are* we going?" Sure it was going to be a tad awkward for the earl to knock on Lady Trumbull's front door in the dead of night and explain to the elderly lady just how her niece had come to have a rather large hole drilled through her shoulder.

Branford didn't answer. Swearing softly, he ducked into a shadowed nook, just in time to dodge the spill of light from a watchman's lantern.

That did it! The earl may be arrogant and high-handed at times, but he didn't deserve to suffer the consequences for her own precipitous actions. As soon as the scuffling steps faded into the mist, she sought to squirm out of his grasp. "You may put me down now, sir. I am quite capable of taking care of myself. I can make my way home from here." That her knees buckled the moment her toes touched the ground did not exactly add support to the claim.

"Don't be an idiot," he growled, scooping her back up to his chest. "Within two steps you would be flat on your arse."

"Oh!" Portia was acutely aware that his hand was resting on that portion of her anatomy. "Well, you needn't be so rude about it. I was merely trying to help you avoid a bit of embarrassment should we be spotted."

"Embarrassment is the least of our worries if we are seen—in case it has slipped your mind, someone just tried to put a period to your existence back there."

"The bullet *might* have been aimed at you," she replied. "Which reminds me of another thing—"

"Another time, Miss Hadley." The earl emphasized his interruption with a sharp squeeze to her posterior. "We must go on very quietly from here." Stepping out from their hiding place, he crossed the street and quickly turned into another narrow alley. Halfway down the rutted way, he stopped to jiggle at a heavy wrought-iron gate.

Portia craned her neck to see what he was up to. "You will never get that open without the proper tools. Besides, haven't we engaged in enough trespassing for one night? If we are caught—"

The gate swung open and Branford stepped inside, quickly drawing it closed behind him. "We won't be."

"How can you be so sure?" She squinted up at the darkened rear of the town house. "I know it looks as if everyone is abed, but there may be a watchdog, or a restless servant, or—" Her breath came out in a choked gasp. "Sir! What on earth do you think you are doing?"

After cutting across the garden path, Branford had taken a sudden turn and was now running lightly up the back steps. With a shove of his shoulder he nudged the scullery door open. "Going inside. I don't have a dog, and I haven't got around to hiring a full complement of servants. In addition to my butler, whom you have met, there are only an aged housekeeper and cook left from my uncle's staff. And not even Gideon's trumpet could wake them from their slumber."

The Earl of Branford had brought her to his town house?

"I—I am not sure this is a very good idea, sir."

"It's a bloody awful idea, but have you a better one?" He stopped long enough to strike a flint to a candle. "That shoulder has to be examined. And by someone more proficient in treating a gunshot wound than Henry or Bertie."

The mention of her brothers sent a cold shiver down her spine. "Good Lord, they simply *must* not find out about this."

"With a bit of luck, we may manage to keep things under wraps. If the bullet passed cleanly through the flesh——" He stopped short at the sound of bare feet tripping down the curved staircase.

"Bullets? What's all this talk of bullets, guv?" Portia caught sight of a wiry little man stuffing the tails of his nightgown into a pair of baggy breeches, a gap-toothed yawn stretching out his sleepy inquiry. "Got yerself winged by a outraged husband? Told ye that ye should stick t' swiving——"

"Stubble the patter, Blaze. I am going to need hot water and bandages."

Blinking the sleep from his eyes, the other man stared for a moment at the earl, and then at the pair of shapely long legs that were draped over his arm. To his credit, his grizzled countenance remained impassive. Shaking off the last vestiges of lethargy, he ran a scarred hand through his hair and snapped to attention. "Right-o, guv!"

Without further ado, the earl rushed by, the Italian Renaissance painting a mere blur to Portia's eyes as he took the stairs two at a time. At the top of the landing he pivoted to the right.

"I thought you said there were no servants——" she began in a halting voice.

"Blaze is not exactly a servant. He has been with me

for more years than I care to recall, first as my batman on the Peninsula and now as a self-styled gentleman's gentleman—though in truth he can't tell a cravat from a crimping iron." The earl continued halfway down the hallway before throwing open one of the heavy oak doors.

"Lord Branford, again I must . . ." Portia found herself unceremoniously dumped upon a large, ornately carved tester bed. Its covering was a rich damask weave of burgundy and forest-green stripes whose muted hues complemented the sherry-colored paneling and heavy brass-handled furniture. It was, she realized, a very masculine room. And despite her stuffy nose, she also realized that the subtle scent of bay rum and shaving soap was intimately familiar.

Had the earl really brought her to his own bedchamber? A strangled protest gurgled in her throat. "Sir, I am afraid this is really highly improper. . . ."

"Given what has already passed between us, I would say that it is a trifle late to be concerned about either your reputation or your virtue." Stripping off his gloves, he began working at the fastenings of her coat.

She wasn't sure whether her sharp intake of breath was made out of anger or because he had inadvertently jostled her wound.

"Sorry," he muttered softly, deftly slipping the garment off her shoulders.

The huff turned into a soft sigh as his fingers began to undo the buttons of her linen shirt.

"Don't turn misshish on me now, Miss Hadley," he growled. "I must have a look at your injury and ascertain whether a surgeon needs to be summoned."

With all the shock and exertion of the evening's adventure, Portia feared she was coming dangerously close to a swoon. His words, however, were more effective than any vinaigrette in causing her to sit up with a start. "No, please!" She sought to push away his hands. "I tell you, it's naught but a nick. If you will simply take me around to the back gate of my aunt's town house, I am quite well enough now to sneak up to my bed without a problem. I can patch up any damage myself, and with a day or two of rest I will be back on my feet again."

"Ha!" he scoffed. "More likely you would be in danger of succumbing to a putrid fever or gangrene." It didn't take much of an effort on his part to parry her weak thrusts. "A hell of a lot of good you will be to your family if you cock up your toes at this point, Miss Hadley. So sit still—" He paused for a fraction—"and put a cork in it."

Portia scrunched her mouth in indignation, but though she had every intention of responding with a scathing retort, what came out was a stifled laugh. "Good Lord, don't tell me Henry dared say that to *you?*"

"If he had, the young pup would be nursing a sore rump. But as it is, both his bottom and his pride are as yet unbruised."

"So it seems," she murmured. "I—I have yet to thank you for your kindness to them. Both of them are in alt over the prospect of accompanying you to Manton's."

"It appears I should have you accompany us as well, so that you may learn to shoot back." His brow furrowed. "Now, perhaps you would be so good as to explain what—"

"Couldn't it wait until the morrow? You did say you were planning to call at my great-aunt's."

"Yes, I had thought it might be nice to meet under civilized circumstances." It may have been a mere flicker of the candle, but she thought she detected a slight twinkle in his eye. "Tea and cakes rather than bullets and brandy. . . ."

Though his fingers moved with a light touch, Portia could not bite back a cry as they probed at the edges of the torn flesh.

"Speaking of spirits . . ." He eased her back against the pillows and hurried to the dressing table, where a crystal decanter on a silver tray loomed large among the simple arrangement of grooming items. Splashing a good amount of Scottish whisky into a glass, he returned and pressed it to her lips.

"Arrgh!"

Ignoring the coughing and sputtering, the earl forced her to drink it down. "If you are going to dress like a man, fight like a man, and swear like a man, you may as well learn to drink like a man."

"So that I may act as foolishly as a man?"

"Apparently you need no help in doing that," he replied dryly. "However, you will find that a nip or two helps take the edge off the pain." He put the glass aside. "I am sorry to be hurting you, but I'm afraid it can't be avoided." Portia was surprised to see his face soften for a moment. It was, she noted, an extremely attractive countenance, especially when he was not scowling like Lucifer.

"I shall wait a touch longer, for the whisky to take effect, then I will have to have another go at it." He leaned in closer. "Will you be all right?"

Staring into his eyes, Portia was sure that the potent spirits had already flooded her senses. The deep sapphire color once again brought to mind the sparkling waters of the Aegean Sea, and indeed, she felt a strong current pulling her into their swirling depths. Suddenly it was becoming difficult to breathe, and she had the strangest feeling that one might drown in a gaze like that. . . .

Branford looked up as the door banged open. With a woozy sigh she felt herself able to come up for air.

The grizzled valet kicked over a small side table and thumped a large tray down upon it. Eyeing the empty glass by the bedside, he gave a wink of approval. "Aye, that's the spirit, miss. A wee nip of the bottle will fortify yer nerve. Puts a bit of hair on yer chest, it does."

"Thank you, Blaze," murmured the earl as he reached for a sponge. "But somehow I doubt that such a thought is of any cheer to the young lady."

"Oh, er, right-o." The flush that rose to his grizzled cheeks nearly matched the color of his flaming hair. "Sorry, missy. Meant no offense."

"None taken," replied Portia with a lopsided smile. Although her chest might not be sprouting follicles, it seemed to her that it was swaying from side to side in the most peculiar manner. Not an unpleasant sensation, merely . . . peculiar. Branford's touch seemed to steady her, and she felt her grin stretch wider. "Really, sir, being shot is not nearly so bad as one might think. Aside from the fact that bloodstains tend to ruin a per-

fectly good garment . . ." She bit at her lip as the earl's
fingers moved back to the wound, but did not cry out.

"You may wish to revise that opinion in another few
moments," he remarked tersely, his mouth compress-
ing to a tight line as he swabbed specks of gunpowder
from the raw flesh. "Damn it, Blaze, stop dawdling
about over there and bring the hot water closer."

With a rather detached sense of consternation, Portia
realized that perhaps she should not allow two strange
gentleman to be standing by the bedside, ogling her
bared shoulder. Not that it was a very pretty sight, but
any vestige of propriety seemed to slipping away, along
with the greater part of Henry's old shirt. A proper
young lady ought to feel a sense of shock, or at the very
least embarrassment, yet somehow she couldn't seem to
bring her anger—or her eyes—into sharp focus. It all
seemed . . . hazily humorous.

The valet hurried over with the basin. "Ohhhh, will
ya look at that," he exclaimed, peering down at the raw
furrow that had been ploughed across Portia's shoulder.
He leaned in for a closer inspection. "That's a right nasty
scrape, but it could be a hell of a lot worse. Appears that
th' bullet has cut clean through th' flesh, guv."

"Yes, I can see that," said Branford through gritted
teeth.

"Kind o' reminds me o' th' time we wuz ambushed
by that French patrol near Badajoz an' ye took a slug
in th' same place," continued Blaze, clearly warming
up to the subject of blood and gore. "However, on that
occasion we had t' dig it out with a rusty knife, as I recall." He shook his head. "Now, if you want t' talk
about nasty, missy, you should ha' seen *that* little tus-

sle. Henninger had three fingers sliced off by a saber, an' Potter ended up with half his guts spillin' out a hole in his—"

"For God's sake, put a cork in it, you blasted idiot!" exploded the earl, slanting a murderous look at his valet before glancing up at her with an expression of concern. "You are showing remarkable fortitude, Miss Hadley," he went on in a considerably milder tone.

"I should consider myself lucky, I suppose." Portia tried to smile, but the earl saw she was slowly turning a rather bilious shade of green.

"Can you bear up a moment or two longer?" he asked.

Not trusting her voice, she nodded in answer.

Branford rinsed out the sponge and prepared to make a final pass over the injury. "That's a brave girl," he said, not bothering to add that she was also a slightly foxed one. Judging by the fatuous smile on her face, the whisky seemed to have fuzzed the worst of her pain. He only hoped that it would not cause a sudden lurch of her insides—he would rather his shirt not be ruined, along with his coat.

"Aye, tough as a seasoned trooper, she is," piped up Blaze. "Ain't never seen a female wot could have half her arm blown off and not fall into a fit of hysterics."

"Blaze . . ." warned Branford in a low growl, finding himself sorely tempted to tear both limbs from the other man with his bare hands.

The young lady, however, appeared to be finding his valet's running commentary highly diverting. "And just how many females have you seen with their, er, arms blown off, Mr. Blaze?"

"Hmmm." A bit of water sloshed on the carpet as he scratched at his chin. "Well, not many," he allowed. "Though there was this whore in Lisbon that the guv was sleeping with . . ."

"Bloody hell." The earl's eyes pressed closed for a moment, but as his hands were full with the delicate task of cleansing the torn flesh, he was unable to squeeze them around his valet's throat.

"Turned out t' be a French spy," went on Blaze, blithely unaware of Branford's glowering expression. "Lucky the Black Cat had nine lives t' play with. Even so, he had t' shoot her in the wrist t' keep th' little witch from carving his liver into fish bait."

"Indeed?" Portia's eyes took on a decided gleam. "It appears that the earl's exploits with the opposite sex have not been exaggerated."

"Hell, no. And then there was that traitorous countess from Naples—she wuz another corker, though th' guv didn't end up havin' t' shoot her t' put an end t' her mischief. It wuz quite a sight, though, I tell ye, as he chased her stark naked through that fancy villa—"

"That will be all, Sergeant Flynn." The earl slammed down the sponge with a force that rattled the tray. "Consider yourself dismissed." Under his breath he added, "And lucky not be marched out before a firing squad."

In spite of the pain that was clearly etched on her features, Portia let out a burble of laughter. Branford set his jaw, not quite sure whether he wanted to laugh along with her or shake her until her teeth rattled.

He *should* be angry with the outrageous young lady. She was reckless, willful, argumentative, and impetuous—all qualities that were extremely unattractive in a female. So why was he finding it so inexplicably difficult to tear his gaze away from the resolute luminosity of her jade eyes, the brave little tilt of her nose, the plucky twist of her lips.

Bloody hell!

His fist gave another hard smack to the table as he fumbled among the other supplies.

The valet's brows winged up in confusion. "What? Did I step out of line?"

"On the contrary," assured Portia. "I'm extremely grateful to you for your, er, diversionary tactics."

"Begorra!" His leathery cheeks once again flamed with color. "Ye didn't really need much help. Yer a mighty brave lass."

"All the same, it was really very gentlemanly of you to keep me entertained, Mr. Blaze."

"Aw, there ain't no mister attached t' me name, missy. It's just plain Blaze." He gave her a toothy grin. "And if I find th' miserable spalpeen wot done that t' yer arm, I'll put a torch t' th' little bugger's arse."

"I am about to light a fire under your own posterior . . ." began the earl, only to have his warning cut off by a question from Portia.

"Tell me, is your name on account of the color of your hair?" she asked the valet.

"That's part of it, missy. But it also comes from th' time we laid siege to a garrison o' Spanish soldiers who'd been givin' our troops a devil of a time. On account o' me wee size, I wuz able t' crawl through a sapper's tunnel an' set a charge of explosives under their guard tower. The engineers sorta miscalculated the fuze, but I still managed t' send it up in a blaze o' glory. Course, it took a few months fer me hair an' eyebrows t' grow back."

"Suppose we dispense with a blow-by-blow description of our military careers, shall we?" Branford felt his frayed temper was coming perilously close to erupting in the same display of pyrotechnics as the guard tower. "Your duties are finished here. Go back to bed."

The other man gave him a mutinous stare. "But, guv, we ain't finished tending t' th' lass. . . ."

Branford put down the roll of bandage to wind his fingers around his valet's biceps. "I shall handle it from here." Turning him toward the door, he gave a small shove. *"March!"*

Blaze marched, although the reluctant dragging of feet was accompanied by a good many words that should not have been uttered in the presence of a lady.

As soon as the door fell closed, Portia let out another low laugh. "He seemed to have been intimately involved in your wartime activities."

She knew Branford had served under Wellington before acceding to the title, but she had given little thought to his actual duties, if indeed there were any. After all, a good many gentlemen of his rank did little more than strut about in their scarlet regimentals, facing nothing more menacing than a desk full of dispatches.

There had, of course, been the vague rumors concerning his orders to his nephews, and how they had been assigned the most perilous position at the forefront of the battle of Badajoz, where death was most likely to strike at any moment. But other than that, she knew precious little about his past.

She stole a peek at his profile as he busied himself with folding a precise padding of lint. At first glance it was a cold, sardonic face, its forbidding angles a grim warning designed to keep people at a distance. Yet, she had seen them soften, if only for rare moments, and knew he was not nearly as hardened as he wished to appear. It was odd—she had the feeling that although he had sold out from the army, the Earl of Branford was still at war with himself.

Why? she wondered. What personal demons was he fighting?

Her musing was cut short by his finally giving an answer to her question.

"Too damn intimate," he growled, laying aside the lint to tear off a length of linen.

"How long have you known each other?"

"Since the flaming little Irish leprechaun tried to lift my purse outside a certain gaming establishment in Southwark. His skills as a thief were no better than his present woeful attempts at knotting a cravat." Despite the attempt at sardonic humor, the earl's voice betrayed a certain warmth.

She kept her eyes upon him. "So instead of seeing him transported, you offered him a position? Why?"

"He was starving and wouldn't have lasted more than a day or two longer in that hellhole," he said with a shrug. "And the price was extremely cheap."

"Ah, well, I guess that explains it."

It was clear that the earl was choosing to ignore her last comment. After applying a liberal sprinkling of basilicum powder, he pressed the lint to the jagged furrow, then snugged the bandage in a tight wrap around it. "There. Actually it's not so bad as I first feared. The wound is tolerably clean, and this should prevent any further bleeding." With a deft twist, he tied off the ends. "However, I must insist that you summon a doctor to check on it in a day or two, to make sure that no infection sets in."

"But—"

"Invent whatever reason you wish—a catarrh, a curse, a case of hives—but you *are* going to do it."

Piqued by his brusqueness, she raised her chin. "I'm not one of your foot soldiers, sir."

"A pity. Otherwise I could have you clapped in irons for insubordination. It would save us both a lot of pain and suffering."

"And if I refuse?"

"Pray, do not."

Portia was about to fire off another salvo when a slight turning of his head caused a glimmer of the flickering light to spill over his features. It threw in relief the fine lines of fatigue that crinkled out from the corners of his eyes, then shaded down over the hollows of his stubbled cheeks and faded back to shadow over the tautly drawn mouth. It was the look of one besieged by more than mere physical exhaustion.

Feeling guilty for indulging in such petty sniping, she bit at her lip. "Very well, sir."

Branford had already risen and poured a glass of whisky for himself. He tossed it back in one long swallow and, decanter in hand, came back to sit on the edge of the bed. "Am I suffering from hallucinations, or have you just acquiesced to a request without a prolonged fight?"

"Am I really so terrible as that?"

"Worse." His mouth, however, twitched upward at the corners. He refilled his glass, but before lifting it to his lips, he offered her the first sip.

After a moment's hesitation she took a small swallow. Whisky, she decided, was an extremely volatile substance, for a suddenly a sweet, tingling heat was coursing through her, setting off sparks in the very core of her being. It *had* to be the potent concoction that was setting her on fire, and not merely the fact that the earl was sitting so close she could feel the subtle warmth emanating from his broad chest.

Another tiny taste confirmed her conclusion. It was naught but the whisky, she assured herself, brushing her burning tongue against the inside of her cheek. A simple reaction of peated grain, distilled water and imported sugar. It had nothing to do with corded muscle, raven hair, and sapphire eyes.

With a choked cough, she thrust the glass back into his hands.

"Not to your liking?" he asked, one of his dark brows winging up in question.

"It's . . . an acquired taste, I suppose."

"Yes." He drained it in one gulp. "So it is."

The little bit she had imbibed must have loosened her tongue, as well as set it afire. Before she could catch herself, a question she would not normally have voiced aloud spilled forth. "Is that why you drink? To drown out . . . whatever it is that you don't wish to think of?"

"That, Miss Hadley, is a highly impertinent question."

"So it is," she said, echoing his own words. "But then, you know I am utterly lacking in all the normal social graces and feminine charms."

Branford's eyes met hers with a fiery intensity. His voice, however, was so soft that the words were barely audible. "Not all."

She dropped her gaze, hoping the tendrils of loosened curls would help hide the flare of longing. No wonder females were warned about the dangers of drink! She had sworn not to let passion overcome prudence, but the stuff had the oddest effect on one's reason—like dissolving it in a swirling vortex of boiling oil!

"Miss Hadley?"

Her head jerked back up.

"If you bite down any harder, you will be spilling more blood." His finger brushed lightly along her lower lip. "Your shoulder must be aching abominably. I shall mix up a dose of laudanum for you."

"That's not necessary, sir," she mumbled. "Actually, I don't feel a thing. You did a very neat job." Her fingers stole up to the bandage. In truth, she didn't feel any pain, only a warm tingling sensation where his touch had grazed her mouth. "Once again, I find myself having to thank you for coming to my aid."

He shrugged and poured out an extra measure of whisky.

If she had been thinking straight, she probably would have left it at that. But the casual dismissal somehow goaded her into further probing. "I know you think me nothing but trouble. So why have you offered to help me?"

"I told you—dodging a duel with a minor is a cursed inconvenience."

"That doesn't explain the risks you took tonight."

"There was nothing noble about it." The earl paused just long enough to drain his glass. "I did it to protect my own hide. Leaving you behind might have given away my own presence."

"What fustian! There is no sane reason for anyone to connect the two of us. You could have easily crept away without being recognized."

He spun the faceted crystal in his fingers. "Well, unfortunately I didn't realize that earlier."

Portia wondered whether she detected a slight slurring of his sarcasm. "Are you planning on getting jugbitten?"

"The thought had occurred to me."

"Well, it's not a very nice one—"

"I am not nice, Miss Hadley." His voice took on an even more sardonic twist. "You have heard the gossip—I ravage innocent maidens and murder young men."

She was taken aback, not by the cynicism of his words, but by what she saw swirling in the depths of his eyes. *Pain? Disillusionment? Self-doubt?* The ripples were gone in an instant, but in that fleeting moment she realized the enigmatic earl was a good deal more vulnerable than he wished to appear.

"The Black Cat is not the only one who has been savaged by the tabbies, Lord Branford. I have heard enough nasty whispers about my own father to put no credence in vicious gossip," she said flatly. "Whatever your faults—and I am sure they are legion—you have shown yourself to be more of an honorable gentleman than most males who lay claim to the title."

"To the devil with all gentlemen. And all titles," he said with a weary bitterness. "Never expected to be a damn earl." The whisky appeared to have loosened his tongue as well, for after a harried sigh he began to ramble a bit. "Not with my two young cousins just entering manhood. Lord, what fine men the scamps would have been. Dead now, and as you have heard, it's all because of me." His mouth twisted in a mocking smile that did not quite hide the spasm of hurt. "I suppose by now I should be used to the ugly rumors that swirl around my name. They have been around since my days at Oxford, when I was accused of fleecing men out of their money."

"Is it not true that you won a great deal of blunt?" inquired Portia.

"Yes, I played at cards and won. But not through cheating. I merely realized that through sharp concentration and careful observation to little details—watching expressions, counting cards, that sort of thing—one could turn the odds in one's favor. All aboveboard, if a bit mercenary."

"Is that how you came by that interesting sobriquet?"

"Aye, I was called the Black Cat because I was bloody bad luck for anyone who sat down opposite me to play. But it was not mere serendipity. I made my own luck." His head slumped forward. "It held until Badajoz."

Portia touched the tips of her fingers to his cheek. "That is beyond luck, sir. That is fate, and no earthly being can control it, no matter how careful one is."

It was several moments before he drew back. "You seem to have forgotten that I am accorded to be a beast, Miss Hadley."

"Well, I am very fond of animals," she murmured, suddenly wanting very much to chase the look of remorse from his features. "I had a whole collection of stray dogs at home. And cats . . ." The attempt at humor broke down in a watery sniff. "That is, at what used to be my home. Thank heavens Emmy Stanfield agreed to take them all in when I had to leave for London." She lifted a sleeve of her brother's shirt to wipe at her nose, only to have the fastening fall all the way open. "Hell's bells," she swore, staring down at her nearly naked breasts. They were covered with only a thin lawn chemise through which the rosy areolas were clearly visible.

She reached down to tug the shirt closed, but the earl was quicker. His hands brushed hers aside and began to rearrange the wrinkled linen. But after a moment of fumbling, they moved with exquisite gentleness to cup the curves of her flesh.

The soft fabric stretched taut across the nub of her nipples, the friction coaxing them to hard little points. Realizing his primal need to hold on to someone other than a ghost, Portia didn't pull away. *To hell with practicality and propriety!* At that moment her need for him was just as overwhelming. No matter that he was a devilish rogue who tumbled women as though they were dice, that he soused himself in the demons of drink, that he chased naked countesses through exotic villas—she wanted his touch to rove at will over her own exposed flesh.

A heated moan escaped from her lips, and she leaned into his grasp, feeling his lithe fingers close around her, as though they were reaching up into sun-warmed branches to pluck a ripe peach. An answering groan, deep and feral, sounded in the earl's throat. He shifted on the bed so that he could bend over and capture her mouth in a lush and lingering kiss.

"Ah, sweeting." He lifted his lips just enough to voice a hoarse whisper. "Be warned—you are playing with fire."

Somehow she desperately wanted to seem as worldly and experienced as the naked countess and the legion of other women who had shared his bed. "I'm no stranger to risk," she replied. "I know what I am doing. And what I want."

"What do you want?" he asked, his words crackling with heat. "Tell me."

Practical Portia disappeared in a puff of smoke.

"I—I want you to take me into your bed," she blurted out, hardly believing her own ears that such words of wanton desire had slipped from her lips. Yet, she had no desire to snatch them back. "Make love to me," she continued. "Just as you did to Lady Roxleigh that night in the conservatory."

There was no longer anything gentle about his touch. While before he had moved with a careful deliberation, his hands now began to plunder her body with reckless abandon. Her shirt was pulled completely off, the soft folds of linen pooling around her waist. And then they were underneath the sleeveless chemise, bare flesh on bare flesh.

Dazed, she fell back among the pillows, desire licking up inside her like tongues of hot flame. The tiny shell buttons of her undergarment seemed of their own accord to come free, exposing her breasts to the lapping light. She heard his ragged intake of breath, then his lips were moving—over her jaw, down the curve of her neck . . .

And then taking her nipple between his teeth!

Portia cried out, though the sound from her throat was not one she recognized as her own. Strange as it sounded to her own ears, the high-pitched moan seemed to fire him with a new urgency. His tongue began a tingling exploration of her peaked flesh.

Suddenly she, too, was hungry for the heat of his naked skin, eager to touch the chiseled planes of muscle. Reaching out, she tugged at the ends of his cravat and pulled the length of linen loose from his throat. The earl raised himself up and tore it the rest of the way off. Another few yanks removed his waistcoat and shirt. She was not quite certain, but she thought she heard the faint sound of fabric tearing and a button or two falling to the carpet. Then he was looming above her, all sculpted shoulders and tanned flesh. In wonder, she ran her fingers through the dark curls of hair.

"I am not hurting you, am I, sweeting?" he whispered as his arms wrapped around her waist and pushed her back against the pillows.

"No! . . . Yes! . . . I don't know!" It was all such a dizzying whirl, she didn't know what she was feeling, except that she didn't want it to stop.

The earl seemed to sense her desire. His hands slipped down to her snug-fitting breeches, stroking the inside of her thighs, then moving up to caress her more intimately. Even through the nubbed wool, the teasing of his fingers were like a lick of fire, drawing a liquid heat from deep within her core. The honeyed wetness drenching her flesh was a strange new sensation, and she found herself drawn into its current, swirling in a vortex of passion.

With a soft cry, she arched into his palm.

"Have you any idea how mesmerizing you are, my tigress?" murmured the earl in a husky whisper, his hands moving up the front of her breeches. Portia felt him undoing the fastenings and peeling the fabric down from her hips.

It was *she* who was mesmerized, she thought. Unable to reply, she was aware only of the racing of her pulse. Indeed, the thump of her heart was growing louder and louder, drowning out all other sound. . . .

"Bloody hell!"

Branford sat up abruptly as the pounding on the door grew more frantic.

"Guv!" came the muffled shout. "Guv, a man has come with a message from th' Saint. Says it's right urgent."

"Christ Almighty, have him wait. I will be down in a trice." He was already reaching over, groping for his shirt among the other garments strewn over the floor. The fiery whisper of a moment ago had taken on an edge that might have been tempered out of cold steel. His face, too, had lost all trace of warmth. "I must go. Blaze will see that you get home safely."

Crossing her arms over her chest, Portia nodded

blindly. And suddenly it spilled over her like a bucket of cold water—this was nothing out of the ordinary for him. She was only the latest in an endless parade of paramours who had slipped between his sheets.

The realization left her feeling naked in more ways than one. Chilled to the bone, she grabbed for her shirt among the covers and pulled it on while he stood to do up the buttons of his waistcoat.

"Take as long as you need to make yourself ready." He had turned away and was running a hand through his hair, trying to restore some order to the tangled locks. "Blaze will wait at the foot of the stairs."

The Devil and the Saint.

What sort of message could not wait until a decent hour of the day to be delivered? Surely not one that augured any good. A shiver brought goosebumps to her bare flesh, bringing with them a resurfacing of all her earlier suspicions.

Just what was the Black Cat up to, prowling the streets of London at night?

The earl moved noiselessly across the carpet. "I—" With a hand on the doorknob, he hesitated for just an instant. "I will still be calling at your aunt's town house later today. After tonight, we have even more to discuss."

Portia found herself wishing that she, like her missing father, could be on a strange ship bound for ports unknown when he did.

Chapter Twelve

❧❀❧

One eye pried open, but as the shaft of light felt like a saber bent on gouging it out, Branford let it fall shut again.

May Lucifer be corned, salted, and pickld in brandy!

Or perhaps port, since by the look of the empty bottle lying inches from his nose he had consumed a good measure of that particular spirit as well. He winced as his unshaven cheek scraped against the woven wool of the carpet. A quick peek at its pattern showed he, along with several other vintage items from his cellars, was lying spreadeagle on the library floor. Which explained why his head was now feeling heavy as a French cannonball and his mouth as dry as Spanish dust.

Despite his muzzy wits, it was all beginning to come back to him. Tony's messenger had delivered a hot tip from one of Whitehall's more reliable informants. However, after combing through the rookeries of Seven Dials, he had found that the stolen items being offered for sale were no more than worthless Turkish trinkets, and the purveyor a petty smuggler who had acquired them on one of his routine trips to Antwerp.

So, he had returned home in a foul temper—tired,

wet, cold, and frustrated. Most especially frustrated. *The devil take it!* He had certainly been in no mood to return to his bedchamber. Not after . . .

The earl winced again. *Satan's prick!* Had he really behaved like a randy alleycat, pawing and snabbering over Miss Hadley as if he were some feral beast? And to make matters worse, he seemed to recall plying her with whisky first, in order to take advantage of her weakened resolve as well as her weakened body.

Recalling Taft's joking comment, Branford found himself thinking that he deserved to be hung upside down from the sultan's gates, so that the crows might pick out his eyeballs. And Tony would doubtlessly be the first to agree, for in the matter of espionage, it was a cardinal sin to allow lust to overrule reason. Why, even the most inexperienced agents knew better than think with his pego instead of his brain.

Even if the female in question was not a prime suspect.

Miss Hadley the enemy? There were still unanswered questions regarding her behavior, yet despite his judgment being fuzzed by drink and fatigue, he was finding it harder and harder to believe that she had anything to do with the treacherous plot that threatened the Crown. Yes, she was clever, resourceful, and daring, but there was not a bit of guile or deceit clouding the flash of her jade-green eyes. Indeed, unless her acting talents were as Shakespearean as her name, he was almost certain she was innocent. . . .

At least in one regard.

As to the other. . . . Her passionate response to his intimacies implied that she was no stranger to a man's touch, and given her apparent refusal to be bound by other strictures of Society, he had no reason to think otherwise. Nonetheless, he couldn't help feeling a tiny twinge of guilt. No matter her previous experience and overt invitation, she was still an unmarried young lady. As such, a true gentleman should have controlled his lust.

In mockery of such prim thoughts, a wave of desire crested up and slammed full force into his groin as he recalled removing her shirt and running his tongue down the lovely arch of her neck and over the delicious curves of her breasts. Shifting against the carpet, he felt his shaft growing hard and aroused again. He had a bevy of willing women ready to tumble into his bed, so why was he allowing himself to be bedeviled by lascivious thoughts of an outspoken country chit?

The memory of her mouth parting for his, her tart indignation sweetening into unfeigned passion, caused him to groan in answer.

Perhaps this strange swirl of exasperation and attraction was hard to explain for the simple reason that he had never experienced it before. The maddening Miss Hadley was unlike any female he had ever encountered. Her fiery temper, headstrong boldness, and unbridled opinions were extremely irritating. And yet it was impossible not to admire her dogged determination, deep compassion, and raw courage. With a wry grimace he realized that if she were a man, he would probably consider her a . . . good friend.

After a moment's thought, the earl shook his throbbing head. He must be completely cupshot to have come up with such an absurd notion. Females were not friends but foes.

He drew in a ragged breath. In his experience they fought with the skill and cunning of trained Hussars, always seeking to maneuver men into some trap. Most especially the parson's mousetrap! Over the years he had gained enough experience to be very good at parrying that sort of hand-to-hand combat.

One of the keys was to know the rules of engagement. In battle, there was a fine line dividing boldness from rashness, and he had become quite adept at avoiding the slips that could lead to unconditional surrender. Another key was to keep a cool detachment from the fray. That had always been easy, for rarely had he been tempted to become emotionally involved. Oh, he had taken—and given—physical pleasure, but he had kept his feelings well guarded. In truth, he had built such a fortress around them, he wasn't even sure a heart still existed somewhere deep within the walled shadows.

Not after the shattered bones and sea of blood at Badajoz.

Well, it didn't matter, as he never meant to make it vulnerable to anyone again.

With a low groan he rolled on his side and drew his knees to his chest. But somehow, despite the circling of his defenses, he could not help feeling another sharp-edged thought pricking at his consciousness. Miss Hadley might not be scheming to betray her country, but perhaps her questionable activities of late were proof that she had some other strategy in mind.

After all, the lofty title and hefty fortune he had inherited would certainly solve almost all of her problems. And no doubt it hadn't taken very long for a clever young lady to figure that out.

He had sensed a subtle shift in her attitude toward him, but did the softened sarcasm and heated kisses mean she thought his offer of a temporary truce could be turned into a more . . . permanent alliance? His jaw slowly tightened. He had been a bit slow to react to a threat from *that* direction, but his battlefield skills had not yet become so dulled that she could steal a march on him. He had evaded too many ambushes over the years to be outflanked and outmaneuvered by a green girl. If she was looking for a quick conquest, she had best look elsewhere.

But after another moment or two, his teeth unclenched. In her defense, Branford admitted that in the heat of the fray she may have . . . misunderstood his signals. She was, for all her intelligence and spirit, still young and inexperienced. Contrary to ugly rumor, he did have a code of honor, and he did not wish to see her hurt. He would, he decided, take pains to give her fair warning that trying to trap him into a marriage of convenience was a strategy doomed to go down in ignominious defeat.

Drawing a deep breath, Branford told himself rather forcefully that with such a strategy he could, in good conscience, consider that gentlemanly honor had been satisfied, as long as he took great care to behave himself and keep a proper distance from the young lady in the future. And yet, despite the show of self-assurance, he couldn't quite silence the small voice in the back of his head that questioned whether his decision had more to do with his own cowardice than any more noble sentiments.

Nonsense. He was a seasoned soldier who had never

quailed in the face of danger. What would he be afraid of?

Ignoring the whispered reply that mayhap it was his own feelings that had him turning tail in confusion and running for cover, he screwed his face in grim resolve. The plan he had suggested to Miss Hadley and her brothers would help ensure that she stayed well out of trouble—and well out of reach of his arms. Which, he admitted with just a twinge of guilt, was a bit like trying to close the barn door after the horses had galloped free. Still, he resolved to rein in his animal urges. . . .

The sudden pounding sounded as loud as the kick of hooves against wood. Perhaps, he thought with a vague sense of foreboding, he had better roll to one side in case the door splintered open and a troop of cavalry mounts charged across the carpet.

Sure enough, the paneled oak gave way.

"He's in there, Cap'n. Leastwise, I see a pair of familiar boots sticking out from behind the desk. Want fer me to help ye scrap him off the floor?"

"That won't be necessary." The sound of a labored limp shuffled across the room.

Branford raised his head and squinted but saw only a black shape silhouetted against the garlands and medallions of the ceiling.

"Bloody hell, Alex, you look even worse than I do." Viscount Davenport poked at the earl's outstretched arm with his cane. "You have a devil of a nerve ringing a peal over my head," he grunted, lowering his gaunt frame into one of the armchairs by the hearth. "It appears you, too, have no wish to inhabit the land of the living."

"M-Max?" Branford managed to sit up. "Christ Almighty, is that you?"

"Were you expecting Charon? Judging by the numbers of bottles on the floor, it appears you expected to be ferried across the river Styx."

"Arrgh." The earl rubbed at his bleary eyes, then suddenly brought his mind into sharper focus. "What time is it?"

"Going on three."

Damnation. There wasn't much time in which to make himself presentable. Still, he decided that a mug of black coffee might do just as much for his appearance as a splash of cold water and a shave. "Blaze," he cried, further dismayed to find his voice was a hoarse croak.

"Yes, guv?" The prompt reply suggested that the valet had stationed himself just outside the door.

"A pot of Jamaican brew, and make it as thick as molasses."

"That's not exactly the warm welcome I had in mind." Davenport hefted one of the brandy bottles and held it to the light. "How rude. Didn't leave a drop for an old friend." The unsteady note indicated he had already downed more than a drop himself. "Have Blaze fetch another, eh?"

"As I recall, you were always quite partial to the Irish imp's coffee." Branford found the sight of his friend's haggard face sobering enough to drain the slur from his own words. "Let us drink to old times with that."

Davenport gave a grunt. His fingers tightened around the glass neck, but after a moment of wavering he let it slip to the floor. "Blaze does not appear to have lost any of his old spark."

"No, he still manages to land himself in the frying pan from time to time, but on the whole, he has taken to civilian life better than I expected. And Splinter? I did not see any sign of him when I paid you the visit." Left unsaid was the fact that the viscount's longtime servant would never have permitted his master to descend into such a hellish existence.

"Left him in Yorkshire for the time being. Had no use for him here, and he seemed happy enough to be pottering around the stables and flirting with the parlor maids."

"Ah, so he, too, has adapted tolerably well to life after the army."

"Unlike some." A humorless smile pulled at the viscount's lips. "Tell me, Alex, was that tale of an important intelligence mission a complete hum? For it does not appear as though you are engaged in any meaningful activities at the moment." His friend's self mocking expression grew more pronounced. "Not, of course, that I am in any position to offer criticism."

"No!" Branford added a mental oath at being caught in such an unfortunate state by his friend. "What I told you was the truth! As for this—it is not exactly what it seems. I was out most of the night pursuing a lead."

"Not much luck, I take it," remarked his friend dryly.

The earl grimaced. "You might say that." The lurching of his stomach had stilled enough for him to get to his feet. Running a hand through his hair, he moved to lean against the hearth. "Look, I should like to explain the whole matter in detail. The thing is, I must go out for a bit."

"You need not humor me, Alex. If you wish to withdraw your earlier request, just say so. Don't fob me off with lame excuses."

"Damnation, Max. Don't go. I really could use your help, as I don't seem to be making much headway on my own." He let out a harried sigh. "I won't be gone long. I have to, er, interview a suspect. She—"

"She?" Despite his expression of assumed ennui, Davenport couldn't disguise the surprise in his voice. "You have as your suspect a female?"

"Not one but two of them." Under his breath Branford added, "And the prospect of interrogating either is daunting enough to drive anyone to drink."

His friend fiddled with the carelessly knotted cravat at his throat. "This is taking a rather unusual turn already."

"Ha! You don't know the half of it," muttered the earl.

"When *am* I going to hear the whole of what is going on?"

Feeling that he owed his old comrade some show of trust for the effort he had made, Branford relented. "Oh, very well. But understand, I only have time to sketch the barest of outlines." At the viscount's curt nod he went on, "Not to wax too melodramatic, but the fate of the Empire may rest upon a document that has gone missing. . . ."

"Bloody hell!"

"My words exactly when Tony explained it to me.

His men have still not turned up any tangible clue as to what has happened to the cursed thing."

"If the Saint has no clue, then how——"

"Damnation, any further questions will have to wait until later. As I told you, right now I have an appointment with a Boadicea in britches."

The arch of the viscount's brow twisted his injured features into a more menacing face. "Well, I doubt I shall be of much use to you with women," he remarked with a cynical grunt. "Unless you wish for me to frighten them to death."

Branford's gaze jerked up from the flames. After a moment's study of the viscount's vicious scar and intimidating scowl, a slow grin spread across his face. "Bloody hell, Max. That's *exactly* what I wish for you to do. When I return from the Warrior Queen, the two of us are going to pay a call on the Lady in Red."

Portia looked up from her pacing and glanced at the clock. Was it not possible to recite some ancient Sanskrit incantation to slow the passing of time? she wondered. Or invoke a spell, or curse, or a thunderbolt from the heavens? Because, barring some miracle, the Earl of Branford would be knocking upon the front door in precisely seventeen and a half minutes.

How was she supposed to greet a gentleman who less than twenty-four hours ago had been kissing her with consuming passion and caressing her bare breasts?

Her education had encompassed a great many unorthodox subjects, but that was not one of them.

It was not that she was feeling overwhelmed with

remorse concerning her actions. She had quite consciously tossed every vestige of propriety—along with a good deal of her clothing—to the wind. Her lips had willingly parted, her tongue had entwined with his, her fingers had sought out the naked planes of his chest. As she thought about it, Portia felt her cheeks growing hot as the coals of the parlor fire. And not from any sense of maidenly shame. The truth was, when he had put his mouth over her nipple and run his tongue in lush, languid circles around the rosy flesh, she had found the new experience exciting beyond her wildest dreams.

But the ticking of the clock as she passed close to the hearth was a grim reminder of reality. Entertaining girlish fantasies about the earl's heated embraces was naught but a waste of time. Especially for an aging country spinster. The chilling change that had come over him on hearing his valet's words, and his abrupt departure, should be ample proof that their intimacies had been nothing more to him than another fleeting dalliance.

Her tongue brushed over her lower lip, still tender from the passion of his kisses. For a brief interlude she had thought she had glimpsed something a good deal more complex than lust in his eyes. But perhaps she had been mistaken.

Portia nearly stumbled as her toe snagged on the edge of the carpet. Had she been allowing emotion to cloud reason? On looking back at recent events with an objective eye, it was nigh impossible to deny that something terribly havey-cavey was afoot.

Her steps slowed. It was highly suspicious that

everywhere she turned, she kept running into the Black Cat. Even more disturbing was the fact that he refused to offer any reasonable explanation for his nocturnal prowlings. A knot began to form in the pit of her stomach. The earl knew Dunster and was, to say the least, intimately acquainted with Roxleigh's wife. And then there was the ungodly summons from the Saint.

Good Lord! Could it be that he was in league with the dastards who had kidnapped her father? She swallowed hard. Regardless of the damning evidence, she was finding it increasingly difficult to think of him as an unprincipled cad. Or a vicious beast. Yes, he was cool and clever. But not cruel. If he mean to coax information out of her or stop her investigations, surely he wouldn't have to resort to such underhanded methods as . . . taking her clothes off.

Would he? After all, his valet's stories had made it abundantly clear that intrigue and seduction were second nature to him. The thought caused any lingering warmth to turn ice cold. . . .

A soft knock at the door caused her to flinch.

"Lord Branford to see you."

She flexed her knuckles. "Show him in, Stevens." If the earl imagined she was naught but a meek morsel, one that he could devour in one bite, he was going to have a rude awakening.

"Miss Hadley . . ."

Portia turned. Despite her resolve, she could not help feeling a certain flutter of excitement at the sight of him. A second glance, however, quickly brought her back down to earth. His hooded eyes and shadowed expression gave him the look of someone who had been up to no good.

"I trust you are not experiencing too much discomfort."

She stiffened, wondering whether he was making a subtle mockery of what had occurred just hours ago. "I have recovered quite nicely from the assault," she shot back. "You, on the other hand, appear to have engaged in another sort of hand to mouth combat last night— one in which the bottle emerged victorious."

Was it her imagination, or did a touch of color darken the earl's cheeks?

"Have a seat, sir," she snapped before he could reply. Her voice was honed to an even sharper edge by the realization that she had nearly bungled her strategy by alluding to the latest Incident with the first breath out of her mouth. She was, however, determined to avoid any further mention of it. "I have been thinking long and hard, sir, and there are a number of questions that need answers. So let us get right down to it."

He took a place on the sofa and crossed his long legs with a nonchalance that set her teeth on edge as well. "Ah. No holds barred, I see," he murmured.

"Stubble the games, Lord Branford." Portia remained standing before the crackling fire. "First of all, have you any idea what Lord Mirkham was seeking last night?"

The earl regarded her with an impassive face. "I can hazard a guess. Can you?"

"Am I *never* to get a straight answer out of you?" she demanded. "I swear, you sound as convoluted as Mirkham." Her nose crinkled. "By the by, what was that oddly sweet smoke? Another of Mrs. Grenville's Indian specialties? She had me taste her spiced *chai*—"

"I should avoid sampling the cannabis weed if I were you," he murmured. "It is even more potent than brandy in addling one's wits."

She glared, hoping her cheeks were not glowing as brightly as the lump of hashish. "Let us cease playing cat and mouse, sir. Just what is it you are up to?"

One dark brow rose toward the ceiling. "Up to?" he repeated.

Her fist smacked down upon the marble mantel. Why, she wondered for an instant, were men able to do that without wincing? Repressing the urge to rub her bruised fingers, she shot him another scowl. "Yes, up to! It can be no coincidence that everywhere I step, you are under my feet."

"As I recall, I am sometimes on top."

"That is quite enough, sir! I have no intention of discussing the, er, latest Incident."

"There was nothing incidental about what happened last night—"

"Sir!" Forgoing another whack at the hard stone, Portia contented herself with throwing the earl a verbal punch. "I will not stand for any more of your devious, manipulative, and calculating machinations!"

His smile faded. "Now, Miss Hadley, that is a low blow. I did not—"

"I have *not* finished, sir!"

His mouth fell shut.

"You cannot deny you have been shadowing my steps, and I demand to know why."

The earl remained silent.

"Cat got your tongue?" she jibed. "Or is there some more sinister reason you refuse to answer?" Suddenly aware that his gaze seemed leveled at her chest, she quickly crossed her arms. "And that is not the only explanation I want. Why did you tell Henry and Bertie you meant to help us? You should be ashamed of lying to children!"

That finally roused him to speech. "I have not lied to you or your brothers," he replied hotly. "My offer was genuine. And a damn good thing it was, considering what happened last night. Bloody hell! With every impetuous step you take on your midnight forays, you are coming closer and closer to sticking your spoon in the wall!" He drew in a breath, then moderated his voice to something less than a shout. "Perhaps it is you who should be ashamed of yourself for taking such brazen risks. Your foolhardy actions nearly robbed them of yet another family member. Do you truly wish to leave them veritable orphans?"

"Speaking of low blows!" Portia bit at her lip. "I have told you, I *have* considered the consequences. And dire though they may be, I feel I have no choice but to forge ahead, no matter the dangers. I have always been the one to look out for all of us."

Branford watched in grim silence as she turned to stir the coals and add a log to the fire. "I don't doubt it," he said quietly, once she was done. "However, this once I am offering you a chance to turn back out of harm's way while I take the lead."

It was several moments before she answered.

"Really, sir, do you think me a complete ninny? I am not quite so naive as to fall for such an obvious ruse."

What the devil was she talking about? He was usually able to keep pace with all manner of Machiavellian thought processes, but the workings of this particular female's brain was leaving him in the dust. "What ruse?"

Her arms tightened across her chest. "Where is my father, Lord Branford?" she demanded abruptly. "And why was he kidnapped."

The sudden shift in her thinking caused the throbbing to begin anew in his head. "I am afraid you have lost me, Miss Hadley," he replied. "How the devil do you expect me to know that?"

"Because your cohorts have got him," she explained patiently, as if speaking to a child.

"What?"

Ignoring his outburst, the young lady continued on. "You wish to trick me into giving up my investigation by pretending to help, is that it? Well, it won't work. I warn you, come hell or high water, I mean to find my father."

"You think *I* am involved in his disappearance?" The earl could not quite believe what he was hearing. "Bloody hell—why?"

Her sneer faded slightly. "Well, you have been acting awfully suspiciously. . . ."

"The same might be said for you!"

She had the grace to flush. "I have been entirely forthcoming with the reasons for my actions, while you, on the other hand, have explained nothing!"

"That's not entirely true," Branford answered through

gritted teeth, trying not to sound too defensive. "I told you I was not at liberty to divulge my reasons."

"Hmmph! That is as spurious an answer now as it was the first time you voiced it, sir."

"Nevertheless, it is the only one you are going to get," he muttered.

"I suppose you will also refuse to tell me who the Saint is," she snapped, "or why he should be sending a message to you in the middle of he night?"

"The Saint has *nothing* to do with you, Miss Hadley. I—" He stopped abruptly as he fingered the fobs on his watch chain. "Look, if I had anything to do with the abduction of your father or your property, why would I be skulking around in your shadow?"

Portia answered without hesitation. "To make sure I don't stumble onto the truth."

"That could be ensured with a great deal less effort, Miss Hadley. You have seen how effective a knife or a bullet can be."

She looked a bit less sure of herself now. "Er, well, it might raise too many questions were something . . . *extreme* to happen to me. . . ."

"You might call having your throat slit or brains blown out rather extreme," he growled.

"So, I imagine you decided to use more subtle methods of achieving your goal."

It took a second for him to comprehend her meaning. And when he did, it took another few moments to master his outrage. "You think I deliberately set out to . . ." His mouth thinned to an angry line before he could finish. Did she really believe he had made love to her as a means of manipulation?

She looked back to the fire, the play of light from the licking flames obscuring her expression.

"You still think me a scurrilous cad, worthy of naught but such scathing contempt?" Branford rose stiffly, surprised at how wounded he felt. He supposed he really had no right to be angry at her accusations, but he was. And hurt. In two quick steps he was by her side, his hand cupping her chin to prevent her from turning away. "I may be guilty of certain lapses of judgment, but not the ones you think. I asked you once before to trust me. I am asking you again to do so."

"Why should I?" Her jade green eyes were molten with misgiving.

"Because—" Branford lowered his mouth so it was nearly touching hers—"I give you my word that you won't regret it."

She blinked, then averted her gaze. "I will continue to consider your offer, sir."

"Do, Miss Hadley. Before things take an even more dangerous turn." His hand released its hold on her. "Speaking of trouble, there is another matter we ought to get straight, in order to avoid any further . . . misunderstandings."

Her brow furrowed.

"Consider this fair warning, Miss Hadley. Ladies with far more experience in the field than you possess have tried any number of ploys to maneuver me to the altar. As you see, they failed. So if you have designs on forcing a marriage of convenience, put them out of your head.

"M-marriage," she sputtered, her features scrunching in patent disbelief. "You think *I* wish to entrap *you*? Good Lord! What ever gave you such a cork-brained notion?"

"Most young ladies wish above all things to be married!"

"Well, as you may have noticed, I am not like most young ladies! I never wish to be leg-shackled. And if I did, it most certainly would not be to *you!*"

Her answer should have elicited a sigh of relief, and yet, he found himself frowning. "Why not?"

She looked taken aback by the question. "We should be here the rest of the day if I were to catalog all the reasons."

The thought that she didn't think he would make a good husband was unaccountably rankling, though he took pains not to show it. "No doubt the list would prove fascinating," he replied with a sardonic drawl. "But unfortunately I have another engagement that prevents me from lingering so long." Out of the corner of his eye he had caught sight of the ormolu clock on the mantel, and loath though he was to leave the conversation on such a note, he could not stay much longer if he was to have any hope of catching the Lady in Red at home. "However," he continued, "you may be assured I will return tomorrow."

The announcement did nothing to smooth the scowl from her face.

"One last thing. Your wound—"

"Is no cause for concern," she said curtly. "Despite your valet's dire observations, it is hardly more than a scratch. A bit of laudanum has dulled any discomfort, so do not give it another thought. I told you, I can take care of myself, sir."

"That may be so," he muttered, taken aback by the sudden urge to shelter her within his arms. "The trouble is, you think you have to carry your whole family upon those shoulders, bullet holes and all." After one more quick glance at the clock, the earl turned and left the room. However, he decided to make one last stop before quitting the Trumbull town house.

The touch of his fingers still singeing her flesh, Portia was barely aware of the heat from the hearth. Her nails dug into her arms as she heard his steps retreat across the carpet and the door fall shut. So much for strategy, she thought glumly. All her plans had gone up in smoke the minute he entered the room.

She had reacted just like some peagoose heroine in a Minerva Press novel, allowing herself to be distracted by the sight of those sapphire eyes and chiseled features, no matter that they had looked a trifle worn by whatever he had been up to. She had thought she had more than feathers for brains, but apparently she was grossly mistaken. For only a birdwitted idiot would have failed to press for the answers to her questions, rather than let the conversation veer so completely off course.

Marriage? Her face took on a dull burn. From anger, she assured herself, and not any spark of regret. She had meant what she had said—she had long ago vowed never to give up her independence. However, that he considered the threat of being forced to offer for her hand so dire that it prompted such a warning was wounding. Much as she wished to deny it, she had come to feel a certain warmth for the earl, and had thought the sentiment returned. She had no illusions as to her attractiveness to him, but the overt rejection had hurt far more than the ball of lead that had pierced her shoulder.

Even worse, not only had she failed to learn anything more about his own mysterious doings and that of the sinister Saint, but everything about Mrs. Grenville and the strange scene they had witnessed the previous evening remained an enigma.

And, of course, there was the tantalizing bit of information she had read in the newspaper, which she had never had a chance to mention.

What the devil was wrong with her? Between her familial responsibilities and her scholarly interests, she certainly had no desire and no need for anything else in her life. Especially a roguish rake who reduced her rational thoughts to ashes. . . .

Though she fully expected it was coming, the knock on the door caused her to jump.

"So?" demanded Henry, not waiting for a response to barge right in. "Did you give Lord Branford your decision?"

"As a matter of fact, I did," answered Portia tartly.

"Well? What was it?"

"That I am still thinking about it."

Bertie's face screwed in dismay. "Thinking about it? But that is just the answer you give us when what you really mean is that there is no bloody way on earth you are going to say yes!"

"Bertram Orlando!"

He cringed. "Sorry."

"I should see that your mouth is rinsed out with

soap and water, young man." But, recalling that her own behavior had been less than spotless of late, she relented. "We will forget about any punishment this time. Just promise me you won't repeat that in front of Aunt Octavia."

"I promise." His toe scuffed at the carpet. "But I wish you would let Lord Branford help us. If you ask me, he's a great gun—"

Portia winced at the mention of firearms.

"—and skilled in the art of warfare. It seems that it would not hurt to have a seasoned soldier on our side."

"I *will* consider it, Bertie. But trust me, there is more to the matter than bullets and brawn."

His lower lip jutted out, but he didn't argue any further. Turning away, he began to poke at the pile of papers set on the corner of the desk.

To forestall the comment she saw forming on Henry's lips, she exaggerated a sniffle. "I'm still feeling somewhat under the weather, so I'm going to lie down for a bit and look over these volumes on Eastern art to see if I might yet come up with a clue concerning the book Mr. Huffington sent over." Hurrying to the escritoire, she reached for the stack she had brought in earlier from the library. The movement, however, sent a jolt of pain through her injured shoulder and she twisted awkwardly. To her dismay, the books fell to the floor.

Henry knelt to retrieve them, but not before fixing her with a searching look. "What's wrong with your arm?"

"N-nothing. My slipper caught on the carpet."

He, too, refrained from pressing her, but it was clear from his expression that the answer was far from convincing. "Bertie," he muttered, "stop dawdling and come give me a hand."

"Oh . . . er, right." The youngest Hadley bent down to pick up the volume by his foot. After passing it to his brother, he held up the piece of paper he had been perusing. "This is really quite interesting. At first glance it's naught but random numbers, but then a pattern appears to emerge. I should like to study it more closely, if you don't mind."

Portia saw it was the list of expenses she had taken from Dunster's desk drawer. She had set it aside as useless, so if for some reason it provided him with a bit of amusement in mathematical theory, she had no objection. "By all means, take it."

"Hmmm." His head was already bent over the columns of numbers. "Look at this. . . ."

Seizing the moment to escape, she snatched the books from Henry's grasp and stumbled for the stairs. *Hell's bells!* she thought in dismay. She wasn't sure how much longer she could keep up the juggling act before all the balls came crashing down upon her head.

"Shot?" Lady Trumbull gave an owlish squint through her spectacles. "How on earth did *that* happen? Despite all the scandalous talk, I cannot imagine that you have taken to dueling with young ladies."

"I did not pull the trigger." Branford could not help but admire the dowager's spark of gritty humor in the face of such shocking news. "Of that I can assure you."

"Well, I did not seriously think you had." The elderly lady's expression turned grim. "Have you any idea who did?"

"Not yet. But I intend to find out."

"Well, you seem to be very clever about that sort of thing." Lady Trumbull's pen tapped thoughtfully against her chin. "I am, of course, enormously grateful for your concern for my niece. I have tried to counsel her to be more . . . cautious, but I fear the words of an old lady have had little effect."

At least one female in the household seemed to appreciate his efforts to be a gentleman, thought the earl with a wry sigh.

"And as for your confidences," she continued, "I assume you have a good reason for telling me this, Lord Branford." He thought he discerned a slight twinkle in her eye. "For I doubt you are much given to acting on mere whim."

"How astute of you, Lady Trumbull." He inclined his head in polite salute, drawing a chuckle from her.

"I am not quite so dotty as I appear," she answered, the flash behind the glass lenses growing a bit brighter.

"I can see one would be making a grave mistake to think you were not awake on all suits, madam."

"Charming as well as clever—I wish I were forty years younger, my dear man."

"You might be in real danger if you were." He draped one leg over the corner of her desk and leaned in closer. "Or haven't you been attending to the gossip making the rounds of the drawing rooms?"

"Pfffph. You mean that drivel about you?" Her gnarled hands gave a dismissive wave before they set to shuffling a stack of manuscript pages. "I think I would take my chances. After all, life is rather boring when one never takes a risk."

"True. But it is my impression that your young relatives are inclined to take that philosophy rather too much to heart. Especially your niece."

"I am afraid it is a family weakness. Sometimes I think I am the only sensible one of the lot." Lady Trumbull sighed. "So, what do you have in mind?" she asked in a conspiratorial whisper.

"Only that you use that good sense to see to it that a physician is summoned to check up on her. If left up to her own discretion, she would let her bloo—er, blasted arm fall off before admitting the need for any help. You might use her sniffles as an excuse for concern, or—"

"Leave it to me, Lord Branford. You need not worry over the details."

"I was counting on as much. In the meantime I shall make some inquiries into the matter." He picked at a crease on his sleeve. "Er, just one or two last things, if I may. It would be best if the boys do not get wind of bullets having been fired. Just as I would rather that Miss Hadley does not suspect that I went behind her back, so to speak."

Lady Trumbull squared her frail shoulders. "Really, sir. I told you I am not a bloody idiot." She dipped her pen in the inkwell and pulled over a fresh sheet of foolscap. "Now run along and let me get back to my Cicero." Her gaze flitted to the marble bust of the ancient poet that sat atop one of her bookshelves. "Though he is not nearly so dashing as the Black Cat."

❧❀❧

Chapter Thirteen

"About time you got back." Davenport lifted a glass to his lips. The earl was relieved to see it contained naught but milk.

Milk? Where the devil had Blaze come up with a glass of milk?

The viscount caught the glance. "Vile stuff. But Blaze insisted. Assured me it would put flesh on my bones."

"Well, that's an improvement in his social skills. Last night he was assuring a young lady that whisky would put hair on her chest."

Davenport nearly choked on the mouthful. "Why would he tell her that?"

"He was under the impression it would encourage her not to faint as I was patching up the bullet hole in her arm."

"How—"

"Don't ask," muttered Branford as he rummaged in one of his desk drawers. He finally managed to locate the small pistol he kept for emergencies and slid it into his coat pocket. "Come along. We have to hurry if we are to catch the lady before she goes out."

The viscount's one visible eye narrowed. "The one who was shot?"

"No, no, I have just come from the Warrior Queen. We are going to see the Lady in Red."

"The Warrior Queen and and the Lady in Red?" murmured his friend. "This whole affair is becoming more . . . extraordinary by the minute."

Branford allowed a tiny smile. "Yes, and you have yet to hear of the children."

"Children!" Davenport shuddered. "Spent a week with my cousin's brood and nearly went out of my skull with boredom."

"Trust me, you will not be bored by these two." The drawer banged shut. "Pull on your gloves, Max. We must be off."

The viscount showed no sign of budging. "Didn't wear any gloves." He gave a low growl and ran a hand through his uncombed hair—a rather difficult task, as the tangle of tawny locks fell nearly to his shoulders. "Not in any condition to visit a lady, no matter whether she is red, purple, or molded out of green cheese."

Branford's gaze traveled up from the tips of his friend's scuffed Hessians, threadbare waistcoat, and soiled cravat to his brooding profile. A three day stubble clung to the lean cheeks and chin, though it did nothing to hide the bony angles revealed by the loss of weight. And while Max's eyes had once been an unusual shade of rich amber, the one not covered by the black patch was so murky as to appear a dull, muddied gray. "On the contrary, your appearance is perfect."

Davenport's head snapped around. "Don't be an ass, Alex. The sight of me and my gruesome phiz will have her cowering under the nearest sofa."

"Let us hope so," he replied, a wicked smile beginning to play on his lips. "The Lady in Red has stood her ground in the preliminary skirmishes. It is time we launch a full-blown attack—perhaps calling in the heavy artillery will rattle her into making a fatal mistake." After one last check of his pockets, Branford started for the door. "Hurry," he urged, giving a tug to his friend's rumpled sleeve. "It's getting late and I don't want to chance missing her."

Curiosity appeared to win out over cynicism. With a grudging shake of his head, the viscount levered himself to his feet. "Never thought I would live to see the day the Black Cat needed reinforcements to face off against a mere female."

"*Mere* female?" Branford shoved his friend's cane into his hands. "Ha! Let us see what tune you are whistling in an hour."

The low rush of the air escaping from a startled Davenport was muffled by the rustle of silk and the slap of sandals. "An unconventional butler," he murmured, watching the turbaned figure pad away down the hall, embroidered tunic flapping around his knees in a flutter of brilliant colors.

"An unconventional lady," replied Branford softly. He took a moment to study the small parlor, with its bold furnishings and juxtaposition of art. "One who appears to be a master of the unexpected." Recalling the servant's deadly prowess with his hands, he narrowed his eyes. "Don't underestimate either of them, Max, on account of their being a female and a foreigner."

"My brain is not quite so pickled that I have forgotten the basic rules of the game, Alex," muttered his friend. "You need not worry about me being taken by surprise."

Nonetheless, the sight of the sultry widow did cause his uncovered eye to widen. The earl, too, could not help staring as she made her entrance into the room. Dressed in a stunning shade of rose pink that set off her ivory coloring and jet-black hair, she certainly cut a striking figure—one that would have most gentlemen thinking of little else but what lay beneath the clinging silk. That, he imagined, was exactly the reaction the daring design of her gown was calculated to cause. If he didn't know better, he would have likened her to an exotic flower, lush and lovely to look at. But he was well aware it would be a grave mistake to think of her as naught but a decorative bloom.

"Lord Branford." Mrs. Grenville acknowledged his bow with a cool nod. "This is a surprise."

"Not an unpleasant one, I trust." As there was no immediate response, he went on. "Allow me to introduce Lord Davenport, an old friend who has only recently returned from the Peninsula. Having heard so much about you of late, he was quite anxious to meet you in the flesh."

"And I have heard of the Valiant Viscount and his exploits at Ciudad Rodrigo." Mrs. Grenville took a step closer to the other man and appeared to be studying the red gash cutting across his face. Branford saw his friend go rigid, as if steeling himself for the inevitable shriek of horror.

The only sound to escape from the lady's lips was a

brusque "Hmmph." She tilted her head to regard the puckered wound from another angle. "What is your doctor using to treat that?"

Clearly taken off guard, Davenport hesitated before replying. "Nothing."

"Idiot."

The viscount recoiled, his wary expression indicating he was unsure just who the epithet was directed at.

"What the English medical profession knows about healing could fit on the tip of a scalpel." The words were punctuated by another snort. "Idiot," she repeated. "It is scandalous that a soldier should have to suffer twice for the sacrifices for Crown and country."

"You speak as if you hold loyalty in high regard," murmured the earl, fixing her with a penetrating stare.

Brow still furrowed, Mrs. Grenville gave no response, save to indicate that they should be seated on the sofa. As the earl and his friend sank down into the lush burgundy velvet, she gave a clap of her hands. "Would you care for tea?"

"Not really," replied Branford, determined to take the offensive by matching her own cool frankness.

The turbaned servant padded in, and after murmuring a few words in his ear she waved him off. "Perhaps a smoke, then?" Her hands reached for the ebony box on the side table.

"What are you offering? Turkish cheroots?" He flicked a speck of dust from his Hessians. "Or perhaps something more interesting—say, Bengali hashish."

The polished wood nearly slipped from her grasp. "W-what makes you think I would have such a substance in my possession," she asked with a casual laugh.

To the earl's ear it sounded rather forced. He smiled. "Why, as a purveyor of the exotic, I imagine you have all sorts of intriguing things for sale."

Mrs. Grenville was quick to recover her poise. "I would not have thought a proper English gentleman would be interested in hashish, Lord Branford."

"Ah, but Davenport and I are not typical tulips of the *ton*. We are interested in a great many things, Mrs. Grenville."

"Such as?"

"Information."

If she was startled by his words, she hid it well. "A great many people here in Town seem to think I deal in more than spices and condiments."

The earl chose a thin cigar wrapped in Virginia leaf and lit it from one of the candles. Exhaling a pungent plume, he watched it drift toward the ceiling. "Where there is smoke, there is usually fire."

She took up a Turkish cheroot and leaned toward the flame. "Perhaps it is merely steam from a hot curry."

Their verbal fencing was interrupted by the reappearance of the servant. Nearly hidden by the billowing sleeves of his silk tunic was a small copper tray, upon which rested a single item.

Mrs. Grenville said several words in Hindi.

The servant turned and with a low bow presented the viscount with the squat glass jar, the top of which was sealed with crimson wax. The contents looked to be a viscous substance the color of crushed mangoes with flecks of lime green and chili red swirled throughout.

Davenport, whose gaze had become rather unfocused, recoiled as if it were a cobra about to spit in his good eye. "What the devil is that? And why is he shoving it at me?"

"It is for that slash across your face. Apply it twice daily and you will quickly find the scar all but disappears."

"You expect me to put that . . . *peacock potion* on my flesh?"

"Suit yourself. Despite the odd appearance, it works wonders." She shrugged. "However, if you wish to resemble a Maori savage for the rest of your years, that is entirely your affair." Ignoring a curse that would have caused most ladies to turn a vivid crimson, the widow motioned for her servant to put it on the side table, then turned back to the earl. "Was there some specific reason you stopped by, Lord Branford? A purchase, perhaps?"

"Possibly. But I have a great many questions to ask before I make up my mind."

"I can give you the direction to my offices. The clerks there are extremely knowledgeable."

"I prefer to deal directly with you."

"What sort of merchandise are you interested in?" she asked after taking a moment to rearrange the ends of her sash.

"Only your most valuable items. Be assured that I am prepared to pay quite handsomely if I see what I want."

"I shall have to consult my inventory."

"Naturally. However, bear in mind that I wish to act quickly. And while others might be interested in bidding for your goods, I should be sorely disappointed to hear I lost out to, say, a gentleman like Mirkham or Dunster."

The hand holding the cheroot shook just enough to send a spattering of ash onto the carpet.

Satisfied that his tactics were having the desired effect, Branford exhaled one last puff of smoke, then made to rise. "Come, Max, we are in danger of staying past the hour deemed acceptable for a social call." Regarding the widow out of the corner of his eye, he added, "Perhaps Lord Davenport and I might return at a more convenient time for conversation. Would tomorrow suit you?"

Unlike her gown, Mrs. Grenville's face had not the faintest trace of color left to it. "I—I fear I may be occupied for most of the day with some pressing matters of business."

Branford placed his card upon the table. "Then I shall await word from you as to when you might be free. But pray, do not delay too long. I understand enough about business to know it is important to move fast if one hopes to best the competition."

His strategic withdrawal was slowed somewhat by Davenport, who had slumped back against the shell-pink pillows, his one visible eye squeezed shut. The earl gave a silent oath on seeing that sweat was beginning to bead on his friend's brow and that his hands betrayed a slight tremor, even though they were clenched into fists. *Bloody hell,* he chided himself. In the heat of battle he had momentarily forgotten that

Davenport was waging a fight of his own. And he had seen enough in the army to know that brandy and laudanum were powerful adversaries. "Come, Max," he murmured again. "Let me give you a hand."

"Your companion does not look as though he will be accompanying you anywhere on the morrow," said the lady softly. "Opium is a good deal harder to give up than hashish. But if you are truly his friend, you will try to make sure that he does. Otherwise it will not be a French saber that sends him to his grave, but a Chinese poppy."

"Thank you for the sage counsel, Mrs. Grenville." Branford hesitated a moment, then slipped the jar of brightly colored ointment into his pocket before getting to his feet. "I shall offer some advice of my own. You, too, would be wise to handle Eastern merchandise with great care. Opium is not the only item from the Orient that may prove deadly if misused."

She bent down to stub out her smoke, the quick movement obscuring her expression. "That sounds suspiciously like a warning, sir."

"Perhaps it is."

Gritting his teeth, Davenport waved off the offer of help and managed to get to his feet unaided.

"Then I had better take heed. If I have heard correctly, you were also involved in the Peninsular campaigns," murmured Mrs. Grenville. "By all accounts, it was a brutal, nasty business."

"War usually is," replied Branford as he watched his friend summon up a last bit of strength to square his shoulders. "But that is all in the past. We are merely two old dogs nursing old wounds. We have laid aside our sabers and are looking forward to enjoying all the pleasures of Polite Society for a change."

Mrs. Grenville had recovered enough of her nerve to manage a cool reply. "Well, let us hope you are not finding civilian life too dull, sir." Her skirts kicked up in a sensual swoosh around her ankles as she moved for the door. Over the whisper of silk, her parting comment was audible to her ears only. "For somehow I doubt that a Cat ever really changes his color. Or should I say, stripes."

Portia tugged at the sash of her wrapper, as if the rearrangement of her garment might help straighten the disarray of her thoughts. Several hours had passed since the earl had taken his leave, and yet, she still was having trouble considering the meeting, and his proposal, with any semblance of cool, rational detachment.

Pulling a handkerchief from her pocket, she blew her nose. If only she could blame these odd surges of fever on some physical ailment. However, she knew quite well that they had nothing to do with a case of chilblains or a touch of catarrh. The only affliction she was suffering from was a growing attraction to a dangerous rake.

And the only medicine was to concentrate on her investigation rather than the arrogant tilt of that acquiline nose or the thick waves of raven-colored hair curling around his collar.

The trouble was, it was not merely his sensual masculinity that had melted her initial disdain. The earl had let slip his mask enough to allow a peek at what lay beneath the show of jaded cynicism. Though he wished to keep it well hidden, he had shown himself to be a gentleman of sensibility, intelligence, and honor. And, if she was not greatly mistaken, one capable of feeling grief, loss, and loneliness. The revelations had only made her like him more.

But could she trust him?

With another watery sniff, she dipped her pen in the ink and forced her attention back to her notes.

Dunster. Roxleigh. Mirkham. Portia stared at the names she had just jotted on a fresh sheet of paper. One of those gentlemen could now be crossed off the list of possible suspects to pursue. That left the other two. And, she realized with a grimace, Roxleigh's demise did not eliminate a myriad of questions concerning what he had to do with her father's disappearance.

If. How. Why. Head bent, she wrote down several headings, but then she paused, and her pen fell to doodling a series of curlicues on the page. A number of tantalizing clues had come to light, if only she could piece them together in a logical pattern. Surely, if she concentrated hard enough, she would find the answer staring her right in the face. . . .

Her breath came out in a sharp hiss as she looked down and saw that her random scribbles had somehow taken the form of a sketchy portrait, the angular features crowned with a mane of thick black hair. Repressing an oath, she quickly added a pair of fangs to the mocking lips. The result caused a momentary quirk of satisfaction, and yet, as she stared at her handiwork, she knew the Black Cat could not be dismissed with a sniff and a stroke of her pen.

Though she had thought him a mere caricature of a drunken wastrel after their first encounter, she had quickly learned that he had a good deal more depth than a scratch of ink. And a good deal more complexity. The image of an indolent rake hid a number of admirable qualities. Yet it also masked a fearsome predator, one with razor-sharp teeth, claws, and cunning.

Dangerous. The word came to mind again.

Portia laid aside the pen and propped her chin on her palm. There was no doubt that the earl could be very dangerous. The question was, whose side was he on? Her fingers felt for her father's ring beneath her wrapper. It was perhaps naive thinking on her part, but she could not quite believe he meant her any harm. He had certainly had his chances to rip her to shreds. But he hadn't. Indeed, despite his occasional snarls and growls, he seemed to care about her and her brothers.

Or was he simply toying with her? The burnished gold suddenly felt rather cold against her skin. Was he merely using such ploys to keep her off balance until it suited him to move in for the kill?

It was yet another question to which she did not know the answer! The realization was chilling, and with her thoughts in a whirl of confusion, she rose and went to stand before the fire. *Did she dare step into the flames?* Despite all her misgivings, she longed to think she might trust him. And what had she to lose? It was not as if things could get much worse, she mused with a rueful sigh. She had taken a number of other terrible chances so far, and somehow managed to survive. So perhaps it was worth the risk. Perhaps she should abandon all caution and tell him everything.

Including what she knew of the Jade Tiger and the *Lotus of the Orient*.

Sparks flared up from a last bit of burning log, then fell into the glowing embers. The crackling still echoing in her ears, she turned away and began to pace.

"Damn it, you have no right to keep me a prisoner here," came the querulous growl from Davenport. "I want to go back to my own bed."

Branford regarded his friend's drawn face and steeled his jaw. "There is no way in hell I am allowing you to return to that cesspool you presently call home." He turned to Blaze. "Help me get his boots off, then make sure he does not stir from under the covers until I return."

The valet gave a grim nod. "Aye, gov. I'll see to it, if I have to lash his limbs to the bedposts."

On noting the fresh set of tremors shuddering through Davenport's frame, the earl heaved a sigh. "I fear you may not be exaggerating."

"The devil take it, get me some brandy," demanded the viscount. "Still have a few bad spells, but a swig of spirits will do the trick."

"Not tonight, Max. We have, however, ordered up a bit of beef broth from the kitchen."

Although he was well accustomed to foul language, Branford winced at the torrent of obscenities that greeted the announcement. "Do I take that to mean you would prefer gruel?" he asked dryly.

Teeth clenched, Davenport lapsed into a surly silence.

"Try to get some nourishment into him," he murmured to his valet.

"Don't worry, guv. If I have to force feed him like a Strasbourg goose, I will see that Cricket swallows something more wholesome than spirits."

"My thanks, Blaze. I shall try not to be long, but unfortunately I have to put in an appearance at Lady Henshaw's *musicale* in order to give Tony an update on how things are going."

Blaze grinned. "Give me regards to the Saint. How is he holding up to the rigors of married life?"

"Quite well, though I daresay Lady Cecilia does not allow him to become too complacent. She can be as formidable a foe as Marshal Nye at times, but our former comrade seems to enjoy the challenge."

"Hmmph." The valet shook his head in disbelief. "Well, I'll tell ye, the only cat's paw I wish to be under is yours, guv."

Branford gave a curt laugh. "I doubt that either of us are in imminent danger of being caught in the parson's mousetrap, so don't fret on it." He tugged at his open collar. "Though perhaps a wife might remember in what drawer my cravats are located."

A starched length of linen duly located and looped into a *trone d'amour,* the earl finished dressing for the evening and set off for his rendezvous.

The soprano's trilling rendition of an aria from Mozart's *Le Nozze di Figaro* only exacerbated the feeling that a corkscrew was spiraling into the back of his skull. He accepted a glass of champagne from one of the passing footmen, figuring that it might help drown out the worst of the warbling. The hostess was known for the quality of her lavish suppers and free flowing spirits, but not for her discernment of musical talent. The only way the performance could get worse, Branford decided, would be if he attempted to sing in falsetto.

To his relief, there was a brief intermission in the program. Joining a number of other guests who appeared equally anxious to retreat from the confines of the room, the earl moved toward the terrace. As arranged, he wandered to the far end, where a trellis of overhanging ivy partially obscured the view, and lit up a cheroot. Leaning back against the stone balusters, he blew out a perfect smoke ring and watched it quickly disappear in the swirl of the night breeze.

"Let us hope your other efforts are not proving quite so nebulous."

"It is *your* document that has disappeared into thin air," replied Branford without turning his head. "And it would help if you and your agents might offer something of more substance than the word of a gin-soaked pickpocket."

Taft shifted in the shadows. "Christ Almighty, I am trying, Alex." He, too, lit up a smoke. "You learned nothing from the surveillance?"

"Only that I am getting too old to be crouching in a sodden pile of rubbish for hours on end, and too slow to be chasing suspects through a maze of rookeries," quipped the earl as he took another puff and regarded the glowing coal of his cheroot. "The tip from your informant came to nothing. However, I might have stumbled onto a much more promising lead." He gave a succinct summary of what had occurred at the widow's town house the previous evening. There was, of course, no way to avoid mention of Miss Hadley's presence, or of the subsequent shot, but he kept the account down to the bare bones.

Still, the story drew a low whistle from his friend. "This whole damn affair is taking on more bizarre twists and turns than one of Scheherazade's tales," muttered Taft. "Yet another gentleman of the *ton* involved with the Lady in Red—shall I put a tail on Mirkham?"

"No, not yet. Let us not do anything that might alert the enemy until I have had a chance to plan my next move."

"Well, remember that time is running damn short. Tsar Alexander is demanding a meeting with our envoy, and we cannot put it off much longer. If the truth comes out that we no longer possess the document, our alliance with the Russian Bear may dissolve as quickly as your ring of smoke."

"I am aware of that, Tony." Branford tossed away the butt of his cheroot. "Any word yet on the inquiries I asked you to make on Lord Dunster?"

"As a matter of fact, I was just going to get to that. Your claws may have grown a bit dull from lack of use, but it appears your instincts are still sharp as ever. Once my men started digging around, they did turn up some rather interesting information." He lowered his voice even more. "Knew him to be a loose screw, just didn't realize how loose. The first bit of probing uncovered some nasty rumors about his involvement with a gambling scheme that has been fleecing young men newly arrived in Town of their fortunes. Nothing that could be proved beyond a doubt, but enough to make me want to dig deeper."

Branford's mouth thinned.

"With the application of some muscle, our shovels came up with even more dirt. We have learned that the marquess appears to have his hand in any number of other sordid deals—from supplying brothels with fresh girls from the country, to smuggling hard currencies, to fencing stolen merchandise."

"Stolen merchandise," murmured the earl. "An interesting coincidence."

"Even more so is the fact that the murdered Lord Roxleigh had been a close crony of Dunster since university days."

Roxleigh and Dunster. The pieces of the puzzle that had been floating around in his head suddenly snapped together. Roxleigh had been one of the other half-naked men with the marquess when Dunster had stumbled upon him and Miss Hadley in the library. *Damnation!* Now, if only he could remember who had been the third. However, try as he might to picture it, that face still remained submerged in his memory. "I am as skeptical about coincidences as you are, Tony. I think it is time I take advantage of my own less-than-sterling reputation to strike up a closer acquaintance with the marquess."

"Word has it he can be found most nights at a certain establishment in Seven Dials run by a Mrs. Wynwood. It is known to the cognoscenti as the House of Flowers."

"I am familiar with the name," said Branford, with a curl of his lip.

"Cecilia would no doubt carve out my liver if I even admitted that much," growled Taft. "However, by pulling in a few favors, I have managed to establish one of our men inside the place. I daresay you will recognize him, for the two of you worked together on several occasions in Lisbon."

The earl smiled. "He should blend in quite nicely."

After a quirk of his own lips, Taft began to tug at the fobs on his watch chain. "What about this complication with the Hadley chit?" His brow furrowed. "You say the young lady was shot?"

"A mere scratch." Having omitted a good many of the details surrounding that particular part of the evening, the earl decided it would be best to downplay the incident. "There is no reason to be concerned about having another dead body on our hands," he said lightly. However, some slight nuance in his voice drew a strange look from the other man.

"Perhaps not. But I cannot like the fact that she keeps turning up under such suspicious circumstances." Taft paused, as if expecting some sort of reply from Branford. When none was forthcoming, he pressed on with an outright question. "Wouldn't you agree that all the evidence seems to indicate that she is in some way involved with our enemy?"

"No." Realizing that he sounded as if he were trying to convince himself as well as his friend, Branford took a moment to regain a measure of control. "Actually, I think it quite likely she is telling the truth, and that she is an innocent pawn in this game of intrigue."

Taft made a face. "I hope that is your brain speaking and not some lower portion of your anatomy."

"Ha!" A disparaging snort punctuated his exclamation. "Don't worry—after all my years of experience, I am not about to confuse reason with lust, Tony. Especially not for a headstrong country miss whose outrageous behavior would put an Amazon to blush."

"I hope you are right," murmured Taft. His expression, however, betrayed a lingering doubt. "Yet, I cannot help but think it would be a grave mistake to ignore the Hadley connection to our conundrum."

Seeing as Hadleys were impossible to ignore, there was little cause for such concern. "I have no intention of doing so."

"Hmmph." His friend still sounded unconvinced. "Whatever it is you have in mind, you had better move quickly."

"I mean to keep a close eye on the widow, as well as to cozen up to the marquess and his cronies. And to have another little chat with the Warrior Queen." At the lift of his friend's brow, he quickly added, "That is, Miss Hadley. Though I believe her innocent, I think she has not told me all she knows." He paused for just a fraction. "At the same time, I'm going to have Max go over the latest information you passed on from Constantinople to see if he can spot something we both have missed."

"Max?" Taft coughed on a mouthful of smoke. "How the devil did you convince him to crawl out of the depths of hell?"

"One step at a time." He shook his head. "But God knows, it won't be an easy climb."

"I fear all of us are treading a treacherously steep slope," replied his friend, "and one slip could mean utter disaster." Straightening the tails of his waistcoat, Taft flicked away the rest of his cigar. "I had best be getting back to the music before my absence is noted. And you?"

"I plan on making a quick exit through the card room. I would rather face a horde of screaming Nubians than another aria from Madame La Noille."

"All joking aside, Alex, you had better watch your step. Our unknown enemy is infinitely more dangerous than an army of savage warriors. And infinitely more cunning. The next bullet that comes whistling out of the shadows may well be aimed at *your* head."

"Well, on that encouraging note, I shall take my leave." After several paces he hesitated. "However, I cannot help wondering . . ."

"Wondering what?"

Branford kept a straight face. "If my assailant were at a distance of fifty yards, using a large-bore hunting pistol primed with top-grade powder, what size hole would be drilled through my skull?"

Chapter Fourteen

❧❦❧

As she made another turn of the room, Portia grabbed up her notes, sorely tempted to consign the lot of them to the flames of the fire. As she did, the scrap she had torn from *The Morning Gazette* fluttered free and came to rest by the inkwell. Her eyes skimmed over the terse announcement, causing the rest of the papers to fall back to the leather blotter with a thump. Smoothing out the wrinkled bit of paper, she reread the lines, then looked up, her face scrunched in thought. Along with a few bare facts, the smudged type seemed to beg the question anew.

Did she dare trust the earl? He had given her no reasonable explanations for his skulking about, only his word that his intentions were honorable. *Were they?* No amount of pacing would bring her any closer to the answer, she decided. She would simply have to close her eyes and make a leap of faith.

Unconsciously, she turned to the window. If she was going to make up her mind, she would have to do it fast. By morning it might be too late to act.

The ticking of the mantel clock suddenly sounded loud as gunfire, each passing second causing her to flinch. A log snapped in the grate, sending up a shower of sparks. Uttering several of her coachman's more fiery oaths, she threw off her wrapper and hurriedly changed into her darkest gown, then grabbed up her cloak.

It was, she knew, only a short walk through the back alleyways to the earl's residence. Having made the same trip quite recently, she had no trouble picking her route past darkened mews and walled gardens. To her relief, the gate to his garden was still unlocked, and as she nudged it open and moved noiselessly over the grass, she was also grateful for the knowledge that no snapping, growling mastiff would be waiting to tear her limb from limb.

However, how a certain Black Cat would react to her trespassing was an entirely different matter.

It was only after tiptoeing up the stairs to the back terrace that the vague sense of unease took the form of an uncomfortable thought, causing her to stop short. While she could not, for obvious reasons, march up to his front door and drop the knocker, just how was she going to announce her presence? Up until that moment she had been so caught up in her own pressing concerns that it had not occurred to her that her arrival might be not only awkward but unwelcome.

Especially if he was not alone.

Her cheeks turned a bit warm, despite the coolness of the breeze. Was she yet again guilty of the sort of reckless behavior that was going to land her in deep trouble? Pulling her cloak a bit tighter, she stood motionless by the stone balusters, debating whether or not to beat a hasty retreat, when suddenly a light flared to life in the room directly in front of her and one of the casement windows banged open.

"Bloody hell, Alex. I have damn good reason for feeling hot under the collar!" A tangle of tawny hair glimmered in the moonlight as a head leaned out over the sill and drew in a deep gulp of the bracing night air. "If I am to join forces with you and the Saint, I demand to be kept fully informed of the latest developments."

Portia shrank back against the cold granite, her eyes growing wide with shock as the face turned in her direction. If this was the sort of monstrous ruffian the Earl of Branford was in league with, then she had no doubt embarked on a fool's errand.

"Or perhaps you don't trust me," continued the gruff growl. "Seeing as the stakes are so high, you may be worried that I will somehow jeopardize your efforts by slipping back to the brandy and opium."

His words sent a frisson of fear down her spine. But despite the trembling of her limbs, Portia abandoned all thoughts of fleeing. No matter the risk, she was not about to give up a golden opportunity to learn what the earl was up to. As the man turned away for a moment, Portia slipped from the railing and took a position behind a large marble urn filled with ivy.

"Keep your chirping down, Cricket. I would prefer we don't alert all of Mayfair to our plans, if you please."

She had no trouble in recognizing the baritone drawl as Branford's.

"Of course I trust you. I merely thought that you might be worn out from your earlier exertions and would rather hear all the details in the morning." The earl had joined the other man by the open window. From her vantage, Portia could just make out his silhouette against the damask draperies. Was it merely a play of light, she wondered, or had his features taken on a sharper, more forbidding edge to them than she recalled?

Branford's companion appeared somewhat mollified by the explanation. "As Blaze has stuffed me with nourishment and forced me to nap, I am not about to be trundled off to bed without hearing whether the Saint had any new information to pass on."

"Indeed he did. A bit of digging turned up . . ." Branford suddenly paused. "Come away from the window, Max. The breeze has picked up, and it would not do for you to catch a chill."

Portia had to bite back an audible oath as the two of them moved back into the room. To her further dismay, the earl's hand appeared a moment later and pulled the mullioned casement closed, causing his words to become naught but a jumbled murmur. Ducking in closer to the limestone facade, she held her breath and strained to catch what he was saying.

To no avail.

Deciding that there was no choice but to employ desperate measures, she slowly lifted her head so that her eyes were level with the granite sill. The glow of the fire revealed that the earl and his companion were standing before the hearth, their attention riveted on a piece of paper that Branford was holding up to the light.

She could not help but blink in dismay at her first

real look at the other man. If the Earl of Branford was said to be Lucifer incarnate, then who in Hades was his menacing friend? With his wild locks, gaunt features, and patched eye, Cricket appeared a devilish apparition risen up from the depths of hell. The impression was only furthered by the strange orange stripe painted across his cheek, its hue looking to her eyes like the color of burning coals.

Steeling her resolve, Portia waited a moment, then removed her glove and inched her fingers toward the window. One by one, her nails managed to work their way under the lip of the frame. After offering up a silent prayer that the hinges were well oiled, she gave a soft tug.

". . . so I am about to take myself off to Little Broome Street, in order to pay a visit to Mrs. Wynwood. With any luck I shall run into Lord Dunster among the guests."

Her mouth went very dry.

The earl's companion gave what might have been a smile. To Portia, the expression was more akin to a wolf baring his teeth. "I expect you will have a pleasant time. She is accorded to be a most accommodating hostess."

Without waiting to hear Branford's reply, Portia crept away from the open window. As soon as her feet touched the soft grass of the garden, she quickened her steps to a near run, not pausing until her fumbling fingers had eased the gate ajar, allowing her to slip out into the sheltering shadows. As she leaned back against the mossy brick, it took a moment or two to still the pounding of her heart.

Yet the echoing thuds hammered home the question that was foremost in her mind. Had she made yet another egregious error in judgment in thinking she could trust the earl? Her hands clenched in the pockets of her cloak. There was, she decided, only one way to find out. Evidently, some sort of grand entertainment was taking place at a lady's residence that night. Seeing as she was becoming quite adept at skulking about in the greenery, she reasoned, it might be possible to overhear a snippet of conversation that would reveal whether the earl's sapphire sparkle was naught but false paste.

In for a penny, in for a pound. Portia took no more than another moment to decide that she had to take a chance, no matter what the cost. After all, the earl and his cohorts were not the only ones playing for high stakes. Keeping a firm grip on the small leather purse she had thought to tuck away in her pocket, she headed for the corner of Curzon Street. Neither Little Broome Street nor the lady in question were familiar to her, but as she had little acquaintance with Town or the *ton*, that was hardly surprising. Surely the direction would be known to anyone who made his living navigating the twists and turns of London.

With such thoughts in mind, she hailed the first passing hackney. It creaked to a grudging halt, the driver's eyes narrowing at the sight of a lone female coming out of the mist. His expression grew even more scrunched when he heard the address.

"Yer sure?" He ran his gaze from the tips of her muddy slippers to the hood of her rumpled cloak. "Ain't dressed in the usual manner fer such a place."

Her chin rose. Well aware that her attire was hardly suitable for an elegant soiree, she sought to sound more confident than she felt. After all, it wasn't as if she meant to stroll up to the front door and seek admittance with the rest of the guests. "Nonetheless, that is where I am going."

"Not in my cab ye ain't. Not 'til ye show me yer silver," he snarled. "Ye look too new at it t' have any blunt."

Although she had no idea what he meant, Portia flashed several of her coins.

He spat out a dribble of tobacco, then held out a grimy palm. "Suit yerself then, duckie." Once the fare had passed hands, a leer spread over his stained lips and he flicked the tip of the whip at the door. "Climb in."

As the streets grew darker and pavement rougher, Portia began to suspect that something was not quite right. And each jolt of the rickety wheels seemed to add another turn to her growing sense of unease. The only spills of light seemed to come from the numerous gin houses dotting the way, and the faces illuminated in the pale glow were hardly the sort she expected to see. Her nerves stretched taut, she peered out of the grimy little window, only to discover she had not the foggiest notion of where she was, or how much longer she would have to endure the fetid smell of stale straw and spilled ale.

She was on the verge of demanding that they turn around when the hackney suddenly lurched to a halt and the driver called out for her to step down. Relieved at finally being able to escape the oppressive atmosphere of the cab, Portia flung the door open and rushed off down the narrow street without so much as a word or a backward glance. By the time she realized the folly of such a move, the vehicle had disappeared in the rising fog.

Had the driver taken her for a ride—both literally and figuratively? The neighborhood certainly did not appear the sort of place where Polite Society might gather for an elegant soiree. Cursing herself for having failed to ask the driver for more specific directions before he bolted, she began turning in slow circles as she walked, looking for any sign of Little Broome Street. So intent was she on trying to spot a glimmer of life among the deserted buildings that she was unaware of another figure's approach until a hand tugged at her elbow.

"Ye lost, dearie?" asked a voice whose dulcet tones could not disguise its humble Southwark origin.

"Errrr . . ." Portia stumbled, but somehow managed not to slip on a mound of rotting cabbage. "Well, I am looking for a Mrs. Wynwood."

"Ye new in Town?" inquired the female, her brow lifting slightly.

"Why, y-yes," stammered Portia, not quite sure what that had to do with anything. "So I am afraid I am unfamiliar with the streets in this area, Miss . . ."

"Oh, ye can call me Suzy." The young woman grinned, revealing a slight gap between her front teeth. That appeared to be the only flaw in an otherwise stunning face. Glossy gold ringlets framed a heart-shaped face and a pert little nose. Her wide eyes, fringed with thick lashes, were a soft shade of robin'segg blue, and the pursed mouth a perfect shade of rosebud red. *Perhaps too perfect.* Portia leaned in a bit closer and thought she detected a bit of paint, as well as a touch of rouge on the rounded cheeks.

"A big city like Lunnon can be an awful hard place t' get along in," continued Suzy. "Especially if ye got no one t' show you the ropes, if ye know what I mean."

Portia had not a clue, but she nodded anyway.

"Well, ye look like a nice sort. A mite skinny, but with the proper attire, pushing up yer chest and all, ye'll do fine."

"The truth is, I wasn't exactly invited . . ." admitted Portia.

The other woman dismissed the confession with an airy laugh. "Don't worry. I'm heading to the same place, so just come with me. I'll introduce ye t' who ye has t' know." Before Portia could utter any protest, Suzy took hold of her arm and dragged her off through a series of zigzags that led into yet another twisting street.

"I'm not really dressed for—"

"Don't give it a thought," said Suzy over her shoulder. "We'll go in by the back entrance. By the by, what's yer name."

"Portia," she answered, too taken aback to consider lying.

"Hmmm." Suzy kept up a rapid pace as she considered the information. "I suggest ye call yerself Patty," she said after several strides. "Sounds a bit cozier. And gents tend t' like simple names."

Feeling thoroughly out of step with what was going on, Portia tripped after her new friend. "But I—"

The faint protest was overridden by the rapping of Suzy's knuckles on a heavy oak door. Set at eye level was a small brass grille, and behind it a panel of blackened steel. For a moment there was no response, but then the steel slowly slid to one side, revealing a single eye.

Suzy gave a flounce of her skirts and a cheery wave. As the other woman's cloak fell slightly open, Portia felt her jaw follow suit. It was not the gown's bodice that caught her attention but rather the lack of it. She didn't think she had ever seen such a small amount of fabric used to cover such a large expanse of flesh. Why, if the neckline were cut much lower, it would be revealing Suzy's . . . navel.

"You know, on second thought . . ." Portia started to back away, but just at that moment the door swung open and she found herself unceremoniously pulled inside.

"Ye be Leroy's replacement?" Her new friend was looking up at the massive doorman with undisguised curiosity.

"Ya, dat I is, mizz."

Seeing the odd expression that had come over Suzy's face, Portia couldn't help but venture a peek of her own.

Somehow she managed to swallow a gasp. Even in her wildest dreams she had never seen anything quite like the sight that now stood before her.

It was not just the faint flicker of the single wall sconce that was giving the man's skin a dusky cast. He was a mulatto—a fact made even more apparent by the fact that he was bare to the waist, his coffee-colored torso glistening with a sheen of scented oil. His thumbs were hooked in a red sash wrapped around his hips, and, like Suzy, Portia found herself staring at the tattoos adorning his massive forearms.

The right one bore a single word, spelled out in an ornate flourish of gothic script that ran from just above his wrist to his elbow. Fascinated by the unusual sight, she had to lean in a bit closer to make out the individual letters.

F-U-C-

Oh, dear. She had encountered it before, in one of the few volumes her father had forbidden her to read. Feeling her face turn as crimson as the fringed silk around the doorman's middle, she quickly jerked her gaze to the other arm. Which only caused her eyes to grow wider. The jet-black ink traced out a figure of a man—a naked man—but . . .

Portia blinked. Surely the artist had got the proportions all wrong.

With a rumbling chuckle the mulatto flexed his muscles, causing the figure's prominent frontal appendage to give a slight wiggle.

She fell back with a strangled squeak.

"Da name is Cane, mizz. Iz short for Hurricane. Dey call me dat cause I can kick up a real storm when I hazto."

Suzy had fallen into a gale of laughter at the unique display of artistry. "Well, ye certainly add a spot of color to the place, that's fer sure."

A flash of gold caught Portia's attention as she tried to look away. Unable to tear her gaze away from the mesmerizing figure, she found herself staring at the mulatto's shaven head. The source of the glitter was a large hoop earring dangling from one lobe, its design that of a snake grasping its tail between its fangs.

Cane grinned at the scrutiny, his teeth gleaming like whitecaps on a storm-dark sea. "Welcome to de House of Flowers."

"Right." Suzy smiled as well. "Come on, Patty, I'll just take ye along to meet Mrs. Wynwood."

The brassy note of a horn rang out, followed by a peal of raucous laughter.

"If you have come to run in the Debaucher's Derby, sir, you had best hurry." The female who had admitted him into the marble vestibule eyed the earl's broad shoulders with frank approval, then let her gaze slip a touch lower. "I wager you have the strength and stamina to make an excellent showing."

"The Derby?" Branford felt his overcoat being removed with a deft twist of her hands.

"Aye. The Run for the Roses. It is the highlight of this evening's entertainment at the House of Flowers." She winked. "Winner take all." With a saucy toss of her auburn mane, she pointed at a set of heavy drapes hanging to the right of a set of mahogany paneled doors. "Care to peek at the rest of the field?"

"Why not?" Affecting an air of casual nonchalance, he went to have a look at what was going on behind the velvet folds.

The room was quite large, but its width had been narrowed considerably by the fact that all the furniture had been shoved up against the wainscoted walls, leaving a long corridor of bare parquet running from end to end. Silver candelabras stood cheek by jowl down both sides of its length, the myriad of flames licking up in a sinuous dance of light. From the far hearth came another loud blast, drawing Branford's attention to a scene of equally heated activity. The Derby was, by the look of things, a race, complete with steed and rider—but one quite unlike any being run on the turf of Newmarket, Epsom, or Doncaster.

First off, he could not help but observe that the jockeys were all females, seeing as they were clad in naught but high-topped leather riding boots equipped with silver spurs. In lieu of racing silks to distinguish her identity, each sported a single rose behind her left ear, every flower a different color. Like their male counterparts, the female riders were mounted astride, but it was not high-priced horseflesh gripped between their thighs. Serving as stallions were a half dozen stark-naked gentlemen who were down on all fours. Saddles were apparently deemed unnecessary for the occasion, but reins had been fashioned out of silk scarves, and one was set between the teeth of each mount. Branford couldn't repress a sardonic curl of his lip at recognizing a particularly pompous bishop and leading Tory politician among those prancing about the makeshift paddock.

Amid a chorus of laughter and ribald advice from a small group of spectators, the jockeys were warming up for the event with a few short trial runs, putting their steeds through their paces with bouncing exhortations and much slapping of the short whips against bare behinds. From what Branford could make of the drunken shouts and scrabbling, a good deal of blunt was being wagered on the outcome, with the peach-colored rose emerging as the favorite.

"Fancy teaming up for a go at it, sir?" The female who had taken his coat had slipped up behind him and now had her fingertips hooked in the waistband of his breeches. "I'm accorded to have a superb pair of hands. Soft yet sure. You won't be disappointed, even if you don't run away with first place."

"Winner take all, you said?" Branford accepted a glass of champagne from a voluptuous serving girl who, like the jockeys, was entirely nude save for a few strategically placed flowers strung in place by thin silk cords. "What's the grand prize."

She nuzzled his ear. "See the gold trophy on the mantel?"

The earl had no trouble spotting the object in question, as it was molded in the shape of a large phallus.

"You win that and a garland of roses. And the right to stand stud to each of the jockeys."

"A tempting offer." He drained his glass. "But I think I shall seek other sport tonight."

"Ah, yes. I seem to recall that you prefer to mount your fillies in a more intimate setting." There was a whisper of velvet as Lord Dunster appeared from behind the draperies. His hooded gaze, flat and unblinking, reminded Branford so much of a snake that he half expected to see a forked tongue flick out from between the marquess's thin lips. "There are a number of private chambers upstairs, which cater to a variety of special needs. For example, the Violet Room is equipped with all manner of interesting flagellants, while the Peony Room comes with an assortment of stimulating oils—and attendants to apply them." He paused, then indicated that the earl should follow him back out to the vestibule. "You see, we are a special sort of place," continued the marquess as he turned into one of the hallways. "One that caters to a special sort of clientele. Tell me, Branford, just how did you come to hear of us?"

"From Roxleigh, before his unfortunate demise."

"Well, I trust you will not be disappointed."

Despite the marquess's nonchalant tone, Branford noted that the other man's fingers tightened on the fobs hanging from his watch chain. "A pity about your friend," he said softly.

Dunster turned a bit pale. "He was in the wrong place at the wrong time. An error in judgment that cost him dearly."

"So it seems. I would have thought he was smarter than that." Slowing his steps to regard one of the erotic murals, the earl added, "From what I understand, the two of you were partners in a number of . . . highly profitable ventures."

The marquess's gaze was no longer unblinking. The momentary flutter of his lashes matched the slight tremor of his voice. "H-how did you—"

"Oh, I have learned over the years that it pays to keep one's eyes and ears open." Branford flashed a knowing smile. "After all, I sense that we are both the sort of gentlemen who understand that luck is not merely due to fortuitous fate, aren't we."

The light from the single wall sconce caught a gleam of speculation in Dunster's eyes.

In emphasis of his last words, Branford buffed his

nails on the jet-colored lapel of his evening coat. "Indeed, I am accorded to have quite a sharp sense of business, but of late I've begun to feel a bit bored with my current pursuits and am looking for new hunting grounds. I thought perhaps, given the circumstances, you might be looking for a new partner. From what I hear, we may rub together rather well."

"An interesting suggestion." A slight commotion at the end of the hallway caused the marquess's head to jerk around. "I will think about it."

"Do." Taking care to keep a casual note to his voice, he pressed a bit harder, in case the marquess might let fall a bit of useful information. "And I imagine that you have other associates who need be consulted. If you wish to arrange a meeting . . ."

"I shall—" A muffled yelp from within the shadows of the archway put an abrupt end to the conversation. Brow furrowing, the marquess turned quickly and hurried toward the sound. Swearing under his breath at the untimely interruption, the earl followed close on the other man's heels.

The realization of just what sort of establishment she had entered finally sunk in. Fighting to keep her wits above a wave of panic, Portia managed to disengage her arm from Suzy's grasp. "Er, I think I have changed my mind about joining the other guests. So, I will just be running along—"

"Don't be turning misshish, sweeting."

Horrified, Portia saw that the hand now wrapped around her elbow belonged to none other than the Marquess of Dunster. Ducking her head, she mumbled some other excuse, which was dismissed with a nasty laugh.

"No need to be nervous, my dear." His grip tightened. "There is always a first time—you'll soon get used to it. Mrs. Wynwood will see you properly dressed for the festivities. Then we shall find you a suitable partner."

"New girl?"

Hell's bells! She did not need to look up to know who had just joined the little group.

Dunster nodded. "Country chit. Doesn't look to be a prime filly, but she will do for those of our clientele who can't afford to be too choosy." He added a curse as Portia stamped on his toe, then gave her a shake that nearly rattled her teeth. "A tight rein and well-handled whip will soon have you broken to the saddle."

"I wouldn't mind having a go at it," said Branford slowly. "I like them fresh off the farm."

"You don't want to take a stroll through the rest of the stable?"

Suzy, who was as adept at rating the fine points of a stallion as any regular at Tattersall's, took the opportunity to display a length of shapely leg. "That's right, sir. Plenty t' choose from. And there's something to be said fer a well-trained mount. Knows when t' walk and when t' gallop."

Branford's mouth stretched into a wicked grin. "No doubt. But tonight I find I am looking forward to a . . . less predictable ride."

Dunster laughed as he relinquished Portia's arm to the earl. After what she had seen and heard earlier that evening, she was not exactly eager to find herself in his grasp, but at the moment he seemed the lesser of the two evils, so she acquiesced without a struggle.

"Don't run her until she is lame. If she is to earn her oats here, she will have to make several turns around the paddock." The marquess looked about to add another ribald jest when someone in the adjoining room spoke his name. Although the whisper was no louder than a zephyr, the effect on him was like a clap of thunder. He went rigid, and through her lowered lashes Portia was surprised to see a sheen of sweat break out on his forehead.

"Go ahead, then, and give her a prick of your spurs," he finished, but a certain brittleness had replaced the bravado in his tone. Without waiting for a reply, he made for the doorway, his boots rapping out a nervous tattoo across the parquet.

Out of the corner of her eye she noticed that the earl was straining to make out the vague profile half hidden by the fluted moldings, but the wavering flame of the single wall sconce blurred the features beyond recognition. He started forward, but the catch of his fingers on her cloak stopped him in mid-step.

"Hell and damnation," he breathed as Dunster and the stranger disappeared from view.

Suzy looked somewhat alarmed at the black look that had come over the earl's face. "Now, sir, ye go easy on Patty. She's new at all this."

"Ha!" Ignoring the quizzical lift of the other woman's brows, he brought his other hand to Portia's shoulder. Before she could mouth a protest, she felt herself being shoved none too gently back into the rear vestibule. There followed a loud thud, which she assumed was the result of the earl's boot coming in swinging contact with the door.

Sure enough, she heard it slam shut behind them.

"This time you truly deserve more than a tongue lashing, Miss Hadley," he snapped. "I have a good mind to follow Dunster's advice and take a riding crop to your derriere as soon as I get you out of this place."

"That, sir, may not be as easy as you think," she pointed out, a tilt of her chin indicating the towering mulatto guarding the door. "He may not be quite as easy to manhandle as I am."

The earl's eyes narrowed for an instant, then relaxed. "Ah, so there you are, Cane. Throw back the bolts," he said in a tone considerably more friendly than the one he had just used with her. "And be quick about it."

To her amazement the other man's broad lips parted in silent laughter. "Yes, sor."

"With a bit of luck, we may be able to get out of this without all hell breaking loose," added Branford through gritted teeth.

"Don't worry, Cat. I can come up wid a story t' cover for ye here." The mulatto worked the heavy iron locks as if they were toothpicks. "But it still look like ye got a devil of a problem on yer hands."

"You have no idea," came the muttered reply. Halfway out the door, he paused for a fraction. "Keep your eyes and ears open. Descriptions. And names— try to suss out who are the regulars who frequent the place. I will want a full report when we meet at the arranged spot."

Portia finally managed to recover from her initial surprise. "The two of you—"

"Not now, Miss Hadley," snapped Branford as he propelled her out onto the steps.

"But—"

With a harsh growl, he brought his lips down hard upon hers, silencing any further protest.

It was not merely the physical force of his actions that rendered her incapable of speech. The rasp of his tongue sliding into her mouth suddenly drove all rational thought from her head, leaving her limbs feeling as though they were made of meringue.

The sensation was, however, over in an instant, as the earl jerked away and gave her shoulders a rough shake. "Now pick up your skirts and start moving, unless you fancy becoming the latest bloom to have her petals plucked in the House of Flowers."

After navigating a maze of slanting byways, they emerged through the pinched gap between two buildings into a narrow lane. Hearing nothing but the rustling of feral cats among the garbage, Branford decided it was safe to slow their pace to a walk. "It isn't enough to risk your life in these dangerous forays of yours?" he demanded raggedly, though it was anger, not physical exertion, that was making his breathing difficult. "So now you risk your virtue as well?"

"I don't recall you being so concerned with my virtue the other night," she shot back, "when you were plying me with whisky and relieving me of my chemise."

"Bloody hell and damnation!" The unfortunate

truth of her words did nothing to improve his temper. "I—"

"And if we are trying to avoid detection, do try to moderate your voice to a normal shout," she added as she kicked a broken jug out of her way. "Unless, of course, you are in league with the enemy and are merely taking me deeper into the stews, where my body won't be discovered for months, if at all."

"I am *not* your enemy, Miss Hadley! How many times must I tell you that?"

Portia's eyes stayed riveted straight ahead. "Why should I believe you? You demand explanations from me, yet refuse to give an even halfway plausible accounting of your own mysterious prowlings! And what about the sinister characters with whom you consort? The murderous fellow I saw you with earlier was—"

"You were skulking in *my* garden tonight, spying on *me?*" Branford couldn't help letting out another string of curses.

It was too dark to see if the color had risen to her cheeks, but she did stumble a bit. "I—I hadn't planned on it. Indeed, I had decided to take you at your word that I might trust you, and had something of pressing importance to tell you. As a lone female, I couldn't very well approach your front door without attracting undue attention. So I came in by the back gate, fully intended to make my presence known until that . . . villainous friend of yours appeared at the window." Her hood was slipping a bit, but in her anger, she made no move to tug it back in place. "Just who is Cricket—an opium-crazed assassin?"

"Miss Hadley—"

"And just who is Hurricane—a trafficker in love slaves?"

"For the love of God, no!"

She stamped her foot, ignoring the fact that it landed with an unpleasant squish. "Then who the devil are they!"

"They are reputable individuals," answered the earl, wondering why it was he always seemed to end up on the defensive with her. "I swear it, but I can't tell you any more than that. For good reason," he added.

"*That* excuse is wearing awfully thin, sir. I would suggest some scenarios of my own, but unfortunately, my imagination does not rival that of Mrs. Radcliffe." She gave an aggrieved sniff. "Cricket. Hurricane. The Saint. Who is going to show up next—the Grim Reaper?"

"He already had a shot at you, if you recall," muttered Branford, taking care to step over the shards of a shattered bottle. "And need I also remind you that he was not on my side? Or do you truly think that I had that entire evening planned?"

Save for a slight intake of breath, she uttered not a sound. Nor did she try to shake off his arm when he made to guide their steps into yet another zigzagging street. After the silence had continued for some distance, he slanted a quick look at her profile, trying to discern what lay beneath the uncharacteristic reticence.

Her lashes were lowered, but not enough to hide the gold sparks in the molten green. *Anger? Contrition? Embarrassment?* Though he had meant to change tactics and take the offensive, he found himself feeling just a tiny bit guilty in spite of his pent-up anger. The questions she had raised were valid ones, but before he could decide on how to go on, she finally spoke up.

"If we are on the same side, I, too, deserve a modicum of trust."

The quiet resolve of her statement caused Branford's lips to compress. "I am afraid I am coming to the same conclusion. Otherwise it seems we will constantly be at daggers drawn, fighting each other instead of the real enemy."

Her grimace grew more pronounced, and she let out a sigh. "The maddening thing about this whole affair is that it appears to have more sides than an octagon."

"And, as you have well noted, our enemy appears to have more tentacles than an octopus. One already has hold of your father." He threw open the door to his carriage. "Get in before another wraps itself around a second Hadley. Then, I think it is time we laid our cards on the table."

Chapter Fifteen

Portia rearranged the folds of her skirt. "As you have more experience in games of chance why don't you go first?"

"Bloody hell! This is no game, Portia. Enough of your clever quips—I want the truth."

She started, not only because he had used her given name, but because he was speaking so softly. Her experience with the Black Cat, though not exactly of long standing, had taught her that he was at his most dangerous when his voice dropped to a purr. "I—I have really told you everything of any importance," she stammered. "Well, essentially everything."

"Tell me again." There was a scrape of flint and a low hiss as he lit one of the carriage lamps. "I have always considered myself to possess a rather agile mind, but I am having a bit of difficulty in following the twists and turns of your thinking." He had taken the seat across from her but was leaning in so close she could not avoid meeting his gaze. "Not to speak of figuring out just what you may consider essential."

A storm of emotions had darkened his eyes to the color of slate, and with a small swallow she realized she had never seen him so angry. She drew in a steadying breath, seeking to keep a modicum of composure. After all, he, too, had a good deal of explaining to do, seeing as she had just encountered him in a bawdy house, in the company of her archnemesis.

"*My* story has not changed a whit," she replied, managing a bit more bravado than she actually felt. "I have been telling you the truth from our very first encounter, which, I might add, is more than you can say for yourself. My family has been cheated out of all our earthly possessions and my father has gone missing. I am trying to discover who is behind such a dastardly plot. And why."

Portia had rather hoped her pointed barb would elicit some twinge of embarrassment, but the earl's face remained as unrevealing as a slab of stone. "Go on."

"Er . . . about what?"

"Do not think for an instant that you are going to get off that lightly, Miss Hadley. There are a great many things you have left unsaid." His voice was also hard as rock. "And though I usually prefer to proceed in a logical order, we will start with the most pressing. What was it you were supposedly coming to tell me when you crept into my garden?"

Satan be singed! He was questioning *her* veracity? Forgetting her earlier misgivings about the wisdom of trusting the earl, she responded hotly with the truth. "That the *Lotus of the Orient* was due to drop anchor at the East India docks on the flood tide."

His mouth tightened, as did his voice. "How did you know the *Lotus of the Orient* was a ship?"

"The explanation is hardly as sinister as you seem to expect. I happened to notice it in *The Morning Gazette*.

There is a small section at the back of the paper devoted to shipping news. It lists the expected arrivals and—"

A low oath interrupted her as the stony facade finally showed a slight crack. "I bloody well know the column."

"Well, don't swear at me. It is not my fault you did not think to read it for yourself."

"I will arrange to have her searched first thing in the morning, though it is most likely that the thing I am looking for will no longer be aboard." He drew in a breath. "Were you aware of this information—as well as the fact that the ship in question is a Grenville and Company vessel—the night we overheard the widow make mention of it?"

She hesitated, but only for an instant. "Yes."

"Hell and damnation! Why didn't you tell me then?"

"Because . . ." Portia's voice dropped to a halting murmur. "If you recall, things were all happening rather quickly. And later, I was . . . somewhat distracted."

There appeared a slight ripple in his gaze.

"Furthermore," she continued, keeping her eyes locked with his, "you have to admit that your own irregular actions have hardly been the sort to inspire an overwhelming desire to confide in you."

He shifted under her scrutiny. "Surely you must have realized that if I meant for you to come to any harm, I had ample opportunity to see to it before then."

"Perhaps," she allowed. "Or perhaps you have something else in mind that better suits your purpose."

"Ah." It came and went so quickly, she wondered whether she had only imagined the look of hurt that passed over his face. "So, you still harbor suspicions that I am in some way connected to your father's kidnapping?"

"Any rational person would," she countered, "seeing as you have not seen fit to dispel such notions."

"We will get to that in a bit." Portia thought she detected yet another slight crack in his composure. "But first, let us finish with you." For a moment he seemed uncertain of how to go on.

Portia frowned slightly. She could not quite imagine what else he might want to know.

"You had no other ulterior motive for seeking out Dunster or the late Lord Roxleigh?" he demanded.

She shook her head, puzzled as to where his questions were leading.

"Or, most especially, the wily widow?" he pressed.

She replied with another negative, then could not help adding, "Why do you ask?"

The earl did not answer directly. "It is . . . understandable how a young lady, alone and worried over her family's survival, could be drawn into a nefarious plot out of sheer desperation."

Now thoroughly mystified, she frowned. "I don't know what you are getting at, sir."

"Then let me be blunt. Are you in any way involved in a plot to steal and sell a certain ancient artifact? The amount of blunt being offered by the person who wishes to acquire it would tempt a saint."

Portia responded with scathing sarcasm. "A Saint! Well, I suppose that begins to explain—"

"That was an unfortunate slip of the tongue," he interrupted. "What I meant was, the amount would seem an answer to your prayers."

He suspected her of being a lying, scheming thief? An explosion of outrage shot through her. "To the devil with your mysterious Saint! And with you, sir! I am *not* an unscrupulous adventurer or a . . . manipulative liar."

"I have not lied." In the faint glow of the lamp, she could see his jaw twitch as he worked to keep his temper in check. "I have already admitted that you are entitled to an explanation of sorts, and while there is much I cannot divulge, I will try to answer you as truthfully as I can. Even with a limited amount of information, I trust you will quickly understand the reason for my previous reticence."

"Y-you really mean to answer some questions?"

He nodded.

"If you are not in league with the people who kidnapped my father, then who are you working for? And what are you after? Are you looking to acquire this item you spoke of and sell it for your own profit. Or—"

Branford held up a hand. "One shot at a time, if you please, rather than a full-blown artillery barrage."

Clamping her jaw shut, she leaned back.

"As you seem to have guessed right off, I am working for the Saint."

"Well, that explains everything," she said with a touch of sarcasm. "Really, sir, if that is all you mean to tell me, I—"

"His close friends have called him that since university days, on account of his being the sole one of our little group who never got into any trouble. But of course, most people know him only as the Honorable Anthony Taft——" Branford's voice dropped a notch despite being in the privacy of his own carriage——"Minister of Eastern Affairs at Whitehall."

"Oh." Head spinning, she felt a certain numbness stealing over her, as if she had just been hit with another slug of red-hot lead. "I suppose that answers a number of the other questions," she said rather hollowly. "I take it Cricket and Hurricane are also a part of your group."

Branford nodded. "Cricket, as you heard me call him, is actually Viscount Davenport, an old friend and fellow officer from the Peninsular wars who won much praise for his bravery at Ciudad Rodrigo. His current malevolent appearance is not the result of some violent misdeed but was come by honorably, at the hands of a French officer."

"I see." Portia's voice was hardly audible above the creak of the wheels.

"As for Hurricane, we have worked together on a number of other missions in the Mediterranean. Don't let his looks mislead you. He is quite skilled at the delicate business of ferreting out information. He arrived several days ago from our base in Lisbon, and given what the Saint—that is, Mr. Taft—had dug up concerning Dunster's activities, he arranged for our mulatto friend to take up a position at The House of Flowers."

A guilty grimace pulled at her mouth. "Where once again I only managed to trip up your efforts."

"You do have a habit of turning up in awkward places." The corners of his lips quirked up just slightly, but there was still an edge to his voice.

Portia swallowed hard. Fear was still sharp in her breast, as was contrition, indignation, and a number of feelings she couldn't put a name to. Thoroughly confused by the tangle of conflicting emotions, she took some moments to form a reply. "So it seems I have, er, been very wrong about your intentions, sir."

"Yes. You have."

Why was he looking at her with such a strange intensity? she wondered. She had, after all, just admitted her error. "I'm sorry," she muttered. "I will be more careful next time. . . .

His fist smacked down upon the leather seat, causing her to jump. "There will be no next time, Portia."

The imperious tone of his voice somehow channeled all her doubts into one explosion of injured pride. "How dare you! You are in no position to order me about." She began to sidle away from him. "Let me out of here this instant. I will see to making my own way home."

He shifted quickly so that his broad bulk was looming over her. "On the contrary, it seems I am in a perfect position to prevent further foolishness on your part."

"Bullying lout." She shoved at his shoulder and sought for the handle of the door.

"Am I?" Branford's eyes were burning with a raw anger. He hadn't budged, and it was clear from the tenseness of his form that his temper was on a short leash. One that was hanging on by a mere thread. "Perhaps, but it's clear you need someone to curb your damnable recklessness"—he caught her wrist in a hard grip—"for you appear to have an insatiable taste for danger!"

Swearing back at him, she fought to free herself, but struggling only seemed to goad him to greater fury.

"What really brought you to a notorious bawdy house, Portia?" he demanded, thrusting her back against the squabs. "You have witnessed naked lust between a man and a woman. Is that what you wished to see again?" There was a tautness to his tone that she had never heard before. And then, with a near audible crack, his self-control snapped. "Or perhaps you followed me because you were looking to have your own skirts yanked up and my cock buried deep inside you?"

She drew in a gulp of air, fully meaning to counter his outrageous accusations with a fiery denial. However, the words that spilled out were a far cry from those she had intended. "P-perhaps I was."

"Then you shall have it!" He twisted sideways and began removing his coat. "But it will not be a furtive groping beneath folds of fabric." His cravat fell to the floor, followed by his coat. "I mean to have both of us stripped to the bare flesh, my dear." Branford shucked off his shirt and, without pausing, managed to peel his breeches down over the polished leather of his Hessians. His linen drawers slid easily from his lean hips, unsheathing his swollen manhood. It jutted out from the tight curls of raven hair, its shaft as rigid as a sword of Toledo steel.

Portia felt herself going very limp as he loomed over her, naked save for his high top boots. "Take off your cloak," he ordered.

"But—"

"Silence!" His voice was steely as well. "For once you will obey me without argument."

To her own amazement, her fingers began fumbling with the ties.

"Now unbutton your bodice."

Sucking in her breath, she worked the tiny fastenings free by feel, finding it impossible to tear her eyes from the sight of his arousal. In the conservatory it had been only a shadowed shape, but now, for the first time in her life, she was seeing a man in all his magnificence. And magnificent it was, she thought with a hard swallow. The broad, hooded head seemed possessed of a potent virility that sent a shivering thrill out to the very tips of her fingers.

"I—I shall need some help in undoing the back of my gown."

The earl reached around and tugged the tapes loose. His hands, however, then set on his hips. "Keep going," he said coolly.

Portia slowly wriggled out of the smooth silk, finding it oddly exciting to do exactly as he said. Anticipating his next command, she pulled down her chemise, leaving herself naked to the waist.

"Excellent." His eyes glittered in the lamplight. "Now slide your clothes all the way off."

The skirts frothed down around her feet. Despite the slight draft, she felt deliciously warm all over. There was just one last—

"Wait!"

Her hands stilled on her thighs.

The earl glanced at his boots, then at her legs. "Leave on your garters and stockings."

Letting go of the ruffled band, she looked up at him through her lashes.

"Admit it, Portia. You want me badly."

The sound in her throat was unrecognizable as any words.

"Say it!" he demanded. "Tell me I don't disgust you any longer!"

The chiseled planes of his body appeared hard as sculpted stone, but at that moment the expression on his face made him look achingly vulnerable. His eyes were an inscrutable winking of infinite blues, light sapphire darkening to near indigo. How had she ever viewed him in black and white, a hardened rake with no redeeming qualities? She reached up and touched his cheek. He didn't flinch but covered her hand with his own.

"No, you do not disgust me, my lord. It's been an age since I have thought of you as naught but a dissolute wastrel." She drew him closer, so she could feel the caress of his breath. "Indeed, I think I see far more good in you than you see in yourself."

All at once he was kissing her with an exquisite gentleness, his fingers trailing a gossamer touch as they caressed over her hair. It wasn't long, however, before the searching softness of his lips slowly took on a fiercer intensity and his fingers tangled in her tresses, sending a scattering of hairpins across the seat. Sensing his need, she wrapped her arms around his neck and returned his embraces with a hunger of her own.

"Ah, my brave, reckless tiger," he groaned. "Don't *ever* frighten me again as you did back there."

Her lips parted in surprise. "F-frighten you?"

"When I realized it was you, and what danger you were in, I was afraid I might murder the bastard with my bare hands." His whisper had deepened to a husky growl. "I don't want any man touching you but me."

She felt his fingers skimming everywhere—her breasts, her belly, the length of her legs—and the trail of pleasure nearly caused her to swoon.

"And my name is Alex," he added. "Considering the other intimacies we have shared, Portia, I think it is high time you use it."

Alex.

The very taste of it on her lips was as intoxicating as his kisses. Fiery as whisky, the four letters caused any last vestige of reason to go up in smoke. Through the haze, she was suddenly aware that she wanted nothing so much as to shout it out to the high heavens as his thumbs began to tease her nipples into hard little points. Reaching up, her own hands moved as urgently, running over the contours of bare flesh, reveling in the feel of the coarse curls and corded muscle.

As a scholar, she had wondered whether men and women could truly experience the intensity of emotions described in certain books. The sentiments—as well as some of the physical descriptions—had seemed greatly exaggerated. But apparently no printed page was a match for empirical research. Anyone with a rudimentary education in the physical sciences should have known that.

And indeed, ever since the earl had first slid his hand over her bare breast and teased it to a tingling arousal, her detached intellectual curiosity had flamed into raw desire. For a moment of madness she would cease to be Practical Portia and allow Passionate Portia to soar.

If only for a fleeting interlude. After all, she was going to spend the rest of her life with her feet planted firmly back on rough and rocky terra firma.

Branford drew a ragged breath. The earlier brush with danger was in part to blame for the conflagration licking up inside him. As was fear and anger—fear over what might have happened to her, and anger over how vulnerable his heart had become.

And so, for all the years of experience at keeping his feelings in check, he had suddenly lost all self-control. Reason had burst into flames, burning away every remnant of measured thought and gentlemanly scruples. The flare had died down somewhat, but the combination of emotions was still a potent heat inside him. As was the simmering desire that had spilled over in a raging boil. He knew he might well regret his own recklessness, yet all that mattered at the moment was how right she felt up against his skin, the warmth of her curves molding to his body, as if some missing pieces of a puzzle had suddenly materialized out of thin air to fill in the blank space.

To the devil with rules and reason!

With a thrusting urgency Branford recaptured her mouth and drove his tongue in deep, hungering to taste every nuance, to explore every contour.

A soft moan escaped her lips as she wrapped her arms around his shoulders and opened herself to the probing intimacy. "Alex," she said in a voice smoky with the same flare of passion he felt searing his own insides. "Alex."

"Lud, I have never wanted anything as badly as I want you now. I fear I shall go mad if I wait any longer," he groaned. "Are you growing ready for me?" Tracing a path over the ruffle of her garter, he drew a palm across the inside of one thigh and pressed it up against the downy triangle between her legs. Heat suffused his fingertips, and a wetness kissed his bare skin. With a primal growl he eased a finger inside her passage, the honeyed slickness giving him all the answer he needed.

She whispered something in his ear—he knew not what, as all he could hear was the roar and crackle of his own emotions. Rasping an inarticulate reply, he levered himself up and replaced his fingers with his shaft, slowly stroking its length up and down against her hardening nub. In the flickering light he saw her eyes widen at the sight of his rampant nakedness jutting out from the dark curls.

She didn't answer save for a ragged quickening of her breathing. Sensing a growing heat in her core that matched his own inflamed senses, he shifted a hand back between her legs and increased the tempo of his caresses, dipping well within her velvety softness.

"I knew your passions would be as fiery as your temper," he murmured.

Her lips were warm and pliant on the ridge of his jaw. "Do you still think my tongue too sharp?"

With a husky chuckle Branford twined a hand in her loosened tresses and drew back her head. "On the contrary, sweeting," he answered after a long and thorough kiss. "On further investigation, I find it quite perfect." He shifted again, so that the curves of her breasts were molded to his chest. "Indeed, I would say that our bodies are very well matched to each other, wouldn't you?"

She uttered a soft cry, giving voice to his own rising urgency. Unable to contain his desire any longer, he parted her thighs, groaning as her nails dug into his shoulders and pulled him closer. The tip of his shaft was suddenly enveloped in an exquisite warmth. Drenched in a feeling of profound exultation, unlike anything he had experienced with another woman before, he groaned aloud. Then, with a deep thrust, he buried himself inside her.

Branford wasn't sure which of them was more shocked.

Portia bit back a yelp of pain, while he pulled back and stared at the faint trace of blood. There was a moment of stunned silence before a rush of breath formed a ragged whisper.

"Bloody hell."

He looked up to see that her lashes were wet with tears.

"M-must you always swear at me?" she said in a voice so low it was almost inaudible. "I know I always seem to make you angry, but—"

"I am not angry, Portia. Far from it. Merely . . . unsure."

"Or disappointed." Her lip quivered. "No doubt because I am not as experienced as your naked countesses or sultry spies. Or as attractive as a b-buxom beauty like Suzy."

"You are quite wrong, my green-eyed tiger." Branford brushed a drop from her cheek. "You are infinitely more alluring than any other woman I have known. And as for experience, I own to feeling a selfish pleasure that you have known no other man's touch."

She blinked in disbelief. "Then why do you no longer want me?"

"Sweeting, I want you so much, it is driving me wild, but I am trying to behave like a proper gentleman rather than a rapacious beast."

"Please, Alex." The carriage light caught the golden sparks in her jade gaze. "I should like you to be the Black Cat for just a while longer."

With a deep growl he slipped his hands beneath her hips.

Surely this couldn't be wrong, thought Portia as she arched to open herself to him. Indeed, never had anything felt so right. The initial prick of pain had given way to a singular sensation that transcended mere pleasure. Alex was inside her, moving with a gentleness that belied his muscled strength, and with each slow thrust she wanted to draw him in deeper. Smiling at the wonder of it all, she ran her tongue over the tanned flesh of his shoulder, tasting salt and a woodsy masculinity. To her delight, she felt him grow even harder in response to a gentle nip.

"My tiger," he rasped, his hands raking over the pointed tips of her breasts as his teeth took hold of her lower lip.

Moaning at the surge of pure heat that shot through her, Portia ran her nails lightly down his back, reveling at the sinewy tautness of his buttocks and the fact that her caresses seemed to arouse him to a more torrid pace. "Faster, Alex," she urged, though she didn't quite know what it was she sought.

He seemed to have no trouble interpreting her need. "Ah, so ready, my reckless one," he murmured, now slipping his fingers between their slickened bodies and adding an intimate, stroking arpeggio to the rhythm of his lovemaking.

She thought she was going to explode any moment in a shower of liquid sparks. "Alex!" she cried out again. Another thrust of his loins sent a pulsing quiver through her, and as his tongue matched the plunging intimacy, overwhelming her senses with the raw force of his presence, she was filled with a searing awareness of him above her, around her, inside her.

An uncontrollable passion shot up from her very core. Burst after burst of pleasure sizzled through her. Somehow she freed her mouth, but whether her voice was a shout or a whimper was impossible to tell, for the only sound she could hear was a roaring in her ears as the conflagration of her climax engulfed her.

The earl had been watching her face, and the sight of her molten reaction seemed to ignite a new urgency in him. She felt the tremor in his touch, heard the quickening of his rasping breath.

Portia was suddenly aware of another roar, a fierce, primal cry as the Black Cat filled her with one last wild, shuddering rock of his hips before releasing himself. A groan followed as he fell spent across her thighs, spilling a white-hot pool of his seed upon the leather seat.

For a long, languid moment she lay perfectly still. It occurred to her that perhaps she should be acutely embarrassed, lying completely naked across a carriage seat, the earl's naked manhood still touching her bare thigh. Yet, it was not shame or regret that had brought a rosy glow upon her cheeks but a sense of profound peace. Feathering a kiss across his tangled locks, she let her eyes fall closed.

The blissful interlude proved all too fleeting. They had hardly emerged from the twisting lanes of the rookeries when the earl slowly stirred and propped himself up on one elbow. "Sweeting, much as I hate to bring up mundane matters at this moment, we haven't much time, and there are certain things we had better discuss before we reach our destination."

"Hmmm?" Still savoring the sensation of her limbs feeling soft and shimmering as jellied aspic, Portia was listening with only half an ear. "Like what?"

"Well, seeing the problems that arose when you doubted my earlier intentions, it seems prudent to make sure there are no further misunderstandings between us," he replied. "Just as soon as our enemy is apprehended, and I have recovered both your father and the missing government item, I will make the arrangements for a special license. . . ."

"Special license," repeated Portia faintly. A hideous premonition came over her as she sat bolt upright. "W-whatever for?"

His expression was unreadable. "I should think it rather obvious."

"As in . . . marriage?"

"Well, that is what most people use it for," drawled

Branford. "As it is rather an expensive scrap of paper, I would prefer that Bertie not scribble his equations across it."

How could he appear so glacially calm when just a short time ago he had been making love to her with fiery abandon? Unless . . .

Unconsciously her chin took on an ominous tilt.

"You need not be nervous, Portia. I will see to all the niggling details and handle all the necessary formalities."

Rather than serve as any reassurement, the announcement caused a chillness to spread through her marrow. *Niggling details? Necessary formalities?* His voice had a cool detachment to it, as if he were speaking about placing an order with his tailor or boot maker.

For a moment her throat was so painfully tight that speech was impossible. Then, blinking back the prick of tears, she managed to make a reply. "Why, you arrogant, odious man! What makes you think I would even consider marrying you?"

"We might start with the fact that I have thoroughly compromised you."

"Ha! It is not as if I didn't lend a hand in the matter." Her fumbling fingers sought for her chemise among the garments on the floor. "It is not as if this was any different from your other casual liaisons," she added after tugging the rumpled muslin over her head. "The number, I assume, is legion."

All trace of humor faded from his face. "The rules are different for an innocent young lady."

"It's not as if we have been playing by the rules from the very beginning!" Determined not to reveal how much his dispassionate manner had cut her to the quick, Portia matched his sardonic tone. "You didn't take advantage of me. I knew what I was doing. A man is free to abandon his virtue when he chooses—why shouldn't it be the same for a female?"

"It simply isn't," he stated with infuriating male logic. "And while we might have ignored one or two minor transgressions, the Incidents—as you so charmingly term them—have gone far beyond a mere bending of the rules. Now that I know the truth regarding your . . . innocence, I have decided we should be married as soon as possible."

"*You* decided? Of all the pompous, condescending . . ." Too furious to go on, she stopped to draw a breath and snatch up her gown. Then, sensing that anger was having no effect on him, she tried a different attack as she wrestled with the tapes and buttons. "What does it matter whether an Incident has occurred one or one hundred times? Nobody knows."

"*I* know," he replied quietly. "And honor demands—"

"To the devil with that," she cried hotly. "Why, you don't have a twitch of tender feelings for me."

He steeled his expression. "That has little to do with the matter—"

"The hell it doesn't!" Her voice rose sharply. "I'll not be manipulated like one of your foot soldiers on the field of battle. I have no intention of marrying anyone—much less an overbearing tyrant—without sharing some . . . mutual feelings of regard."

"Portia . . ." he began.

"*No!* And that is final." She knew she was perilously close to sounding hysterical but didn't give a fig. "I would rather be ruined ten times over than find myself riveted to you for life. Please don't speak of it again. *Ever* again." Her voice modulated to a more measured anger. "Consider your beastly male code of honor satisfied—you have offered, I have refused. So you may breathe a sigh of relief, wipe the sweat off your brow, and leave me in peace."

He gave no sign of doing either of the first two suggestions. The third, however, seemed up for discussion. "You are sure that is what you wish?" he asked as he assumed his breeches and picked up his shirt.

"Fervently," she replied, keeping her eyes averted from the rippling of muscled flesh.

"Very well, then." He had not resumed his place facing her, so it was impossible to make out his expression without being too obvious about it. Yet, by the unperturbed tone of his voice, it appeared he had taken the rejection coolly.

Too coolly, she thought, with a morose little sniff. He could at least have had the grace to argue a bit more heatedly. *Not* that she had any desire for false flattery, or any intention of changing her mind. But he had spoken so dispassionately of duty and honor when only minutes before he had been making love to her with a fiery abandon. It might have been nice if he pretended that the experience had meant something more . . . personal than rules and regulations.

Her hands clenched into a tight knot in her lap. *Of course it had not been personal!* Had she really thought one of the most notorious rakes in London had developed a tendre for her? It was mere animal lust that had aroused the Black Cat.

But she had no right to be angry, she reminded herself. Not with the earl. If she had been seduced by anything, it was her own hubris. She had been sure she could flirt with fire and come out unsinged. If she was now feeling as cold as old coals, she had only herself to blame. Blinking back tears, she steeled her spine. No matter how charred she was feeling inside, she was determined not to succumb to self-pity. The earl had been correct about knowing the rules. She had chosen to challenge him at his own game. It would be wrong to whine or wheedle on discovering she did not, in fact, know how to play.

Gentlemen were not the only ones who possessed a sense of honor.

Her chin rose a trifle higher. "Getting back to business, sir, I have several other questions. Are you still willing to answer them?" she began, somehow managing to keep her voice from cracking.

"What is it you would like to know?"

"A good many things, actually. This item that has gone missing—have you any reason to think it related to my father's disappearance?"

Branford hesitated long enough that she feared he was not going to reply. Then, to her relief, he grudgingly muttered, "Yes." As his fingers started drumming on his thigh, he added, "We have already assigned men to start scouring the docks for any leads concerning your father, and given the discovery concerning the *Lotus of the Orient,* I mean to confront Mrs. Grenville first thing in the morning. As for Dunster, I have brought in reinforcements to help with analyzing what moves to make next."

The sharp logic of his list was unassailable. Unlike herself, the earl appeared to have things well under control. "I do not suppose you can tell me exactly what this item is?"

"No, I cannot."

"Is there anything I can do to help?"

A muscle twitched in his jaw. "At the risk of sounding condescending or overbearing, I would like to suggest that you refrain from any further forays of your own until I have had a chance to pursue those leads. As you have witnessed, things appear to be taking a more dangerous turn lately, and it can only serve as a grave distraction if I must worry about what you are up to, instead of concentrating on tracking down our enemy."

"That is a reasonable request," she allowed. "Will you, in turn, keep me informed of what you learn?"

"That is a reasonable request. As far as the information concerns your father."

Her teeth set at the veiled sarcasm of his replies, but she forced herself to mimic his icy politeness. "Very well." She fell to pleating her skirts into rigid folds. "You see, if we treat each other like intelligent, rational individuals, we are quite capable of working together without all the fuss and fireworks."

"I shall try to keep that in mind." The curl of his lip was coldly sardonic. "Have you any anything else you wish to ask?"

Portia shook her head. "Not at the moment." Folding her hands in her lap, she sat at rigid attention, determined to maintain a modicum of dignity. The earl, she noticed with a sidelong glance, had simply leaned back against the squabs and closed his eyes.

So much for passion and pyrotechnics, she thought glumly. Perhaps they were best confined to the printed page. And perhaps being a bluestocking spinster was not so bad after all.

The carriage finally rolled into the streets of Mayfair. As it eased over the cobbles and turned into the darkened side street that the earl had requested, she was jarred into remembering to raise her hood. A hasty tug set it in place, and several tucks rearranged her curls into some semblance of order. She could think of nothing to say but a rather stiff farewell.

The earl inclined his head with equal reserve. "The passageway directly opposite the carriage leads to the mews of your aunt's town house. Forgive me for not being a gentleman and accompanying you to your door"—he then reached out to smooth a fold in the heavy wool and reknot the tangle of the ties—"but in the event that Henry and Bertie are lying in wait, I would rather they not be given a reason to go charging off for pistols and powder."

Portia colored. For once, she was willing to admit his sarcasm was entirely justified. The Black Cat must be cursing his foul luck in having run into the Hadley family—the entire Hadley family. She, of all people, knew what a sore test of patience the eccentric lot of them must present.

Chapter Sixteen

"Just getting back?" Davenport looked up from the slab of beefsteak on his plate and cocked a brow. "You do not have the look of a man who has just spent the night at one of London's most exotic pleasure houses."

Branford tossed his gloves and walking stick in the general direction of the sideboard and dropped into a chair. In no mood for banter, he ignored the remark, making no attempt to moderate his scowl as he reached for the pot of coffee that had been left on the table. He did, however, not fail to note that his friend had left off wearing the black eye patch. The injury still gave the viscount's expression a twist of menace, but at first glance, the strange ointment seemed to be working wonders. Already the inflammation looked less raw and the puckering of the skin less pronounced.

Rubbing at his bristled jaw, the earl slanted another quick look to make sure he wasn't mistaken, and although his own eyes felt as if sabers were carving up his irises, he was further gratified to see that a good night's sleep had apparently cleared much of the dull haze of opium from the other man's gaze.

All in all, he thought with just a touch of asperity,

Max appeared to have a good deal more appetite for the coming day than he did.

"Why the black face, Cat?" continued the viscount after wolfing down a bite of broiled kidney. "Didn't you get lucky?"

He supposed he should be glad to see that his friend was recovering a bit of his sharp sense of humor along with his looks, but his own feelings were still rather too raw. Biting back a snappish retort, Branford took a sip of the now tepid brew, then slammed the cup back down on the table with enough force to rattle the rest of the china. "Blaze," he bellowed, "if it is not too much to ask, I should like to have something other than dirty dishwater served for my breakfast." Without waiting for a reply, he rose and stalked to the chafing dishes, where he passed up all but a morsel of Yorkshire ham.

"I take it things did not go well," murmured Davenport between munches on a slice of toast slathered with gooseberry jam.

The newspaper unfolded with a decided snap. "Do you mind allowing me to enjoy my meal in peace and quiet before peppering me with impertinent questions?" he grumbled.

"Well, well, somebody got up on th' wrong side o' th' bed," remarked Blaze as he thumped down a fresh pot of coffee by Branford's elbow. "That is," he added, eyeing the earl's rumpled clothing and stubbled chin, "assuming ye made it into any bed at all." Eschewing the slightly more tactful method of interrogation employed by Davenport, the valet crossed his arms and fixed his employer with a gimlet gaze. "So, wot th' devil happened?"

With two veteran soldiers nipping at his flanks, the earl decided any further attempt to elude questioning was futile. Heaving a harried sigh, he balled up the newspaper and threw it on the floor. "Seeing as I won't be permitted a moment of peace until I make a report, why don't you pull up a chair and make yourself comfortable."

Ignoring the obvious sarcasm, Blaze dropped into the nearest seat and cocked his head expectantly.

"Ah!" Davenport pushed away his plate and leaned forward in his seat. "So your trip to The House of Flowers was—"

"Not exactly a bed of roses," finished Branford with a dry grimace. "However, I did manage a few moments alone with Dunster, and was able to plant the seed of my involvement in his business dealings."

"You think it will work?" demanded the viscount.

The earl inspected his cuff. "Hard to say. I had wanted a bit more time to cozen up to the weasel, but unfortunately I was compelled to make an early exit."

"Bloody hell!" blurted out both of his companions in unison.

"Now, why the devil did you do that?" added his valet, not bothering to temper the critical tone of his voice. "Just when it appeared things were getting interesting."

"It had to do with saving a young lady's virtue," he replied somewhat obliquely.

Davenport couldn't refrain from flashing a sardonic grin. "I have heard that Mrs. Wynwood's females offer a variety of attributes, but I would not have thought that either virtue and pedigree would be among them."

"No. Not until Miss Hadley marched through the door."

"Bloody hell!" they repeated, their voices sounding a good deal more incredulous than the first time around.

"How did she—" began the viscount.

"By sneaking up on us and eavesdropping on our plans." Branford pulled a face. "We must be getting old, Max, and woefully dull, to allow a green country miss to get the edge on us."

Davenport's face gave an involuntary squinch, causing a large glop of the orange goo to fall upon his lapel.

"Well, ye have t' admit that Miss Hadley ain't quite like any other young lady," observed Blaze.

As if he needed to be reminded! thought the earl.

"A real trooper she is. Ain't never met a braver lassie. Pluck t' th' bone." The valet suddenly frowned as he ran a hand through his fiery locks. "Ye did see that she got home safe an' sound, didn't ye, guv?"

Not about to allow the discussion to turn in *that* direction, Branford sidestepped the question. "Of course I got her out of The House of Flowers unscathed. As Hurricane was standing guard at the back door, it did not prove too difficult."

Counting on his next words to further divert their attention, he paused for effect, then added, "And the information I learned from her was equally as valuable as anything I might have pried out of Dunster." After repeating what Portia had told him about the *Lotus of the Orient*, Branford wound up his narrative. "So, for the rest of the night, I was busy arranging for a thorough search of the vessel, and for several of Tony's best men to place Mrs. Grenville's residence and warehouses under a constant surveillance."

"I take it nothing turned up aboard the ship?" asked Davenport.

"No," he admitted. "I feared as much, seeing as what we are looking for is so deucedly easy to hide."

Davenport scratched in consternation at his cheek, dislodging a few more dollops of the viscous substance.

"And as for the widow, I've just come from paying an unfashionably early call, only to be told by her faithful retainer that she was . . . not receiving." His mouth thinned to a grim line. "Come this afternoon, she will be receiving, all right—another visit from me, whether she likes it or not. However, as she won't be going anywhere without being tailed, I decided to grab a few hours of sleep in order to be sharp for a final confrontation."

Blaze snapped to attention. "Right-o, guv. You have a doss while I brush up a fresh set o' togs."

The retreating stamp of the valet's footsteps was drowned out by the rustle of paper. "Before you go, Alex, there is one thing I wanted to show you." Davenport took up the small stack of documents that was lying by his elbow and fanned them across the table. "While you were out amusing yourself with the ladies, I was applying my attention to the various papers you received from Tony."

Tired though he was, Branford didn't miss the subtle change in Davenport's voice. "Did you discover something of interest?"

"Take a look for yourself." He picked out one of the items, a crinkled and creased letter, and held it up.

Branford studied it for a moment. "That is devilishly odd," he grunted. The looping French script was widely spaced, as if written by a child's hand, and the message was merely a polite note inquiring about the health of the recipient and his family. It was not until one looked closely, at where a bit of liquid had stained the paper, that another trace of lettering was visible between the original lines.

"The hidden message is written in gallotannic acid," said the viscount on noting Branford's furrowed brow. "When dry, it is invisible. The gaps between the lines reminded me of something similar I had seen in Portugal, so I had Blaze run to the apothecary for a solution of iron sulphate and tested it on a section. Sure enough, the hidden writing came up. Once I have soaked the whole document, the iron will turn the ink to black, and with any luck we will have the real message." Davenport fingered the dog-eared corner of paper. "This sort of technique fits the profile of what we are looking for, Alex. It is used when an agent is rushed and does not have time to construct a complex cipher to encode the meaning."

"Well done," murmured Branford.

Davenport's satisfaction faded somewhat. "But the trouble is, I cannot make heads or tails out of the little that has showed up. The script certainly looks Eastern, but the language is like nothing I have ever seen before. Perhaps if we send to Oxford for an expert . . ." He let out a snort of frustration. "But even then it may take some time to find someone familiar with this particular dialect."

"Still, very clever of you, Max. I would never have spotted the trick."

"That is because I spent most of my time in a field tent, poring over papers, while you entertained your-self with flesh-and-blood opponents."

"Like our mysterious Mrs. Grenville." Reminded of the upcoming clash, the earl set his jaw. "Just as you have wrested secrets from a mute page, I look forward to forcing some answers from the Lady in Red."

Davenport frowned as he fingered the smear of orange on his cheekbone. "You are really convinced she is in league with Dunster?"

"As a female who has managed to be successful in the world of business, she has all the qualities necessary to be one of the main villains—brains, opportunity, a knack for turning a profit, and an instinct for survival," he answered. "And the evidence all points at the same conclusion. Her guilt is obvious."

"Too obvious, if you ask me," grunted the viscount.

"Ah. Has the wily widow added another name to her long list of admirers?"

The flush that rose to Davenport's face was as red as one of the lady's low-cut gowns. "Don't be ridiculous. My observation was purely professional."

Branford lifted a brow. "Even with an eye patch obscuring the view, you could hardly have been blind to her obvious charms."

"Not at all my type," came the gruff reply.

"Come, Max, one unfortunate experience with a heartless jade is no reason to swear off the opposite sex in general." The earl was well aware that Davenport had been engaged to a young lady whose greed turned out to be as great as her beauty. On deciding that his august lineage did not make up for a rather modest fortune, she had jilted him for an aging roué who was said to be rich as Croesus. Over a year had passed, but it was clear from his friend's darkening scowl that the wound on his cheek was not the only one that was still raw.

"My private life has naught to do with Mrs. Grenville. Or you, for that matter."

Deciding not to push too far with his teasing, Branford returned to the more serious considerations. "I am glad to hear you have no interest in the widow, for she will soon be taking her leave from London. A permanent one, as her next tête-à-tête will be with the hangman at Newgate." He tugged off his cravat and hung it over the back of the chair. "However, she is not the only villain we must account for. We have yet to learn the identities of the others involved in this affair, and for some reason I cannot shake the feeling that neither the wily widow nor dirty Dunster is the mastermind of it all."

"Any ideas where to begin looking?"

The earl ran a hand through his disheveled locks. "For a start, I mean to make the rounds of the gaming hells of Southwark tonight. I would like to have a little chat with Newton, who introduced me to Lord Dunster, and perhaps a few of Roxleigh's old cronies, to see who else is considered an intimate of their group."

Davenport nodded. "In the meantime I have asked Tony to send me the file on every gentleman at Whitehall who knew about the existence of the document."

He began shuffling the papers into separate piles. "Along with any further information his men may have dug up on Dunster and his activities. I am going to comb over them for any hidden threads that might tie them together."

"You have certainly made a number of momentous discoveries over the past twenty-four hours." Branford eyed the clock, thinking that the same could be said for his own effort. "I am going to lie down for a bit. I, too, have a good deal of things to sort through."

The strange note in the earl's voice caused a crease in Davenport's brow. "Don't sound so blue-deviled, Cat. You know your legendary luck never deserts you for long. Indeed, it had already taken a turn for the better, seeing as it appears we are finally on the right track in this case."

"Let us hope so, Max."

As he made for the stairs, he wished he could feel quite as sanguine as his friend. There was no denying that it felt good to be back in the hunt again, all senses thrumming with awareness. Tony had been right—he had needed the challenge of intrigue and danger to get the blood flowing again. Yet, despite the heat surging in his veins, a small part of him couldn't help but wonder whether he had been a fool to allow Taft to coax him back to life. Living entailed such agonizing risk. As did loving.

Love. It had ambushed him from out of nowhere, he admitted. Shots had exploded, blades had clashed, sparks had flown. Then, at some point during the heat of battle, he had surrendered his heart to Portia.

Lud, he had been so surprised by the force of the realization, and so unsure of her feelings, that he had been too cowardly to voice his sentiments aloud. His military training had dictated a tactical reteat, but instinct told him he had made a mistake. Had he ruined any chance of winning her hand by remaining silent? His feet paused for a moment on the stairs. He could only hope there would be time enough later to regroup and attack the conundrum of how to change her opinion on matrimony. But first he had better marshal all his concentration to battle the present problem.

With a sigh he turned to regard the Renaissance canvas, his gaze coming eye to eye with the Archangel Gabriel. Noting the sword arm raised in exhortation and the muscular confidence exuding from every brush stroke of the painted figure brought a faint smile to his face. "Aye, wish me well—I have a feeling I am going to need all the bloody luck I can get."

Suppressing a sneeze, Portia thumbed through the first chapter, then laid the book atop several others she had pulled down from the shelves. It was clear form the dust on the bindings that this particular section of Hatchards was not nearly as frequented as the area devoted to offerings from Minerva Press. She sighed and glanced up as she moved along the next row of shelves, finally spotting the last title on her list wedged in between two volumes of *The Arabian Nights*. No doubt the effort at research would prove a waste of time, but she needed to keep busy in order not to think of . . .

Her fingertips fell short, but before she could look around for a stepladder, a gloved hand slipped by hers and plucked it from its place.

"Here, allow me to be of assistance, Miss Hadley," said Mr. Dearborne as he gave the grained leather a wipe with his handkerchief. "Ah, Needingham's *History of the Maharajah Moguls*. An excellent piece of scholarship. Chauncey is considered the leading expert in the field," he added after squinting at the embossed type. "In fact, it is just the volume I was looking for." Although the alcove appeared deserted save for the two of them, he took the precaution of lowering his voice to a whisper. "I take it you are doing a spot of research of your own concerning the Jade Tiger?"

"I thought I may as well take a stab at it." Portia could not keep a note of frustration from her reply. "However, I fear it is rather like looking for a needle in a haystack."

He gave a sympathetic nod. "Unfortunately, it is a feeling with which we scholars are well familiar. But do not be discouraged. I have made a bit of headway, if only to eliminate a number of possibilities."

"Yet, it seems a rather impossible task." She gestured toward the other books she had gathered. "I could search through pages from now until doomsday and still not stumble across any mention of a mysterious green beast."

"At the risk of sounding terribly pompous, let me say that most important discoveries require patience and perseverance."

"And luck," she sighed.

"That too," agreed Dearborne. "Especially as 'the East' encompasses a vast area. I don't suppose you have thought of any other hint your father may have dropped, however vague, that might help us narrow down our focus? No particular country or culture that seemed to have grabbed his attention of late? No odd correspondence?"

Portia bit her lip as she met his questioning gaze. There was a depth to the brown eyes that hinted at a sharp intelligence beneath the rather ordinary color. Unfortunately, too sharp, she thought with an inward sigh, for a look of concern caused them to darken a shade at her continued silence.

"Miss Hadley?" His graying brows rose in silent encouragement.

Still she hesitated. There was a certain reassuring solidity to all his features, from the high brow and aquiline nose to the broad lips and square chin. Yet they rather paled in comparison to the hard, angular planes of Lord Branford's visage. *Not that she wished to be thinking of the dratted Black Cat.* But he did have the look of a gentleman well used to danger, while her father's colleague had the mien of someone more versed in the subtle nuances of books and parchment rather than the grim harshness of gunpowder and sabers.

"I have been racking my brain to recall anything that might be of import," she replied slowly. "But . . ."

He shifted the weighty volume from one hand to the other. "Yes?"

She cleared her throat, stalling for another few moments as she debated whether to involve him any further. There was no reason to think that the scholar was in any danger, she reasoned, as her unknown enemy could not possibly be so omniscient as to know of these private conversations. So perhaps there was no harm in letting him help wrestle with the intellectual part of the conundrum, as long as she continued to take care that he was not exposed to any physical risk. After all, an answer might help free her father.

A slight twinge of conscience also compelled her to admit that she would be able to hold her chin up a touch higher if she could make some tangible contribution to the earl's investigation, considering all the trouble she had caused him.

"I cannot really explain it," she finally answered, "but for some reason I think it may have to do with India."

Dearborne stroked at his chin. "Hmmm. India." Although he looked as if he wished to press further, he contented himself with a mild shrug. "Well, then, let me concentrate my efforts there for the time being and see what turns up."

"Thank you, sir. You are being more than kind."

"Nonsense. Though Julian and I do not see eye to eye on a good many things, I should never forgive myself if I did not lend whatever help I can."

He offered Portia the book in his hand, but she gestured for him to keep it. "No doubt you will make better use of it than I." Ducking away from his scrutiny, she turned for the other books. "Now, I had best go make my purchases and collect my younger brothers. I—I promised them we would stop for some ices at Gunther's."

He tucked the volume under his arm. "I will start right away." He cleared his throat with a strained cough. "Forgive me for saying so, but you seem a trifle on edge, Miss Hadley. Have you any more reason to think you are being threatened by some shadowy stranger?"

"No," she murmured. "I must have been mistaken."

"Well, do take care, my dear. And as I said before, do not be discouraged. I am sure that with a bit of digging—and a bit of luck—we will soon uncover the key to this mystery."

Branford decided he was in need of a new curse—he had said *bloody hell* so often over the past few days it was beginning to lose its edge. Still, as he slammed the door to the neatly organized study and turned back to the turbaned servant, he couldn't help but repeat it in a low growl. He had searched every room, from attic to cellar, and had to admit that the man had not lied. The widow was not there.

Poof. Like a swirl of exotic smoke, she had up and disappeared without a trace.

He clenched his fists. Tony might as well be employing monkeys from the Tower menagerie as agents, for all the skill the two seasoned operatives had exhibited in their attempt at keeping the Lady in Red under surveillance. The earl couldn't help himself. He swore again.

The other man's expression remained inscrutable beneath the bushy black beard and gauzy wrappings of silk.

"Where is she?" he demanded in a loud voice, more to relieve his frustration than in any expectation of getting an answer.

An exaggerated shrug of the shoulders set off a jingling of silver bells decorating the servant's saffron tunic.

Branford ground his teeth in irritation, then slapped

his card down on the rosewood side table, nearly knocking a pair of intricately carved nude statues to the carpet. "When she returns, tell her she is not to leave again, under pain of arrest, until I have had a chance to speak with her. Is that clear?"

The turban gave a slight bob.

Turning on his heel, the earl stalked to the front door, wrenching it open without standing on the usual social conventions.

As it fell shut with enough force to set the brass elephant head swinging wildly from side to side, the servant winced.

"Bloody hell," he murmured, in perfect imitation of the earl's clipped tone.

A rattle of the windowpane brought her out of a fitful slumber. Portia sat up and pulled the coverlet tighter as another gust of wind swirled through the garden. No doubt a branch had knocked up against the glass, she thought. Come morning, she would have to remember to ask the gardener to check on whether the gnarled old elm needed pruning. Settling back against the pillows, she closed her eyes, wondering how long it would take for sleep to come again. In truth she was surprised she had dozed off at all, what with the maelstrom of emotions spinning around in her head.

From her very first foray into the darkened London streets, she had known the dangers she faced, and yet, she had been confident that wits could make up for experience. *Too confident.* She had always believed intellect to be a more powerful weapon than emotion, but perhaps, she admitted with a rueful twist of her mouth, that was because she had never known just how intense elemental feelings could be. Her head might still be whole, but her heart . . .

Her gaze jerked around as another sharp rap sounded against the window. And another. A third pebble ricocheted off the glass before she was able to throw the mullioned casement open and peer down to the garden below. There was, however, no sign of movement among the bushes, save for a fitful stirring of leaves. Puzzled, Portia glanced heavenward. A smattering of rain clouds had scudded in from the east, bringing a damp chill to the night air, while far in the distance a low rumble of thunder presaged a coming storm. Had her imagination, already over-worked, only exaggerated the patter of the first few raindrops? Clutching her night rail to her chest, she prepared to swing the window shut.

The wave of a gloved hand, pale against the black cloak that had materialized out of the boxwoods, was visible for only an instant.

"Who . . ." she began, only to be cut off by a sharp hiss, which was quickly swallowed by a gust of wind.

The gesture was repeated, then the dark shape stole closer to the house. By craning her neck, Portia thought she could make out its progress toward one of the rear doors. Grabbing up her wrapper, she hurried for the stairs.

Upon reaching the entrance to the pantries and kitchen, she paused to light a candle, then, moving more cautiously, she nudged open the heavy oak door leading into the scullery and stepped inside. In the wavering circle of light, the large copper vats and stone sinks took on an ominous cast, slowing her steps even more as she crept over the cold stone floor.

There was no sign of life at the small window to the right of the door. Had her agitated emotional state brought on all-too-vivid-nightmares? she wondered. Drawing a deep breath, she leaned up against the thick oak, trying to still the slight tremor of her hands by telling herself she was acting like one of the hysterical heroines of Mrs. Radcliffe's horrid novels. Such chidings brought a wry smile to her lips, and for a moment she thought the dull thud she heard was but an echo of her racing pulse.

It took a fraction of a second longer to realize the sound was coming from outside.

"Who is there?" she demanded in a taut whisper.

"Olivia Grenville, Miss Hadley." The voice was missing a shade of its usual self-assurance. "Please let me in. And quickly."

Her fingers tightened on the iron latch as she recalled the grim efficiency with which the widow and her servant had dealt with Lord Mirkham. Was this, as the earl had put it, another tentacle reaching out? After all, he was convinced the lady was one of the principal villains, and she had no reason to think him mistaken.

And yet . . .

"Please!"

Something in the urgency of the plea caused Portia to throw caution to the wind. Acting on intuition rather than common sense, she slid back the bolts.

Mrs. Grenville stumbled inside. Her stylish cloak was torn, her elegant red dress was disheveled, and the delicate skin beneath her eye was darkening with a bruise. Portia gasped, then started to speak.

"Ssshhh." The candle was blown out with the same agitated breath. Spinning around, the widow pushed the door closed and shoved the bolts home. Her hand then shot out and pulled Portia down with her into a low crouch, so that both their heads were below the windowsill.

For several moments, all that could be heard was the gulp of ragged breathing, but then a faint scuff of gravel revealed that someone else was moving through the garden. The steps moved quickly across the path and faded away. The widow, however, remained pressed up against the plaster, a sharp squeeze of her hand warned Portia not to move.

Arms wrapped around her chest to control her shivering, Portia gave a tiny nod and held her breath.

A moment later the latch began to jiggle. The door gave a slight shudder as a shove from a shoulder tested the locks. There was a pause, then a harsh scraping as a knife probed at the window. Finding the latches fastened, the blade withdrew. Silence ensued, and it seemed like an age to Portia before a hurried tread signaled that the intruder was retreating.

Mrs. Grenville turned, and after a quick gesture to her lips indicating it still was not safe to speak, she motioned for Portia to lead the way out of the scullery. Keeping low, the two of them crept through the darkness out to the hallway and back up the stairs. Not daring to pause for a light, Portia somehow managed to lead the way to her bedchamber without rousing any of the other occupants of the house. Muffling the click of the latch with her wrapper, she eased the door open and motioned for Mrs. Grenville to slip inside.

The widow moved to the windows and pulled the draperies before venturing to speak. "I apologize for coming here, but I had to act quickly and could think of nowhere else to go."

Portia's face took on a martial expression. "If you are in trouble, you may trust me to do all I can to help."

"I really have no choice." Mrs. Grenville's lips gave a wry quirk. "Not now."

"What—"

"A slight miscalculation. And just as in business, such minor mistakes can result in disaster." The widow examined the rent in her outer garment. "I had not expected them to move quite so quickly."

"Who—"

"It is a long story, I'm afraid." she interrupted. "Perhaps you had better look at this first." Reaching into her cloak, she withdrew a small oilskin packet and placed it on the bed.

"Why—"

"Because it is meant for you."

Thrown off balance by the widow's disjointed explanations, Portia hesitated before picking up the object. She slowly undid the wrappings, revealing a small statue carved out of dark green stone. It appeared to be some sort of stylized cat, she noted vaguely, but what caught her attention most was that around its neck was a gold collar, from which hung a slender book.

The cover was made of an exotic green silk rather than leather, and on closer inspection she could make out several lines of lettering, though the language was foreign to her. Mystified, she flipped through the first few pages. A lengthy interval passed as her gaze took in a seemingly random juxtaposition of tightly spaced text, columns of numbers, and odd little pictures.

"I don't understand—what is it?" she finally asked.

The widow's faint smile became a bit more pronounced. "Why, it is the Jade Tiger."

The shock of the announcement caused Portia to blurt out an unladylike curse. "The devil take it!"

"Yes, well, apparently the Devil would give his right arm to get his hands on it," remarked the other woman with a touch of gallows humor. "And much as I hate to admit that two very capable females may need assistance to keep it in safe hands, I think we had better consider calling in reinforcements."

Chapter Seventeen

With a discreet bow, the earl's butler handed him a folded note, then withdrew from the library.

The earl broke the seal and glanced at the contents. "May Lucifer have his prick roasted over red-hot coals."

Davenport looked up. "That's one I haven't heard before." Shifting the stack of files to one side, he gave a slight cough. "I take it another problem has arisen."

"Quite likely." The earl skimmed over the short missive once more. "I believe Miss Hadley would rather submit to being boiled in oil than request my immediate presence, so yes, no doubt something is damnably wrong."

"Why is that?"

"Why is something wrong?" Branford could not keep the edge off his voice. "With Miss Hadley, I would not dare to venture a guess. My imagination is not up to the task."

Despite the show of sarcasm, he felt his throat constrict. It was true—she would not send for him unless something was dreadfully amiss. But as she had penned the note herself, it was likely not Portia in the thick of trouble this time, but Henry and Bertie. The thought that something might have happened to them caused a strange lurch in his chest. As he well knew, the lads were brave enough—and, like their sister, impetuous enough—to attempt something rash. So far, their pluck had not led them into any real danger, but what if on this occasion they had chosen to confront the wrong gentleman?

The thought of anyone harming so much as a hair of their tousled heads elicited a rumbling growl and another oath. Rising abruptly, he grabbed up his gloves and walking stick.

"No, what I meant was, why would she be loath to seek your help?" The crinkling around Davenport's eye was due more to puzzlement than the fast-fading scar.

"Don't ask." He was certainly not about to go into all the reasons why the young lady considered him an arrogant lout. "And don't dally. You had better come along with me."

Getting to his feet, the viscount followed in Branford's agitated wake, tactfully refraining from any further questions.

Lady Trumbull's elderly butler appeared to be expecting their arrival. Indeed, he seemed almost relieved at the sight of two very large, very imposing gentlemen on his doorstep, and ushered them toward the library as fast as his rheumatic joints could manage.

Portia was seated behind her aunt's desk, and the pallor of her drawn face only increased the earl's sense of anxiety. Before she had a chance to offer a word, he barked out a question.

"The lads—has something happened to them?"

"Henry and Bertie?" She seemed to be staring at his hands.

Looking down, Branford realized he was gripping his walking stick so tightly that it was in danger of snapping in two.

"No," she went on. "Though I cannot blame you for being annoyed at the possibility that they have created more mischief for you. I know they have been an extremely vexing distraction."

It was not annoyance or vexation that had tied his insides in knots, Branford realized as his muscles slowly unclenched.

"However, it was not on account of my brothers that I asked you to call, sir. The latest news . . ."

His rush of relief was quickly overshadowed by a sense of foreboding. "What news?"

She fumbled with something in her lap, then looked away. "Well, er . . ."

Following the direction of her gaze, he caught sight of Mrs. Grenville standing off in the shadows of the bookcase.

The earl found himself cursing yet again. He and several of Tony's men had spent most of the night on their feet, combing the city from the glittering environs of Grosvenor Square to the fetid stews of St. Giles in a vain effort to locate where the elusive widow had gone to ground. His already agitated state of mind was not improved by the realization that she had been here all along—and, he thought with a grinding of his teeth, looked to have spent the night a good deal more comfortably than he had.

A second glance quickly caused him to revise that assessment. The dress was the first clue that something was terribly amiss—the Lady in Red was wearing a gown of pale cornflower blue whose demure cut was not nearly so dramatic as the designs she usually favored. And as she turned her head from the leather-bound books, a small bruise below her left eye became evident.

His own shock was echoed by a muttered oath from Davenport. But before either of them could comment, Portia was on her feet. "I—we—thought that in light of your, er, current interests, you would wish to hear the story Mrs. Grenville has to tell." She directed a sidelong glance at the viscount and seemed to hesitate.

Belatedly recalling that Portia had not formally met his friend, Branford made a hurried introduction. "You may speak freely," he added. "As I told you earlier, Lord Davenport is helping with the investigation. And as for hearing what Mrs. Grenville knows, I have been trying to do precisely that for the last several days." The slight spasm that came to the widow's face caused him to moderate his sharp tone. "Indeed, in light of the glaring holes that still exist in the puzzle, I think it's about time the widow lay whatever pieces she possesses out on the table—if only so that Lord Davenport and I may have some hope of helping the two of you avoid further brushes with disaster."

"Yes," agreed Portia, with a hollowness that he had not heard from her before. "It is becoming more and more evident that despite all my efforts, I have made a complete hash of trying to fit things together." Her shoulders slumped. "Rather like trying to force square pegs into round holes."

Suddenly aware that the widow was not the only

one with dark smudges under her eyes, Branford found himself fighting the urge to sweep Portia into his arms and kiss the bruising uncertainty from her face and her voice. Then, with the harsh realization that such an action would hardly be welcome, he masked the twitch of his limbs with a slight cough and a step back from temptation.

"On the contrary, Miss Hadley," he replied softly, "you have done extremely well in fitting things together, despite your inexperience at such things."

Rather than serve as any encouragement, his attempt at reassurance only brought a fiery flush to her cheeks. "You needn't be sarcastic, sir," she snapped in a low voice, then muttered something else under her breath. It was said too softly for him to catch all of it, but he thought the words included *insufferable* and *ass*.

Davenport, who had been observing with tweaked brows the strained interplay between the earl and the young lady, ventured to intervene. "Er, perhaps we should listen to what Mrs. Grenville has to say without delay." With a brusque gesture he turned to the widow and indicated the small sofa to one side of the desk. "Would you care to take a seat before you begin?"

"Just because I have joined the ranks of the walking wounded does not mean I can't think on my feet, sir," she answered tartly.

"I meant no offense," he muttered.

The gentlemen exchanged rueful glances, and Branford had to admit that for seasoned intelligence officers they were not looking overly smart in their initial handling of the two females.

There was an awkward pause before Mrs. Grenville

broke the tension with a slight sigh. "Forgive my rudeness, sir. I fear I am still a trifle on edge." Despite her rather ragged appearance, she moved with unruffled poise toward the indicated seat. "While you, sir, are looking vastly improved since our last meeting."

"I was a bit under the weather," replied the viscount gruffly.

"And have some ways to go before the clouds are completely cleared from your brow." Her hand came up to touch the puckering near his eye. Ignoring his flinch, she ran a finger lightly down the length of the scar. "However, the ointment seems to be working well. I trust you will not be foolish enough to abandon its use."

This time it was the earl who ventured to rescue his friend from a difficult position. "As Lord Davenport suggested, perhaps we should dispense with the small talk and get down to business."

"Ah, yes. Business." The Lady in Red took a moment to smooth the skirts of her borrowed gown, a slightly bemused look coloring her features at the sight of the unfamiliar blue. "A subject with which I am very familiar. However, I'm afraid the particular transaction you wish to discuss is a rather complicated affair. I hardly know where to start."

"Perhaps with who caused that bruise on your face," replied the earl. "Was it Mirkham?"

"Miss Hadley told me that you witnessed that little encounter." The tightening of her fingers revealed that she was not quite as composed as she wished to appear. "I will get to that, but I think I had better explain a few other things first."

Branford's boots scuffed on the carpet in some impatience, drawing a glare from Portia. "Like your midnight meeting in Lady Fotherington's gardens?" he growled, pretending to have missed the flash of jade.

"So you observed that as well?" The widow shifted against the pillows. "It appears there is very little you have missed, sir."

Ha! he thought to himself. He wished that were the case, but in truth a great deal had escaped his notice until quite recently. Aloud, he merely gave a noncommittal grunt.

"I might as well begin there, as it may clear up a number of your questions," continued Mrs. Grenville. "I did have an assignation, but not one in any way connected with your concerns, Lord Branford."

The earl's frown was directed at Portia rather than the widow. "And how would you know what my concerns are?"

"Because I told her, of course," answered Portia impatiently. "At least listen to the full story before having me marched out to be drawn and quartered."

Branford felt his hands clench at the reminder of bullets cutting into her flesh. Not trusting his voice, he gave a curt nod for Mrs. Grenville to speak.

"You see, my name is not really Grenville. Nor am I a widow."

The announcement elicited a blink from the viscount, but the earl managed to mask his own surprise behind an impassive countenance. "Go on."

"You needn't hear the whole tedious story. I am the eldest child of the Earl of Harkness, an overbearing tyrant who sought to marry me off to one of his dissolute cronies." She drew in a sharp breath. "I was only sixteen, but as I am rather strong-willed myself, I refused to submit to a life that promised only boredom and more bullying."

"Brute," muttered Davenport.

"So I ran away," she continued. "As a gently bred girl, I didn't have any idea what life on the streets might mean, but standing up to my father over the years had toughened my resolve. I had a bit of pin money saved, and somehow managed to make my way across the Scottish border and on to Edinburgh without mishap. From there—well, I won't bore you with the details, but suffice it to say I was lucky enough to be given a chance to earn my keep by a kindly gentleman who took pity on my naïveté."

Portia couldn't refrain from interrupting. "It was incredibly brave of you."

"More likely incredibly foolish." The widow gave a small smile. "But somehow I survived. However, after working a short time at Grenville and Company, it became clear the business, and my benefactor, were on the verge of financial ruin. As I had always had a knack for numbers and practical turn of mind, I came up with an idea. . . ." Her smile grew more pronounced. "After doing some research, and a careful analysis of supply and demand, I suggested we get involved in the spice trade."

"Which, I wager, proved profitable." It was impossible to discern whether Davenport's mutter was prompted by admiration of her business acumen or quite the opposite.

"Oh, highly profitable." The widow cast him a cool look, as if daring a disparaging comment on females and finances. "And when I suggested that we move our headquarters to India, Mr. Colloden was delighted at the idea. The dear fellow was, in truth, more interested in the study of botany than business. To avoid any nasty gossip, it was decided that I should assume the name of Mrs. Grenville. The charade also allowed me to handle the daily operations of the company without raising too many eyebrows. After all, it is not entirely unheard-of for a widow to take over her late husband's business interests."

"Clever." It was Branford's first comment in a while. However, despite his grudging respect for the widow's pluck and resourcefulness, he refused to be distracted from his main concern. "But as to Mirkham and Dunster . . ."

"Yes, yes, I am getting to that, sir." Mrs. Grenville turned slightly to look out at the garden. "I had always been quite close to my younger brother, and I kept in clandestine touch with him, sending letters and money through my old nanny. Unlike me, Thomas is a gentle, amiable soul. And that, I suppose, is part of the current problem." Her mouth thinned. "He is engaged to be married to the eldest daughter of the Marquess of Hollington. The two of them have made a love match, but their happiness is being threatened by our cousin, Lord Mirkham. Even as a child, Louis was a dirty dish, and now he is blackmailing Thomas with the letters he has stolen that show a sister in trade."

Although the widow's voice remained very measured, the earl could see the stiffening of her shoulders. "The truth would, of course, cause a terrible scandal. I did not wish my brother's life to be ruined by the choices I had made in my life. So, as I have a good deal more experience in negotiations than Thomas, and have learned not to be intimidated by even the most weasely of men, I took it upon myself to return to England to . . . handle Lord Mirkham. It was, by the way, a meeting with my brother that you spied in Lady Fotherington's gardens."

"We saw you offer Mirkham jewels and hashish, but that was not enough," said Branford. "What did he want from the *Lotus of the Orient*?"

She sighed. "The answer is not nearly as nefarious as you think, sir. The cargo of the *Lotus* included a small but quite valuable quantity of a new blend of spiced tea I have created. Somehow, in the course of his other shady dealings, Mirkham learned that one of my rivals would be willing to pay a fortune if the sample was stolen." On seeing the twist of disbelief that pulled at the earl's features, she let out a sigh. "It may sound implausible to you, sir, but the world of commerce is not unlike the world of politics. Intrigue, espionage, treachery, even bloodshed are all part of the game when considerable power and profit are concerned."

"And the demand for a new type of tea would, I imagine, generate enormous profits," mused Davenport.

"Astronomical," agreed Mrs. Grenville.

Both of them looked to the earl for comment.

The silver knob of his walking stick slapped several times against his palm before he spoke. "I suppose that gives a satisfactory explanation of your recent actions."

The widow's lips crooked. "Assuming I am telling the truth? I can corroborate all of what I have told you."

"Hmmph. No doubt." The stick gave another slap. "But that still leaves a great many questions unanswered. Such as who coshed me over the head—"

"Allow me to apologize for that, sir," Mrs. Grenville sighed. "Vavek is sometimes overzealous in protecting my interests."

Branford gave a stiff nod. "Very well. But that still does not explain why Lord Roxleigh was murdered in your warehouse. We know he was working with Dunster, and given their other dealings, I doubt the two of them had any interest in tea." As he spoke, Branford found himself fumbling to arrange the new pieces of the puzzle into any recognizable pattern. "I wonder what—"

"You are right, sir. Roxleigh wasn't looking for tea, though Mirkham's employers thought he was," interrupted Portia. "We think he was looking for this."

Out of the corner of his eye, Branford caught a flash of green. "What is it?" he demanded, turning to stare at the small object she was holding up for his inspection.

"The Jade Tiger."

"What the devil—"

She stopped him with a snort of frustration. "Don't ask me what it is for! If only I knew!" Her breath came out in another forceful sigh. "From what little I have pieced together, I think it is a legendary artifact whose arcane markings are said to hold the key to deciphering some ancient mystery. My father had apparently suspected its existence for years, and had set in motion a search to discover its whereabouts—for scholarly reasons, of course. When the unrest and war threatened to engulf the Caucasus, one of the local scholars, who had heard of Father's interest, apparently decided the treasure would be safest in Father's hands. So it passed overland through Tehran and southern Persia, into Baluchistan, and then to the coast of India."

"To Bombay," explained Mrs. Grenville, picking up the narrative. "My benefactor's other hobby was the study of ancient manuscripts, and over years of correspondence he had developed a warm friendship with Lord Hadley. It was, therefore, only natural that the baron sought help from Grenville and Company when he learned that such a valuable item needed transport to England." She took a deep breath. "Mr. Culloden had passed away several months before Lord Hadley's letter arrived. But as I recalled the name and read the urgency of his plea, I decided to send it on the *Lotus of the Orient,* along with my own valuables. As he also included a strict warning to be very careful about who should know of its existence, I was disturbed to learn, upon my arrival in London, that the baron had gone missing under rather mysterious circumstances."

"As if you didn't have enough to worry about," sighed Portia.

Mrs. Grenville's expression turned wry. "I admit, it did add a further twist to an already tangled situation."

Portia smiled. "I can hardly blame you for being so wary during our first encounters."

"I have encountered my share of slyness and subterfuge over the years. Until I was sure you were who you said you were and could be trusted, I decided to be very wary."

"It is not just I who am grateful for your caution," observed Portia. She slanted a look at the earl. "I would imagine Lord Branford considers himself immensely lucky that you were able to keep the Jade Tiger from passing into another's hands."

The earl was so caught up in what he had just heard

that she had to repeat herself. "Yes, I suppose it is a stroke of luck that Mrs. Grenville is both clever and capable," he answered slowly. "However, in all honesty, I would feel a good deal luckier if I could figure out if this Jade Tiger has aught to do with the item Max and I seek." He could not help but frown. "It may, after all, be only a coincidence that someone is trying to steal it. A rival scholar, perhaps?"

Portia shook her head. "I don't think so. Mrs. Grenville showed me the last letter my father wrote to her benefactor. It refers to the Jade Tiger as the Key to the Lion. In scholarly circles, a key means a cipher of sorts—one that will somehow unlock the meaning of some momentous secret.

"Lion?" Davenport's head came up with a snap. "Would you mind if I have a look at your Jade Tiger, Miss Hadley?"

Porita handed it over to the viscount without argument.

"Alex, as you know, what we seek is officially called the Riddle of Rafistan. However, in his missives to Tony, the Tsar's minister kept referring to it by the name used by the locals," he said quietly while thumbing through several of the pages that hung from the statue's neck, "which is the Lion's Voice." The cover closed with a soft snap.

"Bloody hell." Things were finally beginning to fall into place, thought the earl, and a picture starting to emerge from the haphazard bits and pieces. "A Lion, a Tiger, and a missing English baron—an odd menagerie, but one that may be more dangerous than a host of trained armies."

"Yes," agreed Davenport. "My guess is that this little book is nearly as important as the Riddle itself. The trouble is, it will take quite a bit of time to discern the hidden meaning. What with analyzing whether there are recurring patterns, and applying a system of complex equations . . ." His words drifted off for a moment as he considered the magnitude of the problem. "You see, most codes are based on mathematical principles. However, the good ones can be incredibly difficult to figure out. I have some expertise in the subject, but still . . ." He shook his head. "This one looks devilishly tricky, Cat. It could take weeks, even months—that is, assuming I can solve it at all."

Branford's mouth thinned. "We don't have weeks or months."

"I have a good head for numbers," volunteered Mrs. Grenville.

That actually won a grudging smile from the viscount. "I don't doubt it, but to accomplish the type of calculations I am speaking of, in the amount of time we have, we would need a . . . a mathematical genius."

Portia darted an odd look at Branford. "Then perhaps . . ."

He nodded. "By all means, let us summon Bertie and ask his opinion of the problem."

The look on his friend's face clearly indicated that he thought the earl had taken leave of his senses. "Alex," he warned in a low murmur, "I am aware that you possess a deucedly odd sense of humor at times, but this is hardly the occasion for giving it free rein."

"I assure you, I am deadly serious, Max."

"But I was under the impression that the, er, young person in question is only a child."

The earl found his mouth quirking upward in spite of the gravity of the situation. "But a most unusual child. Let us see what your impression is after you have spent five minutes with him."

Davenport appeared unconvinced but acquiesced with a slight lift of his shoulders. "Your pardon, Miss Hadley," he said stiffly after Portia had rung for the butler and asked him to fetch her brother. "I do not mean to disparage the lad's talents, you understand. It is just that the theory involved, and the sort of calculations to which I am referring, would stump any number of Oxford dons."

Her lips also gave a small twitch. "Yes, no doubt they would, sir." Returning to her aunt's desk, she resumed her seat and started sorting her notes into several neat piles.

Once again, a silence descended upon the room. Branford picked up a volume of Latin poetry and chose a section at random while the widow turned her attention to the watercolor hanging over the mantel. After a self-conscious tug at his cravat, the viscount fell to a desultory examination of the papers lying atop the blotter of the worktable by the window. It was not long, however, before a grunt of surprise escaped his lips.

"Have you any idea where this came from?" he demanded, holding aloft a single sheet of foolscap covered with a minute scrawl.

Portia squinted. "I imagine it belongs to Henry. For the last few days he has been occupied with comparing the stylistic nuances of some obscure dialect. Northern Farsi, I believe."

"Dare I inquire who Henry is?"

"The other child—Bertie's older brother," she answered. By way of further explanation, she added, "He is rather gifted with languages."

"Good Lord," he exclaimed faintly. "Alex, I think you have better come have a look at this."

Branford dropped his perusal of Cicero to join his friend.

"Look familiar?" asked Davenport, shoving the document under the earl's nose.

"I have seen a similar sort of zig and squiggle when a fly has fallen in my soup," he quipped. "But in all honesty, I cannot claim to recognize . . ." He left off as his gaze focused in on the jiggly dashes of ink. "Hmmm. On second thought, it does bear a striking similarity to the hidden bit of writing you brought to light on the captured dispatch."

"Precisely." Davenport picked at a few of the dried bits of red sticking out from his cheek as he took another long look at the writing on the page. "Farsi, you say? I, er, think that perhaps we ought to ask both of Miss Hadley's siblings to make an appearance."

The clatter of running footsteps and a scrabbling of hands at the door knob interrupted his words. So, too, did a muffled exchange from the other side of the paneled oak.

"Ummmph! Just because your arm, due to its larger arc, is able to exert more torque on—"

"Put a cork in it!" came the whispered retort. "Now, straighten your collar and wipe the ink smudge off your nose. You don't want to look like a child, do you?"

Branford clasped his hands behind his back. "I believe Henry Falstaff and Bertram Orlando are about ready to take the stage."

Chapter Eighteen

❧❦❧

". . . And then apply one of Twickham's logarithms. Yes, that would probably do the trick." Bertie looked up. "Mind you, it's only a first glance. If I spend a bit more time with it, I may find an even easier solution."

"How long do you suppose it would take you to work through the problems, Bertie?" asked the earl.

The lad's face screwed in thought. "For the mathematical part, maybe a day, sir. As for correlating the data to come up with an actual alphabetical table, that may take a little longer." He shrugged his small shoulders. "I'm not as good with letters as I am with numbers."

"Max?" Branford's brow arched.

"Er, yes, if I have the raw data, I'm sure I can take it from there."

Portia had to repress a chuckle at the stunned expression that had come over the viscount's lean face. Shell-shocked might be a more apt description, she decided, seeing as he had just endured a barrage of highly advanced mathematical theory that would have left most Oxford dons reeling.

"So, assuming we can solve the mystery of the Jade Tiger, how about the translation of the captured dispatch?"

In his eagerness to answer, Henry nearly fell off the corner of the worktable on which he was perched. "If it is any one of the dialects from around Baku or Tabriz, as you suggest, then I should be able to figure out the gist of it. However, there is—"

A loud knocking cut off his words. Before anyone could voice a reply, the door flew open and Lady Trumbull breezed in with a platter of fresh scones, followed by the maid with a large tea tray. "I imagined that all of you might welcome a bit of sustenance."

"How thoughtful, Aunt Octavia," murmured Portia, lowering her lashes to hide her amusement. There was, she noted, a similar sparkle in the earl's sapphire eyes, though it lasted no more than an instant.

A pang of regret shot through her at the glimpse of it. Even under such trying circumstances, the earl had not lost his sense of humor. It was one of the facets she found most appealing about him, along with his patience with her eccentric family, his loyalty to his friends, his strength in the face of danger. . . . She forced her eyes from his profile. There was no point in dwelling on his admirable qualities when her own prickly pride had made certain that she would not see hide nor hair of him again once he had finished his mission for Mr. Taft.

After seeing to the arrangement of the pastries and china, Lady Trumbull dismissed the maid but made no move to follow. Instead, she seated herself amid the plump pillows of the settee and began to pour.

"Er, Alex . . ." Still unconvinced that children should be privy to matters of state, Davenport made a small choking sound. "Do you really, er, think it wise for—"

"If you are about to ask if it is wise for an old lady to be present for the current discussion, young man, you may just put a cork in it." She placed one of the cups on a saucer and smiled sweetly. "Do you take milk or lemon?"

"Er, lemon," croaked Davenport.

"You don't really think I am about to let the lot of you have all the fun?" she continued. "I demand to be a part of whatever is going on in here. Besides, I daresay I have accumulated a bit of wisdom to go along with my years, so perhaps I may be of some help."

Having recovered from his initial shock, Davenport turned to the earl with a frown. "Good Lord, Cat, we are talking about the fate of nations here. Do you really think . . ." His voice became a taut whisper. "Er, that is, considering the danger involved, are you sure we should be involving women and children."

As Branford took his time in assessing the assembled company, Portia made her own surreptitious survey. A scarred veteran, two spirited females, an elderly expert on Latin sonnets, and two lads, one of whom was barely tall enough to stand eyeball to eyeball with the middle button of the earl's waistcoat. Though she kept her opinion to herself, she was forced to admit that perhaps the viscount had a point.

But to her surprise, the earl did not appear to agree with his friend. "It's a bit irregular, I admit. Yet, if you recall, on the Peninsula we fought the French quite effectively with some rather strange allies among the guerrillas." A smile slowly split the grimness of his expression. "And I daresay, Cricket, this bunch is a match for even the most treacherous enemy."

The look of grave concern on the viscount's face turned to one of grudging bemusement. "Oh, very well. I suppose it is worth a shot." His fingers came up to rub at his cheek. "I, for one, have to admit I would rather face off against a regiment of French sabers than cross swords with any of the present company."

"It appears Lord Davenport is actually a great more intelligent than a bug," quipped Mrs. Grenville. Ignoring the tightening of his jaw, she continued, "Indeed, I must admit I am at a loss to see a resemblance to any sort of insect. Except for his present coloring, that is."

Branford allowed a quick grin as the viscount's face went through a series of tiny contortions. Apparently it was not just a theoretical challenge that was stirring his friend to life again. With a slight cough, he looked from the widow to Davenport and back again. "The sobriquet actually derives from his prowess in sport. Max wields a mean bat on the cricket pitch. During play on a makeshift field on the Peninsula, one of his prodigious swings sent the ball in a soaring drive—whereupon it hit smack against Wellington's forehead as he was riding by."

Henry and Bertie stared at the viscount, eyes widened in awe.

"Knocked his hat clean off," drawled Branford, looking to Portia as if he were enjoying the chance to tell the tale. "The Iron Duke had a sense of humor about it, I must say. Threatened to put Max in charge of the artillery, saying that if his aim was as good against Soult and the Frogs, the war would be won in a trice."

There were smiles all around, including a reluctant twitch from the viscount, before Lady Trumbull brought the conversation back to a more serious note. "Well, now that we are allies, let's get down to brass tacks." She set the teapot down with a thump of impatience. "Henry, do go on with what you were saying about the captured dispatch."

"Max, we had best keep in mind that the Hadley females seem to possess a remarkable talent for peering in windows and listening at keyholes," remarked the earl dryly.

"I have very acute hearing for a lady of my age, young man," replied Lady Trumbull, trying to appear mildly offended. The effect was ruined by the dancing gleam behind the gold-rimmed spectacles.

Henry finally managed to get a word in edgewise. "Sir, what I was about to say was, if I knew more of what this whole matter is about, I would have a better chance of interpreting things correctly."

"Much as I hate to admit it, what the lad says makes some sense," said Davenport after a brief silence. He turned to Branford. "In for a penny, in for a pound, Cat."

The earl took a deep breath before continuing. "As we have gone this far, there is not much point in holding back the rest. However," he stressed, raking all of them with a stern look, "you must all recognize the gravity of the situation and swear not to breathe a word of this to anyone. I am deadly serious in this. The slightest slip could result in death to any one of you. Miss Hadley and Mrs. Grenville have experienced firsthand just how ruthless our enemy can be, so they can attest to the truth of my warning. Are we agreed on this?"

There was a solemn nodding of heads.

"Very well." Portia thought the earl did not look quite so amused as earlier, but after only the slightest hesitation he proceeded to explain about the stolen government document and his suspicions concerning Lord Dunster.

"I say, sir—" began Bertie, only to be cut off by his sister.

"Well, the picture certainly becomes a great deal clearer," she observed, "now that we have filled in a number of the glaring holes." In a lower voice she added, "We might have avoided a good deal of trouble had you been more forthcoming from the very beginning."

His eyes darkened a shade, but whether in anger or contrition she could not tell. Not until he opened his mouth.

"Forgive me," he said in a slow drawl that made his sentiments perfectly clear. "I must be a slowtop, as well as an arrogant and insufferable lout, for failing to comprehend the innocence of your own actions."

"Sir—" Bertie attempted to speak again, but was drowned out by Davenport's hasty attempt at staving off further skirmishing between Portia and Branford.

"Er, let us not waste time in fighting among ourselves. There is a great deal to do."

Unable to contain his impatience, the lad raised his voice to a near shout. "Lord Branford!"

"Put a cork in it, Bertie," chastised Henry.

"I'll be damned if I will!" he replied hotly.

A sudden silence descended over the room, save for a slight rattle of china as Lady Trumbull put down her teacup.

Portia drew in a sharp breath, not quite sure what to make of the youngest Hadley's transgression. "Bertram Orlando—"

The lad's chin took on an unrepentant tilt. "Wash my mouth out with soap if you must, but before you do, Lord Branford may wish to hear about the meeting Lord Dunster is planning."

"*What* meeting?" demanded both the earl and his friend at once.

"The one spelled out in the boot maker's bill Portia took from his desk." Bertie let just a touch of smugness creep into his answer. Seeing he had everyone's full attention, he went on to explain. "I noticed that the pattern of the numbers looked odd, so I asked Portia if I might take a closer look. Well, sure enough, it proved a rather simple code, one straight out of Bertolli's manual on the subject. Even a child could have figured the transposition of letters for numbers."

"Bertie, if it is not too much to ask, might you forgo the theoretical explanations and tell us what it said?" asked Branford.

All in all, Portia gave the earl credit for showing great restraint.

"Oh." The lad rubbed at his nose. "Yes, sir. The message was this—'The Bee will come for the Lion on the evening of eight thirteen at Hawthorne Hall. Arrange the usual diversions.' "

"Eight thirteen. August thirteenth—why, that is tomorrow evening!" Branford began to pace. "B? B?

What the devil does it stand for? An initial?" he wondered out loud.

"B-E-E," spelled Bertie.

"Hmmph. Another beast for our menagerie," growled Davenport. "And one just as puzzling as the Lion and Tiger."

For several moments the only sound was the thud of the earl's boot heels on the thick carpet. Then, with a slight clearing of her throat, Lady Trumbull ventured a suggestion. "While the bee has long stood for prosperity in classical allusions, of late, it has been adopted as Bonaparte's pet symbol. Could Bee refer to an agent of the Emperor?"

"By Jove." The earl stopped in his tracks long enough to plant a kiss on the elderly lady's hand. "Speaking of brass tacks, I think you have hit the nail on the head, Lady Trumbull."

Two spots of pink appeared upon the elderly lady's cheeks. "Haven't lost all my marbles yet," she murmured.

"Nor any of your other considerable charms," replied the earl with a rakish wink.

Portia felt a little lurch of her insides. It had nothing to do with the glint of Branford's eyes when he smiled, she assured herself. If she was feeling a trifle unsteady on her feet, it was only due to lack of sleep and the fact that the room had all of a sudden become rather stuffy.

"Hawthorne House is Lord Dunster's estate in Kent," she said rather thickly as she moved to open a window. "Not much more than an hour's drive away."

"No doubt you have it timed to the minute," said Branford, a smile still lingering on his lips. "I don't suppose you managed to purloin a floor plan of the place. It might come in handy."

Assiduously avoiding so much as a glance in his direction, she threw open the casement. "Sorry. Must have misplaced my picklocks and ropes somewhere along the way." As her back was turned, she missed seeing how her shrill tone brought a slight crease to his brow. It was gone as quickly as it came, replaced by a steeling of his features as he marshaled his attention to mapping out a plan of attack.

"It is a long shot, but I mean to return to The House of Flowers this evening, and see if I can learn more about what is planned for tomorrow. With any luck, I may even convince Dunster to include me among the participants."

"It is worth a try," agreed Davenport. Taking up pen and paper, he began to scribble some notes. "In the meantime, we will have to alert Tony and arrange for the area to be surrounded by his best men."

"Let us hope they are more effective than the idiots he used to keep watch over Mrs. Gren—er, that is, Lady Harkness."

"I think it best if you stick with Mrs. Grenville," a wry note was evident in her voice. "It has been so long since I used my real name, I probably wouldn't respond to it. And I would also prefer to keep my return from the dead a secret from my father and the rest of Society until my brother's happiness is ensured."

The earl inclined his head. "As you wish."

Davenport's pen continued its faint scratching. "I am sure Tony will see to it that no one will slip through the noose this time. Meanwhile, I would like

Master Henry to come with me and see if he can make any sense out of the strange dispatch." Seeing the youngest Hadley's crestfallen expression, he hesitated, then tugged at his cravat. "Er, and perhaps Master Bertram should come along, too, and begin a preliminary study of the Jade Tiger."

Both lads made a beeline for the door.

Branford paused in his pacing. "And while you are at it, take another look at the files Tony sent over. I still cannot shake the feeling that I am missing one last piece to the puzzle."

"I will keep at it, but, like the Saint, the others from Whitehall seem quite exemplary gentlemen." Davenport gave a curt laugh. "Indeed, the only vice I have spotted so far is the fact that Lord Lochern plays in a weekly hand of whist with fellow members of the Historical Society, where the wagering runs to the enormous sum of a shilling a hand."

"Hardly a lot to strike fear in the heart of the Crown," grunted the earl.

The viscount's mention of scholars jarred Portia from her glum study of the scudding clouds that were fast turning the blue sky to a dull gray. Rather like her own mood, she mused before heaving a small sigh. "No, I have to agree," she said aloud. "A good many of the members are friends of my father and have gone out of their way to express concern over his disappearance. Indeed, Mr. Dearborne was kind enough to offer his assistance in helping discover what the Jade Tiger could be." Out of the corner of her eye she noted the darkening of the earl's countenance but chose to ignore it. "Of course, now I can inform him that he need not go to any more trouble."

Branford's walking stick began a slow, rhythmic tapping against the side of his boot. "You knew about the Jade Tiger before last night?"

She knew the softness of his voice augured ill, but was in no frame of mind to engage in one of their heated duel of words. "Oh, what does it matter now? Let us not start brangling about past decisions when we have more important concerns to occupy our attentions."

The earl looked as though he wished to argue the point, but contented himself with a wordless grumble. "Very well," he muttered. "But I must insist that you not say anything more to Mr. Dearborne for the moment. It will do no harm for him to keep his nose buried in a book for another day or two."

Aware that the others were following the exchange with undisguised interest, she bit back an acid retort and merely nodded.

"We had best get moving, Max. While you return home with the lads, I will make arrangements with Tony, then try to meet up with Hurricane, in case his efforts have turned up anything useful."

Branford was halfway to the door when Mrs. Grenville called one last question. "The males have all been assigned useful tasks. Is there nothing we ladies can do to help out?"

Although he studiously avoided any glance in her direction, Portia had no illusions as to whom his next words were directed. "At the risk of sounding pompous or overbearing, may I ask you ladies to refrain from taking any action of your own until we have a better idea of what we are up against?"

Lady Trumbull brandished her teaspoon as if it were a saber. "Only if you promise to report back to us as soon as possible. We insist on being kept abreast of the plans."

He shrugged in harried defeat. "Much as I would like to refuse, I would rather have Lucifer and his legions up in arms against me than three such formidable females."

Formidable. Portia felt anything but that as she curled up against her pillows and buried her chin in the coverlet. Her great-aunt had assumed command with the same brusque efficiency as a general after the gentlemen had taken their leave, insisting that the two younger ladies lie down for a few hours of rest. Mrs. Grenville had been marched off to one of the guest rooms, and in truth, Portia had not been in any frame of mind to put up much of an argument when she, too, had been ordered to her own quarters.

She didn't need Bertie's expertise in mathematics to know her chances of regaining even a small measure of the earl's regard added up to naught. Or Henry's flair for linguistics to comprehend what a dreadful hash she had made of expressing her feelings. Suppressing a sigh, she sought to control the quiver of her lips. Every time she opened her mouth, she seemed to say the wrong thing, perhaps because her own emotions seemed to be speaking to her in strange tongues.

It was impossible to translate into words the odd little lurches and flares of fire that surged through her core. This sort of love—a roar of flames rather than the soft, steady glow of familial affection—was a new language, one she was having great difficulty mastering.

The earl, on the other hand, appeared to be having no problem making his sentiments known. The clouded color of his eyes, the grim set of his mouth, the clenching of his fists, the sharp edge of his sarcasm—all spoke volumes on how irritating he found her company. And while there had been several inexplicable exceptions, she recalled with a watery sniff that they had, for the most part, occurred after he had imbibed quite a bit of brandy. So no doubt the explanation was that he had not been thinking clearly.

Portia supposed she could hardly blame Branford for being annoyed. However unwittingly, she had placed him in a number of awkward situations, not least of which had finally forced him to make an offer of marriage, despite his avowed reluctance to march to the altar. It had been duty, rather than any more tender emotion, that had wrenched the words from his throat.

Just as it had been relief that had flooded over his features at finding himself excused from the onerous obligation of honor.

Blinking back the tears that threatened to spill over her cheeks, she found her own spirits turning nearly as black as a certain Cat. She had only herself to blame, she admitted. She had known she was flirting with disaster the night she had climbed into Lord Dunster's study. Well, she had met it in spades! It was perhaps a fitting irony that all of her risky actions had resulted in naught but her losing her virtue—and her heart—

to a roguish earl who was likely to bedevil her dreams for some time to come.

Sure enough, when she closed her eyes, Portia could only picture waves of thick black hair framing a pair of sapphirine eyes, a subtly faceted blue that mirrored the depth and complexity of the earl himself. *Black and blue.* She hugged her knees to her chest. Indeed, she was feeling rather bruised in both body and spirit.

But as she drifted off into a fitful sleep, she took some small measure of solace in thinking the chances were good that her father was about to be saved, no matter that it was at the loss of her own peace of mind.

Branford awoke the following morning with a splitting headache, due as much to the prospect of the coming meeting with the Hadleys and Company as to the copious amounts of brandy and champagne he had been required to down at The House of Flowers. In that instance, however, the present pounding in his temples had been well worth it. After several hours of drinking, gambling, and groping the girls, he had finally managed to cozen up to the marquess. It took a few more shared bottles and a number of pointed hints of how useful a man with deadly skills and no compunction about using them could be, but a gleam of interest had finally come to Dunster's bleary eyes. The invitation to meet with the marquess's partner to discuss a business arrangement had been tendered for the coming evening.

So his aching head was a small price to pay for such a victory, thought Branford, throwing back the covers and easing his bare feet to the floor. Now, if only he might come through the next engagement without suffering a more grievous injury, he hoped, only half in jest.

"I had better brush out a fresh coat." Blaze had stomped into the room at the first sign of life and was now wrinkling his nose as he scooped up the discarded garment from the carpet. "Wouldn't want you to go visiting Miss Hadley with the reek of that musky perfume clinging to your collar. She would likely want your head on a platter."

"Hmmph!" The idea that Miss Hadley might be the slightest bit jealous drew a snort from the earl. "The young lady might wish to see my head parted from my neck, but not for any amatory reason. I assure you, she finds me arrogant and odious." There was a tiny pause before he added, "Not to speak of pompous and overbearing, if I remember her words verbatim."

The valet gave a swipe to the offending sleeve. "Very perceptive of the lassie," he replied. "I see she is not only extremely brave but extremely intelligent."

Branford wondered whether the muzzy state of his head had affected his hearing. "Words of praise for a female? Thought you were not, on principle, very keen on the fairer sex."

"Aye, but Miss Hadley appears t' be a real trooper. If we are t' have a lady around, might as well be one who can stand up t' your ornery temper or flying bullets without blinking an eye."

"Hmmph," repeated Branford, grimacing as the first splash of cold water slapped against his cheeks. "Who says we are going to have one around?"

The valet tossed the coat over the back of a chair. "I

may not be the brightest fire on this planet, but I have learned enough about the ways of Polite Society to know that sooner or later an earl has an obligation to set up his nursery."

His scowl deepened. Hell would likely freeze over before the lady in question consented to be part of those plans! He refrained from expressing such thoughts aloud, however he was rather surprised at how sharply he felt the stab of such sentiments. He should be glad of Miss Hadley's refusal to consider his proposal, for with her fierce streak of independence, she was altogether too fiery to make a proper sort of wife. And yet, he wasn't. Not at all. She—along with her delightfully eccentric family—had lit a rare spark in the cold ashes of his life. Even now he could feel the warmth of it deep within his breast. She had made him laugh, she had made him swear, she had made him think. . . .

In short, she had made him feel alive again, from the roots of his hair to the tips of his toes. How was he to prevent the flame from being extinguished?

It was yet another conundrum to wrestle with. But first he had to solve the mystery of the Riddle of Rafistan. Finishing his ablutions in moody silence, he pulled on the proffered fresh shirt. "Has Max risen? I should like him to meet me in the breakfast room as soon as possible. We can plan strategy over a pot of coffee—"

"Or tea," suggested Blaze dryly, "seeing as it is nigh on four in th' afternoon."

"Bloody hell." Quickly tugging his cravat into a haphazard knot, the earl rushed for the stairs, his valet trailing along with an immaculate navy superfine coat draped over one arm.

His friend was in the library, seated at the massive desk with several stacks of books and papers spread out before him. Without looking up, the viscount slid a paper across the leather blotter. "Bloody genius." Branford was fairly certain the compliment was not directed at him. "Actually, you had best make that plural," continued Davenport. "Both lads are, er, rather extraordinary. No wonder Dunster and his cronies kidnapped the father. If he possesses even a fraction of his progeny's intellect, the Riddle of Rafistan will prove no more difficult than a nursery rhyme to figure out."

"What is this?" Branford started to read the neatly lettered page.

"Henry's translation of the captured dispatch that was en route to the Emperor's informant in Constantinople. It confirms what we surmised—a French agent has a rendezvous here in London to purchase the answer to the Riddle. It also mentions that the trail to the Tiger has finally been uncovered and that they are hot on its tracks."

"Well, it seems our erstwhile widow was lucky to stay a step ahead of her pursuers," he murmured. "And Miss Hadley's outlandish story of being cheated out of her home and possessions begins to make more and more sense. Our enemy did not know whether the baron had received the Jade Tiger, so he contrived to take possession of the baron's entire library in hopes that it would be secreted among the other books."

"Cunning of him," remarked the viscount.

"Oh, yes, our enemy is a clever fellow. But while he

planned for most every contingency, he did not reckon on meeting with the likes of the Warrior Queen."

Not that *anyone* could be prepared for an encounter with the likes of Portia.

However, he had no choice but to walk into the lion's—or rather, tiger's—den. "And much as I would like to avoid a meeting with the lady in question, I have pledged my word to report in. I assume the lads have already informed the ladies of what you discovered."

His friend squirmed a bit in his seat. "It seemed unreasonable to order them to keep mum. Er, besides we agreed to share information, did we not?"

"Only because I am an experienced enough soldier to know when not to fight a losing battle," groused Branford. Letting out an exasperated sigh, he reached for the cup of coffee and plate of buttered toast that Blaze had set upon a corner of the desk. "Let us go marshal our forces and outline the final plan of attack."

"Ah. Then you, too, managed to learn something of import?" Davenport was already busy shuffling papers into a slim portfolio. "What is the latest?"

Branford took his time in finishing his toast and coffee before replying. "As I prefer to go over it only once, I will explain my plan once the ladies are present."

A bemused twitch of his cheek caused a bit of the orange ointment to fall on the viscount's collar. "Ha!" he said with a trifle more of his former humor than the earl cared to hear at the moment. "I look forward to hearing what maneuvers you have come up with to keep them well out of the action."

Ha! And the Devil would look forward to having his cloven hooves shod with red-hot nails! Branford doubted his friend would be looking so amused when he heard exactly what the earl had in mind.

One outraged officer he could handle. It was facing off against not one but three fiery females that was going to test his true mettle.

Chapter Nineteen

Mrs. Grenville was the only one whose countenance remained impassive, noted Branford. He shifted slightly and suppressed a wince. As for the others, it was not at all difficult to discern their reaction to his plan. If the daggered looks flashing his way had been forged of steel, he would have been chopped into mincemeat several moments ago. He supposed he should be grateful that they had all agreed to exclude the lads from the current meeting. Things were daunting enough without having to fight off their looks of wounded outrage as well.

"Damn it, Alex, you cannot think I will go along with that." In the first blush of anger, the viscount forgot enough of his usual reserve with the opposite sex to let out an oath.

"You are free to walk away from the field of battle, if that is what you wish," shrugged Branford.

The volley of invectives that followed would have blistered the ears of a seasoned soldier. He noted, however, that none of the ladies so much as batted an eyelash.

". . . as if I would desert a comrade in the heat of the action," finished Davenport, his jaw working so vigorously that the orange stripe flickered like a hot flame.

"Then you will obey orders. I assure you, it is a vital role."

His friend crossed his arms and glowered.

"Let me get this straight." It was Portia who finally punctured the awkward silence that ensued. "You wish for the ladies to remain here, within the confines of these walls—"

"Working on our embroidery, no doubt," sniffed Lady Trumbull. Branford did not fail to note that had the jab of her pen been aimed in his direction it would have skewered his liver.

"*And* you mean to post Lord Davenport as a guard," continued her niece, "to make sure we do not set foot out the door?"

The earl cleared his throat. "Not exactly. It's for your security as well. The enemy is no doubt growing desperate to find the Tiger and may come looking here." Seeing the gold sparks coming to light in her jade-green eyes, he made one last stab at appealing to logic. "As to my part of the plan, I shall explain it once more. I dropped a blatant hint about having a highly valuable item to dispose of, providing I could find the right buyer, and Dunster seemed to take the bait. The only sensible strategy is for me to proceed alone, for the slightest misstep will ruin everything."

"But—"

"No *but*s, Miss Hadley. What else do you suggest? That we all charge in hell for leather without knowing the lay of the land or the enemy's strengths?"

The question, uttered with just a touch of an edge, did little to douse the fire in the young lady's gaze, but it did cause her to hesitate in answering.

It was, he mused, still a source of constant wonderment that she could possess such stubborn courage. However, he wasn't about to have her exposed to any further risks. And besides, absurd though the notion might be, a small part of him wished to accomplish the mission unaided—recovering both the Riddle and, with luck, her father—so that he might rekindle a spark of admiration in her eyes.

He missed that light. She had stormed into his life, all flash and thunder, illuminating every nook and cranny—even the places he wished to keep hidden from himself. He had fought to extinguish the flame, but now he wasn't quite sure he would ever be content to dwell in the shadows.

Squaring his shoulders, he quelled such thoughts for the present and pressed on. "Taft will have men surrounding the area, so even if I trip up, the bastards will not slip through the noose."

"I still don't like it that you mean to go in there alone," growled Davenport. "If something goes wrong, you should have someone to—"

The earl waved off the argument. "Bringing a companion would only serve to raise Dunster's suspicions. If something goes wrong, I shall simply have to . . . improvise. In the past, you know I have always managed to land on my feet."

"Aye, Cat. But who knows how many of your nine lives are left?"

"Well, I shall just have to chance that there are one or two."

To the earl's surprise, he found an unexpected ally in the widow. "It is hard to argue with Lord Branford's reasoning," she observed, once the grumbling had died down. "I have learned in the course of business that one must be careful not to let emotion take precedence over expediency. Indeed, it is often necessary to give way to practical considerations in order to be successful."

"How heartening to see that someone else here has a modicum of common sense," murmured Branford. "Now, if there are no further questions, Max and I had best return home and finish off the final details. He shall return here at the same time that I leave for Hawthorne House." Making a conspicuous display of consulting his pocket watch, he added, "Which, according to the schedule I have mapped out, should be in exactly two hours and twelve minutes."

Snapping the gold case shut, he congratulated himself on handling an extremely volatile situation without having it blow up in his face. That the first skirmish of the night had been a clear victory was a very good omen, he assured himself. It boded well for having the rest of the mission run with the same smooth military precision.

Had he seen the looks exchanged among the three ladies as he turned for the door, or heard the scrambling of two lads away from the keyhole, he might not have felt quite so sanguine.

"It was by no means an unconditional surrender, Miss Hadley." The self-styled Lady in Red toyed with the ends of her slate blue sash. "I was merely pointing out the advantages of keeping a cool head under fire. If the earl chose to interpret my words as a firm commitment to sitting at home and twiddling our thumbs, then he may find himself much mistaken."

"He may?" Portia allowed her chin to drop just a notch. "And please call me Portia. After what we have been through together, the formality seems rather silly."

"I should be delighted to. And you both must call me Olivia. Given the charade of names, it is the one I am most comfortable with." Mrs. Grenville sipped meditatively at her tea. "Getting back to Lord Branford, I take it you are not overly pleased at being ordered to stay clear of the action."

"Indeed, I am not"—Portia couldn't help but resume her agitated pacing along the perimeter of the carpet—"especially by an overbearing, arrogant martinet." Her boot kicked at the knotted fringe. "Odious man," she added under her breath.

An odd little ripple stirred in Lady Trumbull's pale blue eyes.

"And how dare he place us under house arrest?" The more she thought about it, the more incensed she grew. "Hmmph! Short of shackling me to the newel post, Lord Davenport may find his assignment not quite as uneventful as he seems to expect."

"What do you have in mind?" asked the widow.

Portia started on another turn of the room. "Give me a moment to think on it," she muttered. "I suppose it would be rather churlish to contemplate bodily harm, seeing the injuries he has already endured for King and country."

"Perhaps a little laudanum in a glass of port would do the trick," mused Lady Trumbull. "Of course, we would have to calculate just the right dose. Too little and he won't fall asleep fast enough, but too much may cause a number of adverse effects."

"You are determined to go, despite the earl's objections?"

"The earl can holler from here to Hades," replied Portia, "but it is my father whom Dunster is holding hostage, along with the Riddle of Rafistan, and his flesh is as precious to me as that scrap of paper is to the Honorable Mr. Taft. I simply cannot sit here with my fingers crossed and hope that things turn out for the best."

The widow's mouth turned up at the corners. "Well, then, let us put our heads together. I doubt we will have to resort to violence with Lord Davenport. There are other ways of getting him out of our way. And once we have done so, I have an idea. . . ."

By the time the viscount arrived back at Lady Trumbull's town house, the ladies were ready. They had indeed been busy plying their needles, but not over the usual dainty embroidered flowers or neatly stitched samplers expected of such highborn females. Mrs. Grenville was, however, immensely pleased with the results of their handiwork.

"Trust me, gentlemen are easily distracted," she said, holding up the evening gown and inspecting the dramatically altered neckline. "I have found that a splash of color and certain other design elements ensure that they see what you wish them to see. Like the Lady in Red rather than the runaway daughter of the Earl of Harkness."

"How very astute." Portia found her respect for the other lady's acumen growing by the minute. "But I have, er, few of your assets to work with."

The widow's mouth curved in a cynical smile as she ran an appraising eye over her companion. "Oh, I think you greatly underestimate your assets. Even though I could not show quite as much of them as I wished, on account of the bandage, I promise you, they will prove every bit as distracting as we hope. Indeed, I doubt very much whether anyone will recognize Baron Hadley's daughter, especially after we have rearranged your hair and made judicious use of a few cosmetics." Her hand came up to the bruise on her cheek. "Hmmm. That is our one problem—my town house is likely being watched, so I dare not send for my collection of potions."

"Actually that should not be a problem at all. I imagine I have everything you need in my dressing room." Lady Trumbull allowed a small smile. "At my age, one may be forgiven for resorting to a bit of rouge and paint."

"Well, then, everything should go smooth as silk."

"Would you care to join us in a hand of whist, sir?" inquired Lady Trumbull as the viscount was shown into the parlor. "No doubt you dashing young gentlemen are used to much more lively entertainment, but perhaps we ladies might help to keep boredom at bay."

"I don't care much for cards," replied Davenport. Portia was slightly dismayed to see that the sight of three brilliant smiles fixed on his person did little to soften the viscount's stoic expression. "You needn't feel obliged to keep me entertained. I have brought some notes to finish transcribing."

"All work and no play, sir?" murmured the widow.

Davenport's bearing turned even stiffer. "I am not a very playful fellow."

For a moment Portia feared their plan was going to prove more difficult to implement than they had imagined. But rather than abandon the fight quite yet, her great-aunt gave a wistful nod. "Of course, sir. I should not have imagined you would wish to partner a dotty old lady for a penny a point."

There was a tiny hesitation, and then good manners won out over his natural reserve. "On the contrary, Lady Trumbull." Setting aside his document case, he approached the card table. "I had not considered the numbers—if I am needed as a fourth I shall be happy to sit down with you." Though his expression remained very grave, Portia thought she detected a hint of humor flash in his eyes. "And no one, least of all me, underestimates the sharpness of your mind."

Ha! She ducked to hide her grim smile.

The first few hands were played amid a polite exchange of small talk. It was not until Davenport's jaw relaxed slightly and his spine lost a bit of its rigid set that Mrs. Grenville made the next move.

"I do hope Lord Branford is not marching into mortal danger." A shudder caused her hands to waver in dealing the cards. "No doubt you soldiers are hardened to the idea of your comrades facing death"—she heaved a small sigh—"but for me to imagine the earl alone, with no friend at his shoulder, is quite . . . unnerving."

"Alas, let us pray he comes to no harm," murmured Lady Trumbull, taking a moment to remove her spectacles and dab at her eyes with a handkerchief. "However we should not be speaking of such morbid things. It is not as if it is Lord Davenport's fault that he allowed the earl to ride off on his own."

Portia wondered whether they were doing it too brown, but the viscount appeared unaware of the theatrics being played out for his benefit. Scowling, he gave a tug to his cravat, as if it had suddenly become several sizes smaller.

"No," agreed the widow. "Of course it isn't." Her tone hinted at just the opposite.

There was a dead silence as the ladies picked desultorily at their cards and the viscount reached for the glass of lemonade by his elbow.

"No doubt a soldier dare not disobey orders, even when he is no longer in uniform," said Portia, just loud enough to be overheard.

A choking sound ensued, followed by the thump of the glass. "The deuce take it, ladies! Do not imagine for a moment that I wish to abandon the Cat to a pack of wolves, but we must also think of your safety."

"Oh, what fustian! I have lived here since you were in leading strings, young man," exclaimed Lady Trumbull. "You don't seriously think that any harm can befall us here in the middle of genteel Mayfair, within the cozy confines of my own home?"

Brow furrowing, he picked at his cheek.

"Indeed, it would be terrible if a misplaced sense of chivalry kept you from your real duty," pointed out Mrs. Grenville.

"I do not like to think of abandoning my post, but—"

"But sometimes victory can only be achieved by a bold change of strategy," suggested Portia.

"Like Hannibal in the Alps, or Wellington at Assaye," chimed in her great-aunt.

The viscount raked a hand through his locks.

Sensing a wavering resolve, Mrs. Grenville launched the final salvo. "But of course we are forgetting that Lord Davenport is not at full strength. Perhaps his injuries prevent him from acting as he would like—"

"Bloody hell!" Exploding out of his seat, the harried officer began to march around the card table. "There is still time."

"Your carriage can be readied in minutes," assured Lady Trumbull with a smile of encouragement.

"Y-you ladies won't stir from this room?"

"Don't worry about us, sir. We would not dream of doing anything rash," promised Portia, her utterance backed up by earnest nods from her co-conspirators.

Just as she had hoped, the viscount was too caught up in the heat of battle to notice the nuance of her answer. With a squaring of his shoulders, he took no more than a moment to make up his mind. "The devil with Alex's orders. You are right—he may need someone covering his flanks. If you are sure—"

"Yes!" they exclaimed in unison.

"You had better hurry," urged Portia for good measure. "There is not an instant to lose."

The ladies waited until the thud of his steps had died away in the hallway before springing into action.

The bundle of clothing was retrieved from behind the sofa, along with an assortment of vials and jars.

"Ha!" Portia's voice held a measure of grim satisfaction. "Soldiers are not the only ones capable of the quick maneuvering and complex strategies necessary to execute a plan of attack."

Unfortunately, her words were all too correct.

Amid the stomp of boots and the swoosh of silk, the sounds of two shadowy figures slithering down the ivy vines and into the boot of the earl's carriage went unnoticed.

Branford made a show of draining his glass, though most of the brandy had been spilled into the tasseled pillows plumped under the whore's bare shoulders. There were three other gentlemen in the dimly lit boudoir, their partners in the same state of undress as his own. That made seven so far that he had seen since his arrival at Hawthorne House. All but two he recognized as members of the *ton,* so the list of suspects for the French agent had been narrowed considerably. He would have to contrive to keep a close watch on the both of them.

Reaching for the champagne on the side table allowed him to steal another quick glance around the room. Where was the marquess? he wondered with some impatience. Much as he wished to learn the identity of Bonaparte's messenger, it was not nearly as important as discovering the shadowy enemy who was masterminding the treachery against the Crown.

He feigned a long swig from the bottle, then rolled from the divan and exaggerated a drunken stagger into the hallway. From there his steps became a good deal more steady. Moving lightly, he crept along close to the wall, pausing at every doorway to listen for a moment. At the fourth one he heard something other than breathy panting and heated moans.

"It's nearly done, I tell you," came a raspy whisper. "Your ruler may scour the length and breadth of his empire, but he will not find a scholar anywhere near as suited to the task as the one I have working on it."

"How much longer?"

The angle was such that the earl could not see the two men from where he stood. Swearing to himself, he pressed up against the wainscoting and strained to recognize either of the voices.

"A day or two at most."

The reply was inaudible, but he dared not move in closer.

"I promise you, he will judge the wait to be well worth it."

"The price you are asking is . . . astronomical."

"Not really, when you consider that what you are receiving is priceless."

There was something devilishly familiar about the mocking laugh that preceded the words, but try as he might, Branford simply could not connect it to a name or face.

"I will have to think—"

The snick of a door knob being turned caused the earl to duck into the opposite chamber. A voluptuous brunette, wearing naught else than the satin sheet draped over her thighs, lay across the ornately carved bed. Tugging off his coat and cravat, he quickly lay down beside her. And not a moment too soon.

"Ah, I see the Black Cat has found one of our kittens to pet." Dunster moved from the doorway, his lidded gaze following the slow tracing of the earl's thumb over the rouged nipple.

"A nice bit of fluff," he grunted. "But if I were merely interested in kittens, they can be found purring in a great many houses in Town. I came here tonight thinking we might have a mutual interest in felines of a different stripe."

The dappling of moonlight showed the marquess going very still. "What sort of feline did you have in mind?"

Branford propped himself up on one elbow and ceased his caressing of the naked woman. "Oh, one a bit more . . . tigerish, perhaps?"

"Tiger." Dunster's voice tightened to a croak.

"Yes. Haven't you heard? There are rumors that a certain exotic beast has recently made its way to England. One that might be of particular interest to a man of your business dealings. Indeed, it seems that several parties are anxious to track it down."

"Be off." With a jerk of his hand, the marquess indicated for the doxy to take her leave. Something in his tone caused her to scurry from the room without bothering to scoop up the frilly undergarments that were draped over a bedpost. "What do you know of such big game?" he demanded.

The earl took his time sitting up and refastening his shirt. "Enough to have done some stalking of my own. And as you have no doubt heard, I'm quite a skilled hunter. I can be counted on to make the kill." Sensing the other man's mounting tension, he paused to grope among the sheets for his cravat, then draped it casually around his neck. "I imagine the bounty on such a beast would be quite high."

"What sort of price do you have in mind?"

"It is not money I want. It is opportunity."

Dunster ran the tip of his tongue over his lips. "Opportunity?"

"To take Roxleigh's place as a partner in your various business endeavors. Pleasures come at a price, and the earldom I've taken as my trophy has regrettably shallow coffers. In return for a share of your profits, I think you and your friends would find a man of my abilities and scruples—or lack of them—a very useful sort of fellow to have around."

"Wait here," whispered the marquess.

As soon as the sound of the hurried steps receded, Branford moved to the window and checked his pocket watch. All was quiet in the surrounding woods, but by this time Tony's men should have every road, lane, and cart path leading away from the secluded estate cordoned off. The noose was slowly drawing tighter around the neck of the traitor, he thought with grim satisfaction. He just hoped his own was not caught along with it.

The gold case clicked shut. He still had several hours to find the document—and Miss Hadley's father—before all hell broke loose.

Mrs. Grenville stepped back and admired the results. "Excellent. That should do the trick."

Portia sucked in her breath as she stared in the mirror. "No one could possibly recognize me," she mumbled, the tip of her finger touching her ruby lips. "I don't recognize myself!"

"By the by, you should wear that shade of smoky emerald more often. It accentuates your magnificent eyes and the tawny highlights in your hair."

She looked down at the plunging cleavage. "Good Lord, I am afraid this dress accentuates a good deal more than that."

Her great-aunt coughed gently. "Perhaps it goes a bit further than is proper for a normal social occasion, but Olivia has a point. It is a shame to hide yourself under those strangling collars and voluminous sleeves you usually favor."

"As if anyone is interested in the view . . ." muttered Portia, trying hard not to think of the earl's torrid embraces. And even if some of the looks he had slanted in her direction had not been scowls, she had, with her sharp tongue, made sure they would not be repeated.

The arch of Mrs. Grenville's brow was made even more apparent by the heavy shading of kohl, but she refrained from comment. Placing the pot of lip color, the powders, the rouge, and the hare's foot back into the inlaid rosewood box, she snapped the lid closed and took up her cloak. "We had best be off."

"Owen is waiting in the mews with our carriage." Draping a wrapper over her own bare arms, Portia followed the widow to the door. "Aunt Octavia, we will be back as soon as—"

The rest of her parting words were arrested by the

sight of the very large and very cumbersome carriage pistol that the elderly lady now hefted in her gnarled fist. Dropping the length of muslin in which it had been wrapped, her aunt clamped her spectacles more firmly upon her nose and stood up.

"Er, you cannot be thinking of—" began Portia, once her jaw had resumed its normal position.

"Of coming along for the ride?" A flash of light winked off the glass lenses, as well as the polished steel of the weapon. "Ha!" The unladylike snort was punctuated by another wave of the barrel.

"But—"

"If you are about to add that I am unfit for a bit of adventure, you can damn well put a cork in it! I don't care to be told by you that I am too old, any more than you care to be told by the earl that you are too . . . female."

In the harsh glare of such reasoning, Portia was forced to acknowledge that her aunt had a compelling argument.

"I admit that I am, er, a trifle too wilted to participate in your little masquerade, but I can remain in the carriage, ready to fly for help if things go awry."

"Or, by the look of that cannon, blast anyone within half a mile clear to eternity," murmured Mrs. Grenville dryly. "By the by, Octavia, you may wish to remove your finger from the trigger until we get a touch close to our target."

"Oh. Right." Lady Trumbull gingerly lowered the weapon and rubbed at her wrist. "What a deucedly awkward thing to aim, in any case. I shall have to ask Henry to show me the proper technique."

Mention of her brother spurred Portia to action. "Another time, perhaps. For now, if you insist on bringing it, hand it over and I will carry it. But hurry! We had better start moving, before my brothers get wind of what we are up to. As it is, I am surprised there has not yet been some sort of explosion from the other side of the keyhole."

To her relief they made it down the stairs and out through the kitchen door without encountering any servants or siblings. The carriage was indeed waiting, with Owen taking in a notch on the last buckle of the harness. Looking up and seeing the approaching trio, he rubbed at his eyes, then fell to muttering.

"God help the poor devil who is gonna be receiving this merry little party."

Portia gave a toss of her head as she yanked the door open and stepped aside for the others to climb in. "Don't be impertinent."

"I ain't being impertinent, Miss P. I'm being truthful! A man may deal with one, maybe two strong-willed females, but Lucifer himself ain't got a prayer in hell of standing up to three!"

Keeping further grumblings to a minimum, he checked the traces one last time and heaved himself up to the box. Once the wheels started rolling, Portia took great care to brace the pistol at the far end of her seat, then joined the others in settling back against the squabs for one last review of strategy.

"You seem quite confident that you will have no trouble in gaining admittance to the manor house," began Lady Trumbull, curiosity evident in her voice.

"As Portia has witnessed, the servants employed by

a gentleman such as Lord Dunster will be expecting a certain type of female visitor. No one will look overly closely at faces."

The elderly lady gave a delicate cough. "You seem to know a great deal about exactly what goes on at these evenings. Not that I mean any offense," she hastened to add.

Mrs. Grenville smiled. "None taken. My familiarity with such debaucheries comes not from empirical knowledge but rather from doing a bit of careful research, as a practical business consideration. It pays to know what the competitors are providing in the way of incentives to close a deal. That way, while I may not be able to provide the same sort of entertainment, I can figure out an equally attractive offer." She paused. "My office manager is an enlightened fellow who has none of the usual prejudices concerning the fairer sex, so he had no qualms in explaining what occurs when men gather together to indulge in a night of play."

"How very resourceful, Olivia." Intrigued, Lady Trumbull could not help asking, "Did you figure out a way to compete?"

"Of course. There is more than one way to appeal to a man's greed or vanity."

"You seem to have an excellent understanding of men and the way they think." Portia sighed. "While I, on the other hand, always seem to say or do the wrong thing."

"Is there someone in particular with whom you are experiencing difficulty?" inquired the widow after a discreet pause.

"N-no, no. I mean in general."

"In my experience, one rarely gets in a pucker over theoretical situations."

Portia felt her cheeks turning rather warm. "Well, perhaps there *is* a specific individual. It does seem that the earl and I tend to go at each other like . . . cats and dogs"—she sniffed—"as you have no doubt observed."

"What I have observed was that the Earl of Branford seemed to be quite concerned with keeping you out of harm's way."

"What he was trying to do was keep me out of his hair!"

"Really?" Her great-aunt took a moment to remove her spectacles and polish them on her sleeve. "It did not look that way to me." Eschewing further elaboration on the statement, she perched the lenses back on her nose. "If you want my opinion, Lord Branford has been a true gentleman from the very beginning."

Ha! Portia refrained from saying it aloud, but her expression must have spoken for itself.

"You seem determined to view him in naught but an unfavorable light, my dear."

"No more than he wishes to view me," she replied softly. "The truth of it is, I find him arrogant, overbearing, and odious, and he finds me headstrong, opinionated, and shrewish."

"Ah. I see the relationship has distinct possibilities." Mrs. Grenville gave a tweak to her skirts. "As we have a while to go to reach our destination, perhaps it might be useful to discuss a different sort of strategy."

Chapter Twenty

"Come with me."

The earl followed on Dunster's heels, feeling the old, familiar frisson of anticipation at finally closing in on the enemy.

"In here." Dunster's hurried steps finally drew to a halt halfway down the long hallway. Moving aside, he gestured at the closed door.

Branford took hold of the knob and swung it open.

A single taper cast a flickering glow over the rows of leather-bound books and a collection of classical sculpture grouped in one corner of the crowded study. In the faint light, the marble fragments took on a rather ghoulish appearance. A head, a torso, a single hand—they rather reminded the earl of the severed limbs he had seen in the aftermath of a deadly skirmish.

Hardly the most encouraging of thoughts. However, a cool smile curled his lips as he looked around for his flesh and blood enemy.

"So, the Black Cat claims to have an intimate acquaintance with another species of feline?" The desk was so hidden in shadow that the voice appeared to be coming from thin air.

With a deliberate show of smoothing a fold from his striped waistcoat, the earl nodded. "In my experience, predators have a way of finding each other."

A chair scraped back over the thick weave of the carpet. "What exactly do you know of tigers, Lord Branford?"

"Enough to realize that the bounty on the one that is loose here in London must be quite high. After all, the longer such a dangerous beast eludes capture, the greater the chances that some disaster will occur."

There was a short silence. "So the Black Cat is offering to hunt down the Jade Tiger?"

"Those who have encountered the sharpness of my claws know that when I choose, I can be quite effective in moving in for the kill," he replied.

"It is true," offered Dunster from his position near the door. "The Cat is rumored to have left a number of victims ripped to shreds at gaming tables. And then, of course, there was the matter of his nephews. . . ."

"I am well aware of the earl's history." The words, though uttered softly, caused the marquess to cringe.

Branford's face gave a twist as well. Searching his memory, he sought to recall where he had heard that voice before, but with no luck.

"Indeed," continued the silky tone. "I have found that a careful study of the past ensures that one does not repeat the mistakes of others who are now dead."

"A wise philosophy," murmured Branford. "But then, I would expect no less from a man of your obvious intelligence."

The zephyr of sound might have been one of dry amusement. "Cats are known for possessing a certain cunning and stealth as well. Tell me, why do you seek to offer me the spoils of your hunt instead of keeping it all for yourself?"

"I am not in a position to take full advantage of my catch. You, of all people, know that a prize is only valuable if you are able to put it to good use." The earl kept his gaze focused on the nebulous shifting of shadows. It might have been his imagination, but he thought he detected a ghost of a profile slowly moving closer to the aureole of light. "There is also another reason. While I have had my share of luck in making a killing or two, there is bigger game to be had when one hunts in a pack."

"Again, why me?"

Branford took his time in replying, sensing that his answer was crucial to his chances of success. "Because you are said to be the king of the jungle."

"Ah." The face that suddenly appeared above the candle was smiling, though the harsh play of light and dark gave the features a rather sinister cast. "It would seem that we are beasts of a similar stripe."

"I was hoping you would see it that way." The earl began to congratulate himself on playing a clever game of cat and mouse. "Does that mean we may be able to do business together?"

"Oh, yes, Lord Branford. I believe you and I have a great deal of business to go over."

The words caused an unaccountable prickling at the back of his neck, but he put it down to taut nerves. He was, after all, still a bit out of practice in all his old moves. However, things were going even better than he had dared hope. He now had a face, and while as yet there was no name to go with it, he recognized the gentleman as the other half-naked man who had been with Dunster and the doxy on the night of his first encounter with Miss Hadley.

Dunster, Roxleigh, and . . .

"You see, Dearborne, I told you we were not making a mistake in considering the Black Cat to take Roxie's place." The relief in Dunster's voice was unmistakable. "I am sure a man of his instincts will prove a great asset to us."

Dearborne? Hell's teeth! Was that not the name of the scholar Portia had mentioned?

As the flame caught the glint of polished steel that was now pointed at his chest, the earl cursed himself for a damnable fool.

"Idiot," snarled Dearborne at his crony. "Would that your brain was as active as your cock. Don't you recall that Lord Branford was the one in your study the night the papers you so casually left lying about went missing."

The marquess blinked in confusion. "I—I seem to remember the earl was at my desk, but only because he was mounting a filly. . . ." His throat tightened in a convulsive swallow. "The drawer was locked, I swear it. How would he have known—" Once again, his voice choked off.

"How, indeed?" Dearborne's eyes, reptilian in their black, unblinking gaze, turned on Branford.

"What papers? What the devil are you talking about?" bluffed Branford, knowing his only choice was to chance a brazen bravado. "I assure you, the only thing I was seeking that evening was a good and thorough swiving. Which," he added with a pronounced smirk, "was exactly what I got."

"Oh, you were caught with your breeches down, Lord Branford. And I intend to find out exactly why."

Reaching over to the corner of the desk, he grabbed a small bell and gave a sharp ring. Almost immediately two figures materialized from behind a side door. "Take his lordship down to the cellars and lock him up. We shall have time enough after we settle our business with Levesque to make the Cat yowl out some answers. Jumanot, here, is quite skilled at skinning strays who wander into places where they should not venture."

One of the men, a hulking brute with a broken nose and several knife scars cutting across his pocked cheeks, gave an evil leer.

"You are making a grave mistake, Dearborne . . ." began the earl, as hands took rough hold of his arms.

"On the contrary, Lord Branford. It is you who have made a fatal misstep."

Bloody hell! It was deucedly odd, but what bothered him most as the butt of the pistol came crashing down upon his head was not the prospect of his imminent demise but the look of withering reproach that would spread across Portia's face when she learned of what a hash he had made of things.

Davenport paused in picking his way through the trees, just long enough to be sure the faint rustle of leaves behind him was not an echo of his own careful steps. He had ordered the carriage to halt halfway up the winding drive, choosing to approach the rambling stone manor house on foot. He had not yet decided how to seek entrance, but now it appeared that bit of strategy would have to wait. He had a more pressing problem coming up from the rear.

A twig snapped, followed by a muffled grunt.

It appeared there were two of them. The viscount pressed up against the trunk of a gnarled oak and withdrew the blade from his boot. Taft's men had orders not to move in for another hour or two, so his pursuers could be naught but the enemy's henchmen. Inching around for a better angle, he waited for them to make their move.

The first one crept out from a thicket of pines and came forward in a low crouch. Davenport waited until the fellow was nearly past him, then whipped a hand around his pursuer's collar and pressed the point of the knife to the back of his neck.

"Ouch!"

"Put a cork in it, Bertie!" came a harried hiss from behind. "Or I'll be forced to leave you—" Seeing his brother in the grasp of a hooded stranger caused Henry to stop dead in his tracks.

With a low oath, the viscount shoved the knife back in its sheath. "Bloody hell, what the devil are you two doing here? This is no place for child's play." On noting the wounded expressions that came to their faces, he moderated his tone. "Hurry, let us move into the shadows."

"We wanted to help," replied Henry, manfully controlling the slight quiver of his jaw once they came to a halt. "After all, haven't we proven we are capable of handling a tricky task as well as any man?"

Davenport acknowledged the truth of the words with a grimace. "So you have, lads. But, dash it all, your sister would have my guts for garters if she knew you were here."

"Well, it would be the pot calling the kettle black," piped up Bertie, "seeing as she and Aunt Octavia and Mrs. Grenville are hot on your heels."

"But they promised they wouldn't leave the house!"

"No they didn't." The youngest Hadley rolled his eyes. "You don't have much experience with females, do you? They promised they wouldn't do anything rash. Trust me, there is a big difference."

"Bloody hell."

"Er, perhaps we shouldn't waste time in arguing," ventured Henry. "They will no doubt be here shortly, so the sooner we make sure Lord Branford is not in need of any help, the better."

Stifling the urge to swear yet again, the viscount looked from one earnest face to the other. "I suppose you are giving me no choice," he muttered, "save for beating a retreat with you two in tow and leaving the Cat to fend for himself."

"No, sir, we are not."

A sigh signaled a harried surrender. "On the field of battle, a soldier must obey orders without question, or other lives may be put at risk. Understand?"

Both Hadleys gave a solemn nod.

"Come along, then." One hand shot out just in time to keep Bertie from plowing into a tangle of brambles. "Though my brain must still be a bit fuzzed with opium . . ."

"Good Lord, Bertie, try not to stumble around like

a babe in the woods," exclaimed his brother in a harried whisper.

"I'll have you know that I am not—"

"No quarreling in the ranks," warned Davenport, his words effecting an immediate silence. His expression took on a touch of bemused irony as he turned for the distant manor house and set off. "Hell's teeth," he sighed, rubbing a hand over his cheek. "Let us pray that a bit of the Black Cat's legendary luck has rubbed off on my own scarred hide."

"So, love, where d' ye want us?"

Portia watched in wonder as Mrs. Grenville assumed a sinuous tilt, causing her cloak to fall open at the bosom.

The servant standing guard at the door took a long moment to ogle the view before answering. "Wid yer legs wrapped round me hips, sweeting," he grunted, letting his tongue run over his lower lip. The sound of approaching footsteps quickly recalled him to duty and he jerked a thumb toward the hallway to his left. "Drop yer wraps back there, then take th' back stairs up t' the next landing. Ye won't have no trouble finding th' party."

"More of them? Thought they'd all arrived by now." Eyes narrowing, the other man surveyed the newcomers with a pinched expression. "Yer late."

The widow dismissed the accusation with an airy wave. "Had a stop t' make on th' way. And ye know th' bleeding toffs—they don't appreciate a working lass has got t' stick to a schedule. So sometimes ye got t' take a bit longer t' get th' job done than ye had allotted for."

That drew a grudging bark of laughter. "Aye, bloody toffs," he murmured. "Well, ye better hurry. The master don't like fer th' girls t' be shirking their dooties."

Without further ado, Portia found herself being hustled across the polished parquet. "You were sublime," she whispered after they were out of earshot. "I wonder if, with a bit of practice, I might learn to manage men with half as much cleverness as you."

"That was merely the opening act. From here, the role gets a bit more challenging. Just follow my lead, and remember, if things get dicey, just smile and giggle." A loud thumping from above caused the widow to draw to a skittering halt as they were about to turn the corner. Pressing back into the slanting shadows, she then ventured a guarded peek at what was going on.

"Damnation."

Portia was at her shoulder in an instant. "Hell's bells," she added in a vehement whisper at the sight of the earl's lifeless form being dragged down the narrow flight of stairs. At least it was not his head that was bouncing from step to step with such a decidedly unpleasant sound, she thought—though, judging by the trickle of blood dripping from his temple, that part of his person had not escaped its share of rough treatment.

"How far we got t' carry th' bleedin' mort?" demanded the smaller of Branford's two captors as he paused to wipe the sweat from his brow.

"Ye heard th' master. He's t' be locked away in th' cellar fer th' time being. The old wine vault has an iron gate an' a sturdy lock. We'll use that. An' you kin stand th' first watch"—a nasty twitch tugged the other man's lips into a parody of a smile—" 'cause I need t' sharpen me blade if I'm t' be given th' task o' skinning a cat."

His cohort had looked about to argue, but promptly shut his mouth at the mention of honed steel and began moving again.

Amid another series of bumps and thumps, the two of them wrenched open the door at the foot of the stairs and disappeared with their burden behind the heavy, iron-banded oak.

"Now what?" breathed Portia, the question directed as much at herself as her companion.

"We wait—"

"But—"

"—until that bloodthirsty villain with the knife reappears and goes off to find a whetstone," quipped the widow. "As soon as he is out of the way, it should be a fairly easy task to take care of the other fellow."

"Er, if you don't mind me asking . . ."

"I will distract him and then you will smash him over the head. You don't, perchance, have any scruples about hitting a defenseless male?"

"None whatsoever. What I am wondering, however, is how you mean . . ." A bright smile eclipsed her words. "Ah. Of course."

"I imagine there will be something hard and heavy lying about."

"Don't worry." Portia flexed her knuckles. "I'll get the job done, even if I have to employ my brother's lessons in the art of pugilism. I throw a very credible right cross."

The door opened and the villain with the blade stomped off, whistling a merry little tune that set Portia's teeth further on edge. Despite the outward show of bravado, she felt a piercing worry at the thought of the earl lying injured and helpless. What if he was already—

As soon as he turned the corner, she made to rush across the vestibule, but her companion kept a restraining grip on her arm. Finally, after what seemed an interminable wait, the widow indicated that they should remove their cloaks, then led the way on tiptoe to the cellar entrance.

"Remember what I told you—in a business negotiation, it never pays to let emotion override reason." After a last moment appraisal of her own attire, Mrs. Grenville tugged her bodice an inch lower. "Let me initiate the first offer."

The guard was leaning back in his chair, but the legs came down on the dirt floor with a thump as he caught sight of the two ladies.

"Oh, dearie me, must've taken a wrong turn." The widow's voice had taken on a silly, simpering quality that caused Portia to stare in openmouthed fascination. It had the same effect on the marquess's minion, but for entirely different reasons.

"We was looking fer th' party, but it don't appear there's anything goin' on down here." With a flounce of her skirts, she stepped closer to the gaping guard and craned her neck in a show of looking around. The twisting movement caused the fabric of her gown to slide even lower.

His eyes grew even wider.

"We could, of course, change that. There looks t' be plenty of bubbly, and we got a couple o' nice gents." A deliberate stumble landed her square in the guard's lap. Giggling, the widow waved a hand at the earl's prostrate form lying behind the locked bars. "What's th' matter with yer friend? Already been wetting 'is whistle?" With a broad wink, she nodded at Portia and tittered, "I'm sure me partner, here, could revive 'im."

"Ferget about 'im." The guard, his gaze glued to the mounds of flesh hovering inches from his face, gave a wolfish grin. "I can show ye ladies a good time all by meself."

"I'll drink t' that, love." She wet her thumb and ran it lightly over the man's lower lip. "Don't suppose ye got th' key t' that door?"

His fingers clawed at his pocket and withdrew the iron ring.

Portia needed no signal to swoop in and snatch it from his hand. "Don't you two move. I'll just fetch us a bottle or two t' get things started." Quickly freeing the rusty padlock from the hasp, she grabbed up two champagne bottles by their necks. One would no doubt do the trick nicely, she decided, but it never hurt to have a spare.

"Here we are. These look t' be a smashing vintage." Echoing the widow's dulcet tones, she sidled up to the man's shoulder. With a sweeping flourish, her arm came up over her head. "Shall I uncork one?"

"Let 'er pop," said the grinning guard, his gaze still riveted on the delicacies dangling right before his eyes.

The sound was more of a dull thud.

There was a low gurgling noise, then his chin fell forward, coming to rest in the widow's cleavage. Pushing him roughly aside, she scrambled to her feet, letting him continue his slide downward until he tumbled headlong onto the damp earth. Portia couldn't resist adding a sharp kick to the man's posterior as she stepped over his bulk.

Mrs. Grenville was already kneeling beside the earl. "There is quite a nasty lump on his brow," she said with some concern. "And it appears he is still unconscious."

Fearing that even the slightest show of her true feelings might cause her to come completely undone, Portia forced a cool quip. "Don't worry, he has a very hard head." She pried the cork out of one of the bottles and splashed some of the champagne over Branford's face.

"W-what the devil . . ." Coughing and sputtering, the earl opened his eyes. It appeared to take him a moment or two to bring her face into focus, but as the recognition sank in, he looked about to say a great deal more. Then his gaze dropped several inches and his jaw remained suspended in midair.

After several abortive trys, he finally regained the powers of speech. Barely. The whisper of "Bloody hell!" was hardly audible through his gritted teeth.

The rasp of his voice—no matter how rough— caused Portia's heart to give a little leap, though it was clear the reaction was not mutual. "You know, it might be nice if just once you could manage a civilized greeting when you see me." Concealing her rush of relief with a show of tart efficiency, she began dabbing at the blood on his forehead with the end of his cravat.

"It might be nice if just once we met under civilized circumstances," he growled.

She slanted the widow a look of exasperation. "See what I mean?" The folded linen scraped against the torn flesh, drawing a sharp intake of breath from the earl. Staring down at her fingers, she realized they were still a bit shaky from worry. "Obviously the blow was not a serious one, for it has not altered his usual manners one whit."

Wincing, Branford pushed away her hands and sat up. The change in position did nothing to alter the scowl on his face, she noted. Indeed, it became a good deal more pronounced as the details of her appearance became less cock-eyed. "What in the name of Hades are you doing dressed like that?" he demanded in a choked voice.

"Apparently some men do not find the view so objectionable," answered Portia with an edge of asperity. "For which you ought to be extremely grateful."

Mrs. Grenville stood up and dusted off her hands. "If you don't mind me interrupting, I would rather that one man in particular does not view us here when he returns with his well-honed blade. Are you recovered enough to move, sir?"

The earl's scowl turned to a rather sheepish grimace. "Quite." Heaving himself to his feet, he made short work of locking the guard in the wine cellar, then took up the pistol that had fallen behind the chair. "Follow me."

Weapon at the ready, Branford proceeded cautiously up the darkened stairwell. At the top of the landing, he paused with his hand on the handle of a closed door. "I did not have a chance to check out this part of the house."

"The corridor on the left leads to the front entrance, where two of Dunster's lackeys are standing watch," volunteered the widow.

"To your left are several doors that appear to be locked, as well as the back stairs leading to the upper floors. On your right is a small room where the females are supposed to deposit their outer wraps," added Portia. "I imagine it will be deserted right now."

His nod was one of grudging approval for their powers of observation. "Then we will duck in there for a moment while I decide on my next move."

"*Our* next move," breathed Portia as she hurried after him, though it was uttered softly enough that he pretended not to hear.

Leaving the door slightly ajar, Branford took a moment to check the priming of his pistol. "What can you tell me of your friend Mr. Dearborne?"

In the faint moonlight he saw her face screw in concern. "Dearborne?" Although she looked as if she wished to answer his question with a number of her own, she hesitated. "My impression is that he has a rather high opinion of himself as a scholar, and takes any criticism of his research badly," she responded after some thought. "Indeed, several years ago he and my father had a disagreement over the interpretation of a discovery which turned unpleasant for a time. The controversy seemed to blow over, but I did wonder whether he was the sort who might hold a grudge."

Her hands knotted together. "You think he is part of this?"

The earl nodded. "The ringleader, in fact."

She looked stricken. "Good Lord, yet another foolish blunder I have made."

It took considerable resolve on his part not to drop his guard for just a moment, so that he might gather her in his arms and kiss the look of remorse from her face. Prudence, however, won out over passion, and he contented himself with a whisper of encouragement. "Don't rake yourself over the coals, sweeting. We would never have picked up his trail in the first place if it were not for your dogged determination." Branford did not realize he had used an endearment until he caught sight of the sudden spasm of her expression. Covering the slip with a gruff cough, he peeked out into the hallway before going on. "Both of you ladies have proved very, er, resourceful, but from here on in—"

"If you are about to tell us to stay put, save your breath," interrupted Portia, her wide-eyed surprise narrowing to a stubborn squint.

"But it is much too dangerous for you to be involved in what I have planned!" he argued.

Mrs. Grenville, who had been observing the interchange between the two with a great deal of interest, finally joined in the discussion. "Might I point out that we managed to extract you from a very deep tangle of briers without getting scratched? By the by, what *is* your plan?"

"Well, er, as to that, I was just, er . . ." Stalling for time, he made a show of edging the door open and surveying the empty hallway.

"It had better be an awfully good one," replied the widow dryly. "It seems to me that you haven't a prayer of moving more than a few steps from here without being spotted. Unless . . ."

She glanced at Portia—a calculated look that sent a chill down his spine.

"No, and that's flat," he said through clenched teeth as he watched her begin to undo the ribbons on her bodice.

"I am afraid you have precious little choice."

"If you are going to suggest—"

"It's the only way sir. A gentleman appearing to be making sport with the hired females will be far less noticeable."

"Bloody hell." He searched feverishly for a retort to her suggestion, but was forced to admit she was right.

"Strip off your coat, sir. And unfasten your shirt."

Reluctantly he complied.

She reached up and tousled his locks to even greater disarray, then draped herself over his shoulder. After surveying the curve of her body, she tugged one side of her gown down to expose a breast. "Must appear believable," she said in a clipped, businesslike tone. Her mouth slowly rounded to match the sinuous curves of her body. "Smile, sir. You must also remember to play your part."

Somehow he did not feel in the least like smiling as Portia took up position on his other side. "Over my dead body," he growled, catching hold of her hand in the act of following the widow's example. A surge of possessiveness gripped him, causing his fingers to tighten.

Her brow furrowed but she made no attempt to pull away. "Why?"

Perhaps his wits were still a trifle addled because rather than answer with a facile retort he blurted out the truth, and with a vehemence that took even himself by surprise. "Because I'll be damned if I allow any other man to ogle your charms."

"My charms?" She blinked and her features took on an odd scrunch. "I didn't think I had any to speak of."

He pulled her closer. "We will speak of them, all right—"

"But *not* right now," interrupted Mrs. Grenville. "Entertaining as it might be, a lovers' spat will have to wait until business has been taken care of." She gave the earl's arm a sharp tug. "Let's go."

Chapter Twenty-one

❧❀❧

Davenport squinted up into the gloom of the crenelated ramparts, searching for any sign of movement.

"Don't worry, sir. Bertie is quite good at this sort of thing. We have filched many a strawberry tart from the window ledges of the local tavern on account of his agility." Despite the air of confidence, Henry's taut shoulders and craning neck betrayed a certain amount of trepidation.

The only response from the viscount was a further narrowing of his eyes. His gaze then shifted from the shadowy ledge to the twist of vines clinging to the limestone wall. "Damnation," he muttered. "I should have gone myself."

"It would not have held your weight. Or mine," he added with a sniff of resignation. "My brother is never wrong on those types of calculations. When you consider tensile strength multiplied by the mass of—"

"Yes, yes. I do not doubt the veracity of his equation." Davenport looked up again, the muscles of his jaw set hard as stone. "However, if the imp does not make himself known in the next few moments, I am going up, regardless."

Both of them strained to catch some sound from above, but there was nothing, save for the usual night noises. Leaves rustled in the freshening breeze, gnarled bark rubbed against rough stone, and the hoot of an owl sounded in the distance. The viscount shifted his weight in obvious impatience, then reached for the vines.

He managed to duck just in time to avoid being thumped on the head by the coil of knotted rope that dropped without warning from out of the darkness. Heaving a sigh of relief, he grabbed for the tail end and gave several hard jerks.

"Don't worry, sir. Bertie is very good with knots," assured Henry.

"I am beginning to wonder if that little prodigy is endowed with supernatural powers. Are you sure your father did not discover him in some ancient lamp?"

The elder Hadley gave a reluctant grin. "He is actually quite human. Indeed, there are a great many times when he can be annoyingly childish."

"You could have fooled me." Davenport tested the rope once more before bracing his feet against the base of the wall. "Wait here."

Henry's face crumpled. "But, sir . . ." By the way he had been rubbing his palms together, it was clear he had fully expected to get his own hands wrapped around the hemp.

"No argument. Orders are orders," said the viscount gruffly. He was about to start hauling himself up, but paused to add, "It is the only sensible strategy." The defensive note in his voice made it sound as if he were trying to convince himself as well as Henry.

The set of the lad's jaw made it seem as if his teeth might crack.

"Take cover behind these vines. You will be safe enough on your own—even if a guard happens this way, there is little chance he will spot you in the shadows."

Henry marched stiffly into position.

Davenport's hand tightened on the rope and his boot scrabbled against the smooth stone as he began to climb the wall. He hadn't gone more than several feet, however, when he paused again.

"Oh, bloody hell," he whispered roughly. "No doubt I should be hauled before a court-martial on charges of temporary insanity, but come along."

The widow giggled and pulled the earl's head down so that his chin was resting on the creamy curve of her breast. "La, ye sure knows how t' show a girl a good time."

Portia swayed slightly, angling her shoulders to further obscure his features. "Here now, don't be hogging th' gent's attention," she chided.

"Aw, don't worry. A man 'is size 'as got plenty t' satisfy us both," she answered with a wink and a leer.

Ignoring the cackle of feminine laughter that followed the comment, two liveried servants brushed past them without a second glance.

Mrs. Grenville let her head loll back, using a fluttering of her heavily blackened lashes to mask her careful scrutiny of the passage. "The coast is clear," she murmured. "Let us hurry."

They made it to the top of the stairs without incident and found themselves facing a dimly lit room. At first the only thing the earl could make out within was a jumble of vague shapes and silhouettes. But as his eyes adjusted to the reddish glow of the tinted candle glass, he was able to discern the forms of several couples in various stages of undress locked together on the carpet.

A low gasp from Portia caused his eyes to shift to a recessed alcove close by the open door. Backlit by the taper's flickering flame, Dearborne's profile appeared to undergo a series of grotesque transformations as he stood in close conversation with another gentleman, the shifting light causing his nose to resemble a wolfish snout and the tufts of silvery hair to take on the shape of pointed horns.

The scholar turned abruptly.

Branford quickly let out a guttural moan and drew the two ladies closer, burying his face in a swirl of silk and flesh. The ploy seemed to do the trick, he noted, trying to keep an eye on his quarry while ignoring the tantalizing curve of Portia's left breast pressed up against his cheek.

Not that there was a great deal of time to dwell on the subject, he reminded himself harshly, wrenching his attention away from the sight of the emerald silk stretched taut by the bud of her nipple.

Dearborne passed by them, and Branford was relieved to see he took no notice of the trio of debauched revelers as he continued his hushed exchange of words with the other man. A whisper of French confirmed the earl's hunch that the marquess's companion was the agent from Paris.

The scholar and his companion headed down the hallway to their left, which Branford knew led to the series of private chambers. As soon as the steps grew fainter he snapped upright. "No telling how long they will be, but I shall have to chance a search of the library while he's gone." He made to rush off, but Portia's hand prevented him.

"Two can make quicker work of it than one." Her mouth quirked. "And as you know, I have some experience in the purloining of papers."

"I'll wait here," offered Mrs. Grenville. "Perhaps, with the right sort of delaying tactics, I can gain you a few extra minutes if he returns before you are done."

He looked from one determined face to the other and decided not to waste his breath arguing. Besides, he admitted, the two ladies were proving themselves the equal of Wellington when it came to bold shifts in strategy.

"Don't try anything foolhardy," he cautioned the widow. "Just a shriek of laughter will do, to warn of his approach. You needn't engage in any hand-to-hand combat with the enemy."

"Leave the diversions to me, sir. I have more than my share of experience maneuvering among dangerous gentlemen."

Portia tugged at his arm. "Come on."

The library was deserted. Branford closed the door noiselessly behind them and stole over to the desk. Striking a flint, he lit a single candle and set it down on the floor. "Damnation," he whispered, giving a quick tug at the top drawer. "I trust you brought your hairpins."

"Locked, is it?" Portia knelt down beside him and plucked one of the ornaments from her artfully arranged curls. "After a certain snide comment on professionalism, I took the liberty of having these made up." A knot of delicate silk flowers disguised a shaft of tempered steel, its thickness twice the norm.

His earlier irritation suddenly gave way to wry amusement as he regarded the implement. How was it that one young lady could be so maddeningly, cleverly, beautifully outrageous? Inserting it into the lock, he couldn't help but utter a low chuckle. "Brings back fond memories of our first encounter."

"Given your jug-bitten state at the time, I am surprised you have any memories of that evening—fond or otherwise."

"Trust me, an ocean of brandy could not drown the recollection of such a singular experience."

She made a face. "I don't suppose you will ever allow me to forget it."

"No," he agreed. "How could I, when it was so unforgettable?" A soft snick sounded. "Ah. Excellent. As always, my dear Portia, you are a source of constant wonderment." He handed her the hairpin, along with a handful of documents. "You check these while I go through the rest of the contents."

He noted with an inward smile that her jaw had gone rather slack and her fingers nearly let the papers flutter down to the carpet. Then, exercising the stalwart spirit he had come to adore, she recovered her wits and fell to a careful examination of the first letter that came to hand.

"Really, sir," she muttered, her eyes studiously

avoiding his. "This is hardly the appropriate occasion for displaying your strange sense of humor."

"My name is Alex." He tossed aside several dog-eared maps and a leather purse. "In case it is you who are having trouble with your memory."

"My brain recalls with perfect clarity the fact that we are supposed to be searching for a priceless Riddle, not indulging in odd quirks of whimsy." A sudden crease appeared on her brow and she looked up, peering at him in some concern. "Are you sure you are all right? I have heard that a hard blow to the head can sometimes result in a delayed addling of the wits."

"Quite sure." A bundle of letters joined the discarded items. "Speaking of riddles, there is something I have been wanting to ask——" His voice broke off sharply as his fingers fell upon a slim morocco case at the back of the drawer. He lifted it out and held it close to the candle.

Jewels winked madly in the light. It took the earl a moment to make out that the gold-encrusted design was the letter *R*.

"The Riddle of Rafistan," breathed Portia. "Well, what are you waiting for? Open it!"

He undid the filigreed catch and opened the lid.

The box was lined in black velvet that age had faded to an indeterminate shade of gray. The change in color might not have been so apparent, noted Branford with some detachment, if the box had not been so glaringly empty.

"Bloody hell." It was Portia who said it first.

"My sentiments exactly." He snapped it shut. "Dearborne must have it on his person."

Portia hitched at the sheath of silk hugging her hips. "It should not be so very difficult to hide behind the door and catch him by surprise when he returns. After all, you have a pistol—"

"So do I."

They both looked up to see a glint of steel as Dearborne nudged the library door all the way open. "And so does my friend Jumanot. His, I might add, is currently pressed up against the forehead of the lovely Mrs. Grenville. So if Lord Branford does not toss his weapon over here by the count of three, the widow will have new reason to be called the Lady in Red."

"Well done, Bertie." Davenport reached down and helped Henry up and over the top of the ramparts.

"When we sailed to the Hebrides with Father last summer, the captain showed me all sorts of useful knots. The clove hitch is particularly suited to loads of—"

"Put a cork in it, Bertie," wheezed his brother, as soon as he managed to catch his breath. "We are not in the schoolroom, in case you haven't noticed."

Bertie's lower lip took on a defiant jut. "In case you haven't noticed, I have been putting my knowledge to practical—"

"Shhhh!" Davenport reached out and yanked the lads into the shelter of the stone wall. "And keep your heads down. The first thing raw recruits must learn is not to give away their position to the enemy."

Both Hadleys turned a flustered shade of pink. "Sorry," they whispered in unison.

With a flick of his wrist, the viscount drew in the

last bit of dangling rope and looped it into a neat coil. "Another basic lesson is that when one is entering dangerous territory, it is prudent to ensure a quick means of escape."

They nodded.

He threw a sidelong glance at them as he checked the priming of his pistols, looking for any sign of fear. The two faces were drawn, but the steely resolve etched on their boyish features matched that of battle-tested soldiers.

A small smile tugged at the viscount's lips, causing his scar to twitch. "Good work, men. You have performed like veteran troopers."

Even had he not warned them to silence, the lads looked incapable of speech.

"From here, we best go on at a crawl."

Davenport made one last survey of the area before flattening out on his stomach. So far, there had been no sign of patroling guards, but he decided to exercise extreme caution. Motioning for the lads to follow, he slithered toward the arched wooden door in the far wall. As he had hoped, it was unlocked.

Once his eyes had adjusted to the gloom, he saw that it was a storage room. Crates of slate roofing tiles, coils of rope, bags of nails, and casks of pine tar were stacked in a jumble along one wall, while opposite them, sections of the spiked wrought-iron railing leaned up against the peeling plaster.

"Stay here."

Henry and Bertie went still as statues.

The room was at the end of a narrow hallway. What other doors he could discern along its length were shut tight. Indeed, there was no sign of life, save a faint spill of light farther on that revealed a stairwell.

Davenport thought for a moment, then retreated several steps and signaled for his troops to advance. "We must see where that leads," he explained in a low whisper. "Stay close—but not too close."

Like the hallway, the stairs were deserted. After a slight hesitation the viscount started down, one tread at a time. On reaching the lower landing, he caught the first sound of voices, then the scuff of footsteps approaching fast. Looking around quickly, he spied a linen closet that had been left open.

"Hurry," he mouthed, not daring further words. To his relief the lads scurried into the cramped space with nary a noise. Edging in behind them, Davenport was just able to draw the door closed as two figures turned the corner.

"Ye heard th' master. Yer mine when he's done wi' ye, so I suggest ye start talkin' t' me real sweet."

"Yes, I heard Mr. Dearborne," came the cool answer. "His exact words were to keep your paws and your prick in check until further notice. As he looks to be a man who does not tolerate disobedience, I suggest you do as he says and unhand my neck."

Though the words were uttered softly, the viscount had no trouble recognizing Mrs. Grenville's voice. Gritting his teeth, he sank into a crouch and cracked the door open so that he could observe what was happening.

The widow's captor, a towering brute who looked to be as broad as a bull in the shoulders, did indeed have the hairy fingers of one hand on the widow's bare throat. The other hand was holding a pistol inches from her temple.

"Bitch," snarled the man. However, he slowly let his palm fall away from her neck. "Ye'll be bloody sorry fer that. I don't likes a female wi' an ornery mouth, so I'll teach ye some manners." He bared his teeth in a wolfish grin, revealing several blackened gaps, and proceeded to describe what he was going to do to her in excruciating detail. "Heh, heh, heh." His laugh was rough and ugly, like the rest of him. "And by th' time th' lesson is over, ye'll be beggin' fer mercy."

Mrs. Grenville didn't so much as bat an eye. "Don't count on it. In business, one learns not to assume a deal is done until the goods are actually in your hands. Before that, anything can happen."

For a moment he was too confused to react, then his face purpled in rage at her cool composure.

The viscount winced, fearing the brute's spasm of anger might cause him to inadvertently pull the trigger. Raising his own weapon, he took dead aim at the other man's forehead, but hesitated and let the gun fall away.

"It was a clear shot."

The viscount hadn't realized Henry had moved up to his shoulder until the lad whispered haltingly in his ear.

"Why—"

A hard nudge to the lad's ribs warned him to keep silent.

The pistol, meanwhile, had ceased its wild gyrations around the widow's head. Still snarling threats, her captor moved around behind her and shoved it up against her spine. "In there," he ordered, pushing her toward the door of a small sitting room. "Trust me, when th' time comes, ye'll wish I ha' pulled th' trigger, fer a bullet would ha' been quicker an' kinder than me blade."

Davenport inched the linen closet door open a bit wider. Next to the sitting room was a billiard room, the massive table looming heavy and black in what little moonlight filtered in from the elongated windows. Deciding that the angle of view should keep them from being spotted, he took hold of Henry's sleeve and motioned for him to make a run for it. He sent Bertie next, then followed, pistol held at the ready.

"You should have drilled the bastard," whispered Bertie, once the viscount had drawn the door shut and joined the two lads in a crouch beneath the billiard table. "Lord Branford would have hit him right between the eyes." He blinked several times in succession. "But maybe you are not as good a shot as the earl."

"The earl would *not* have taken the shot, either," explained Davenport somewhat defensively. "First of all, it was too risky at that range, what with the angle and the way the miscreant was bobbing and waving around so close to Mrs. Grenville. Second of all, a shot would have alerted the entire household that something was wrong, putting the whole mission in danger." Shifting his grip on his pistol, he added, "By the by, I'll have you know that the earl and I are evenly matched when it comes to culping wafers at Manton's."

Bertie ducked his head in apology. "Sorry. I see I have a lot to learn about soldiering."

"Thank heavens there is some subject you have not mastered." The viscount's faint smile lasted for only an instant before his lips compressed to a thin line. "Trust me, I, too, would have liked to have blown the bastard to kingdom come. However, there is yet another reason why it would have been foolhardy to announce our presence. If Mrs. Grenville is here, so is your sister—as well as Branford. And if the widow is a prisoner . . ."

"Bloody hell," swore Henry.

"So, until we know exactly what is going on, our hands are somewhat tied."

"Isn't there *something* we can do?" asked Bertie.

The viscount picked at the last few specks of orange that were left clinging to his cheek. "I'm thinking."

Dearborne kicked the earl's weapon aside. "Well, well, speaking of surprises, this *is* an unexpected turn of events." His gaze shifted from the earl to Portia, and the sneering tone took on a sharper edge. "But then, you were always a headstrong, troublesome chit, poking your nose where it didn't belong, even at age twelve."

Portia couldn't help firing off a retort, despite the earl's warning nudge. "You mean, because I ventured to point out that your dating of the Illyric vases was off by two centuries? And that the stylistic interpretation was a shoddy piece of scholarship, with a number of glaring errors that even a child could see?"

The scholar's face darkened. "You Hadleys! Always lying and conniving to cheat me out of my due recognition with the Historical Society! For years your father slandered my research, or stole my ideas for his own."

"That's not—" This time it was impossible to ignore Branford, for his arm had snaked around her middle, squeezing the air out of her. She remained silent, admitting that under the present circumstances, it was perhaps not the best of strategies to goad the man into a raging temper.

"But I shall have the last laugh on all of you. History shall credit *me* with solving one of the great scholarly conundrums of all time." His cold chuckle sent a chill down her spine. "And that is not the only reward I shall receive for dear Julian's labors."

"Very clever, Dearborne," murmured the earl, before she could respond. "It must have taken pure genius to pull off such a complex plan as this. Tell me, how did you manage it?"

Her father's nemesis was not the only clever man, thought Portia in some admiration. While she had reacted without thinking, the earl was showing a cool head—in spite of all the abuse it had taken of late—and seeking to gather the information needed to trap all the conspirators. She sighed inwardly. Dearborne was right. She *was* a headstrong, troublesome chit.

The scholar's mouth turned up in a smirk. "Actually, it was all rather easy, especially as I was dealing with idiots." It was clear the earl had been right in sensing that Dearborne was eager to boast of his deeds. "Lord Kenwick, a regular at our weekly games of whist, proved woefully easy to pump for information. A question here, a question there, and the old fool was soon led to disclose a number of things about the secret doings at Whitehall. All in confidence to trusted scholars, of course."

"Including the transporting of the Riddle of Rafistan to London."

"Precisely. I had made handsome profits off of his previous disclosures, but the Riddle was a prize that offered the opportunity of a lifetime. Armed with Kenwick's information, I had no trouble arranging an ambush for the special courier between Portsmouth and London."

"I see." Branford straightened. "But how did Baron Hadley fit into all this?"

"I suspected he was about to take possession of the key to unlocking the secrets of the Riddle. Julian had been mumbling for years to some of his cronies in the Society about his search for a Jade Tiger."

Catching the lift of Branford's brows, Portia gave a slight shake of her head. "I honestly don't recall mention of it. But then, Papa was interested in so many rare treasures, it was hard to keep track of them all."

"Not if you know what you are looking for." Dearborne gave a wolfish smile. "When my sources in the East learned that such a beast was linked to the Riddle, I began to question him more closely—under the guise of scholarly interest, of course—on the progress of his quest. As always, he was annoyingly vague, but on further probing I discovered that he let slip enough thinly veiled hints to his friends to make me suspect it had been found."

"So you kidnapped him?" She forced her voice to remain calm but couldn't help adding, "Was that because he was the only one capable of deciphering the Riddle?"

Dearborne's face took on a malevolent twist for an instant, then relaxed. "Why should I go through all the effort, when I had someone else to do the drudgery?"

The earl shot her a frown, then looked back up at the scholar. "Why the false wager, turning all of the Hadley possessions over to Dunster?"

"The baron was going to have need of an extensive collection of reference material in order to figure out all the arcane references contained in the Riddle. I decided that things would go much more quickly if he had his own library at his fingertips."

"As I said, very clever of you."

"But without the Jade Tiger, even so learned a man as my father won't be able to solve the mystery of the Riddle," murmured Portia, half to herself.

"I've tracked the elusive beast to Grenville and Company. And while the widow managed to slip through my fingers on several occasions, you, my dear Miss Hadley, were obliging enough to deliver her to my doorstep. I am sure that when Jumanot and I have a little chat with her, she can be convinced to reveal its whereabouts. Once it is in my possession—along with you, as an added incentive to get the job done quickly—your father will be able to fill in the last few missing gaps in the Riddle"—he fingered the plain buttons of his waistcoat. "And I will be a very, very rich man. So you see, Miss Hadley, you are really no match for my intellect, for rather than providing any real opposition you have made things exceedingly easy for me."

Portia felt her shoulders slump. For once, the despicable man was right in his interpretation of the facts. She had made a terrible hash of things, and her own impetuous actions had put not only herself at risk but the widow as well.

Not to speak of the earl. . . .

He must be searching for a whole new string of invectives to express his ire over the misfortune of having made her acquaintance. His mission—and his life—would certainly have been a great deal simpler if he hadn't had her dogging his steps at every turn. And now, in no small part because of her interference, the situation was looking awfully grim.

From under her lashes she ventured a sidelong glance at his profile, fully expecting to see the familiar twitching of temper upon his lips. To her surprise, however, his countenance appeared unperturbed, as if he were unaware of how perilously close they both were to shuffling off their mortal coil.

Surely, behind the mask of unconcern, he was furiously mapping out a strategy for taking the offensive, she thought. At least, she fervently hoped he was, for at the moment her usually vivid imagination was an absolute blank.

"Yes, it is clear you thought of everything," Branford said slowly. "The only small slip was Roxleigh's demise."

Dearborne shrugged. "It was of little consequence. He was becoming quite unreliable. I was saved the nuisance of having to dispose of him myself. And while I hadn't expected someone else to have learned of the Jade Tiger's arrival on these shores, my men moved quickly to eliminate any rival. They shot whomever was skulking outside of the widow's town house. . . ."

Portia gave an involuntary wince.

"One of Mirkham's minions, no doubt, for I learned it was he who had ordered the search of the warehouse and was shadowing Mrs. Grenville's movements. But I took care of that problem rather easily as well last night. With his dissolute habits, Mirkham was piti- fully easy to follow into the stews and leave dead in the gutter."

Eyes narrowing, Dearborne fixed his unblinking gaze on the earl. "I know Mirkham wasn't working on his own. He hadn't the brains or the nerve for aught than petty crime. That leaves you, Lord Branford."

The earl inclined his head politely.

What was he really up to? wondered Portia, surrep- titiously looking around for something that might be used as a weapon. He would have better luck trying to charm a basketful of cobras than a snake in the grass like Dearborne.

"I give you credit for initiative in thinking of en- listing the widow and Miss Hadley in your attempt to steal the Riddle from me," continued the scholar. "But as you see, you were a fool to think mere females could be of any use against someone such as me." He raised his pistol. "In any case, your clumsy attempts at thwarting my plans have become somewhat of an an- noyance—"

With a gurgled gasp, Portia abandoned her search and made to throw herself in front of the earl. After all, she reasoned in the split second she had to make her decision, if she hadn't been as stubborn as a mule and snappish as a stray dog, he would likely have completed his mission long ago.

Branford, however, seemed to anticipate her thoughts, for without so much as a glance in her direction his arm came up to block her move. At the same time he drawled softly, "Before you pull the trigger, you may want to be sure you are not putting a period to your only hope of capturing the Jade Tiger."

The barrel wavered.

"Think on it," he gave a safe, sardonic laugh. "Surely you don't really believe I entrusted it to one of the ladies?"

For the first time a flicker of uncertainty appeared in the other man's eyes.

"W-where is it?"

The earl's lip curled. "You have one part of the puzzle and I have the other. As I suggested earlier, perhaps we should strike a deal."

Chapter Twenty-Two

❧

"I'm not sure this is going to work."

Bertie removed his shoes and stockings. "It will work, sir."

"It's too dangerous." Davenport puffed out his cheeks. "Especially for mere, er, raw recruits."

"Actually, sir, we have quite a bit of experience in this sort of thing. When Father explores ancient castles or ruins, it is often necessary to climb up and around in awkward places to read the inscriptions." Henry knotted the rope around his brother's waist.

"Better use a bowline," advised Bertie, testing the knot.

"Besides," continued Henry as he retied the rope and gave a hard tug, "I remember reading in LaRoche's *The Art of War* that a surprise diversionary tactic can be extremely effective."

"I do not need you to quote tactics to me, lad," groused the viscount. Hands on his hips, he surveyed the jury-rigged web of ropes, rails, and bundles they had just finished setting into position according to Bertie's precise specifications. "My wits must have been permanently addled by opium," he added under his breath.

"Addiction to milk of the poppy is a common oc-curence in—"

"Not now, Bertie!" hissed his brother, emphasizing the warning with a jab of his elbow.

"Er, sorry." Ducking his head, the youngest Hadley hefted the length of iron bar by his bare feet, then measured out the length of line tied around its end. "Ten feet six inches. That should do the trick. I'm ready."

Seeing the viscount's face take on a mutinous twist, Henry sought to head off any squashing of the plan. "Honestly sir, it is not as risky as it appears." He looked over the parapet. "The bastard hasn't changed his position in over a quarter hour. He is still sitting in the chair with his back to the open window. Once Bertie reaches that ledge over there, he has a clear trajectory."

"Weight and mass, combined with the arc of the swing—and smash! The bastard won't know what hit him."

Davenport picked at his scar. "Let us pray you are right." He hesitated. "His pistol—"

"Is currently aiming at the floor," assured Henry. "The bastard is so overconfident, he isn't bothering to keep it pointed at Mrs. Grenville."

"No swearing in the ranks, else your sister and your aunt will be wanting to cut out my other eye."

"Sorry." With a conspicuous display of effort, Henry hoisted his brother to the top of the wall. "Er, La Roche stresses in his treatise that speed is of the es-sense. . . ."

"Bloody hell, am I really taking orders from

striplings?" He shook his head. "All right, all right. Count to thirty to give me time to get in place, then let it fly, Bertie."

"Right, sir."

"Wait another five minutes before letting go with the main diversion, Henry." Davenport eyed the heavy assortment of slates, nails, and iron bars that were hanging out over the parapet. "That will certainly make one hell of a racket when it hits the terrace. You have the knife to cut the ropes?"

Henry grinned and held up the blade from the viscount's boot.

"All right, men. Let's swing into action."

"What sort of deal?"

Branford's mind was racing but he knew he had to tread very carefully. The scholar, for all his overweening conceit, was still an extremely shrewd and extremely smart gentleman. *He was also extremely nervous.* The earl was too experienced in the field of battle to miss the subtle signs—the brittleness of the voice, the tic of the jaw, the whiteness of the knuckles on the butt of the pistol. He supposed there were any number of reasons for the other man to be on edge. Whatever they were, they made for a volatile combination, one he would have to take great care didn't blow up in his face.

Especially given the explosive temperament of the young lady by his side.

Hell's teeth! Had she really been about to throw herself into the path of a bullet meant for him? He wasn't sure whether he wanted to throttle her senseless or kiss her witless. *That was not entirely true,* he admitted, stealing a furtive look at the tight silk molded around the curves of her breasts. What he wanted to do with his tigerish lady involved a great deal more than kissing. However, that would have to wait until he had her properly wed. . . .

A glint of light winked off the pistol, mirroring the spark of impatience in Dearborne's eyes. "What sort of deal?" he repeated, jerking the weapon up a touch higher.

Forcing his mind to stop wandering, Branford reminded himself that a marriage license should not be the foremost piece of paper in his thoughts at the moment. "We each have a client for whom the Riddle of Rafistan is of incalculable value," he answered. "If we pool our resources and proceed cleverly, perhaps we can make an even greater profit by selling it to both sides—a clever forgery might do the trick. Or at the very least, we could incite a bidding war."

As the spark of impatience turned to a gleam of speculation, the earl felt he had guessed right.

"Who are you working for?" demanded the scholar.

"Oh, let us just say that it is someone who is quite anxious to keep it out of your client's hands."

"Hmmmm." Dearborne advanced into the room, fingering the tip of his chin.

The earl relaxed slightly. His strategy seemed to be working. If he could draw out the negotiations a bit longer, surely he could maneuver the other man into dropping his guard, if only for an instant.

"What sort of share of the profits do you expect?" The scholar had rounded the corner of the desk and paused, just out of arm's reach. With another step or two . . .

"Fifty-fifty does not seem an unreasonable split."

"Equal partners," murmured Dearborne. His boot slid forward across the carpet. "Isn't that a rather audacious proposal for one in your position."

Branford looked up with a calculated smile. "Perhaps." Just an inch more, and a hard jab to the knee, coupled with a sweeping blow upward, would send the scholar reeling into the desk, knocking off his aim. "But then again, some men might think they deserved the lion's share of the money for finding the Tiger."

"Oh, the Cat will get what he deserves."

The smile was still hovering on the earl's lips as the other man darted forward and whipped the barrel of the pistol across his temple with a vicious crack. A blinding pain shot through his skull, and before Branford could utter an oath, everything went black.

"I was wondering if you were ever going to show up." The widow looked from the viscount to her erstwhile captor, who now lay unconscious on the carpet, a lump the size of an apple rising upon the back of his skull. "However, if you are here, then who—"

"Never mind that right now." Davenport ripped off a strip of the draperies and began binding the other man's hands. "Where are Branford and Miss Hadley?"

"Dearborne must have them. They were in his library, searching for the Riddle, while I waited in the hallway in order to engage in, er, delaying tactics if necessary."

"I won't ask what those might have been," growled Davenport as he directed a gimlet eye at her gown.

"I trust that is not a reproach," she replied tartly. Having dropped to her knees, she wound several loops of silk cording around the fallen man's ankles and gave it a vicious tug. "The earl might very well have been chopped up into mincemeat by this brute had Portia and I not employed what weapons we possess."

"And formidable ones they are," he admitted, finishing off the job.

Her expression turned wry. "Unfortunately, not formidable enough. Dearborne was not so distracted that he failed to recognize my face. "What—"

Before she could finish, the viscount had jerked her to her feet and pointed her toward the door. "Hurry. We have approximately two and half minutes to be outside the library door."

"Why?"

"*Must* you ask so many questions?" His steps took on a more cautious tread as they reached the top of the stairs.

"In business it pays to know in advance what problems one might be facing. I imagine the same is true for the battlefield," she whispered, keeping close at his heels. "Turn right at the foot of the landing."

His acknowledging grunt had a conciliatory note to it.

"We must pass an open parlor, but the guests are not apt to take any notice."

"Sixty-three, sixty-four, sixty five . . ." came the soft count of the passing seconds. "Damnation, how much farther?"

*   *   *

"You see, Miss Hadley, much as you and your father have maligned my abilities at research, I am able to manage quite a thorough examination of the facts when it comes to a subject that affects my own interests."

As he wiped the barrel of the pistol across his sleeve, Portia had to dig her nails into her palms to keep from trying to scratch the smug expression from his face. *Think!* she railed at herself.

"After Dunster mentioned Lord Branford's interest in my affairs, I did some digging into the earl's past. It took a bit of diligent probing, but I discovered that he was rumored to have been involved in the selling of secrets to the French during his time in the Peninsula." Dearborne's gaze held a mocking malevolence that was chilling to behold. "An interesting coincidence, is it not, that all his collaborators ended up dead or in English prisons, while the earl somehow escaped with his skin intact? Well, I am much too smart to fall into his trap. I know what he intended—a double cross, betraying me to the authorities while he ran off with all the money. He will soon find out that I am not as easy to do away with as his two nephews."

As usual, the scholar had jumped to the wrong conclusions, she realized. Now, if only she could think of a way to use it to her advantage . . . A quick glance at Branford showed no sign of life. Indeed, his face was still as carved marble, its pallor accentuated by the fresh trickle of blood running down his cheek. *Was he . . . ?*

The thought brought on a wave of dizziness, but Portia forced her swaying knees to steady. While there was still a breath left in her own body, she must not give up the fight.

Keep stalling, she told herself. Though things were looking extremely black, perhaps the Cat's luck—and her own—had not completely run out. There was still a chance that Lord Davenport had reached the estate and would reach them in time.

"Y-you have truly shown yourself to be superior to all of us," she stammered, needing little conscious effort to affect a tone of fear. "He betrayed me as well, promising to free my father if I helped him." Much as it pained her to do it, she shot out her arm and administered a hard jab to Branford's midriff. "The mangy tomcat. It was only tonight that I realized he was lying through his teeth." Praying that the scholar would not notice her palming the gold watch and chain from the earl's waistcoat, she withdrew her hand and gave an aggrieved sniff. She wasn't quite sure what she meant to do with it, but as it was the only solid item within reach, it might prove useful to have in hand. "W-what do you intend to do with us?"

"I am not a vindictive man." To her eyes the ugly shade of his expression said otherwise. "In fact, I shall see you are reunited with your father immediately, for he is here, secure in a section of the cellar that I designed especially for his comfort. As soon as he finishes with the Riddle, you both will be free to go home."

Ha! And pigs might fly!

As if sensing her thoughts, he tried to smooth his features. "It won't matter if you talk—even if anyone believes you. I will be rich beyond my wildest dreams, and shall be long gone from dreary old England. I have always fancied a villa in Rome, complete with all the sumptuous pleasures enjoyed by the Caesars."

Like Nero or Caracalla? She bit her tongue to keep from uttering a barbed comparison concerning the more deluded and debauched of the ancient rulers.

Dearborne laughed. "As for the earl, his penchant for wenching and carousing is well known among the *ton*. No one will be overly surprised to hear that he suffered an unfortunate accident while in the throes of a drunken stupor. I believe he is going to fall from the balcony and break his neck."

"I have another idea," she ventured, hoping to sound suitably spiteful. "Why not leave him alive to take all the blame? You could make it look as if he, and he alone were the culprit." She assumed a petulant scowl. "That way, he would suffer the ignominy of the hangman's noose, rather than be afforded a quick death."

"Hmmmm." The weapon dipped a touch.

If only she could distract him for just a moment, she might have a chance to—

Suddenly, as if in answer to her prayers, there came a thunderous crash, sounding for all the world as if the heavens had split in two.

"What in the name of God—" The earsplitting noise caused Dearborne to jump. Looking slightly dazed, he jerked around to stare at the narrow casement windows, which were swinging wildly on their hinges, half of the glass panes shattered by flying debris.

Recovering her own wits, Portia seized the opportunity to hurl the earl's pocket watch at Dearborne's head, at the same time launching herself at his weapon. The heavy gold missile caught the scholar square on the bridge of the nose. He gave a yelp of pain, adding his voice to the cries of panic and confusion that were erupting from the nearby parlor.

"Bitch!" he screamed, trying to bring his pistol back on target. But her fingers were already wrapped around the barrel. Abandoning all pretense of gentlemanly scruples, he struck out at her, landing a shuddering blow to her shoulder.

Responding in kind, Portia resorted to the unladylike tactic of biting down on his wrist. Hard.

The pistol clattered to the floor as, with a howl of pain and outrage, the scholar wrenched his arm free. Staggering back a step, he let fly with a few more choice epithets. She paid him no heed, but swept up the heavy weapon and sought to draw a bead on his bobbing form.

Seeing the flash of polished iron, he snarled a last curse and bolted for the broken windows, scrambling over the splintered sill with the agility of a much younger man.

Portia gave chase for several steps, then stopped and dropped the firearm. Flinging herself down beside the earl, she cradled his head between her hands and pressed her lips to his bruised brow.

"Oh, Alex, please swear at me! Invoke the wrath of Lucifer! Consign me to the darkest corner of Hades—anything, as long as I may hear that wonderful growl of yours."

"S-swear at you?" His eyes slowly fluttered open, though their sapphire hue looked a trifle dimmed. "W-why the devil do you want me to—"

She cut off the rest of the groggy question by covering his mouth with a flurry of passionate kisses. "I was so afraid you would never open your eyes and snap at me again," she cried, a ragged catch in her voice.

To her embarrassment, the admission was accompanied by a spill of tears. Having no handkerchief, she dabbed at her cheeks with her scraped knuckles. "Let me see to your head," she muttered, seeking to cover the slip of emotion with a flurry of efficiency. As the much-abused cravat had been discarded somewhere along the way, she began to stanch the trickle of blood with the tail of his shirt.

"This is getting monotonous," he said thickly.

"I know. I have been a source of constant aggravation, sir. But you may take heart in the knowledge that you will soon not have to lay eyes on me." Stifling a sob, she started to draw back. "Ever again."

With a low groan he sat up and pulled her hard to his chest. "I did not mean *you,* sweeting. Nothing about you is remotely monotonous. Indeed, one never knows what to expect."

"I know. I am a sore trial," she said in a small voice.

"On the contrary, you are a wondrous delight." His hand slid over the taut silk of her bodice and cupped her breast. "A most wondrous delight," he repeated softly, his thumb tracing the low-cut ruffle. "I—"

He was, however, cut off by a martial shouting in the hallway that drowned out the shrieks and cries of confusion. An instant later the library door banged open as if it had been hit with a battering ram.

The ensuing sight was a formidable one. Brandishing a pistol in each hand, Davenport exploded from the shadows, the widow right behind him. Having acquired a heavy brass candlestick somewhere along the way, she held it poised at shoulder height, ready to deliver a blow.

"Alex! Miss Hadley!"

"Over here." Portia raised a hand in salute. To Branford she murmured, "It seems that reinforcements have finally arrived. I was keeping my fingers crossed that your erstwhile comrade in arms would eventually charge in to the rescue."

The earl appeared to be suffering from some lingering grogginess, for it took him a moment or two to grasp her meaning. "Bloody hell!" he exclaimed, his face darkening into a scowl. "What the devil are you doing here, Max? I gave you explicit orders to stand guard over the ladies."

"Then you should have provided me with a regiment of the Royal Horse Artillery."

Portia saw the earl rake a hand through his hair, then wince as his fingers came in contact with the lump on the back of his skull. She supposed that, given the circumstances, he could be forgiven for snapping at his friend. "So, where are the rest of them? I'm surprised Henry and Bertie aren't also hot on your heels."

"Well, actually, I told them to stay upstairs—"

"*What!*"

The viscount quickly changed the subject. "Never mind that right now. What about Dearborne?"

"Ahem . . ." Branford was forced to clear his throat and look to Portia.

"Out the window," she said. "Perhaps you had better go after him, to make sure he doesn't elude Mr. Taft's men."

Davenport looked rather relieved to be given a new assignment and hurried toward what was left of the leaded glass. After a quick assessment of the situation, the widow followed after him without pausing for comment.

The viscount paused just long enough to bark a gruff order over his shoulder: "Stay here! It's too dangerous for you to come with me."

Mrs. Grenville paid no attention. However, as the widow moved past her, Portia thought she detected a surreptitious wink.

The sound of their pursuit recalled her to her own senses. With a squeak of dismay, she pushed away from the earl and, with an awkward tug to her tight skirts, got to her feet. "Papa! Good Lord, I—I nearly forgot! Dearborne said he is locked away somewhere in the cellars." There was, she admitted to herself, another reason for her somewhat precipitous leave-taking. A part of her feared it was only a temporary addling of Branford's wits that had him murmuring endearments.

Huffing a grunt, the earl rose stiffly and caught at her arm. "Not so fast, Portia. After all we have gone through, I think it only fitting that we make these last few steps together."

The glow of several oil lamps showed a figure hunched over a desk, the frail form dwarfed by the stacks of books and papers piled precariously on either side of him. At the sound of the creaking hinges, Baron

Hadley looked up from his labors and a soft smile wreathed his lined countenance. "Ah, there you are, my dear." He tucked a wisp of silvery hair behind his ear and touched the tip of his pen to his chin. "You would not believe what an astounding project I have been engrossed in for these past several days."

"Actually, I would, Papa," she said gently. "And it has been weeks, not days."

His brows drew together. "Has it?" A wry smile pulled at his mouth. "As usual, I fear I have lost track of the time."

Clasping his hands behind his back, the earl was surprised to find a lump forming in his throat as he watched Portia approach her father and enfold him in a heartfelt hug. Was he really turning into a sentimental fool in his old age? he wondered, unable to keep an odd little smile from curling his lips.

Baron Hadley stroked a gnarled hand over his daughter's curls. "Dear me, I can be a dotty old fool about a number of mundane things, can't I? But I wasn't mistaken in thinking that Dearborne was up to no good, no matter his efforts to mislead and confuse me."

"No, you were not."

"Hmmph. Only a shallow mind such as his could imagine using scholarship for evil purposes." He gave a sad shake of his head. "I knew I could count on you to outwit him, despite his dire threats to the contrary, so I simply stalled for time, pretending that the task he set for me was inordinately difficult."

"I appreciate your confidence in my abilities, Papa, but actually I am afraid all my efforts would have been for naught if not for the help of Lord Branford." With a tiny tug, Portia directed her father's gaze to where he was standing. "Without him looking out for all of us, things would have been very dark indeed."

"Ah. I have heard talk around the club about the Black Cat," said the baron after a blink or two. "Now, that is an interesting sobriquet, sir. In early Anglo-Saxon culture, the black cat became a symbol of bad luck, though why, I have never been able to—"

"Let us put off any lecture on that subject until another time, Papa. In this case it was a momentous bit of good luck that we ran into each other."

Luck. Branford's smile crooked a bit wider. Since that first cosh on the head in Lord Fotherington's garden, his luck—and his life—had certainly taken on a different direction. He could only hope that her earlier ardent embraces had not been mere hallucinations brought on by the most recent blow to his skull, because . . .

"You see," she went on, a slight hitch in her voice, "he was assisting Whitehall in capturing a dastardly traitor."

"Ah." Her father's brow furrowed in consternation. "I wasn't quite sure what Dearborne was up to, but I had a suspicion it was something nefarious, so I concentrated my efforts on drafting a false translation for him. It was an interesting challenge, crafting a document close enough to the truth to fool him, yet with enough errors to render it useless." He carefully withdrew several folded sheets of paper from one of the leather-bound books by his elbow. "Of course, I couldn't resist noting the real answers to the arcane questions. Now, if only the Jade Tiger has not been lost . . ."

"It arrived, safe and sound."

He let out a rapturous sigh. "I knew I could count on Grenville and Company. Is it as wondrous as I imagined?"

Portia smiled. "Even more so."

"Oh, I should love—" His reveries were interrupted as the clatter of footsteps echoed on the stone stairs and the room suddenly became a good deal more crowded.

"Papa!" Henry and Bertie skidded to a halt before their father's chair, their faces alight with joy.

"Ah, there you are, Julian!" Lady Trumbull had been escorted through the doorway by the Honorable Anthony Taft, who had also taken charge of her ancient carriage pistol. "Delighted to see you hale and hearty, of course. However, I am afraid you are in for a stern lecture from me, as well as those hugs and embraces from your amazing offspring." The twinkle in her eye softened her scold. "But I shall refrain from ringing a peal until a bit later."

Branford cleared his throat and addressed Taft. "I take it that your men have Dearborne in hand, Tony."

"And the French courier." He hefted the aged pistol and shot the earl a wry grin. "I must say, the methods and, er, manpower you employed in ferreting out the enemy were even more unorthodox than usual."

Branford, too, was grinning. "But they got the job done. I trust Lady Trumbull did not put a period to anyone's existence with that cannon."

"Hmmph! I don't see why men get to have all the

fun of shooting at dastards." She flexed her frail fingers. "I had a perfect bead on that miserable excuse for a scholar as he came charging through the bushes, but Mr. Taft insisted that we leave him in one piece for questioning."

A harried grunt sounded from Davenport, who, along with Mrs. Grenville, had remained by the door. "Tony, perhaps you will fill me in on the secret of getting a lady to actually obey your orders. I seem to have no skill whatsoever in mapping out a strategy."

The widow's cool gaze took on a steely cast. "There is no great mystery to it, sir. To begin with, you might speak to a female as if a brain were not the smallest portion of her anatomy."

The fire that lit for an instant in the viscount's eyes gave Branford pause for thought. But the baron quickly headed off any further exchange of words on that front with an observation of his own. Leaning back from Portia's embrace, he suddenly squinted. "Speaking of the female form, my dear, is that a new gown?" Removing his spectacles, he polished the lenses on his sleeve, then clamped them back in place. "Rather different than your usual style, but it is very, er, becoming. You know, in ancient Minos, the young ladies wore garments that left their breasts completely exposed. . . ."

The earl noted with some humor that Portia's face turned nearly the same hue as the widow's favored crimson. "Let us put off any lecture on that subject until another time, Papa. At the moment I believe Mr. Taft would like to ask you a number of questions concerning the Riddle of Rafistan."

"Ah. The Riddle. What a special piece of parchment." A faraway look came to his eyes. "With the help of the Jade Tiger, I think I may finally solve its tantalizing mysteries." His expression grew even more wistful. "It got me to thinking of sailing across the oceans to the Orient! I would dearly love to travel to the Oman's palace, so that I might view the actual inscriptions surrounding the inner sanctum where it rested for centuries." He gave an embarrassed cough. "But, of course, I would, er, not think of undertaking the journey and leaving my children alone for such an extended period of time. . . ."

Branford made a sound in his throat as well. As there was no easy way to broach the subject he had in mind, he decided now was as good a time as any. "Actually, you needn't worry about that, Hadley. You see, I happen to have a rather special paper of my own—one that will allow me to take responsibility for your daughter." Out of the corner of his eye, he saw Portia's lips part. "And your sons," he hastened to add, before she could manage a word. "That is, if they have no objection to living with us whenever you are traveling."

The baron tugged at his ear, then slowly a bright smile dawned on his face. "Ah! You mean a special license? Do I take it you are offering for my daughter's hand?"

"Yes—"

"No!" Portia was staring at him in wide-eyed disbelief. Swallowing hard, she rushed on, though she seemed to be having difficulty in arranging her thoughts in any coherent order. "That is to say, the earl doesn't . . . he hasn't . . . he isn't . . . thinking clearly. He has suffered a number of hard blows to the head, so no doubt he is not entirely aware of what he is saying. . . ."

"Put a cork in it, Portia!" Henry fixed her with a look of horrified disbelief. "Only a complete ninny would think of turning down such a great gun as Lord Branford!"

"Right!" Bertie's mouth scrunched in dismay. "He is a one in a million gentleman. Or, to be exact, one in two million three hundred thousand and—"

"I must say . . ." chirped Lady Trumbull.

The earl held up his hand, and an immediate hush descended on the room.

"Much as I have appreciated the group effort in solving our earlier conundrums, this is one problem I would prefer to work out on my own. Would you all mind giving Portia and me a few moments in private?"

The two lads fairly tripped over their own feet in their haste to hustle their father from the room. Lady Trumbull elbowed Taft in the ribs, and Mrs. Grenville, repressing an enigmatic smile, spun Davenport back toward the stairs.

Once they were alone the silence grew even more pronounced. After an awkward moment or two, it was Portia who ventured to speak first. "I thought we had agreed not to mention that particular subject again," she said haltingly.

"Why? Is the idea of marriage to me really so very odious?"

She swallowed hard. "You don't really wish to marry me."

"I don't?"

"How could you? Sparks always seem to fly between us."

"You have to admit that it brightens things up," murmured Branford.

"We argue."

"Argument is very stimulating. Keeps the blood flowing." He touched at his forehead. "Not that I have had much trouble with that."

She dropped her gaze to her feet. "But . . . you don't even like me!"

"No," he agreed. *"Like* is certainly not the word I would employ. It is much too mild and meek a verb." His mouth crooked slightly. "And there is nothing remotely mild or meek about you, my love."

Love? Had she heard him correctly? Even if she had, it was an awfully oblique reference.

"So, getting back to a certain piece of paper—"

"I have had it up to my ears with documents. Of any kind." If it was merely a sense of honor or duty that had prompted the proposal, rather than any other emotion, she didn't care to hear it. "Let us drop all this talk of papers, if you please."

"I quite agree."

Before she could react, his lips came down on hers with a searing intensity. "I've no desire to speak about inanimate parchment and dribbles of ink, my love," he added after a lengthy interlude. "Let us confine the discussion to things of a very different nature."

"L-like what?"

"Like my very own Jade Tiger."

"I'm not sure I understand."

The sapphirine glitter of his gaze took on an intensity that nearly caused her to stop breathing. "I am speaking of a spirited, green-eyed creature far more precious than any mystical talisman from the East. One who has helped me understand a secret even more important than the ones hidden within the convoluted scrawls of the Riddle of Rafistan."

She forced herself to look away, for fear he would see the fierce longing in her eyes. "I am tired of riddles.

The earl took her chin and turned her face back to his. A tentative smile had come to his lips. "Ah, I see. So you wish for me to come right out and say how much I love you."

Portia hesitated, but only for an instant, before deciding to bare her soul. "Yes. That's exactly what I wish." Her fingers ran lightly from the bruise on his forehead across his cheek to trace the curve of his mouth. "Oh, Alex, much as I have tried to deny it, I . . . I think I have been longing to hear those words from you ever since our first clash in Dunster's study."

He slowly kissed the tip of each finger before enfolding her in a long and lush embrace. "It has certainly taken both of us enough time wrestling with the mystery to discover how simple the answer is. Indeed, it was staring us in the face right from the start." The quirk of humor then faded from his face, and the flickering candlelight illuminated a stark need that looked every bit as hungry as her own. "I never meant to love anyone again—"

"Much less a hot-tempered hoyden." Her lip quivered. "Y-you needn't feel that honor obliges you to say—"

"To the devil with all that! My feelings have naught to do with rules and regulations!" His tongue left a trail of fire along her jaw. "My rash and reckless darling—you showed me that one can't be afraid of taking a risk or two in life."

"Alex—"

"I do love you, Portia. More than my paltry skill with words can ever express." His torrid embrace pressed her back, until she was lying flat atop the massive oaken desk. Caressing her skirts up above her knees, he stepped between her thighs. "Now, about that license. Must I resort to extreme measures, as I did that first evening, to bend you to my will?"

It was late afternoon and an amber light was bathing the bedchamber in a golden glow. For a moment, Portia simply basked in its warmth, then shifted slightly to resume her nibbling at the lobe of Branford's ear. "You no longer need to employ brute force, my lord. As you see, I am firmly in your power," she murmured. "So you may loosen your grip on my person."

His throaty chuckle grew muffled as his mouth captured hers. "Unhand you?" His fingers slid beneath the sheer lawn of her night rail and trailed up the length of her bare leg. "I think not."

"Arrogant man." Working the dressing gown off his shoulders, Portia watched the heavy silk slither over his naked back and buttocks on its way to the floor.

"Headstrong hellion." Several shell buttons popped off as he opened her bodice to the waist. His head ducked and his tongue grazed the nub of a nipple.

"Rakish rogue." With a light nip to his neck, she rubbed her palms in slow, sensuous circles against the flat planes of his chest, marveling at how the texture of taut muscle and crisp curls still turned her insides to jelly.

"Brazen bluestocking." His fingers were now at mid-thigh. "However, it appears at this moment that your leg is quite lacking in a covering of any color." They moved higher. "Ah, no garter, either," he murmured as he stroked up a notch and began to tease his touch through the most intimate folds of her flesh. "How very naughty."

"A-Alex!" Her voice turned husky with passion as she gasped in pleasure. "The door is ajar . . . you are naked . . . and I hear Blaze and the boys on the stairs, returning from target practice. . . ."

"Don't worry, my love. After all, I have had a great deal of experience in making sure you are not caught in a compromising position." Branford tugged out the last of her hairpins with his free hand and sent them skittering across the carpet. "However, to ensure that Henry and Bertie will not be tempted to put a bullet in my bare behind, I shall see to the lock." A wicked smile played on his lips as he added in a low murmur, "I trust, Madame Wife, you have not forgotten how very good I am at manipulating delicate mechanisms."

His hip nudged the door of the master bedchamber shut, causing the brass latch to fall neatly into place.

Snick.